THE BEST OCTOBER

JACK DEBNEY

Copyright © Jack Debney.
ISBN: 9781980313953

http://www.amazon.com/author/jackdebney

All rights reserved. No part of this publication may be reproduced, copied or transmitted in any form without written permission from the author.

First published 2017.

Design and Editing © Alexander Debney

DEDICATION

For Alexander and Eva, to whom I wish many years of happiness.

Contents

I. The Dancing Lamp	1
II. Straighter than Straight	10
III. Nosh for the Prodigal	17
IV. The Rescue	24
V. Families and Secrets	36
VI. Two Old Men	50
VII. A Merry Sprite	70
VIII. The Errand	88
IX. The Smarmers	102
X. In the Land of the Two Rivers at One A.M.	118
XI. A Piratical Appurtenance	137
XII. Knives and Forks	145
XIII. The Absentees	157
XIV. Fate and Mr Gordon	170
XV. Mr Marston Solves the Cuban Missile Crisis	181
XVI. Mrs Shufflewick and other Heroes	201
XVII. The Battle of the Titans	217
XVIII. Three Cross Chapel Street	240
XIX. Badges and Wrestlers	265
XX. Toothache and Biblical Matters	273
XXI. Saturday Night at the Pier	280
XXII. The Best October	310
Author's Note	319
About the Author	320
By the Same Author	321

JACK DEBNEY

I. THE DANCING LAMP

From my hiding-place among the bushes I saw the old man come shuffling along, muttering to himself. He carried an old cloth shopping bag, almost trailing it on the ground. From time to time he stopped and looked from the path on the rise to the hummocky ground that sloped down to the stream.

I'd seen him a couple of times before but I hadn't taken much notice of him. He was sort of disgusting, with his haggard, unshaven face and shabby clothes. His top shirt button was open, showing a scraggy neck, and somehow that seemed to me to be the worst of all, almost like someone displaying his sores. My grandfather had died a few months ago and, when we'd visited or when I'd stayed with him, I'd never seen him without a tie, even at breakfast. I didn't much like ties on me, but it seemed all right for old men. Respectable, dignified like my grandpa.

So this codger didn't exactly measure up to him, but maybe I was being a bit harsh. Some chuntering old bloke who looked as unhappy as I often felt these days, he really wasn't of much interest to me. My chief concern was that he might spot me looking at him from the bushes, but he didn't even glance in my direction. Let him go, so I could lie in wait for more interesting "prey"! That's how I liked to think of the passers-by I spied on, although I never did anything. But even to say the word to myself was exciting, as though it gave me secret power.

I felt that to have followed people would have destroyed that, made me too open to discovery, merely mortal again. So I just took a mental note of the few who came by. It was a bit like trainspotting, except I had no notebook to jot my human "numbers" down in.

What made me follow the old man that afternoon, then? After all these years, I still can't properly account for it. I did make a note in my diary afterwards about what had happened, but you can't expect the full story from that or from memory. Even when you try to slot them together, it's tricky sometimes.

Perhaps it was something very basic that triggered off my leaving the hide and tracking the old man. Not because the dark was falling – that wasn't so bad – but simply because it was getting chilly and I needed a bit of movement. Perhaps, though, it's best just to put it down to fate, a mysterious quality like that.

I followed the man almost to the end of the path where it joined a row of detached houses. But he turned a sharp left just before the junction, and for a moment he disappeared from sight as if he'd noticed me after all and had just been biding his time until he could give me the slip. Thinking he was cleverer than I was. That put me on my mettle.

But I found out quickly enough it was a track he was going along, if you could call it that – a narrow line of bent and crushed grass. I hadn't discovered it and that annoyed me for a bit, because I prided myself on having mapped out the place pretty well.

I had to keep my wits about me, be careful not to brush the odd branch and brambles which reached out to grab me. I didn't want to bring myself to the old man's notice and then get accused of being a nosey parker, told to push off.

I don't think I need have worried. The old bloke was so preoccupied I could have walked on his heels and he wouldn't have been aware of it. The muttering was getting louder now and it became like a kind of moaning, as if he was in horrible pain. He kept repeating what I thought then was "Christ", but later I found out it was something rather different.

I can't say that I was frightened at that point. On edge, ready to run if I had to, but not scared.

The man came out into a small space at the top of the area. There was the fence of one of the newish houses nearby, and a big tree, a beech I think, and plenty of low bushes. A clear vista, better than mine further down, but there would have been nowhere to hide here. I suppose this place had the best view in the whole stretch, which I liked to call "The Land of the Two Rivers" because I'd been reading about ancient Babylon and Mesopotamia in one of my grandfather's books.

He'd lived alone after his wife's death, ages ago so that I hardly remembered her and now he was dead too: April, 1962. My mother had inherited his house and everything in it, including the shelves of books. That was one of the reasons we'd come back to Ketilsby, the main one, I suppose.

Of course, there was no Euphrates or Tigris here, nothing like them, but I gave the stream the first name and a tiny tributary that disappeared under a hummock of soggy ground, the second – not very flattering to the mighty rivers of history, because my local Tigris was hardly wider than a flooded drain. Anyway, it was enough for me. Imagination would do the rest.

I watched the codger fetch out a lamp from the shopping bag. A spirit lamp. Then he revealed a little vase and a few flowers. They looked as if they were dying of thirst, but they were roses, expensive unless he'd grown them himself. Slowly, he bent to put the vase down and insert them, re-adjusting the blooms fussily as if they had to face a particular direction, at an exact angle. Yet there wasn't any water; he hadn't thought to bring some with him or scoop it up from the stream. This seemed odd to me, unless he meant the flowers to die as quickly as possible, but then why carry them here in the first place? Perhaps he was just forgetful, as most old people were reckoned to be. If I wanted, I could always go down the rise afterwards and fetch some water.

He pumped up and lit the lamp, talking away to himself, more loudly all the time. "Christ" seemed to come into it frequently now. I wondered if this man was what they called a religious maniac. I'd heard about such people but never encountered one before: somebody who let his beliefs rule him too much and went a bit funny in the head. It was interesting to a born watcher like me, but it was also getting a bit creepy. I could feel the hairs tingling on the back of my neck.

Then the man went completely silent, standing stock-still in front of the roses and the lamp, staring down the rise. I think he was weeping now. At least, his face was screwed up as if he was, although in that dim light I didn't actually see any tears.

After a short while, he lifted his bag and started to move off, back the way he'd come. I just had time to get out of sight, although I don't think there was much chance of his seeing me, as I said. He shambled off, with the empty bag squigged up in his hand.

I stayed where I was for a bit longer. I'd lost any appetite for tracking the old bloke. It was all too weird for me.

Evening was coming in quickly now; the red light of the lamp shone more clearly. I was completely puzzled as to what the strange old man had been up to. The best I could think of, and it wasn't so far off the mark as it proved, was that he'd made some sort of altar and had conducted a short service there, a bit like a minister in chapel.

Something happened now that rendered the strangeness

of his behaviour almost normal.

I was staring at the red light. I didn't think I'd find any answers there, but in the darkness it was an obvious focus. Then I found myself becoming transfixed by it and, after a short while, the light began to move about, still within the lamp on the ground yet at the same time somehow free of it. At first the light edged up a bit and then moved more quickly, to one side and the other. After that, as though it had tested me and found me not wanting as an audience, it seemed to soar, at least half-way up the tree that stood near.

Now I was scared stiff. I kept telling myself that what I was experiencing must be an optical illusion. I'd read about mirages in the desert and so on, but nothing like this – only in ghost stories, and that thought didn't make me feel any braver. Anyway, this felt absolutely real and terrifying, as if the light were dancing before me in mockery, a dance of power too, showing me what it could do whether I liked it or not.

When I was coming to the hide, I used to tell my mother that I was staying behind to play with some boys at school and that generally pleased her. It was a fresh school for me and she knew that it was difficult. 'Oh, so you're making friends, then?' Beyond giving a fumbled sort of nod, which could have meant anything, I didn't answer her, being reluctant to tell an outright lie. I didn't tell her about my den either. I hadn't told anybody about that.

Even so, there were limits and I should be off home now. Mum would be making tea and she'd be angry if I burst in when it was getting cold on the plate or drying up in the oven. I'd have to eat it either way. She'd watch over me to the queasy end, her favourite punishment for my inconsiderate lateness.

The lamp went on dancing when I stared at it. If I blinked it stopped still for a few seconds, as though taking a rest, then started jigging around again. An optical illusion, that's what it must be – something happening in my brain, with no real life outside it. But, as I said before, it didn't seem anything like that, and that was the greater truth then.

I was strongly tempted to believe the dancing lamp boded evil. It was trying to put me under a spell, lead me away into some shame or disaster I could only vaguely guess at. But, more practically considered, I was getting colder the longer I stayed there and risking a ticking-off at home. I had to break away or give in altogether.

I wanted to run off immediately, but I took what courage I had left in my hands and walked right up to the lamp. The nearer I got the less it moved and that made me bolder. Now I was within touching distance. If I simply bent down... The flame, flickering in the wind, on the edge of guttering, kept to its place and the fear I had began to recede. It was almost as if I'd tamed the strange thing.

Once again, I wondered why the old codger had brought the lamp there and the flowers. This wasn't a cemetery or anything. Ah, but perhaps there was a body buried beneath, right here in this waste area!

The flame seemed to shake its head and laugh, but also to indicate that I was getting warm – which I wished I was, literally considered. It was 'damn parky', as Dad was prone to say, doing up his overcoat in the hall before he went out to the pub in the evening. 'Be back in an hour!' he'd call out to my mother. No response from her apart from the resentful silence, but if Roy were home he'd give a satirical laugh and make some sarky comment about our father's notion of what an hour actually was. Mostly, he was just needling Dad for the sake of it, because sometimes, when they were getting on better, he'd join him in the pub later on. But with Mum the anger went deeper.

Stepping away again, I was gazing at a friendly lamp now, (if I can put it like that and make any sense), surprised but pleased that my feelings about it could change so quickly, and for the better.

'Hey, you there!' a furious voice blasted from over the fence nearby. I looked up and round. I could only see the blurred outline of a thickset figure. 'I've told you before and I don't see why I should have to keep on telling you! What the hell do you think you're up to? That lamp could be dangerous, especially if you just leave it blazing as you usually do. Tipped over, the whole bloody place could go up in flames! So take it away. And if this happens again, I'll be informing the police, you can be sure of that!'

I was glad that in the darkness he'd mistaken me for the chuntering bloke. I didn't even touch the lamp now – briefly wondering whether its owner brought a new one each time , or just reclaimed the lamp he'd used, the next morning – but simply turned and ran back down the track.

The angry neighbour must have twigged then that I wasn't the old man, who could never have got up the speed I did. Even so, he still seemed to hold me to blame, shouting after me to come back, as though it were my duty to act as the codger's surrogate. Well, he could turn off the lamp himself if he was that worried.

In my mind's eye, I saw the dancing lamp again and how calm it had become. I had these strange feelings – fear and fascination mainly; also that strange, nervy one of making friends with a former enemy – and I didn't know what to tell about what had happened, or even if I could ever say anything.

Anyway, I skedaddled. That was another of Dad's words, although I couldn't imagine him skedaddling anywhere. He was short and round, in shape not unlike the gingerbread men Mum had helped me to make when I was small. Watching him go off, he seemed to roll down the avenue where we lived; coming back, he'd sometimes be lurching very slightly. Talks with clients, he told me – mostly potential clients, it turned out, in various stages of being convinced of a deal, or not.

Mum was different, taller and thinner, too often on edge these days. She'd be nasty to Dad if she caught him when he was a touch unsteady and red in the face. There was often a quarrel then, and Dad's face would turn even redder and shinier. That was a kind of lamp too, although not one that did much dancing.

I'd want my elder brother, Roy, near to me at such times. We didn't get on all that well, but better some refuge than none. He was away at university mostly, though I knew he was coming home this next weekend. He often made snide comments but when our parents were quarrelling he was much less hostile, allowing me to sit in his room and play quietly, banging the door shut to show how he disapproved of the raised voices below. Then he'd return to his desk, poring over his books as if nothing else existed.

He was the clever one of the family, as I was always being told – or made to feel, not least by him. If I were being particularly obtuse in his eyes, he'd yell at me: 'You little clot!' – a word which I can't remember other people using when they were calling me names. Perhaps I associate it with him because he'd often add on a short lesson – for example, telling me that "clot" was "klods" in Danish and "Klotz" in German, obviously the same word originally, sighing as though he were spending his knowledge on someone who could never appreciate it.

When Roy came home again at the weekend, if I told him what had happened – the dancing lamp and the muttering old codger – he might laugh and accuse me of having been at Dad's secret bottle of "hospitality" sherry. That is, if he were in a good mood. Otherwise, he'd just tell me to buzz off.

Mum, especially at this hour of the day, would only listen absently, her face intense over what she was cooking, or some other worry.

Dad, in the right, mellow, expansive frame of mind, would sit and mull over the whole question and, in so doing, unintentionally make me look ridiculous, like somebody pretending to be a lawyer in court: 'Did my boy really see this strange old man and the dancing lamp? Members of the jury, I ask you to consider...'

And there was nobody at school I could tell. So I kept the whole thing to myself and tried to write a story out of it, which was almost like talking to another person.

II. Straighter than Straight

There was certainly no skedaddling from the school lines. Every time I had to stand in attendance, I wished there was. Or why couldn't you just turn invisible and drift away, your real self I mean, leaving a mechanical shell behind, like a robot?

'Come on! I want to see these lines straight! Straighter than straight!' roared Mr Marston, the teacher on yard duty. He was our form master and taught us English, history, geography, RK (religious knowledge), most things really, apart from art, maths and woodwork. Mr Marston was tall and skinny with black hair and moustache and a pale, thin face which you always thought should be dark, dark as a plotter in the shadows, but wasn't. There was often a shaving rash on his chin and sometimes his hair was full of scurf. Boys said they'd counted the pieces falling out, as big as cornflakes some of them, they claimed. I saw nothing remotely that size when I checked from behind as he passed amongst the desks, bending down to comment on some pupils' work here and there.

You daren't do anything like that to his face, of course. He'd accuse you of staring, he'd want to know why, and when you couldn't answer he'd convict you of insolence and provide summary punishment – mostly a clip over the head or an ear-twisting; sarcasm was his strongest weapon, though.

'Brace up! What did I say, school? Straighter than straight!'

We shuffled our feet and tightened our hands against the sides of our trousers, but I couldn't see that it made much difference. However, it pleased Mr Marston, because the extra little effort made it look as if we were eager to obey his orders. He loved this air of command, as though Heaven for him would turn out to be a gigantic parade ground – or at least the entrance to Heaven would, because inside the classroom he had much more to offer and took his role as teacher very seriously.

Now he was going along the lines, pushing boys into position, barking sneery remarks at others. There was a student-teacher, Mr Askew, supposed to be helping him, but he didn't do much. Perhaps he wasn't allowed to.

'Heads up! Don't stare down at your shoes, Edwards! It won't make them look any the less dirty. In fact, anybody heard of boot polish in this line? That boy there – Robertson!'

'Roberts, sir.'

'Didn't I tell you, hands behind the seams of your trousers! The seam is not where your nose is and you won't find it anywhere within either. Disgusting habit!'

Mr Marston had introduced me to my class, 2A, the first day of the term, two weeks ago now. The new boy. He'd brought me to the front of the room and asked me to say something about myself, but being on show like that made me stumble-tongued and I couldn't get out much that made sense. In addition, I started to go red, as I often did when I was embarrassed. The eyes of the boys were on me, the master's too.

Mr Marston waited till I was trapped in a longer pause than usual. Then he strode up to me and put his hands flat before my face, as if in front of a fire.

'Hmm. That'll keep us warm against the griping autumnal damp.'

When the class laughed and I went even redder, within an inch of tears, Mr Marston peered closely at me, then turned me towards my place, as though helping a blind person, and said, not unkindly: 'Just joking, Palmer. You've got a nasty eye-watering there. Wipe it dry. You're not used to our keen easterly winds yet.'

'I've been to Ketilsby before, sir. My grandfather lived here.'

'Ah yes,' said Mr Marston, as though distantly recollecting some information he'd been given. 'Anyhow, welcome to 2A and God save you from the flotsam and jetsam that's drifted in here. Translate, Kilbertson.'

'Can't, sir.'

'Good lad.'

My family had only moved to Ketilsby that summer, not long after my mother had inherited the house in Langtoft Avenue. When I'd failed the 11+, we were living in Preston and my parents had sent me to a private C of E school there. They couldn't afford to do anything like that now – besides which, the local church school had gained a bad reputation, some scandal that had not quite been hushed up; my parents wouldn't tell me what it was all about – so here I was at Willow Road Secondary Modern.

The big, grim-looking building actually housed three schools: the Junior Mixed on the ground floor, the Senior Boys in the main body of the building facing the road, and the Senior Girls in the wing that stretched back along by the playground, where we boys were lined up now, to the sports field. Our forming-up times were staggered (the Juniors actually went straight to their rooms), as were the playbreaks for all three schools.

Soon the Headmaster, Mr Gordon, would appear to inspect us, and Mr Marston wanted everything to be just right for him. That must have accounted for the quick look at his watch, his last few commands, the hurried way he pushed at Derek Fraser, who was standing just in front of me, accusing him of slouching. I didn't like the way he placed his hand in the small of Fraser's back, as though he were adjusting his vertebrae.

Derek Fraser was a bit taller than me. His cap of black hair bounced up and down as Mr Marston moved on. I think he would have given his retreating figure the V-sign if he hadn't been afraid of Mr Gordon watching us from the staffroom window through his binoculars. Derek said something in an undertone, though. I didn't catch it, but boys in the adjacent lines did and sniggered and covertly grinned.

Mr Marston knew that he was being made fun of and glanced back angrily, but he couldn't prove anything. The grins would be completely gone and I'm sure that Derek's face was once more a mask of innocence.

After we'd been allowed to file in, we'd be having school assembly. The partitions of the two furthest classrooms were scraped back to make a temporary assembly hall, then the small piano was wheeled in, the dais hastily under construction from old wooden bases, a table placed in the middle with a portable lectern positioned in the centre of that. It was like arranging a stage in a theatre and it had some of the same function.

But, for the immediate moment, it was the cold and waiting for Mr Gordon.

I was facing the main door of the school. That's where he'd have to emerge from, or you'd think so if you applied common-sense logic. So I kept one eye on the entrance, just in case he tricked us and did what people might expect him to do. The other eye I tried to make rove, as best I could. From his slight head-twitch I guessed that Derek was doing the same thing.

There were side-entrances to the place, small doors low down, as though made specially for dwarfs with curvature of the spine, which was one way of describing Mr Cransby, the caretaker. These cellar regions, containing the malfunctioning heating apparatus and the school debris of several generations, were his domain, but there was nothing he could do if the Headmaster chose to walk through and exit from the building that way.

I imagined Mr Gordon slipping out and sneaking along under cover of the bike sheds and then behind the temporary classroom they'd put up near the sports field, so that he could approach his boys via the back of their heads. That's what he'd choose for today.

I was right.

Mr Marston was as silent as the rest of us. His eyes seemed to be standing to attention and his thin lips looked as if they'd disappeared into his face. I glanced quickly at Mr Askew. He was petrified.

'Good morning, Mr Marston,' came that familiar grating voice, advancing from behind me.

'Good morning, Headmaster!' replied our teacher. He didn't quite click his heels and snap into a salute, but it was the next best thing.

'Good morning, school!'

'Good morning, Mr Gordon!'

I could hear the meek bleating that was my part of the response and wished I had the courage to remain silent or just move my lips, as I sometimes did in chapel when I didn't want to join in the hymn. But I was far more afraid of Mr Gordon than I ever was of the minister and always had the feeling, stupid though it might be, that somehow he'd find out if I didn't fulfil my small portion of the daily ritual.

Derek Fraser, of course, sang out his greeting extra-loudly, which maybe was his manner of keeping essentially quiet and hidden. I hardly knew him well enough then even to speculate.

I noticed that Mr Gordon didn't greet Mr Askew. Perhaps he'd forgotten his name, or just regarded him as a lower breed altogether that you didn't communicate with at all unless you had to. However, he must have nodded in his direction or something – smiling didn't really come into it –

because I saw Arthur (nicknamed after Arthur Askey the comedian, naturally!) check a simper and, instead, with a bit more dignity, dip his head slightly. He hardly looked older than some of the senior boys in the Fourth Year. He'd done a few practice lessons with us, under Mr Marston's vigilant eye and so we hadn't dared to play him up.

Everybody stiffened as Mr. Gordon approached. He appeared tremendously old to me then, but he couldn't have been more than in his mid-fifties. The thing you always noticed about him was the expression of lofty severity he wore, as if from some world-turning battle within. I suppose that was one of the things which made him so terrifying, because there was nothing particularly remarkable about his appearance otherwise. He was a spare man, only a little taller than my father, with short white hair and a lined face of high colour. People would have noticed the dry, rasping voice too, though.

Mr Gordon passed down the lines, making one or two corrections here and there, but never touching any boy, as Mr Marston tended to do. Just a short command was enough.

Apart from these and the sound of his shoes, absolute silence ruled. Young, nervous Mr Askew was at the side, Mr Marston at the front, facing us. I had a nickname for him, but a private one. I was an English Civil War buff even then, reading everything I could find on the subject, so perhaps it was inevitable I should call our form teacher Marston Moor, after the battle in 1644.

It would have needed explaining to the other boys, I was too timid to try, and I don't think they would have found it very funny anyway. But I liked imagining Mr Marston in the combat gear of that time, it didn't matter whether Royalist or Parliamentarian, roaring orders which nobody obeyed – this was the bit which really amused me – or perhaps his getting hurt in an unfortunate place, not badly hurt, and running from the battlefield squalling like a baby.

Mr Gordon finished his inspection and went to the front to confer with Mr Marston. Arthur was deputed to order the lines in, the first time, I think, that he'd enjoyed this privilege. He started with the first year, moving up to the seniors, as was normal. But when he gave the order for our class, 2A, to move, an unexpected, good thing happened.

Whilst Mr Gordon's and Mr Marston's attention was distracted, Derek Fraser glanced back at me, his face showing the mischievous smile it often had. I envied him that smile and had even practised it in the mirror at home, but it didn't look right on me. Derek quickly pulled his features into a caricature of my expression: anxious and wary – and then grinned, before turning to the front again. His little trick had worked like comedy can, both cutting you down to size and picking you out, making someone special and ridiculous at the same time. I'd had virtually no contact with him, although I admired him, particularly his spirit, the way nothing seemed to get him down for long.

The moment was over and we were filing into school. I was glad, because Derek had caught me off-balance; I wouldn't have known how to respond to him. And I'd still be too bashful to make any kind of overture, although his sudden teasing seemed to invite it.

We clattered up the stairs, past the Juniors' floor and then into our part of the building.

III. Nosh for the Prodigal

"Nosh" was a word that my brother Roy had introduced to the family. Etymology was one of his chief interests and he'd given us the low-down on this choice acquisition too. It was a Yiddish word, he told us, derived from German "naschen", meaning to eat or nibble. It had come into English use through the linguistic influence of the Jewish community like, for example, "schmutter" for clothes.

'Schmutter? Schmutter?' said my father incredulously. 'Never heard it before in my life. It takes a Leeds boy to find out things like that.'

But he took to "nosh" with enthusiasm. Virtually all our meals became "noshes" for a time.

Roy had returned to university for the start of the winter term. He had spent much of the summer vacation away, working at factory jobs and then travelling abroad, living on the money he'd earned. He'd sent us postcards from France and Spain, but had gone straight back to Leeds when he returned to England. Both my parents were put out at this, taking it as the snub it was probably at least partly meant to be, my mother in particular.

Now, in spite of her sense of affront – a repeated sniff, a few tart remarks about being taken for granted and other maternal gripes – she set about making him one of his favourite dishes: steak and kidney pie which she did very well, especially the crust, making it both crispy and succulent. This would be in honour of his visit.

Roy duly arrived, in duffel coat and carrying an old kitbag he'd acquired somewhere. He was still wearing his CND badge, which had caused a lot of trouble with my father on previous occasions.

'Campaign for bloody Nuclear Disarmament! We had all that disarmament rubbish in the 30's and look where it got us!'

'This is nuclear, Dad. You get four minutes warning and that's all.'

'You won't find your Russki friends giving up their bombs. Even less likely than the Americans. '

'Not yet, but *we* could. Someone's got to make a start.'

'Here he comes!' announced my father now, on watch at the front window. 'Here comes the prodigal! '

I remembered how Roy had scolded me after I'd failed the 11+, and several times since for that matter. I was "thick", or just hadn't made an effort, I'd let them all down. He nagged me much more than my parents had, as though my failure were a deep personal shame to him. In retaliation, I'd messed up the papers he was working on at his desk. He'd chased me from the house then but, however hurt I felt, I had got my own back on him, after a fashion, besides which I'd escaped, leaving his hands smacking on thin air.

So I was shy of my brother now, and still a bit resentful, which was a pity, because there had been a time when we were something like friends. While my father was exuberant on greeting the "prodigal", and my mother affectionate-cum-reproachful, I hung back in a surly, rather ungiving manner.

Roy chaffed me, accusing me of turning into a young tearaway, at school with all those trawlermen's sons. I couldn't help enjoying that because it made me sound tough, which I wasn't, and at least he wasn't accusing me of being stupid. In a strange sort of way, it sounded now as if he approved.

His accent was definitely changing. I'd noticed that in passing at the beginning of July, after his first year at Leeds, before he went away to work in York. A chocolate factory, but he didn't send us any free samples. He could have got a job at one of the frozen food places here in Ketilsby, as he'd done before, but he'd spurned that. He'd helped us with the moving to Grandpa's house, but he didn't seem to like being there. Given the atmosphere between Mum and Dad at times, I can't say that I blamed him much.

It wasn't that Roy, the first university student in our family apart from a remote cousin I hardly ever saw, was going posh or anything, as you might have expected. Quite the contrary. He'd discovered that the proletariat was the key to everything, including the best way to speak. Yet one of Roy's few open snobberies was a pride in his vocabulary, which seemed to be growing ever vaster. He grabbed at new intricate words, as though they were manna in the wilderness. This was rare enough in our social class, let alone among the trawlermen.

The roughening of Roy's accent was much more obvious now. He'd been practising! Or maybe it was simply the effect of the long period we hadn't seen each other. As my mother took Roy plus kitbag upstairs, to my grandfather's old room where he'd be sleeping, Dad shook his head, saying mournfully: 'What's that all about, Colin? He sounds like the writer bloke, what's his name? John Braine – *brain*! That's not what I'm topping up his grant for.'

He was breathing heavily. I couldn't tell how serious he was with this irritation. I smelt the "hospitality" sherry on his breath, but it was fresh, hadn't got sour yet.

'And look at this!' He indicated the duffel coat, slung over the ornate wooden nub at the bottom of the bannisters.

'He had that last winter too, Dad.'

'Did he now? I can't remember. But what I'm asking myself is if we're producing a beatnik in the family or something? – an angry young man even!'

Now he was making a determined effort at lightheartedness, but unfortunately that wasn't how the mood stayed when his son came down for his welcome-home nosh, the Palmer equivalent of the fatted calf. The special wine my father had bought for the occasion should have helped – that was the intention – yet it didn't. I wasn't allowed any, of course, and my mother had only a drop, so the bottle was effectively shared between Dad and Roy.

Firstly, as we settled down at table in the front room (kept for Christmas dinners, formal visits or celebrations like this one) there were approving comments about the food, well up to Mum's best. Then there was the catching up on what Roy had been doing, his adventurous summer abroad.

All that bit went smoothly, my father sighing as he chomped, nodded, sipped, filled Roy's glass and his own, thinking back to his days as a youthful traveller before the war: cycling tours in the Low Countries and just over the German border: 'You could tell trouble was coming from those arrogant swine!' as he was fond of saying. Roy preferred Provence and Spain.

It was when he was going on about Barcelona and Catalonia and the repressive regime of General Franco that my father stopped him.

'Granted, granted. But the – what do they call him? – ah yes, the Caudillo! That's the one. Well, he does maintain stability, doesn't he?'

'Only at great human cost, Dad.'

'Maybe. But there would be even greater human cost if you had riots in the streets, another civil war.'

'There doesn't have to be either.'

'You've got to admire Franco's cunning, the way he fobbed off Hitler and kept Spain out of the last lot.'

'It might have been better in the long run if he hadn't.'

'Eh? How do you work that out?'

'Then Franco would have fallen along with Mussolini and Hitler.'

'Take in Portugal as well, do you reckon? Snooker the lot? It wouldn't have worked! Where the Latin temperament's concerned, democracy's just a word.'

'That isn't true,' said Roy, unable to keep the exasperation out of his voice. He was starting on about Italy but Dad scornfully interrupted him: 'Italy! They change governments with their clothes down there. Mind you, the ice-cream's good.'

Such as it was, the harmony was broken and the prodigal relapsed into a defensive sulk. When he did speak, it was in snapped-off sentences with an even stronger Yorkshire accent than before. And that was the second bone of contention at the dinner table.

'Why are you talking like that?'

'Like what?'

'As though you've just finished a shift down the mine or something.'

'I wasn't aware of anything unusual.'

'Well, perhaps you should be.'

'This is how most people around me in Leeds speak. '

'At the University?'

'Quite a lot, yes.'

'Do you reckon that's the purpose of your expensive education? So that we can hear you talk like "most people"?'

'The University isn't a finishing-school, Dad. You can get elocution lessons elsewhere, if you want them. '

'What puzzles me is why you should go to the trouble of imitating the riff-raff.'

'Who says they're riff-raff?'

'My experience tells me they are. But I suppose it's inevitable that you bolshy types should take them as a model.'

And then they were off, further and further into contentious politics. Dad, who spoke Standard English with a slight Birmingham accent when excited and who described himself as a businessman (small but rising) was a dyed-in-the-wool Conservative and Roy, particularly at such heated times, quite the opposite.

I switched off as best I could, inwardly going through a brief survey of the Civil War, from the King's raising his standard at Nottingham in 1642 to the execution in January, 1649, taking in the major battles: Edgehill, Marston Moor, Naseby and so on – getting them mixed up as I sometimes did, especially when relying on the Civil War instead of counting sheep.

Whilst I dreamed, more or less historically, and Dad and Roy went at it hammer and tongs, a grimly aggrieved Mum cleared away the plates and brought in the lemon and meringue pie, another of her specialities. She did make an attempt to intervene then and calm the two men down. It didn't work for more than a couple of minutes. Both of them were seething and still had plenty to say. If I'd had the courage I would have told her that it was useless: my father and brother in this mood were like a blaze that just had to burn itself out.

Now Dad was on about strikes and the unions, how they'd got far too powerful, much worse than the bosses they were challenging. Roy tried to counter that one, citing poor wages and conditions, still far too prevalent, and the right to withhold labour, defend hard-won rights.

Then they moved to the US versus Russia, Mr Khrushchev, President Kennedy, the Berlin Wall and, if it was so good in East Germany, why did they have to build such a monstrosity to keep their citizens in?

'Because the GDR is losing a lot of its best people, the best qualified, to the West.'

'Well, there you *are* then.'

'No, Dad, there we're not. They're being lured across, offered well-paid jobs and...'

'There you are, then! What's wrong with that?'

'Because it's a bribe, that's why, a propaganda ploy.

They'll soon discover what a capitalist society is really like when they're trapped in it, particularly one in which carefully re-branded old Nazis wield so much power. America's behind it all, of course, because they want to build up a strong, anti-Communist buffer state.'

How far Roy believed all this, I don't know. A lot of it, I think, but he was putting himself in an extreme position, as was my father too. As you do in quarrels.

'I love these family get-togethers,' said my mother with heavy sarcasm when she went out to make coffee. That shamed them a bit. There were hasty, belated compliments about the excellence of the lemon meringue pie that just sounded insincere now.

My father fished out some mint chocolates to go with the coffee, and fired one last shot at my brother.

'Tovarich Roy! Meet the comrade, Red Roy, my son!'

'Well, that's what the name means.'

'No, you're wrong, Professor! It means "king" in French.'

'That may be one of the roots – or what people assume to be its origin. But it means "red" in Gaelic. Hence Rob Roy: Red Robert.'

'Interesting, interesting,' said my father, seizing on this fact, as if only now was the conversation really beginning.

But it didn't get going; it was too late for even the semblance of cordiality to be established that evening, and we just sat awkwardly on at the table, drinking our coffee and crunching on the slightly stale chocolate. Then Roy (choose which derivation you prefer) and I went to the kitchen to do the washing-up, leaving my mother to chide my father for ruining the evening.

IV. The Rescue

During the mid-morning break I generally didn't have much to do with anyone. I'd stroll up to the edge of the sports field, wanting to look like an interested spectator of whatever game was going on there, eagerly awaiting an invitation to join in.

And sometimes I went along the touchline to the point where the view from the school was blocked by the temporary classroom. I was afraid of Mr Gordon at the staffroom window, catching me in his binoculars, picking me out as a solitary kid and coming down heavily on me for that, as though it were a deliberate transgression.

The temporary classroom – it'd already been there three years I was told, and would probably last for ever – was a large wooden bungalow, raised up from the ground on brick supports, so that there was a short flight of steps up to the door and space beneath the structure. Some of the First Form boys – it was 1B's classroom – used to play under it, crawling about and making themselves all mucky. If caught, they'd get into trouble, but they seemed to think the risk worth it.

It happened when I was well out of sight of Mr Gordon's relentless glasses. There were three of them who came at me – two boys from my class, Doran and Witherow, and one great hulking lad from the final year called Svenny Olsen. I didn't know him but once seen, never forgotten. He was like the first turn in a bad dream, the one who set you whimpering, if not screaming – not yet at least.

Everywhere he went, lumbering through the playground with intense concentration as if each step cost him great thought, he provoked fear – most of all in his victims, naturally, but also servile deference in his allies, which was nothing other than fear at its heart. These new friends never lasted long before being clouted and slammed into hasty retreat, and they tended to be smaller, weedier kids, like Doran and Witherow.

They must have bribed Olsen for his help: sweets, chocolate, any cigarettes they could lay their hands on. These were the fees he normally took but also, like any knight setting out on a noble mission, he had to be convinced that he had justice on his side. It added righteousness to each blow, like an invisible knuckleduster.

Doran and Witherow held me, each clasping tightly onto an arm. Olsen loomed up in front, bending so that his wide pasty face, only given colour by acne and an incipient moustache, glared closely into mine. There was a simplicity of mad fervour in that look. Many boys said (not in his hearing!) that Olsen should be in a special school for mentally subnormal pupils, but somehow he struggled on at Willow Road, always at the bottom end of the lower class in his year. When he left, he'd most likely ship out on a trawler like his dad. It was either that or the army or sweeping floors in one of the factories.

'Cat got your tongue?' he said. 'Say something, kid.'

Terrified, I managed a few shaky words.

'What do you want me to say?'

Olsen paused, his face searching mine for signs of resistance or fault.

'Anything. Entertain us.'

Doran and Witherow dutifully tittered.

'But nothing dirty, mind. I hate dirty talk,' said Olsen fiercely. Then, in a softer, slyer tone: 'Unless I'm doing it, goes without saying.'

He grinned broadly, revealing two layers of yellow teeth and a rush of breath that smelt of old cereals, burnt toast and sour milk.

'How about a nursery rhyme?' suggested Doran.

'Yeah. That's good. Go on, kid.'
'I can't remember any. I...'
'Bloody well go on!'

I should have recited "Old King Cole" or "Hey Diddle-Diddle", something like that. I knew scores of them, but unfortunately in my panic I started on the first one that came into my head.

' "Mary had a little lamb,
Its fleece was white as snow,
And everywhere that Mary went,
Her lamb was sure to go".'

The three boys laughed derisively. Olsen mimicked my diction, making it high and lisping. I reddened, hating to think I might sound like that.

'Oh yes, her lamb was sure to go and don't spare the mint sauce!'

The teacher on playground duty that morning was Mr Askew, anxiously trying to exert an authority he didn't yet possess, and the last time I'd seen him he was on the far side, near the school entrance.

Olsen thrust his horrible face right up to mine.

'Are *you* a bit of a Mary?' he asked pugnaciously.

'I don't know what you mean.'

'He doesn't know what I mean!' mocked Olsen, again in that high false voice.

He instructed Doran and Witherow to hold me tighter still, to make my muscles smart – that is, he added balefully, if I had any.

'You think you're better than us, don't you?'

'No, I don't!'

'I reckon you do. Perhaps this might make you change your mind.'

His slap was a hard one, stinging my cheek, making my ear crackle and buzz.

'Convinced?'

I neither nodded nor shook my head, just looked through swimming eyes at the ground beneath me. Some other boys, their attention attracted, had gathered round – but at a safe distance.

'Now you've got a burn on one side, but you're still white on the other. Should be some form of balance, shouldn't there?'

The second slap.

Then there was a series of stern accusations, as though Olsen thought it only fair he should tell me what I was guilty of and had to be punished for.

Apparently, I looked at Doran and Witherow as if they were dirt; I was posh and let everybody know it, like the snob I was; I answered too often in the history class, showing everybody up – a right little canny-knickers! – and I wouldn't help the other kids if they asked me something; even pushing in front of his friends here like some kind of lord and not saying sorry. Now, that was downright rude, wasn't it? So, all in all, I was pretty disgusting, the way I flopped around like a little girl. He believed they'd put the wrong clothes on me and sent me to the wrong school. Olsen leered, displaying a thick, splodgy tongue. Well, there was a sure test to find out whether that was true or not.

'Show us, then!'

My lips were trembling, out of control, and I was afraid I would wet my pants.

'Not going to co-operate, eh? That's not nice, not nice at all. What do you think, lads?'

Doran and Witherow laughed agreement.

'Right. Hold this little tyke as strongly as you can, then. It looks like we'll have to find out for ourselves what it is.'

He eased his hand inside the top of my trousers. Desperately hoping that the bell for the end of break would go soon, I began to struggle at long last.

'He's a wiry bugger, isn't he?' growled Olsen, reaching

further down. 'Hold him tighter, you two! We're nearly there.'

But all of a sudden his hand jerked away and his face retreated from me. Doran and Witherow's fingers snapped off like broken locks. After gaping in fearful amazement, the two accomplices sloped off as quickly as they could.

Someone had jumped up on Olsen's back and thrust an arm round his neck, evidently half-choking him. The figure was leaning rearwards and Olsen staggered back a few steps, seeming as if about to topple. I couldn't see who he was at first and then Olsen, roaring like an angry giant, shook him to the ground with a great heave of his shoulders and a furious working of his elbows. As the boy picked himself up and closed with Olsen again, I saw that it was Derek Fraser.

Olsen was taller and broader than Fraser, with more brute strength, but he was still taken aback by this unexpected assault. He wasn't used to such challenges and I think he couldn't quite believe it to begin with.

'You leave him alone!' shouted Derek, crouching low before Olsen as if about to spring at him like a cougar.

'What's it got to do with you? Do you want to get a bashing too?'

'Try it!' said Derek, and then I saw what I'd never expected to see. Olsen actually faltered. There was something about Derek's anger which seemed to transform his flesh into steel. Even to Olsen he was now a daunting figure.

But, by his own rough code, he'd still have been obliged to lay into Derek, if it hadn't been for two things.

Young Mr Askew had moved into view and had at last noticed that a disturbance had broken out on his watch. Now he was running towards us, yelling in his thin, hoarse voice. He was not an impressive figure, but at least he wore a teacher's baggy tweed jacket, whatever his junior position, and behind all his feeble efforts there stood the authority of

Mr Gordon.

And, just at that moment, the bell rang for the end of break.

'What's going on here?'

'Just larking about, sir,' said Olsen, as airily as he could.

Mr Askew could see it was more than that, but the boys involved – me, Olsen, Derek, (Doran and Witherow must have hidden somewhere at the back of the crowd by now), had moved well apart from each other and Arthur was left without a fragment of evidence.

Our faces must have hinted at something of the story but they also hid the rest and nobody was going to do any explaining.

'All right, in you go! And if I catch you causing trouble again, you lads, Mr Gordon will hear about it!'

Flustered as he was, he was trying his best to act tough. Although he didn't take our names, I was pretty sure he knew who Olsen was. Everyone encountered that 'witless oaf' – as I'd heard Mr Marston shout at him once in the corridor – sooner or later.

***

Derek didn't approach me at all during the rest of the morning. I feared he was deliberately avoiding me, contemptuous of my timidity, lack of fight. I should have shown some defiance, however useless. So I was wary of going up to him, shy of even saying a simple thank-you.

I noticed he singled out Doran and Witherow to glare at. It had its effect. The two small figures looked even smaller and more furtive and kept out of Derek's way, sometimes glancing over at him worriedly. I wondered if they'd try to smarm up to him when the atmosphere had cooled down a bit, try to find little favours they could do for him.

Derek Fraser was normally good-humoured and full of play. So his defending me, facing up to Olsen, made an even bigger difference. I'd never even seen him angry before, let alone in the impressive but controlled fury he'd displayed.

To turn to more mundane things – I was getting hungry.

For lunch it was going to be cold beef and chips with lettuce and tomato that I could douse in salad cream. Something to look forward to, but there was the journey home first and that might prove tricky. Once outside the school, I'd be in danger. Doran and his chum wouldn't try anything again, not yet, but an aggrieved Olsen was another matter. He might go for Derek, of course, because he was the one who'd shamed him, yet Derek's challenge had knocked him out of kilter, as if he'd been made to realise for the first time he was not invincible. I was by far the easier target and, after all, I'd 'caused' the fight anyway.

But when I left the school, trying not to look scared, I found Derek at the gateway. My first thought was that he'd ignore me again, that he was waiting for someone else, but he smiled and fell into step beside me.

He didn't talk about what had happened nor did he brag about his intervention.

'Where do you come from?' he asked me now. 'You told old Marston your grand-dad was from here, but you're not.'

'My Mum was. We live in her father's house now, since he died. But we've been in different places before. The last one was Preston.'

'Preston? Lancashire?'

'Yes.'

'You didn't get your accent there! That's Gracie Fields and George Formby country. Or thereabouts.'

He put on a daft grin like George Formby and strummed an invisible ukulele: ' "I'm leaning on a lamp-post at the corner of a street"...'

It wasn't a bad imitation at all. It made me smile anyway.

As we walked along Willow Road – thankfully, no sign of Olsen anywhere – we swapped information about each other.

'After I failed the 11+, my parents sent me to a church school.'

'Private?'

'Yes. But I think they also had scholarships.'

'You speak posh. But not so posh it makes your ears ache. Nothing like a Ketilbarian, though. '

'A what?'

'Someone who comes from this dump.'

He motioned with satirical affection around him; a ringmaster introducing the circus. I wanted to laugh, but felt too shy as yet and just managed a smile, hurriedly getting back to what we'd been talking about.

'It was a Church of England school.'

'So?'

'Well, there are a lot of Catholics in Preston.'

It sounded irrelevant even as I said it.

'So?'

His voice was sharper and I thought for a moment I'd put my foot in it, that he was Catholic himself. Not that I minded. Most of the kids I'd played with in the avenue off Garstang Road where we'd lived were Catholic and they didn't seem any different from anybody else, apart from the crosses and medallions they wore and their regular attendance at church. But my parents minded, to judge by the sarcastic remarks they allowed themselves, although I didn't understand why.

But I hadn't caught Derek on the raw. It was simply that he couldn't see the significance of what I'd said and he didn't like to be puzzled.

'There's a C of E school in Ketilsby,' he said.

'My parents were thinking of sending me there.'

'The headmaster was a strong bloke, something like Mr Gordon, but he took some kids on a school holiday to France, got drunk and went funny with them. They sacked him after that.'

'Funny?'

'Well, you know.'

I was just about to try and glean something more definite from him when he laughed and burst out with a new idea.

'You can't imagine Mr Gordon getting drunk and misbehaving, can you? Falling down pissed in assembly – that'd be good! Our teacher, though, you could imagine *anything* of him!'

It was my turn to be perplexed. Mr Marston wielded considerable authority too, and I couldn't honestly see him as ever stepping beyond the bounds of correct conduct. He probably ticked himself off in the mirror if his tie was slightly crooked.

'What does your father do?' asked Derek.

'He was a sales rep.'

'A what?'

'A commercial traveller. But he's setting up his own business now. He's always going on about being "financially embarrassed".'

Derek repeated the phrase with delight, adopting a lofty but slightly stuttering tone, like a bashful aristocrat.

'I'll use that when I'm trying to get more pocket money out of Mam and Dad. It's no shame to be skint, though. When Dad was a skipper, he never knew how much he'd be earning from a trip. Well, he got a basic rate but the real money was in the percentage on the catch he'd be due. If it was bad and the market was down, his wallet stayed thin. But if things were good – bonanza! Free candy floss and ginger beer for everybody!'

'Isn't your dad a skipper anymore?' I asked, wondering whether Mr Fraser had lost his job or something.

'He gave it up and went to work for Norlind. He gets a good regular wage – or salary, since they made him a manager. But he doesn't like it. He'd go back to sea like a shot if he could.'

'Why couldn't he?'

'Too uncertain and he claims he's getting too old for that kind of job. Besides, my Mam wouldn't let him. Says she wants a proper family life. Three weeks away and then three days back in port – what kind of existence is that? She says.'

'Yes, but…'

'Old trawlermen always moan when they're on land,' philosophised Derek. 'They don't have time to moan when they're bringing in the fish or keeping their tubs afloat, they're that knackered!'

I made a prim mental note that, if Derek and I got to know each other better and I had a chance to invite him home, I'd have to steer him clear of vocabulary like this. My mother was particularly strict about swearing and what she regarded as 'common' speech. She was fond of invoking the rare but valuable example of Skipper Tom Beeston, a friend of my grandfather's, a man who'd achieved something of a parsonical status on the docks because he never swore, and didn't allow it within his hearing on trawlers under his command.

We came to Shore Road. Our house was in the avenue directly on the other side.

'I sometimes deliver Sunday papers up there,' said Derek. 'Not much call for the *News of the World* in Langtoft Avenue.'

'Where do you live?'

'Willow Road. About a hundred yards up from our school.'

I said nothing, embarrassed that he'd come so far out of his way to protect me from Olsen. For one awful moment I thought Derek might post himself outside our door, like a security guard, and then escort me back.

Instead, he stopped at the kerb.

'I'm going to leave you here. Mam packed me some sandwiches. Corned beef and pickle. Dee-licious!' He pointed to a bulge in his jacket pocket, which I hadn't noticed before. 'It's a nice day, so I'm going to eat them in the park. See you back at school.'

He didn't say anything about waiting for me at the entrance or nearby, but I was certain he would and then pretend it was a chance meeting.

I realised that I hadn't even tried to thank him for rescuing me.

'Listen, Fraser, what you did. I just want to...'

'Derek.'

'I'm Colin.'

'I never would have guessed.'

I made a second attempt and it was worse than the first one. I was genuinely stammering; there was no play-acting about this. Sometimes I got an attack if I was particularly nervous.

'What you did was...'

'Forget it!'

I was trying to get my lips round the word 'brave' so that it would come out in one clear syllable, but his next words mercifully forestalled me.

'I've got an idea, Colin. We have art tomorrow, right?'

'Yes. A double period in the afternoon.'

'You remember Miss Barber said she'd allow us to work in two's, if we could show that we were serious about it. Are you any good at art?'

'Not really.'

'Better than me, I bet. Well, what do you say if we go to Miss Barber at the beginning of the class and tell her there's a special picture we want to do together?'

'What of?'

'I don't know. We'll think of something,' said Derek shortly, as if that were the least of our problems. 'What do you think?'

I simply nodded, but Derek understood exactly what I meant. He was teetering on the kerb-edge while he made his suggestion, pretending he was on a precipice and in danger of falling off.

'OK. We'll do that then.'

He grinned at me.

'You'd better get across now. The road's clear.'

He turned round and started back the way we'd come, briefly waving when he saw that I was over the road, standing on the other pavement. After waving in return, I ambled up Langtoft Avenue, not thinking about the cold meat, chips and Heinz salad cream awaiting me so much as about Derek. I was exhilarated with gratitude and the sense of acceptance, so much so that I could almost have found it in my heart to say kind things about Olsen and his pals for inadvertently having made this possible. But that would have been stupid. To forgive your enemies – eventually – is one thing, but I wasn't going to thank them!

What helped to boost my pride now was the conviction that Derek hadn't just protected me because he'd felt sorry for me and hated Olsen's bullying, but also because he really wanted us to be friends.

V. Families and Secrets

Miss Barber did let us work together, although initially reluctant to do so, sceptical about our joint artistic mission. But Derek, with the kind of cajoling charm that he could turn on like a tap if he wanted something, managed to persuade her and she ended up beaming like an indulgent auntie. Then, as if fearing she'd relaxed too far, she became the teacher again, warning us not to fool around.

'And work hard.'

'Yes, Miss.'

We were allowed to put two tables together at the back of the room. I noticed Doran and Witherow on the other side, near the front. They were drawing separately and didn't seem to belong to each other anymore. They gave the impression of being absorbed in their work and didn't look our way once.

Of course, we'd outlined a project – mainly my idea initially – to Miss Barber.

It'd be a circus picture but with some amazing things going on, not just what you'd expect. After all, the circus ring was already a centre of fantasy, so why shouldn't it be easy to add to that?

In a small sketch, we worked out roughly what we wanted to depict, but the actual doing was, naturally enough, much more intricate – and correspondingly more difficult. Derek assigned me the animals and the trapeze. I laboured away, with his encouragement and occasional intervention. The main difficulties were that my grasp of shape was not very sure and my line uncertain. I tended to rub out and smudge and in the end, if I wasn't careful, it would all just look a mess. Derek checked me in this. That was his best suggestion. 'Let it stay!' he'd urge. 'It's not bad as it is. Don't spoil it!'

Eventually, I got a soulful-looking lion standing near the edge of the ring: outsize eyes and a massive mane. The feet were ridiculous, pointing directly into the ground like thick, clumsy tent pegs.

Miss Barber came along to inspect what we were doing.

'Hm. Very Douanier-Rousseau, Colin,' she judged.

'Who, Miss?'

She explained about the French painter, his attempt at exact realism which became more than that, like a very precise but strange dream.

Miss Audrey Barber was the only woman teacher we had and the only one who called us by our first names. It seemed right in her – a nice continuation from junior school – but it would have been strange and uncomfortable if the men teachers had done that.

'Keep at it, boys. Considerable promise there. I'll bring some Douanier-Rousseau pictures next lesson to show you more clearly what I mean.'

She was young, rather dumpy, with a broad face on which she slapped too much make-up, probably to try to hide the bad skin you could see when she was close, but she was still attractive. It was her personality mainly, the fervent and humorous manner.

'I saw her with her boyfriend last week,' whispered Derek as she went away.

'Where?'

'In Hinchley's. I was in the café with Mam.'

'What was he like?'

'A tall, cheery sort of bloke, with a laugh even louder than hers. Tweed jacket, leather patches, so he's bound to be a teacher. Teachers tend to marry one another, you know, like a tribe, but Miss Barber's not got that far yet – not even an engagement ring.'

'Congratulations, Sherlock!' I said.

'That's me. Shall we put Sherlock Holmes somewhere?

With a big pipe hanging from his mouth and a magnifying glass? Looking for clues amongst the sawdust!'

It wasn't a good likeness but just about recognisable.

'He's on loan to the clowns,' said Derek. 'Can you do a clown now? I need a bit of a rest after all this thinking.'

A white-faced, red-nosed clown, with baggy trousers and huge shoes – that was easy. He was already a caricature and I felt happier when exaggerating a shape. I put him next to the soulful lion, in the act of stroking his mane or dangerously ruffling it, I wasn't quite sure.

'That's good!' enthused Derek. 'Now you stand aside while I populate the high wire.'

The figures that he sketched were not circus types but pop-singers and entertainers, about whom Derek knew a lot.

'Here he is, then, the Billy Fury of the high wire!'

It wasn't like Billy Fury, or anyone really, except that the Elvis signs were there: the hair, the guitar, a mouth twisted in what was meant to be a surly pout. I looked at the face dubiously, and made some comment about the more famous singer.

'Well, Billy Fury models himself on Elvis, doesn't he?' said Derek, put out at my lack of appreciation. Then, as we worked on, at a leisurely pace though because we'd have two sessions for this picture, he gave me a semi-whispering version of "Last Night Was Made For Love", in a husky, yearning tone which was remarkably like Billy Fury's – allowing for the fact that Derek's voice hadn't yet broken, although it was lower in the scale than mine. Perhaps that was what would happen, his voice just sinking until it became like a man's. Better than cracking from falsetto to baritone and back again, as had happened with Roy.

'Well?' Derek asked when he'd finished.

'Great! You sound just like him.'

He was pleased, his self-esteem fully restored, preening himself in such a way you had to laugh.

'I'm a better imitator than painter. Still, it was a good idea, wasn't it? Next time I'll do a Frank Ifield.'

He'd just started on "I Remember You" when the bell went. Miss Barber told us to get our things together, make sure the water jars were emptied and the brushes cleaned, and to put the papers and paints in the art cupboard. Then we should depart in a quiet, orderly fashion.

'Those pictures that are still wet – just leave them where they are. I'll look after them. And make sure your names are on your work. We don't want these masterpieces wrongly attributed for posterity, do we? Derek and Colin, don't crowd your circus overmuch. The focus – or foci – should always be clear.'

The art class broke up. The final period of the day was history, the only subject in which I was the acknowledged star, not that that had gained me much popularity if Doran and Witherow were anything to go by. Derek remarked how he could always see my head swelling up after history and how it was a good thing we didn't have school caps at Willow Road, because they'd never find one to fit me. But this teasing was all right; from Derek it was like disguised praise anyway.

***

We started going round to each other's houses. The first time at the Frasers', naturally I was introduced to his parents – 'This is Colin, he's an escaped criminal, wanted by the police on two continents' – who were friendly and welcoming, and then to his sister, Becky, two years younger than us, in the last year at junior school.

She was black-haired like her brother, with the same darkish, rosy complexion (a gift from neither of her parents, as far as I could see), with similar features too.

There was no doubt in the family's mind that Becky would pass the 11+ with flying colours. She was regarded as brainy and sometimes given the kind of respect which reminded me uncomfortably of all the fluttering around Roy when he'd got his place at university.

Becky could be pert and, in my view, self-regarding, although she always put herself out to be pleasant to me. I was shy of her at first and it was a while before I could accept her presence with me and Derek as anything less than an intrusion.

When in a good mood, which was most of the time, Derek didn't mind her being top at school in everything and although he sometimes sighed that, compared with her, he was 'useless', he felt nothing of the sort – and was never made to by his parents. I envied him that.

Mum and Dad were glad to see I'd made a friend and took to Derek straight away. My mother smiled broadly, looking fifteen years younger at least, whenever she saw him, and judged that Derek would be good for me because 'He'll lift you out of yourself'. What she meant was that I brooded and sulked and hid away in my room too much. As for my father, he always made a great fuss of him but even 'Sunny Jim', as he tended to call Derek, could see that the atmosphere at our place was very different from his house, where the rule was generally cheerful and tolerant, only firm when it had to be.

At home my mother either fussed about everything or let it go altogether, lost in some gloom of her own. She and Dad were even more often at loggerheads, especially since my father had commandeered the spare bedroom as his temporary office, while he was setting up his company: paper products of a 'superior' nature mainly, such as slightly scented notepaper and fancy cards for all occasions. My father, who'd spent most of his working life as a rep, saw what he was starting on now as a bold and positive move, whatever his wife's caustic remarks about the size of the bank loan, the perilous uncertainty of his venture. But, until he could find an office and storeroom at a reasonable rent, it did mean that he was much more under my mother's unyielding scrutiny.

Neither of Derek's parents had been to grammar school, as mine had – up to the end of the fifth year anyway. Derek's father had gone straight to sea after leaving school and, before she got married, his mother had worked in a shop. Yet, in spite of all my father's dictums about 'getting on' and his pride in being an independent businessman, it was Derek's dad at Norlind who seemed to be rising. Boxes of stationery and cards arrived at our house and I helped to shift them up to the makeshift office, but not many of them were parcelled up to go out again. Every time I popped my head in there, it seemed that the barricade of goods around my father's desk was growing.

The assumption at the Frasers' was that, whereas Derek might not be academically inclined, he'd make his way in life somehow. His buoyant nature and everyday quickness would carry him through.

He hadn't told them, save perhaps in a passing flippant remark, what he truly wanted to be. He hardly let on even to me at the beginning, and then it came out in a sudden mad rush, as if he were mocking himself to pieces or protecting a shyness I didn't even suspect he had: Derek proclaimed he'd be a better singer than Billy Fury and Elvis combined, he'd be both the Everly Brothers in one and, if he became a comedian instead – or as *well* – he'd be funnier than Ken Dodd, Tony Hancock and Benny Hill at their very best!

Then, setting his sights a bit lower, he reminisced wistfully about Butlin's holiday camp in Filey where he and his family had gone for two weeks before he started at Willow Road. Some of the redcoats there doubled as entertainers – singers, funny men and even a juggler – as well as organisers. What a smashing life they led! What a great job!

My family, including Roy, the great proletarian, looked

down their noses at Butlin's, the provider of regimented vacations for the masses, so it shocked me to hear Derek going on enthusiastically about it.

My parents certainly worried about what I'd become. Roy was going through a rebellious phase, but he'd get over it and achieve a good result in his final exams. With that kind of degree to flaunt in front of employers or those in charge of awarding research scholarships, you could do anything. Such a qualification would be an unlikely aim for the dullard of the family, but I'd have to find something respectable when the time came, something that wouldn't disgrace them or me.

It was assumed that I'd go to the College of Further Education when I left Willow Road, try to get a few 'O' levels. Then I might be able to get into a bank or the lower reaches of the civil service. There was even some airy talk about my being accepted by a training college further south in the county, where the entrance requirements were startlingly low. So I'd become a teacher, not as accomplished as Mr. Marston, who had a degree, (my father reckoned that he wouldn't stay much longer at Willow Road, that he was simply waiting for a suitable vacancy at the Grammar School), most likely instructing juniors, the kids of that age being reckoned as more tractable and easier to teach.

Such a prospect dazzled me about as much as the others, but from time to time it was held out as the summit of the hopes I could entertain, and then only if I stopped dragging my feet and made more effort.

There were only two things I reckoned I excelled at: history, as I've mentioned – and writing stories, which were kept hidden away in a box, on show to no one apart from me. Now, though, after Derek had been round to my place a few times, I took courage in both hands and told him about them. He was eager to read my efforts.

We'd bought some pikelets on the way home and

toasted the lot in the kitchen, lathering them with butter. Then we put them on a big dinner plate and carried them carefully up to my room. I was afraid of one – perhaps more! – sliding off the plate and leaving great smears of butter on the stair-carpet. Mum didn't like food being eaten anywhere in the house except the kitchen, or the front room on more formal occasions. I stored biscuits and chocolate up in my room sometimes and always tried to make sure there were no tell-tale crumbs or wrappers left around. I'd been caught that way before and got a bad telling-off.

That afternoon my mother was out at some chapel meeting or other, so we were in luck. We could hear my father in his temporary office telephoning somebody. The door was closed but he was speaking in a loud, cajoling voice. He must have been asking heavily for a favour, trying to fix something of advantage for his fledgling firm, but I didn't hang around to find out. My room was at the other end of the corridor and we got in there with the maximum speed we could, our plate of pykelets unspilt though we were giggling and fooling around. I closed the door firmly behind me.

First of all, we tucked into the food, then I showed Derek the stories. Soon the pages had buttery fingerprints all over them, but I didn't mind that – it became like a seal of approval, because he liked the stories and made me promise that I'd copy some of them out for him later on.

I had another secret-laden shoebox too, but I didn't show him that. On the top it contained some old birthday and Christmas cards I liked. They were also camouflage for the diaries I kept beneath. I'd started writing them the year before the 11+ and I was on the third one now. I'd even worked out a sort of code to baffle Mum if she started snooping, though I don't think she ever did. I was supposed to keep my room tidy, but every so often she dusted and hoovered it. She must have seen the shoeboxes yet I'm pretty sure she never looked inside them; the rubber bands I put over the cardboard to keep the lids tight were always in exactly the same position. Still, you couldn't be too careful.

Not that my diaries contained anything scurrilous, but that month they were getting more interesting at least, startling too – I'd already written an account of the chuntering old man and the dancing lamp. They were diaries which only allowed a short space for each day, so I often jumped ahead of the calendar, by trying to make my writing as tiny as possible to include as much as I could. Nowadays, I can only read these minutely-inscribed entries with the aid of a magnifying glass but, making allowance for my years then, the best of them give the essence of what we experienced that October.

Naturally, Olsen's bullying and Derek's rescue of me took up a lot of space, more than that given to describing my hide and the Land of the Two Rivers. They'd been the stars of the show before.

***

It must have been around that time that I told Derek about the muttering codger and the lamp. He was intrigued and not long afterwards we went to the hide and kept a kind of vigil for the lampman.

'This is a den all right!' said Derek from inside. I'd told him where to squeeze through the bushes. I was pleased he approved.

I'd found two wooden boxes at home which I'd lugged here to use as seats. I covered them with plastic bags to keep out the wet, as best I could. And from the inside wall of the biggest bush I'd hung an old tobacco tin I'd found in my grandfather's bedroom, and in it I put things like biscuits or sweets. Although I'd cleaned the tin thoroughly, I couldn't get the tobacco smell completely out. That worried me at first, but in the end I wasn't bothered. It didn't seem to spoil the stuff I put there, in fact probably flavoured it a bit.

Besides, this tin reminded me of Grandpa and that was reassuring, especially when the place was cold and damp. Then the tobacco smell would be stronger than it actually was, somehow a warmth coming off it too, however slight. I'd liked and respected my grandfather, even if I hadn't been particularly close to him. He was an austere and self-possessed old gentleman, who always made an effort to be kind to me.

But he had a contempt for my father he could never completely disguise. In his view, Dad was a posturer and a ne'er-do-well, a poor match for his daughter. In contrast, he praised Roy and often said how much he would have liked to have studied, but that 'You followed your father into his business in those days and there was no further talk about it.'

Yet he was always judiciously brief in his praise of Roy, as if quite aware of the jealousy it might provoke in me. One of the things I remembered him most fondly for was the way he'd get me to recite the dates of the English monarchs, starting with the Tudors. I could do that almost without thinking. This little performance pleased both of us. Taking his pipe from his mouth, he'd grunt and, broggling it out with a pipe-cleaner, proclaim: 'You'll make your way, young Colin, don't worry about that.' It was the kind of comforting prophecy I needed, and I called it back often enough later.

Of course, I was taking a risk putting Grandpa's tin there, the wooden boxes too. Anybody might have discovered them. Other kids wandered through the Land of the Two Rivers – I'd spied on them from the den, fearful lest they'd come up the path and start exploring. But they didn't. They were much more interested in the lower part of the waste area, where the stream and its meagre, muddy tributary flowed and trickled.

My Tigris and Euphrates! A thick clump of bushes and a stunted tree on the rise seemed to have no allure for them, but they certainly had for me.

Derek as well now. He started suggesting various ways the place might be improved.

Some of them sounded a bit fanciful and self-defeating to me, as if we'd be advertising our presence, simply inviting people to raid us, so I hummed and havered, trying to calm his enthusiasm without dampening it altogether.

I reminded him of what we were really here for, this time: to see whether the shabby, chuntering old bloke would come along this path again. Judging by the comments of the irate neighbour, he'd formed the habit of doing so. Whilst Derek and I kept a sharp look-out, we munched the biscuits I'd stored in the tin – tobacco-flavoured ginger nuts! – and swigged from a bottle of lemonade I'd brought with me.

There were one or two false alarms and we had to hang around getting cold but, finally, we were in luck. Along the man came, muttering away, with his shopping-bag, no doubt containing the lamp. He was tieless again, but today the lamplighter, as I began to nickname him, was wearing a scarf loosely tied across his scraggy throat to ward off the edge of the chill.

'Look!' I said excitedly, as I saw the figure approaching. I felt vindicated because Derek had been getting impatient, starting to put down what I'd told him about the codger as one of my 'stories'. He used to do that sometimes as a kind of teasing rebuke, if he felt I was getting too full of myself or letting my imagination run away with me.

In turn I would accuse him of showing off, which was a bit like telling a dog not to bark or a horse not to neigh. That was his nature and, even timid as I was then, most of the time I delighted in it.

Derek gave a start as he peeped out at the old man and

began to say something, then stopped as if he wasn't quite sure. But when the figure drew abreast of our hide, very close to, he let out a breathy sort of whistle.

'What's up?'

He didn't answer, intent on the old man moving to the left of us now but suddenly stopping and staring down at the bag he was carrying, gob-smacked, as if he hadn't seen it before. Then he shambled away.

'What's the matter, Derek?'

'Nothing. Come on.'

Derek was smiling and that curious, secretive smile stayed on his face more or less the whole time as we followed the codger and watched him go through the same ritual as when I'd tracked him first: planting the lamp, lighting it, looking down the slope to the stream. He didn't have any flowers this time, though, and he wasn't weeping, but his face was set and sad.

I kept well out of sight as before, but Derek sometimes leaned out too far. There wasn't much chance of his being spotted, however, because the lamplighter's gaze was fixed so rigidly.

We kept him within our snooping eyes until he moved off on his return journey. It was getting towards dusk. The lamp was still burning but this time it didn't start dancing. Oddly, Derek didn't seem disappointed that I hadn't delivered on that.

I was about to turn the lamp off, apprehensive that the irate neighbour might appear again, but Derek stopped me, his hand on my forearm.

'No, let it burn.'

I began to protest.

'There's no risk,' he scoffed. 'It'll be down to nowt soon. See how weak the flame is.'

He was grinning to himself all the way back, which irritated me a lot. I'd thought that what I had to show him would be a pleasurable extension of what I'd told him, but it'd all gone flat and this mysterious joke of his was part of the disappointment. It was as though he were flaunting something over me now.

So I couldn't help feeling resentful. I'd let him into a secret – three secrets, really: the hide and the old man and, before that, my stories – and all I got was that smug, superior expression!

My annoyance must have shown clearly because, just before we parted at the end of Langtoft Avenue, he gave me his open, fully amiable grin, a world away from the horribly cryptic smirk.

'Don't get mardy, Colin,' he said. 'Something tickling me, that's all. And I'm being a bit mean hoarding it up like this, I know, but I want to see your face when I let you in on the truth. Come on!' He took up a boxing posture. 'I'm Randolph Turpin and you're Sugar Ray Robinson.'

'Who?'

'Before your time, little boy? The night Turpin took the World Middleweight Championship for Britain. My Dad told me about it. He can still go through the fight round for round. He was listening to the commentary on the radio.'

He planted a soft blow on my chest. I swung at him and missed. Derek landed a couple of taps against my cheek, and then abruptly broke off the game – just as I was preparing to charge in wildly – by skipping away altogether, saying he'd be late home if he wasn't careful and get a real slaughtering, fifteen rounds non-stop, from his Mam.

He turned round, just as he was crossing the Shore Road and shouted back: 'Come round to our place after school tomorrow. Ask your mother if it'll be all right. There's bacon and egg pie and nobody makes that better than Mam!'

I called out, thanking him, and saying I was sure that'd be fine. He waved and then was gone towards the Park, but for a second or so I could hear his voice coming back to me, pitched eerily, like a ghost bawling through a megaphone: 'And all will be revealed!'

VI. Two Old Men

Before we were treated to the bacon and egg pie, Derek said that he wanted to show me something 'really interesting'. This necessitated going outside apparently, as he was already putting on his coat again.

'Don't be long!' called Becky. She was in charge of tea, as both the elder Frasers were out. 'I'm turning on the oven now. When the pie's heated up right, I'm putting it on the table. I'm not going to let it burn to a frazzle.'

'How about turning the oven off when the food's ready and leaving it in?' suggested Derek.

'It'd dry up. If you ever helped with the cooking, you'd know that.'

She sounded quite bossy but funny too, like an imitation mother.

'We'll be back,' said Derek. 'And if we're late – a little late – we'll eat it cold. Good that way too.'

'Mam thinks it's better warm.'

'Mam would give us the choice.'

Derek motioned me to get my coat and follow him.

Their house was part of a terrace, but it had a short front garden and the sitting room had a bay window, just about, a very shallow recess, much smaller than ours. On my first visit, Mrs Fraser had been quick to tell me that they didn't live in a council house, but that it wasn't a very satisfactory place either. They needed more space and something was always going wrong, besides which she was tired of renting – just pouring money into the landlord's pocket! She wasn't sure they could afford to buy a house yet, though, even on a mortgage. Her husband thought they'd be able to manage, but he was one of nature's optimists.

Derek set off at a fast pace and led me round several corners, sudden, abrupt ones that you hardly expected. I didn't know this part of town at all, the area behind Willow Road. It was simply called the Marsh. Firm enough underfoot now, a close maze of tarmac and brick, although Derek told me with fanciful glee that there were spots he knew of which they hadn't been able to dry out and reclaim.

'You could die in one of those holes, if you just stumbled in. Sink down, like the quicksands at low tide. One moment you're looking over at Yorkshire, the next you're tucking into as much sand as you can eat, and more. Not much good when you can't breathe, though, is it?'

I'd had nightmares about these fabled quicksands. Everybody had a story to tell about their killing powers, but everybody also seemed to have heard the story from someone else, and on it went. Grandpa had been sceptical, but he didn't actually deny their existence.

The houses were growing meaner, flat-fronted dwellings of scanty width in longer and longer terraces, it seemed to me. They looked straight out onto the pavement.

And then, suddenly, Derek stopped, and stopped me, before a very shabby-looking place.

'This is the one.'

As he was raising the doorknocker, he whispered to me: 'Get ready to run. Across the road, into that ginnel there.'

Then he gave the knocker not just one polite tap, but what sounded like a whole tattoo of thunderous blows. Even the police, certain they'd tracked down a criminal, wouldn't have been that loud.

'Quick!' urged Derek and we sprinted over the road, flattening ourselves against the side of the alley.

'Who lives here, then? What are you after, Derek?'

He shushed me.

Whoever he'd summoned didn't come to the door, although an old woman from two entrances further on did , looking up and down suspiciously before going inside again.

Derek was disappointed, as if the possibility that his quarry might be out had never occurred to him.

I was getting tired of the mystification and what appeared to be this pointless fooling around.

'Come on, Derek. This is silly. Let's go back.'

'Hold on a bit.' He considered the matter. 'What do old men do a lot?'

'Grouch.'

'Yes, yes, and?'

'Eat. Stuff themselves.'

It struck me that neither had been true of my grandfather and I felt guilty, as if I were telling lies about him.

'*Sleep*, of course! They spend so much time sleeping you sometimes wonder why they bother to wake up.'

That hadn't been true of Grandpa either, but this time it was Derek who'd said it.

'So there's still a chance.'

He bent and looked around at his feet. When he straightened up again and moved out under the street light, I saw that he'd collected some pebbles, one or two of them quite big.

I followed him back across the road.

Standing just off the pavement, Derek sighted the upper window of the house. It was all in darkness. No one could be there, that was clear to me. Even old people didn't go to bed that early, unless they were ill, and then a lamp would be left on somewhere, for comfort.

'Derek, what are you up to now?'

'Going to be somebody's alarm clock, that's all.'

I was already on edge. Now I became afraid. I tugged at the sleeve of his throwing arm but he shook me off impatiently and took aim.

The first pebble, the smallest he'd got, struck the window frame.

'Derek!'

The second one hit the edge of the glass which gave a sharp ping.

'Contact!' he yelled.

'Nobody's at home. Let's get out!'

The next throw got the centre of the window. I saw the alert neighbour drawing back the curtain of her front room, squinting at us from an angle.

'That woman's watching us!' I hissed.

'Right. Time for disguise.'

'It's a bit late for that.'

'Maybe.'

He whipped a balaclava helmet out of his side pocket and quickly put it on. That hid his mop of black hair and much of his face, particularly the forehead and ears.

'What about me?'

'You're all right. No one knows you round here.'

I moved as far as I could out of the range of the streetlamp. I had the shameful impulse to run off and leave Derek, yet at the same time I couldn't imagine not standing near him.

'One last time.'

He was hefting the largest pebble he'd picked up.

'Don't! I've told you, the house is empty!'

'Just this last one. Promise.'

He took careful aim and hurled the stone upwards. It seemed almost as fast and hard as a bullet to me. I turned my eyes away, not able to look, fearing the inevitable.

But the inevitable didn't quite happen. There was a cracking sound but somehow the window didn't smash into pieces as I'd expected. Looking up now, I saw a diagonal line across it, running from top right to lower left. No saving the glass. A new pane would have to be put in.

'Oh Derek, you idiot!'

Having been brought up to possess an almost religious respect for other people's property, I was terrified now, imagining this grubby street to be suddenly alive with angry citizens dragging us off for punishment, let alone the scolding that would come from my scandalized parents. And, although he was fond of citing Proudhon's famous dictum about property being theft, I don't think Red Roy would have approved either. For him, what Derek had done (and I'd unhappily gone along with), would just be the violation of a lofty principle by an act of petty hooliganism. And I didn't reckon that Derek's tolerant, open-hearted parents would have been exactly chuffed about the incident.

What actually happened was that, only a couple of seconds after the window had cracked, there was a huge bellow of anger – alarm too – from beyond it, sounding like a monster rudely awakened in its lair.

'You see?' Derek turned to me with an air of triumph. 'I knew the old bugger was in there somewhere. Come on!'

We ran back to the entrance of the ginnel to watch.

There was hardly enough time to hide before the door opposite us was flung open and a dishevelled old man appeared, glaring angrily around him.

'Take a good look, Colin,' Derek instructed me, holding on to my arm so that I shouldn't stand too far out. 'Do you see who he is?'

Even in that artificial, somewhat uncertain illumination, it wasn't hard to recognise him: the lamplighter. I was too taken aback to be annoyed with Derek for holding out on me, crowing over his secret. But he had a further surprise in store.

'That's Mr Marston.'

'*Marston!*'

'Senior. Our esteemed teacher's father.'

Derek read my mind easily enough.

'Yes, I could have told you earlier. Yes, I kept it back – just for a bit of devilment, as Mam would say.'

In the near-darkness he pushed his face right into mine, to check my reaction. Then he moved back, wagging a mock-threatening finger at me.

'But don't take the hump, young Colin. Let's not be "infantile" about this.'

This was a word often hurled at our class when 2A was kicking up.

Now Derek's whisper rose into a chuckle and afterwards into a fit of laughter. He was giving our position away! But that sound was infectious and, whatever the risk, I couldn't help joining in.

Old Mr Marston was still roaring vengeance, yet not loud enough to smother our glee. He peered towards the dark hole of the ginnel, then started to advance in a totter across the street.

'Hey, you lads! Come out of there!'

'He's properly on the warpath,' said Derek into my ear. 'Time for us to go!'

He turned and pelted down the ginnel to the other end. Close on his heels, I followed him. There was no way the old man could keep up with that and he didn't have anyone to help him, especially the younger, speedier allies he needed. That neighbour woman wouldn't be any good, not that she'd done more than look out of the window.

It wasn't long before we were emerging from the maze of streets and getting close to Derek's house.

'Not a hint about what's happened,' he insisted, 'and particularly not in front of Becky. She'd have the whole story out of you in a trice – and, if she didn't, she'd make one up, twice as harmful.'

***

By this time, Mrs Fraser was back, but her husband was still at Norlind, at a managers' meeting, as she told us. He'd be eating there, so we weren't to save any of the bacon and egg pie.

Minus the slices Becky and her mother had taken, this was now on a big platter in the centre on the table. It wasn't really a pie in the full sense, as it had no crust over it; more like what my mother would have called a flan, but I didn't say that.

'Completely cold,' said Becky accusingly, as though our tardiness had spoiled the treat.

It was still very good and I tucked into mine. Derek said he needed Branston pickle with his meal and put a great dollop of the stuff on the side of his plate. He hacked a clump of bread off the loaf, and then a slightly more elegant one for me.

'I can see you at Buckingham Palace eating cucumber sandwiches with the Queen!' said Mrs Fraser, as she brought a fresh pot of tea to the table. 'I've heard of not standing on ceremony, but this is ridiculous. I don't want people to think that you're being dragged up, Derek.'

'You've got a hard job there, Mam,' said Becky.

Mrs Fraser nodded in a rueful way and then turned to me.

'Well, do you like the pie, love?'

'It's excellent, Mrs Fraser,' I said, with an attempt at aplomb.

They all burst out laughing and, although I reddened, I was pleased too, as if at a further sign of inclusion. This was nothing like enemy laughter.

'Yes, I think it's rather excellent as well,' said Derek, adopting a lofty tone like some lord in his club. 'I say, pass my serviette ring, will you? The solid silver one with my initials on it. Look lively, serf!'

'I think Colin speaks very well,' said Becky. The smile she gave me was a little practised, but uncannily like Derek's.

'Of course he does,' said Mrs. Fraser. 'You could take a leaf out of his book, you children. Colin'll be good enough for Parliament.'

'No, he's a born history teacher,' Derek told her. 'He knows as much as Mr Marston, already. Don't you?'

'Well, I don't think so. Certainly not! I...'

Derek got me to do my kings and queens party piece, which I started on slowly and bashfully, gaining more confidence as I moved closer to the present, very aware of Becky's approving gaze on me. At the end, she admitted that my performance was better than she could do, but countered with an abstruse series of geographical facts about South America, which was one of her favourite interests at the moment, she said. I complimented her on her knowledge. The cracked window suddenly seemed far away, almost as if it had never happened. I knew guilt and worry would hit me, but I was glad to keep them at bay for a while.

'Two clever clogs – or cloggses – at one table,' moaned Derek mock-despairingly. 'What did I do to deserve this?'

'Have you got anything for us, then?' asked Becky pertly.

'Funny you should say that.'

Derek got to his feet and took up a Billy Fury pose.

'No, thank you very much!' said his mother, plonking him back into his chair. 'You do a good imitation, but not now. Everything in its place.'

'That's not fair, Mam!' said Derek indignantly.

'Strictly speaking, it is unfair. But you're more in the spotlight in this house than anyone is. You've got to admit that. Besides, it's mealtime.'

'What's that got to do with it? You allowed Colin and Becky.'

'Stop your wailing, my lad. Right now!'

She put another slice of the pie on my plate and a smaller one on Derek's.

'And don't smother it with Branston.'

'What's Dad going to eat at the factory?' asked Becky.

'Nothing like this, I'll be bound,' Mrs Fraser replied. 'He told me the canteen's putting on something special, but he was a bit vague about it.'

'De-frozen fish, de-frozen chips and de-frozen peas!'

mocked Derek.

'That's not so bad, is it?' responded his mother. 'I've never known you turn your nose up at it. Where did you get this kind of sneering talk from?'

'Colin, of course,' said Derek. 'He's simply full of sedition.'

Sometimes Derek surprised me with the words he came out with. He seemed to hoard up a few choice difficult ones, waiting for the right moment to spring them on people – the specially sharp arrows in his quiver. He was pleased now to observe Becky's puzzlement.

'Colin?' said Mrs Fraser, smiling. 'I find that hard to believe.'

'No, I didn't... I'm not, honestly.'

She patted my shoulder.

'He's just teasing you.'

'He never stops,' contributed Becky, 'even when it's *not* funny.'

'It must be terrible to have no sense of humour.'

'Pipe down, both of you!' commanded their mother.

When we'd finished, she wrapped up the rest of the pie in greaseproof paper and put it in a plastic box. 'There we are!' she said, pushing the lid down firmly. 'Now, I'd like you lads to run a little errand for me.'

'What sort of errand?' asked Derek suspiciously.

'Just nip down to Grand-Dad's and give him this.'

Derek groaned elaborately, as if being tortured, which I guessed was the stock response to his mother's requests and didn't signify much.

'I'll do it!' jumped in Becky eagerly.

'Thank you, love, but let the boys go. You can help with the washing-up and then we'll look through one of those intelligence tests you showed me yesterday.'

'Oh, I can do those almost without looking. They're so easy!'

'Even so, a bit of practice won't do you any harm.

They're an important part of the exam.'

That was enough to convince Becky. She'd set her heart on passing the 11+ well. Although the grades weren't announced, beyond pass or fail, she'd *know* she'd excelled and that knowledge would be sufficient to carry her on a wave of triumph into the girls' Grammar School.

I knew something of ambition from Roy, but to see such drive in a girl as young as Becky was both more impressive and more worrying. What on earth would she be like at twenty? An intimidating super-brain but it was odds-on she'd be pretty too.

'I'm taking Colin home,' said Derek. 'We'll drop in at Grand-Dad's as we go.'

His mother told him automatically not to get up to any mischief.

'What? Between here and Langtoft Avenue? Chance would be a fine thing.'

'You'd get into trouble just by standing still.'

I glanced at her nervously. For one instant I thought she'd heard about the window, but she *couldn't* have! – besides which, she was smiling. I felt reassured.

I thanked her for having me to tea, saying once again how good the pie was (without using the word 'excellent' this time), all in that formal, rather stiff manner in which I'd been taught to show a proper gratitude.

Mrs. Fraser seemed touched, though. She mussed my hair affectionately, then rebuked herself: 'Now look what I've gone and done!' She hastily welsh-combed my locks into some kind of order, laughing: 'Don't worry, Colin, my hands are clean. I'm glad you don't use any of that awful hair-jollop.'

She was called away by the telephone ringing – a friend or relative, as far as I could gather; anyway, at least not a furious old Mr Marston. It was Becky who saw us off, asking if I could go further back in history than Henry VII in 1485. I said only with big gaps here and there. I got the impression that it wouldn't be long before she'd do some extra learning, to be able to fill them in for me.

She talked with friendly respect, saving the tartness of tone for her brother.

'There's no need to see Colin home,' she said, following us to the gate. 'I should think he knows the way.'

'We've got to talk about something,' he said. 'Just him and me.'

She took the snub badly.

'You're only trying to avoid homework and you don't get much anyhow!'

'Well, do it for me, then. Tell you what, I'll pay you one and a half Smarties for each correct answer. Can I say fairer than that?'

'Yes, lots! Besides, I don't like Smarties.'

She was talking to us from the other side of the gate now, swinging on it.

'Goodbye, Colin. It was nice to see you. Look after my daft brother, if it's not too much trouble to ask.'

'Not half as daft as some I could mention.'

This bickering too had something of the air of familiarity about it, but it was threatening to develop into a silly squabble; a good thing that Becky chose that moment to flounce back into the house.

Derek and I set off.

'Becky's not always as bad as that,' he said.

'She was quite nice at times.'

'Yeah?' Derek eyed me cynically. 'If you had any little sisters you'd know they're *never* nice. Take my word for it.'

'You should try elder brothers,' I said, thinking of Roy at his arrogant, bullying worst, but pleased when Derek laughed as at a smart answer.

***

At first it looked as if we were making our way back to

old Marston's and I felt renewed alarm, although I managed not to show this to Derek. Then we turned off at the next corner to the house of danger, as I'd already come to think of it.

Derek suddenly threw the plastic box in the air, nearly fumbling the catch but managing it just as it seemed certain that his grandfather's slice of pie would tumble to the pavement. I had visions of it flying out of the box, escaping the greaseproof paper and splattering along the gutter – a welcome and unexpected gift for a hungry dog.

'Here we are.'

We stopped before a terrace house, very similar in size but less run-down than Mr Marston's. There was a light on in the hall. Derek knocked and almost straight away I could hear heavy, deliberate footsteps coming towards the front door.

Whilst his grandfather turned the key in its stubborn lock, Derek said hastily, in an undertone: 'Colin, Grand-Dad's got a thing about the Bible. He opens the pages at any point and reads out the verses he finds first. He claims that it's meant, that God guides his hand. A bit funny when God mostly seems to choose the gloomy bits! I'm just warning you, that's all.'

The door finally opened and before us stood a short, very broad man, his frame virtually filling the width of the space. He looked something like you'd expect an old boxer to look and that impression was strengthened by a nose which had been squashed at one time and knocked askew and great, meaty hands that seemed to close naturally into fists ready for combat. In fact, as Derek told me later, his grandfather had rarely been involved in any fights at all until quite recently, after he'd seen the Light and chosen to testify regularly at the dock gates, preaching, exhorting, and sorting out the blasphemers.

The other thing that made an impression on me was his hair. It was as silver as an old man's should be, but right at the front there was a startling quiff which was still mostly red, something like a horn.

Mr Reynolds led us into the parlour at the back where there was a blazing fire and a rocking-chair close to it into which he carefully lowered his bulky body. Close to the light of the fire, you could see that his hair had all once been bright red. There were still glints of that throughout, but the quiff held the colour by far the best.

After Derek had introduced us, Mr Reynolds quizzed me a bit at first, annoying me by assuming I was from the south of England. Dealing quickly with my father's Midlands origins, I established my mother's lineage, emphasising how her family had lived for generations in Ketilsby or that area.

'Ah well, it's the way you speak, you see.'

'He never says "barth" for "bath", things like that,' said Derek, defending me.

Mr Reynolds nodded.

'All God's children, wherever you come from.'

'Especially north of the Wash, eh Grand-Dad?'

He smiled affectionately at his grandson.

'I'll not alter what I've said, whatever your ribbing, you scamp.'

He was overjoyed at what Derek had brought him.

'Your Mam's bacon and egg pie! That'll make a lovely supper.'

He put the plastic container on the table, next to a big black book which could only be his Bible. The cover was battered and worn and the splits along the spine had been taped up to keep it all together. Derek glanced at me meaningfully.

I thought Mr Reynolds, as his eyes lingered first on his supper-box and then slipped over musingly to the Bible, would start on the game Derek had mentioned – but not yet.

He had his duties as a host first. Derek told him that

we'd just popped in, we had to go soon because he was walking back to my place with me, but the old man insisted on our having something to eat and drink. He fetched out a bottle of dandelion and burdock and a rusty old biscuit tin. Then he stretched up to a shelf for two glasses.

The dandelion and burdock was flat and the biscuits were soggy. I felt a bit queasy even after just sipping and nibbling as, judging from his ill-concealed expression of discomfort, did Derek.

But Mr Reynolds didn't notice because he was staring intently into the fire, sighing, 'The world we're living in, O Lord, the world we're living in!' as though working himself up to a sermon.

'I think we'll have to be going, Grand-Dad,' said Derek.

'Take your time, lads,' he said reassuringly. And then – to us, himself and the universe: 'That young President ... he hardly looks more than a boy, but he's going to have his hands full over Cuba. God guide us aright and bless us all with deliverance!'

Derek watched with a kind of horror as the thick fingers reached over to the great black book.

'Here's something that will always sustain you, boys – come drought, flood, pestilence or storm. Now, let's see.'

He gave his Bible a judicious look, as though calculating whether it'd act favourably today, then closed his eyes briefly while he opened it.

I forget now where the reading came from, perhaps the Book of Hosea; anyway, some savagely colourful Old Testament passage dealing with sinners, punishment and redemption – if you were lucky.

Mr Reynolds certainly had a preacher's voice, deep and resounding, made even more so in that small sitting-room. He sounded almost as if he were shouting the biblical warning directly across to both Moscow and Washington.

'Grand-Dad, I think Colin and me should...'

But the mighty voice couldn't be stilled so quickly. It

had a little further to go before a stop could be made.

Meanwhile, I found myself looking at a framed black and white photograph on the wall opposite the fireplace. It was of a woman, a very beautiful woman, perhaps in her middle twenties, smiling not quite directly at the photographer but a little to one side, either because her attention had been distracted by someone else or, in spite of the strength shown in her expression, because she was shy. Her hair was blonde, drawn back against the sides of the head and fastened at the back. The cheekbones were prominent, her eyes large and wide, the whole face finely outlined.

His reading from Holy Writ at an end, Mr Reynolds sat brooding in a silent amen, which gave Derek, who'd noticed me staring at the photograph, a chance to spring one more surprise.

'That's our teacher's mother.'

I was slow to catch on.

'You know,' continued Derek with laboured sarcasm, 'the bloke at the front who takes the register every morning.'

'I can't see any resemblance.'

'Well, it is her,' confirmed Grand-Dad Reynolds. 'Krista, spelt with a "k" at the start, no "h". She was German. Half-Jewish, but brought up a church-goer. Even so, she wasn't safe in Hitler's Germany. She was able to get out early, 1934 that was, and came here. Her family weren't so fortunate. Most of the Jewish ones were killed.'

'In the concentration camps?' I asked. I'd seen some awful pictures: piles of bones, the hollow-eyed skeletal faces of the survivors.

'That's right,' said Mr Reynolds. 'And her father died in prison, tortured to death most likely. He was a Protestant but he hated the Nazis and didn't hide it.'

'What did she do when she came to England?'

'Krista was well-educated but the only job she could get

at the beginning, being a refugee, was skivvying. A maid, at one of the big fish merchant's houses around the Park. She did better than that later on. During the war she worked as an interpreter for the military. There were quite a number of German POWs around here and most of them were ordinary working lads who didn't know much English.'

'Who's she looking at in the picture, Grand-Dad?' asked Derek in a skittish sort of way. The story of Krista Marston was one he'd evidently heard before.

'Not at her husband, that barmpot!' said his grandfather spiritedly. 'I was standing beside him when he took that picture, and I suppose I must have cracked a joke – made an amusing remark anyway, which he wasn't very good at.'

Mr Reynolds got laboriously to his feet and stood before us, stout legs splayed to get his balance.

'No, she was looking at me all right. And I'd have gone on looking back at her for ever, if things had been otherwise. But that's not for young ears like yours. Anyhow, I was married and took my vows seriously. Your mother was a little girl then, Derek. '

I was puzzled.

'But that would make our teacher quite young,' I blurted out incredulously.

'He's about twenty-seven,' said Derek. 'Too peculiar to have a wife of his own, a girlfriend even, although he's trying hard enough.'

Taken aback, I realised the teacher wasn't all that much older than Red Roy, although I'd always imagined him as being middle-aged, something like forty. Perhaps it was the moustache that did it, or maybe simply the schoolmasterly air he assumed which put more than a decade on him.

'Marston and Krista got together soon after she arrived here. In fact, she was carrying your friend, the teacher chap, before they got married.'

'Friend!' scoffed Derek.

'That caused a bit of scandal, but not as much as it

might have done because people liked her and were sorry for her. Marston was Krista's senior by far. Well, I would have been too for that matter.'

He allowed himself a rueful smile.

'Is she still alive?' I asked, sounding stupid, because I guessed the answer.

'No,' said Mr Reynolds sombrely. 'She died last year. Far too soon, far too soon. Cancer. The way he troubled her, when she was getting weaker by the day, the pain she was going through! He treated Krista as if the illness was *her* fault. Behaving like the worst of bullies. I told him so, in no uncertain terms, I can tell you. There we were – in this very room – the two of us shouting the odds, but my voice overrode his.'

'I bet it did, Grand-Dad,' said Derek admiringly.

'It didn't do much good, though. Well, he quietened down for a bit, grew gentler, but soon slid back into cruel transgression. I've never spoken to Dennis Marston again since that time, though I've prayed for him often enough.'

Derek told him about how I'd seen old Mr Marston with the lamp. At first his grandfather seemed interested.

'Yes, he and Krista used to go up there quite a lot, when the weather was fine.'

'Colin says he was crying.'

'He's a lot to cry about. Let's hope it wasn't just self-pity. If it's a true sense of loss – well, too many have that thrust upon them.'

It suddenly seemed strange to me that the three old men in my mind – my grandfather, the lamplighter and Grand-Dad Reynolds – were all widowers, as though this was the way of things, even if people generally reckoned that it was women who lived longer.

Mr Reynolds clearly felt he'd said too much and made signs of impatience.

'Come on, young Derek! If you're going to walk Colin home, you'd better do it. Your Mam will be wanting you back before midnight.'

'Imagine what would happen if I turned up then.'

Mr Reynolds shooed us before him out of the house, remembering his manners on the doorstep: a genial remark and a clap on the back for me (it had me staggering a little!) and a reminder to Derek to thank his mother for the pie.

The last sight of him before he closed the door was the massive hand held up in farewell and his red, hornlike quiff.

***

Outside, as we started on our way, I taxed Derek: 'You never told me that Mr Marston was half-German.'

'He isn't. He married one.'

'No, I mean our Marston.'

'I did tell you. '

'You didn't. '

'I did! Perhaps you had your cloth ears on.'

'You didn't! '

We went on like this for a while, like a panto act. And, naturally, the insistence on both sides got heavier as we sped on, as if beating time to our movements. In the end, we just let the matter drop, both of us convinced we were in the right.

'Does he speak German? Our teacher, I mean.'

'I don't know. But I noticed his eyes lit up when he mentioned Hitler.'

'Liar! They wouldn't anyway if his mother was partly Jewish.'

'It was a joke, turniphead.'

'Some joke!'

'He certainly doesn't take after his mother. She looked really nice in that picture, didn't she?'

'What picture?'

'The one on Grand-Dad's wall. I saw you gawping at it.'

'Oh, that. Yes, she looked all right.'

'All right! Don't pretend. You were smitten with her – besotted!'

'Where did you get that one?'

'Not from you. I can read as well, you know.'

'Congratulations. I thought you'd never get there.'

He gave me a cuff across the head, not quite as friendly as it might have been, and ran on, laughing, when I tried to hit him back and missed.

Derek was the only real friend I had, but I didn't want my awed admiration for the young Krista Marston of the photograph to be weakened by having to share it. I wanted to write about that face with its tied-back blonde hair, the mixture of beauty and shy kindness, in my diary: to re-create it in words, pay homage like that. But when it came to the task, I couldn't do it. Everything I tried to put down about her seemed inadequate or just wrong and soppy. Yet when I described the other events of the evening, my pen wasn't half so inept.

Derek and I crossed the Shore Road and went up Langtoft Avenue. For a little while Derek was unusually silent, then he said in a dulled, embarrassed voice: 'I didn't mean to break that window.'

It was contrition of a sort, but I couldn't believe it – especially as we hadn't been found out. Later, I thought he was rehearsing for if or when that did happen, putting on these meek tones which didn't suit him at all.

'You didn't mean to? What do you think happens when you hurl rocks against glass?'

He grinned at my verbal flourish but added anxiously, like a troubled conspirator: 'Keep your lips sealed!'

'Who do you reckon I'd tell?'

'No one. Not deliberately. You're not like that, Colin. But you might just drop a hint by accident.'

'Of course I won't!'

I felt hurt that Derek didn't have complete trust in me; annoyed with him too because I thought he'd lumbered me unfairly with guilt. But, really, I'd become complicit the moment he'd thrown the pebbles and I hadn't stopped him. I might as well have been urging him on from the beginning.

'Good old Colin. I can rely on you – until death and beyond!'

He roared out this extravagant declaration and started laughing again. His noise seemed to echo between the two rows of discreet, semi-detached houses. It was nothing like old Mr Marston's shouting, but it sounded just as mad.

VII. A Merry Sprite

After the last morning class, Mr Marston ordered Derek and me to stay behind. It was the day after the pebble-throwing.

'Out to the table, you two.'

The tone was as firm as it normally was, but somehow calmer. Yet I couldn't take much comfort from that, thinking of Dad coming out with another of his stock phrases, the one about the lull before the storm.

On our way to the front, I managed to avoid exchanging glances with Derek. That would have been a dead give-away, though Mr Marston in this mood might have read guilt in zealous avoidance of eye-contact as well. I'd scrutinised the picture in one of my history books of a Spanish inquisitor. Mr Marston's expression now was a pretty good likeness.

'Did you two boys go near my father's house yesterday evening?'

'Where, sir?' asked Derek, too innocent by half.

'Dunstable Street, Fraser. Don't claim you don't know where it is. You live not far away.'

'Oh, Dunstable Street!' exclaimed Derek, as though Mr Marston had mispronounced the name.

'That's what I believe I said.'

'Yes, we probably went down it, sir, because Colin – Palmer here- came round to us for tea. Afterwards, we walked back to his place. Dunstable Street's on the way. Or it can be.'

Our teacher steepled his fingers and let his jaw gravely rest on them. I studied the bald patch on the crown of his head. He couldn't still be in his twenties! Even given my current state of anxiety, I tried to find "young" signs about him and failed dismally.

'Just when do you think you might have flattered poor, shabby Dunstable Street with your presence? '

'Eh? You mean, sir...'

Derek was cleverly and cloudily approximate about possible times.

'You didn't linger, especially in front of one particular dwelling?'

'People don't linger in Dunstable Street, sir.'

'You're turning into a social observer, Fraser.'

'I hope that's good, sir.'

'What's the Party line, then? Can we take it that neither of you even slowed your steps in passing my father's house?'

'Yes sir!' we both said emphatically together.

There was an ominous pause before Mr Marston continued.

'Because, you see, he was pestered by two young louts last evening. They banged repeatedly on his front door when he was trying to take a nap and then these dolts managed to break one of his windows. Rotten behaviour to inflict on anyone but particularly so on a nervous, frail old gentleman, wouldn't you think? They should take responsibility and, after due apology, recompense my father for the damage. Right?'

'Yes sir.'

Mr Marston was now watching us very sharply.

'Whoever carried out this deed did something very wrong, even if it might not have been maliciously meant.'

'Yes sir.'

'And things like that can't remain hidden.'

'Your sins will find you out, sir,' piped up Derek brightly.

'What?' snapped Mr Marston, his colour, rising.

'I didn't mean *your* sins, sir. I meant...'

'Impersonal use. I understand. *One's* sins. But it's a

strange thought for a cheerful livewire like you to have, Fraser.'

'It's something my grandfather says sometimes, sir. He reads the Bible a lot.'

'Mr Reynolds of Hallam Street?'

'Yes sir.'

Mr Marston nodded his head. He must know the whole story, I thought: how the two men used to be good friends and had fallen in love with the same woman, our teacher's mother, and how later they had quarrelled to such an extent that they were no longer on speaking terms.

But I didn't think he knew about the lamp and the ritual the old man performed in the Land of the Two Rivers. It was my guess that that remained Mr Marston senior's secret, because his son was a great eradicator of things irregular or unconventional, and I was pretty sure that if he'd known about this aspect of his father's behaviour he'd somehow have tried to curb it.

'The Bible, eh? It might do you some good to take a look at your grandfather's copy, Fraser.'

'I do, sir. I like the bloody bits, all the fighting.'

I thought this was unnecessarily cheeky, given our situation, and would just enrage the teacher, getting us into further trouble, so I wasn't prepared for what came next.

Mr Marston leant back in his chair and grinned. This was so unusual it disturbed me almost as much as his previous sternness. He did look younger then, briefly alight with easy humour, and I could just about imagine him as still being in his twenties, bald patch or no bald patch.

Rising from his chair, he advised: 'Try the New Testament, Fraser – the Gospels and the Acts of the Apostles. Don't just scoff the mince-pies.'

'No sir.'

Mr Marston tugged Derek's thick black hair, as he tended to do in class if he was in a playfully sadistic mood, that or tweaking his ear and sometimes pinching his cheek with his sharp fingernails. There were quite a number of masters who enjoyed that kind of thing; they chose the boy they wanted to work on, as if this were one of the more tolerable duties imposed on them.

'You're incorrigible, Fraser.'

'Incorri… what, sir?'

'Incorrigible. Do you know what that means, Palmer?'

'I'm not sure, sir.'

'Look it up, then. Both of you. I'll test you tomorrow. You're a merry sprite, Fraser, and I doubt you'll ever change. There, I've just given you the meaning of that tough word I used. Check it, all the same.'

Now he took pains to revert to his earlier, admonitory mood, as though he'd forgotten himself and we'd taken advantage of his leniency.

'Two boys not, as far as I can gather, unlike yourselves in size and appearance, were seen hanging around my father's place yesterday and then running off up the alley opposite. Vague glimpses from ageing eyes, but even so. I shall be looking into the matter and I intend to bring the culprits to book, whoever they are. Is that understood?'

'Yes sir.'

I wondered whether it might not be better to own up after all, and it was as though Mr Marston could read my thoughts because he said, more gently: 'You know, if you've anything to say, it would be better to say it now. Of course, there must be punishment for those at fault, that's in the nature of things. But it'd be less severe than after a confession dragged out from a pile of lies.'

He paused. I was looking at my feet. Later, Derek told me that this was almost as good as saying I'd smashed a dozen windows, but I couldn't help it. Worse still, I was going red. I could feel it, like a fever.

'Are we speaking the same language? Fraser? Palmer?'

'Yes sir.'

Mr Marston stared at us both with an odd, pitiless

sorrow, and then brought the sticky interview to an abrupt end, not that there wasn't the implied promise of others to follow.

'Very well. Go away and consider carefully what I've said.'

***

Outside, as we lingered in the school playground, Derek remarked: 'I think I got the "incorri" word he used, but what's a "sprite" when it's at home?'

'It comes from "spirit", I think,' I said. 'Or it sounds like it does.'

'Alright, but is that what it means now? Is he saying I'm a kind of ghost or something?'

He made sinister whooshing noises and flapped his hands up and down like wings, obviously with vampires in mind as well as graveside ghouls who looked as if they were wrapped in bedsheets.

'No, he thinks you're a sort of elf or goblin, but a larky one.'

'The...!'

Derek blew out his cheeks and pursed his lips, as though to trap a particularly foul expletive, then let out the air in a huge farting rush. He obligingly repeated the performance for some kids near us who had enjoyed it the first time round. I noticed Doran and Witherow amongst them, making a great show of smirking approval.

Glancing up at the school building, I caught the glint of field-glasses reflected in the autumnal sun. Mr Gordon was surveying his charges again and, at that moment, I could sense the focus settling on us. I urged Derek to make haste and we passed round the side of the building, out of the Headmaster's sight.

Walking along Willow Road, I told him that Mr Gordon had been spying on us.

'So what? That was no reason to drag me away. I could have given him a special encore, though I don't think he would have heard me up there.'

He drew his hand through his dark glossy hair. I watched him push some untidy strands into place.

'I don't know why you let Mr Marston maul you around like that.'

'I don't think I've got much choice,' Derek replied,' especially now we're suspects.'

A bit further on, just past the shop where we'd bought the pikelets, he announced boastfully: 'But don't worry. I can handle the Marstons of this world any time.'

He paused, and then moved up closer, as if about to challenge me.

'But you don't know how to, little boy. That's why you need protection!' He made a gangster-face, narrowing his eyes and twisting his lips. 'Capito? Obey, you sawney! Otherwise...' He passed his finger across his throat and mimed the dreadful gushing of blood. 'Where would you be without protection?'

'Where am I going to be with it? That's the question.'

'Trapped either way!' Derek gave a spine-chilling laugh, like an evil master of the universe.

Whatever unease there'd been in him now vanished in a trice and I felt both more grateful and reassured than I should have. It was though we hadn't told anything but white lies and our teacher wouldn't be able to prove our "guilt" in a thousand years, not even if he were Sherlock Holmes himself.

***

Mr Marston was telling us about medieval village life: the strip-farming, the duties of the villeins, the rights and demands of their lords, what they all had for supper, if there was any supper to be had. Even he sounded less than fascinated. I was interested in history, but not in this dreary, day-to-day stuff.

As compensation, I was away back in the Civil War, daydreaming. Prince Rupert had just had a flaming row with the King in Newark, in the upper storey of a house with low ceilings and beams across them. It was now a tea-room, which I'd visited in the summer with my parents. I think the King and his nephew must have been wrangling about tactics and, if they weren't, it didn't matter. My imagination spun out the rest.

Then, by association, I was at Marston Moor. It looked as though the Cavaliers would carry the day, until Oliver Cromwell broke through with his horsemen in a flanking attack. I dwelt on that, the way the Royalists were put to flight, Prince Rupert hiding in a bean field until he could make his escape. The teacher droned on.

This was clearly not one of Mr Marston's inspired mornings, and the realisation seemed to depress him. He stopped speaking and went over to the window, staring out on a drab, rain-swept street. It was a bad sign.

But diversion came quickly and from an unexpected quarter. It was a relief for Mr Marston and for all of us.

A boy I hardly knew called Kilbertson raised his hand and, when acknowledged, said, out of the blue: 'Sir, do you think there'll be trouble over Berlin?'

Mr Marston breathed heavily.

'For heaven's sake, Kilbertson, where are we? As far as I can recollect, we were discussing medieval strip-farming, serfs and boon work, things like that. Forgive me if I'm being dim, but I just can't see the connection with Berlin.'

'No sir, you're not being dim.'

Kilbertson spoke respectfully, solemnly even, but put an unfortunate stress on the last word, which made it sound like the least of Mr Marston's problems. There was a titter around the room, quelled by the master's glare.

'I'm forever in your debt for that kind judgement,

Kilbertson.'

'Sir? No, I meant...'

'Go on, boy, go on!'

'There isn't any connection between medieval times and what I wanted to ask you, sir.'

'So glad to hear it. For a moment I thought my powers of reasoning were defective. Well?'

After his initial boldness, Kilbertson, tall and gangling, became tongue-tied. He stood behind his desk, eyes down, shuffling his feet as if counting them and always arriving at a different number. While he was summoning up the courage to speak, we heard the noise of the Juniors being let out for their break and, beyond our classroom, the dinner ladies moving about in the makeshift canteen, starting to get things ready for the mid-day meal. Both Derek and I preferred going home to eat. School dinners weren't bad but they had a dish-rag smell to them sometimes.

'Oh, come on, Kilbertson! Otherwise, we'll be here till Doomsday.'

'It's just that I'm a bit worried, sir.'

'About what?'

'My brother's in the army, sir. He's stationed in a place called Celle.'

'North Germany. Yes, I know of it. And?'

Mr Marston paused, an expression of consideration replacing the bored, caustic look on his face.

'The Berlin crisis was last year, Kilbertson. Geographically, we've moved elsewhere for this year's hotspot.'

'But what if there's a build-up of troops, on both sides, and my brother's sent to Berlin? It's like an island. They're surrounded there, sir.'

'I don't think you need worry too much. The fact that the East Germans have put up that obscene but strangely useful wall to divide the city should be indication enough.

The line's been drawn, literally. The greatest danger to peace isn't Berlin anymore.'

I couldn't resist shooting up my hand. I was possessed with a burning idea, or rather someone else's burning idea.

'Yes, Palmer? You want to be excused?'

'No, sir, I just ...'

'Not an urgent message from a desperate bladder?'

Some sniggering and open laughter. Permitted this time.

'Go on, Palmer. Entertain us.'

'Sir, they put up that wall in Berlin to stop people getting out.'

'Obviously. Now don't be dull. You can sparkle better than that.'

'Yes, but highly qualified people they needed, like doctors and engineers.'

'Everybody is needed, although I wouldn't like to assert the proposition concerning some of you. Doran and Witherow, are you counted before the throne of the Most High? There are days when I have my doubts, others when I desperately nourish hope. But go on, Palmer. I did you an injustice. Highly qualified or not, these people were fleeing to liberty, weren't they?'

'No sir, they were just fleeing to better jobs and more money. That's how West Germany got them. It was like bribery.'

I was parroting Roy, bringing out his words almost verbatim. I remembered Roy's angry fervour and something of that was carrying me on now.

Mr Marston looked at me curiously.

'There may be some truth in what you're saying, Palmer, but it's a little simplistic. Freedom was a motive force for many of those who chose the Bundesrepublik. Tell me, what paper do your parents take at home?'

'*Ketilsby Evening Telegraph*, sir.'

'No, no! That hasn't had an idea in it since Lloyd George visited the town in 1912. I meant, national newspaper.'

'*Daily Telegraph*, sir.'

'We get the *Mirror*, sir,' someone called out, and then there were rival claims for different papers, like the *Express* and *News of the World*. Mr Marston shushed the class into silence.

'They don't sound very much like the *Telegraph*, your ideas, Palmer, unless it's changed radically since I last looked at my father's copy. Curious. The sentiments you voiced would be more at home in *The Daily Worker*.'

That was the paper I'd seen Roy reading, much to my father's disgust: a thin publication, with angry headlines all about how the proletariat was being cheated and trodden on, and how much better things were in the Soviet Union.

'Never heard of it, sir.'

Another lie, and even delivered with a certain aplomb – borrowed from Derek. This was a harmless one, though, just a fib.

It excited me too that Marston had me down as a secret communist, or at least that I could imagine he did. I understood then, without being able to express it, why Roy was attracted to this world: it made you special, a protector of the underdog, a truth-seeker, in the vanguard of something worth fighting for. And from the thoughtful but somehow sympathetic look our teacher gave me I suspected he might belong to this privileged club too. Perhaps there were secret emblems so that we'd recognise one another – a hammer and sickle inked on the wrist! In red, of course.

'Sit down, Palmer. You've made an interesting contribution to the class discussion. Controversial maybe, but all the same it will get you a plus in my mark-book.'

As I took my place, Derek stared at me scornfully as if I were the slimiest of toadies. There was real anger in his expression and while that disturbed me it also pleased me to steal some of his thunder with Mr Marston. But whatever tension existed between us didn't last long. I gave him a covert V-sign, the first time I'd done that to anybody, and he grinned at my unusual boldness.

Now enlivened, our teacher had definitely left the hovels of the Middle Ages behind him and was giving us the benefit of his wisdom about Mr Khrushchev.

'You've seen pictures of him: fat, squat, pug-nosed, a broad grin when he's amused, a scowl when he's not. Much man-of-the-people bonhomie on occasion. A bit of a clown, wouldn't you think? Bonhomie? No, I'm not going to explain that. Look it up!' He wrote the word in big letters on the board. 'In addition, Khrushchev's a braggart and we don't like that, do we, gentlemen? And don't forget that, whatever this astute Ukrainian has been saying about the horrors of life under Stalin, he was one of the dictator's top lackeys, always there to do his bidding. He knew perfectly well what dear old Uncle Joe was up to.'

Pausing, he surveyed the class. He had all of us hanging on his words now.

'Define "braggart", Fraser. Not a word, I hope, that sits too easily in your vocabulary. '

'Someone like a boaster, sir. You're not calling me big-headed, are you, sir?'

The laughter from the class and Mr Marston's knowing smile gave Derek his answer, but he didn't mind, revelling in the attention and the opportunity to give us a display of injured innocence. It was much more of an exaggeration than when we'd been questioned by Mr Marston, so I reckoned we were still just about safe.

Our teacher briefly returned to his theme.

'Well, are we clear what a slippery customer Nikita is, and that President Kennedy will have his work cut out to deal with him? But, however ruthless the Soviet leader can be, I still don't believe he's insane, bent on the destruction of hundreds of millions of lives.' He stared searchingly at us. 'Yet, if he over-reaches himself, or Kennedy does, then we'll have to start saying the kind of prayers we never even dreamt of before.'

A sombre, frightening note to end his speech on and he must have seen its effect on our faces.

'I think that's enough gloom for today.'

'Cheer up, it may never happen!' Derek called out in one of his funny voices. That was enough to start us giggling and even Mr Marston's face relaxed.

'You've given us exactly the right words, Fraser.'

'That's what my father says when things look bad, sir.'

'A wise man.' He looked at his watch. 'In precisely one minute forty-five seconds the bell will go for the end of class. At the first opportunity, go and get yourselves a huge ice-cream or something similar. Seek refuge in gluttony!'

'An ice-cream in October, sir?'

'Why not? All right, let's compromise on a Fry's chocolate cream or a Mars bar, or a big bag of crisps!'

'Are you paying, sir?'

'One day, Fraser, I'll reveal the miserable pittance I receive for trying to keep you lot this side of ignorance.'

***

The idea of the Berlin Wall began to grip our imagination. Dividing a city just like that was incredible enough but what if, on the drawing-board at least, we should extend the wall, divide not only a city but a continent, a world even? A barricade, a rampart, across the globe!

Derek and I decided to ask Miss Barber about it. Our new joint project. We'd finished the big circus picture, which had gained us praise from her and some of the boys in the class, including Doran and Witherow. Derek viewed these two with intense scorn, deaf to any favourable comment they made. But there seemed to be no renewed alliance with Olsen, as far as we could see. Baleful and scowling, he shambled about the playground, accompanied by different fawners and supplicants.

We were in Miss Barber's good books and she agreed to our ambitious plan with only the minimum of hesitation. In fact, she helped us to join three large sheets of paper together at the edges. These we laid out on a long table at the back of the art-room. In no time at all, our creation was shimmering into what appeared to be an impossible distance. Of course, we didn't forget watchtowers, guards and marauders here and there, although the perspective wasn't good, far more enthusiastic than accurate.

At first Miss Barber identified our picture as an interpretation of Hadrian's Wall, but when we extended it to both margins of the triple sheet, she dubbed it: ' "The Great Wall of China as Perceived Uniquely by Fraser and Palmer" – and there's a title that's almost as long as the thing itself!'

It was more than a fanciful representation of a manmade structure, at least for me. I began to get an exciting sense of infinity as we worked on. It was a heady concept; I couldn't have described the feeling it gave me, not even to Derek.

He got tired of the stretching line, declaring that it looked bare and, despite the guards and marauders, was starved of people. So he began to populate it, borrowing some figures from our circus painting. Naturally, Billy Fury, or some pop-singer likeness, had to appear too. Derek was mucking the whole thing up, in my view. I could protest as much as I liked, but it didn't change anything, and that's when my interest in the picture started waning.

'This is getting more and more surreal, Derek,' said Miss Barber, as she observed him at work. 'You know, like something in a dream.'

'Well, so long as it's not a screaming nightmare, Miss.'

He got on to another tack, leaving aside the world of pop-singers and big top performers. Proudly, he showed me a shape like a dumpling, with a much smaller dumpling for a nose. This creature appeared to be sitting on his haunches, but was thrusting out one podgy leg. I asked Derek who it was supposed to be, if anybody in particular.

'Mr Crush, or whatever he's called,' answered Derek. 'I saw a photo of him in the paper yesterday. You know, the bloke Marston was on about. He's doing one of those Russian dances. Don't you think it's good?'

'No,' I answered, honestly but irritably.

'Well, you're not up to much – just drawing boring lines at the edge of the paper. Anybody can do that.'

It wasn't long afterwards that we abandoned our wall-project or at least brought it to a halt. We declared the picture to be "finished", and Miss Barber seemed to agree, nodding her head, I thought, with more than a little relief.

***

Derek and I left the school together, as we usually did. Often he went with me as far as the park end of Willow Road, and sometimes to the bottom of Langtoft Avenue, that is if we hadn't arranged to go round to each other's houses. Normally, we talked about anything interesting that had happened and made plans. Today, however, I was sunk in silence and, uncharacteristically, that shut him up too.

He must have felt there was something accusatory in my attitude and, in part, he was right. Otherwise, I was thinking of our picture, what a wonderful idea I'd had and how in the end it had been botched. All I needed now was for Derek to break into his Billy Fury routine and I'd be racing ahead – alone.

Increasingly ill at ease, Derek stopped me and asked: 'What's the matter, Colin?'

I hesitated before saying: 'Don't you think we should own up, as Mr Marston said?'

'No!' replied Derek adamantly. 'Are you mad? That'd only get us into more trouble than we deserve. Marston can't prove anything, whatever he suspects. We've just got to stick to our story.'

'Just keep lying, you mean.'

Now Derek's face was hardly that of the "merry sprite" our teacher had invoked. It wasn't exactly that he looked guilty, but he took on a set, rather grim expression, like an ill-fitting mask.

'Owning up at present would be disastrous,' he said with flat deliberation.

'You mean there might come a time when we *can* own up?'

'Why not?' Derek said, but I didn't miss the uncertainty in his voice.

Clearly, he didn't think such a time would ever present itself and neither, if I were being straight with myself, did I, but it was a straw to clutch at, helping to ease my troubled conscience, although I knew it shouldn't.

'How much would it cost to repair, that window?'

'Haven't a clue,' said Derek. 'It'd need a new pane and glass is expensive. Then there's labour costs. Oh, a few quid at least.'

An idea struck me all of a sudden: a solution. It seemed so commonsensical that I was surprised I hadn't thought of it before.

'Why don't we pay for the damage bit by bit, but secretly?'

He gawped at me, amazed at first, as if I'd discovered that the earth had a second moon. Then the familiar wide smile broke over his face and he was Derek again.

'Sometimes, Colin, just sometimes, you're not as green as you're cabbage-looking! Brilliant!'

I pursued my notion eagerly while it was still fresh, making it more feasible by the second.

'Of course, we couldn't afford to give much at a time, but say we each took a shilling out of our pocket-money...'

'Yes, and a bit more when we can afford it, birthdays,

Christmas.'

'Still take us months to pay off, yet...'

'Making amends on the never-never!'

'But how shall we do it? We can't simply leave the money on the doorstep for anybody to take.'

'No, that'd be daft. Just post it – chink, chink! – through old man Marston's letter-box. '

'But what if it puts him on the alert and he watches out for us?'

'Elementary, my dear Palmer,' Derek pronounced in superior Holmesian tones. 'We vary the times of the drop – but always when it's dark, mind. We'll do it together, if you like, but you must follow my instructions to the absolute letter! I'm a master at this type of manoeuvre, or soon will be.'

The first time, we wrote the old man a one-word note: 'SORRY', in block capitals on the back of a paper bag into which we put the coppers and small silver we could spare.

'They'll never be able to trace it back to us,' said Derek with satisfaction. 'Big letters, the way we've done them. It's hardly a signature, is it?'

I wasn't quite so sure – the writing would probably reveal we weren't adults, for a start – but the most important thing was to show our good intentions in practical terms. These grubby coins we'd put into the bag were a beginning at least.

We did keep it up for a while, this piecemeal compensation. But later, towards Christmas, our thoughts were more on buying presents and the contributions to the mend-a-window fund flagged. Still, that didn't seem to matter so much because we planned to go on regularly when we could. It wouldn't even be a bad thing if we went over the amount Mr Marston senior would have to pay for the window, but 'Let's not go mad with generosity,' warned canny Derek, drawing the last shilling from his pocket and looking at it ruefully – the last, that is, until the Skipper paid him his next pocket money on the following Saturday morning.

Most of that would go the same day, whereas Becky tended to save hers. Derek had worked up an excellent mime in which he imitated his sister polishing her every last penny and adding them fussily to the hoard in her piggy bank. I had no idea whether she did anything like this, but I could imagine it, so Derek's version amused me greatly. I wouldn't be challenging Becky about it, however.

Derek did the drops whilst I was the look-out. He revelled in his role as the beneficent ghoul of the night, moaning and groaning his way down the street at first, until I told him to shut up – he was attracting attention from passers-by.

Sometimes he crept into Mr Marston's back yard and put our offerings on the filthy mat outside the door. The old man was bound to step on them when he came out to feed the birds or whatever, Derek said, and would notice something amiss. Whether he could actually bend down to pick the coins up was another matter. Our teacher would do it for him, if need be.

Derek even claimed that once – when I wasn't with him – he'd seen old Mr Marston in a shop and had sidled up to him unnoticed, slipping some loose change into his coat pocket. I was sceptical about this story, mainly because Derek didn't demand that I pay him my share, but it could have been true.

At such times, I saw that our attempts at reparation were more a game to him than a desire to put things right and that did worry me a bit if I was in a solemn, pensive mood. Otherwise, so long as we were doing it, reducing the amount we owed, I didn't think it mattered a great deal. Mischief was the motor on which Derek ran and, anyway, I wouldn't have liked to have been without that.

I'm running ahead of myself, though, and if I'm to be a faithful chronicler, I must return to October, *that* October, in which the world outside nearly came to an end over Cuba but our world grew and shone and became magical.

VIII. The Errand

The bell went for the end of afternoon school. Mr Marston dismissed the class.

'Fraser! A word before you dash off. And Palmer too – the inseparables.'

He waited until the inquisitive stragglers had left the room; just the three of us remaining now. You wouldn't have said that our teacher was in an ear-tweaking mood exactly, but he seemed milder in manner at least – not sitting there and eyeing us like a stern judge.

On his desk there was a parcel wrapped in brown paper, tightly secured by string.

'Old books and documents I borrowed from my father. I meant to drop them off tonight, but I've been called away to a meeting in Horncastle. I wonder if you'd deliver them for me on your way home. Possible, Fraser?'

'Yes sir. '

'Probable? In fact, a racing certainty?'

'Sir.'

'Excellent! I'd appreciate the kindness.'

Neither of us trusted this strangely affable, favour-begging Mr Marston, who was looking us straight in the eye: man to man, or rather chap to chap, as he might prefer to think of it now. I could tell that Derek was instantly on his guard. As for me, I felt very nervy, as if I were groping around in the dark, not knowing what I could bump into.

Mr Marston tapped the parcel.

'Mostly stuff to do with my mother's family and background. Especially since her death, my father has been reluctant to let anything of hers out of his sight, so I did promise him that I'd get these things back to him today.'

Why was he letting us into these family confidences?

Mr Marston leant back in his chair, hands clasped behind his head, as if he'd solved a ticklish problem and at last had the situation completely under control. He didn't look unkind but something of the teacher's sarcastic expression had returned to his face.

'Do you think young fools who cause trouble and disturb elderly people have consciences, Fraser?'

'I don't know, sir. I suppose it depends on the young fools involved.'

'Quite. And you, Palmer?'

'I agree with Fraser, sir.'

'How unusual.'

He unlocked his hands from around his neck and placed them before him. Something about those long arms reminded me of a spider's tentacles.

'A curious thing is happening. Small sums of money have been arriving anonymously at my father's place. A few coppers, the odd shilling and, most recently, a full half-crown. Some little rogue's scruples must have been touched extra strongly that day, or he'd just had a visit from a benign uncle, well in funds! Why are you going red, Palmer? Is it the thought of benign uncles and their generous impulses?'

'I don't know, sir. Perhaps I don't feel too great, sir.'

'Strange. You looked the picture of rude young health a moment ago. And there's no "perhaps" about such matters, surely? Either you feel up to par or you don't. Or have I said something to upset you?'

'I don't think so, sir.'

'Palmer often does go red, sir,' Derek interposed, a little too eagerly. 'And for no reason at all. His mother even took him to see a doctor about it, sir.'

One more to add to the heap of falsehoods we were accumulating, but Mr Marston ignored the comment anyway as something too obviously fabricated to bother with.

'In my view,' he said, 'and I don't think it needs an

Einstein to work this out – yes, I think we can conclude that our two miscreants are behind these payments. The desire to make amends is not dishonourable. Of course, it'd be far better if they had the backbone to own up properly. This sneaky sort of behaviour won't do, even the flourish of the brand-new half-crown.'

He looked at me particularly hard then.

He was about right – not a generous uncle in fact but a generous father, flush with the rare success of winning a contract with a local company to supply their office paper and stationery, and sharing it with me to the tune of a bonus half-crown. In a sudden rush of moral zeal, I'd donated the coin to the Dunstable Street Lamplighter's Benevolent Fund, immediately afterwards thinking I'd been a bit of a fool when I delved into my pocket and found it empty again.

'But there's another problem,' continued Mr Marston. 'As my father gets older, the proverbial bees in his bonnet gather ever more thickly and he becomes prone to attacks of alarm. He's already obsessed with these piecemeal payments. To him, they're marks of fresh intrusion, renewed trespass.'

So much for my brilliant scheme. It was having the opposite effect to what I'd hoped.

I tried hard not to look troubled.

'He's even started watching for likely figures approaching, although his eyesight isn't the best. Imagine if he leapt out and attacked some innocent person, a child with absolutely no evil on his mind, let's say!'

'Does it disturb his sleep, sir?'

'Not yet.'

'That's good, sir. He goes to bed early and takes a lot of naps. He may be worried, but he's not missing out on all that.'

I found it hard to restrain a gasp. To me it seemed as though Derek was throwing himself into a trap, or at least teetering wilfully on the edge of one.

'And how do you know that, Fraser?' Mr Marston asked with some sharpness.

'That's what people of that age do, sir,' Derek replied, both adroitly and blankly.

'You're talking from personal family experience?'

'For the most part, sir. But I sometimes see old folk nodding off on benches in the park.'

'Indeed, Fraser?'

'Oh yes, sir.'

Mr Marston narrowed his eyes slightly, then sighed. He scraped his chair back, as if about to get to his feet. The interview, much to my relief, was almost at an end.

'Don't forget to take Palmer with you. My father will be pleased to meet such a well-spoken boy. He's always lamenting the decline in standards of speech amongst the young. '

'Oh, I know your father, sir,' I said incautiously, pleased – if embarrassed – at the compliment.

'How come?'

'I mean by sight, sir. Fraser pointed him out and I've seen him walking on the Bumps as well.'

'Yes, he goes there about twice a week, so he told me. Sometimes more. It was one of my mother's favourite places. I never quite understood why.'

Indicating the parcel, our teacher said solemnly: 'I'm entrusting you with this, Fraser. You too, Palmer.'

'Yes sir.'

'One last word. If the miscreants, as we've been calling them, are ever persuaded to own up, I couldn't do otherwise than condemn their stupid prank. But...'

He let the word dangle, as he were holding a gold medallion on a chain before our eyes.

'Sir?' prompted Derek.

'But I'd try to say something in their favour too – to their parents and, obviously, my aggrieved father. The reasons? One, the boys would have admitted guilt at last and, two, for the attempt, however furtive, to recompense him. A fair judgement, don't you think? Of course, punishment must ensue, but I'd do my best to prevent the matter getting to Mr Gordon's ear. You know how much he cares for the reputation of the school, the way it's reflected in the behaviour of his boys, both here and in the town.'

'He might get very upset,' said Derek but in a peculiarly strained tone.

'And we wouldn't want that to happen, would we?'

There was a hint of humour in Mr Marston's voice, but none in his face.

He began drumming his fingers on the old scarred table, then stopped abruptly, looking down at some official document before him.

'Well, that's all. You can go now.'

***

'Don't you see what the cunning bugger's up to?' Derek asked me angrily. 'First of all, Marston's Special Offer!' He put his hands before him as if he'd been handcuffed and adopted a stage-whine: ' "I'll come clean, guvner, it's a fair cop".'

Needless to say, I was carrying the parcel at the time – heavier than I'd expected – as we hurried away from the school.

'He's such a bighead! He thinks he's being so clever!' fumed Derek.

He was a perception ahead of me. I was just starting to think better of Mr Marston now that he wasn't before us.

'You don't get it, do you? You still think he's asking a harmless favour.'

'Maybe, he's…'

'And this, to cap it all!'

'What?'

'He's making us revisit the scene of the "crime" – and we'll have to deal with the so-called victim too. The aim is to make us break down and blubber out a confession.'

That seemed ridiculously far-fetched to me, yet Derek's rancour was compelling.

'It wouldn't be enough to make us break down, though,' I ventured.

'Perhaps not,' Derek said. 'But what if a certain party starts blushing and stuttering?'

Taken aback, I replied indignantly: 'I don't do that often. And, besides, I can't help it.'

'You don't *want* to help it.'

His words were cruel, yet dangerously near to a truth I hated to consider, let alone admit. So, understandably, I took the hump, thrust the parcel into his hands and made as if to leave him and cross the road.

'OK, if that's your opinion – it's better you go alone, then.'

'Don't get mardy again, Colin.'

'I've got good cause to!'

He grabbed me by the sleeve of my coat. I tried to wriggle free but couldn't have done that without leaving the coat behind.

'Let go! You're a bully, just like Olsen.'

'No I'm not, but what happens if I turn up without my lah-di-dah friend, depriving the old loony of the pleasure of meeting you? It's me who'd get bollocked by Marston.'

'That's your problem.'

He released my sleeve, rubbed at his eye as though he had some grit in it, and then said, slowly and with great effort: 'All right, I was being mean. Sorry. I was just worried, that's all.'

He hefted the parcel to his other arm.

'Well, don't take it out on me,' I retorted.

I was half-turned away from him, but Derek knew I

wouldn't run off now.

'I've apologized, haven't I? Look, all you've got to do is concentrate on being "well-spoken", as our esteemed teacher called you.'

'Does that worry you, then?'

'Oh yes!' His grin was as wide as an open door. 'Furiously jealous! Tell you what. I'll take elocution lessons from that fellow they're all talking about, Professor Colin Clarence Montmorency Posh-Palmer. That'll do the trick. How now brown cow!'

He stretched out the vowel in the phrase preposterously and we both started laughing.

As we continued on our journey Derek fell silent. I thought he was mulling over our tiff, but he'd gone a bit further back than that.

'And Marston would stick up for us after we'd told him everything! I bet!'

We duly arrived in Dunstable Street, parcel intact, slowing our pace when we were within sight of the old man's home.

'Don't stare up at the window!' warned Derek, an instant before, unthinkingly, I was about to do so. He knocked loudly at the door, this time with success.

***

The person who opened the door looked as wild as on the night we'd cracked the pane and as shabby and unkempt as when I'd spotted him from my hide in the Land of the Two Rivers. At least he wasn't chuntering away to himself this time; all his energy seemed to be in the glare he was directing at us, as though: Here they were! The louts, the layabouts, the young hooligans, the culprits of culprits who'd finally presented themselves before him! Divine justice (or something along those stern unrelenting lines) had directed us to his door. This mad certainty of our guilt was probably the sanest thing about him at that moment, but naturally we couldn't tell him that.

Derek hastily introduced us and explained, holding up the parcel, what our mission was, moving us smoothly back into blamelessness. I felt as if I were living two lives, more so than when we'd been lying to Mr Marston even. Split apart or seeing myself double? It wasn't a comfortable feeling either way.

You could see the lamplighter's face relaxing now; the deep creases like scars were becoming milder, like the wrinkles I remembered from my grandfather. Mr Marston claimed he was beginning to recollect something his son had told him when he'd popped in the previous evening, about sending a couple of lads round with the books and documents. But I also saw that a little disappointment remained in the old man's eyes; he'd been thwarted of his proper prey.

He invited us in and, knowing everything would get back to our teacher anyhow, we saw no polite means of refusing. All we wanted to do, of course, once we'd carried out our errand, was to be on our way as quickly as possible. Now there was the threat of a trap again.

'You do find some good youngsters about. It's easy to forget that at times and tar everybody with the same brush. That's quite wrong!'

Inside, I spotted two things straight off: first, small piles of coins on the sideboard, arranged according to size, the half-crown in lonely, silvery splendour at the end. Our guilt-money. Mr Marston senior had been totting it up, reckoning the amount against what he'd have to fork out to get a new pane; also, I thought, keeping the coins in constant view as evidence.

The second thing was the picture, the enlarged, framed photograph on the wall. It was the same one as in Grand-Dad Reynolds' house, and in the same kind of prominent position too, as though that had been agreed between them before, like ancient children, they'd decided to squabble.

Mentally, I compared the living quarters of the two men. Both places had that funny smell which old people often give off, but it was much worse here. It wouldn't be unfair to say the place stank. You could imagine a heap of rotting food left out somewhere, or piles of clothing last washed in 1066. At Grand-Dad Reynolds' the smell was more like vinegary sweat, mostly overlaid by the odour of strong soap, the cheerful fire in the parlour too – as if he'd made it with specially resinous wood at the base.

From there, it was only a short distance to my grandfather. What I remembered of him in an olfactory sense ('Look it up, Fraser, look it up!') was mainly a rich mixture of tobacco and fish. Even after he'd retired from being a merchant, he seemed to carry the smell of the pontoon and the early morning fish market with him – and I would have sworn that simply wasn't my imagination hard at work.

There was no fire here, at least not a proper one; only a miserable-looking two-bar radiator which gave out a sputtering heat and a whiff of burning dust.

The house, what we saw of it, seemed bare too, as though the best furniture had been stored away, perhaps even given to his son, our teacher – who knows? The wallpaper of the room where he'd seated us was dingy, but newly dingy, it occurred to me, as if the decay had quickened recently, since his wife died.

Most likely that was true. It was hard to think of the beautiful woman in the picture ever allowing a house she lived in to get into this dilapidated condition. She'd have made a good, cosy home of it. But then, according to Grand-Dad Reynolds, she'd suffered from a long illness. She wouldn't have been like the woman in the picture any more when that got hold of her. I didn't like to think about that.

I looked round surreptitiously for the little lamps he

used for his altar in the Land of the Two Rivers. They were nowhere to be seen.

The old man eased himself down into a battered armchair and gazed reflectively at the meagre bars of the radiator. Sighing, he came to himself again abruptly, catching me glancing at the far door, then a small table, other things, making a mental inventory of a room I simply wanted to get out of.

'No, it's not much of a place, is it? We were always at the edge of moving somewhere better but never got there. And then, when the cancer kept on getting worse, my poor wife lost her will to live. Without that, you can't do anything. You've got to fight, fight all the stronger the more pain there is. After all she'd been through earlier in her life – to give up! It broke my heart – but you're too young to know about things like that. And a good thing too!'

He paused, his eyes welling up with tears.

'I used to go on at her, I admit that. A bit rough, but I meant it for her own good.' Taking out a massive handkerchief, almost as big as a drying-up cloth, he wiped his eyes hurriedly. 'Though there's some who'd tell you different. But never mind that now.'

He turned his gaze fully on us.

'Is my son a good teacher?'

'Yes, Mr Marston.'

'He did well for himself. He was always clever. Puts you through your paces, eh?'

'Yes, Mr Marston.'

'He wants me to leave here, move into an old people's home. He's got one picked out already. What do you think?'

We were nonplussed, left to guess at the proper response to this tricky question.

'Well, maybe...' began Derek bravely, but the lamplighter cut in, as though regretting asking us our opinion.

'I suppose he's right. This area's going downhill. Kids running wild.'

He then gave a long, embroidered account of our stupid prank, making it the culmination of a series of torments by local children. I began to understand something of how epics came about. Whether he really had been badly treated I'd no idea, but he believed it and the story'd grow and grow, celebrating his grievance. As he continued, it was clear that it was the cracked windowpane which piqued him most, followed not far behind by the insolent, sly attempt to recompense him.

'They think they're so smart, but they'll be laughing on the other side of their faces before long!' he said menacingly. 'I'm on the look-out for those two street Arabs night and day and I'll catch the little scum, don't you worry! My son warns me not to wallop them, just give them a good talking-to and make sure I've got their names and addresses. But he's too soft at times, too modern.'

He peered closely into our faces, which were turned a little away from him.

'Is he soft with you in the classroom?'

'No, he's not!' said Derek with feeling. This exclamation and the memories that fuelled it prompted him to jump from his chair. More slowly, I rose to my feet too and stood beside him. I hadn't gone red. If Derek didn't notice, I'd tell him later, very pointedly.

Mr Marston stared at him, renewed suspicion showing in his face.

'I think we'll have to be going now, if you don't mind,' said Derek with awkward formality.

'Don't you live around here, young man?'

'Not far away. On Willow Road.'

'I'm sure I've seen you passing by.'

Or lingering with intent, his tone might also have suggested.

'Oh yes, I've seen you all right.'

A long-legged boy, dressed in jeans and a black jerkin, a balaclava pulled down over his ears, running off down the ginnel into darkness, together with his accomplice, a slightly slimmer figure, dark blue mackintosh, unconcealed fairish-brown hair. I was scared that I'd be put on the spot there and then, but I was comparatively new in Dunstable Street and the old man's look was fixed on Derek, rather than on me. Not that that would help me if he did identify him.

'You might have caught sight of me, Mr Marston,' he replied calmly. 'My Grand-Dad lives just round the corner.'

Initially, I thought this was a bad slip which could put us into danger, but regarding the expression on Derek's face and listening to the level tone of his voice, I realised it was quite deliberate – that he'd chosen not to be anonymous, not here and now at least.

'Oh aye? What's his name?'

'Alfred Reynolds.'

Derek was even smiling a bit now, enjoying the effect of his bombshell.

'Alfred Reynolds!'

The old man was shouting the name in a terrible voice, as though, unwittingly, he'd invited treachery into his house.

'In fact, we must have met when I was smaller and you and Grand-Dad were still friends.'

'Yes, we *were* friends, then, the best, before he...' He broke off, his lips trembling, his rheumy bolting eyes staring at Derek. 'But I suppose you know all about that?'

'Not much,' said Derek. 'Grand-Dad tells me it isn't my business.'

That wasn't quite accurate, as I knew, but at least it was diplomatic.

'When you trust someone as I trusted Alfred... and then he turns on you, makes you worse than a nowt!'

I thought both the old men were barmy in their different ways, yet I liked Grand-Dad Reynolds as I couldn't Mr Marston. But now I felt some sympathy for him all the same, engulfed in furious obsession and sorrow as he was.

Yet he made an effort to be dignified now, drawing himself up and assuming a stiffly humorous manner.

'Thank you for bringing this stuff, lads. It's very precious to me. I'll make sure to tell my son about your good deed and the nice talk we had. Who knows? Your marks might shoot up after this. Stranger things have happened.'

'His marks can't shoot up much higher anyway,' said Derek, indicating me.

'Bit of a class swot, is he? He ought to have thick-rimmed glasses for that.'

I made the mistake of glancing up at the picture of his wife one last time, remembering how he'd called out her name with such desperate feeling in the Land of the Two Rivers. He caught the direction of my look and said brokenly: 'There never was another woman like that. Never!'

He motioned us to go by him. His eyes were wet again and he was reaching for his big handkerchief.

'I'll be all right in a moment. It takes me this way sometimes.'

I felt as if we should do something to help, but I didn't know what. To be honest, my predominant feeling was still to put as much speedy distance between myself and Dunstable Street as I could. That didn't seem right, though. I felt Derek's prompting hand on my elbow and heard his nervous voice just behind me: 'We'll see ourselves out, Mr Marston. '

Back in the street, we were silent as we dashed away.

'I'll not go there again,' muttered Derek at last. 'His precious son can run his own errands from now on.'

'He couldn't have known the lampman would get so upset.'

'Don't you reckon?' replied Derek sceptically. 'He knows the state his dad's in. Odds-on he'd behave like that. No, it's all part of the Marston BA master plan, Colin.

Remember what I said before. Cunning. Stirring it up. That's what they teach them at university, beyond all the froth.'

We'd arrived at the park, at the avenue of trees that went much of the way around it.

'I don't think old Mr Marston could have treated his wife as badly as your Grand-Dad said. Look at the way he was crying.'

'Remorse,' declared Derek shortly. 'Blubbering after the damage is done.'

Suddenly, he challenged me to a race along the avenue of lime and conker trees. I was generally faster on the sprint than him, but he gave me a shoulder-charge at the beginning that almost sent me sprawling, so I lost a few seconds while he ran off, whooping with glee. But I caught up and nearly managed to trip him over towards the end, mocking his protests and the accelerated stagger I'd forced him into. He got back into his stride without much trouble.

It was a dead heat of sorts, I suppose, but both of us claimed to have won by a whisker. We were puffed out from the exertion, bent over, hands on knees, trying to get our breath back; feeling tired but invigorated when we did the last small stretch together, before Derek turned off at the Shore Road. It was as if we'd expelled the visit to old Mr Marston from our systems and were clean again.

IX. The Smarmers

Derek had an aching tooth which was getting worse; he was to go to the dentist's that morning. His mother phoned through to the school and Mr Marston, taking the register, grudgingly allowed this to be a legitimate reason for absence as he ticked the class-list. He wasn't so tolerant when Mrs Fraser phoned again, much later in the morning, and said that Derek was still in pain after seeing the dentist – it'd been a tricky extraction – and that she felt she had to keep him at home for the day.

'Isn't it strange,' he mused, gazing hard at Derek's desk, as if willing his shape to appear, even in ghostly form, 'how some people need an hour at the fang-wrenchers and then they're back at work, while others... well, apparently they need a day in bed, propped up by fluffy pillows and cosseted by hot water bottles, replenished on the hour. Strange indeed. This could be an attitude which'll pitch the country downhill at an alarming rate. Your judgement, Palmer?'

'I don't know, sir. But I'm sure Fraser is suffering, sir.'

'Oh, without doubt! The mask of tragedy is only the obverse of the mask of comedy, after all. Will you be seeing him today?'

'Yes sir. I'm going round to his house after school.'

'Commendable! A friendship worthy of David and Jonathan. David – and who? I can almost hear the puzzled query. Context anybody?'

'Could it be something in the Bible, sir?' ventured Doran.

'Something in the Bible,' Mr Marston enunciated slowly

and in capital letters. 'What targeting! But at least you sent the arrow in the right direction, Doran. Just out of interest, how many boys in this class possess a Bible, or their families do, a remote ancestor even?'

Virtually everybody's hand went up. Mr Marston seemed gratified.

'Far better than I'd anticipated. Now, when you go home, take it down from the shelf, brush the dust off and – let's see – ah yes! Try the First Book of Samuel, chapters eighteen and twenty. If I'm not mistaken, you'll find the story of David and Jonathan there. Of course, we could also take Achilles and Patroclus, but that might mean plunging into deep classical water. Enlighten us, Palmer?'

'I can't, sir.'

'Homer. *The Iliad*. But I think we'll stick to the family Bible for the time being. Now, line up and off you go to Miss Barber's. She's waiting to discover the Picasso of Ketilsby.'

'Pee-gasso, sir?' a podgy boy called Forrester asked, more out of denseness than cheek. He had short, spiky, damp hair, as though it had to force its way through an inch of suet. Now he looked around, gobsmacked at the laughter he'd caused.

Mr Marston didn't answer him. Instead, he put on a pained, martyred look and cuffed him over the head, afterwards wiping his hand carefully on a very white handkerchief. The class giggled. Sarcasm was our teacher's signature, but there were many different tones to it, some you were meant to enjoy (unless you were the victim), others not.

I was near the end of the line. Mr Marston tapped me on the shoulder.

'When you see our young friend, wish him a speedy recovery and tell him that we hope to see him back in his place tomorrow.'

It wasn't just that Mr Marston was missing his favourite ear to tweak or hair to pull or neck to pincer. The "merry sprite" and I were still in his good books because of the delivery of the parcel. He'd checked the next morning, rather hesitantly asking how his father had been. Derek and I were as diplomatic as possible, and the teacher had taken that as a good sign. No disasters. The only thing he'd said before dismissing us, once more with thanks, was: 'I'm afraid my father gets very lonely these days.' He looked a bit lost for a moment, as if he'd revealed too much and made himself weak, but then quickly snapped back into schoolmaster mode.

After that brief glimpse of the inner Mr Marston, I was reluctant to go along with Derek's line that he'd set a trap for us, but I couldn't dismiss his suspicion either.

In the art-room, I stared down at the clean sheet of paper, not knowing what to do now that our two big pictures were finished. I doodled around for a bit, producing dead shapes.

'Don't worry it, Colin,' advised Miss Barber. 'Something will come if you let your mind relax. Or do you want me to give you a subject?'

'Not yet, Miss.'

She took me over to the window and made me look out.

'A dull, grey, wet piece of road. If you're really stuck, you could always draw this. But if you do, make the dullness *sparkle*! Do you understand what I mean?'

I thought I did. I knew she wasn't saying that I should populate our part of Willow Road with Billy Fureys and Elvises, but somehow make everything I drew count, as though anxious to announce itself.

Her idea, I decided, was a good one but it didn't work out in practice. Nothing did that morning.

At the end of the class, disappointed, frustrated, I glanced up and saw Doran and Witherow standing before me. They seemed pressed in on themselves as if trying to become even smaller. Since the day Derek had turned the tables against Olsen, these two had all but disappeared from sight. I mean, we were still all members of the same class, but Doran and Witherow had the gift of being utterly inconspicuous when they chose, stuck away in a corner of the room, or bringing up the tail of any group.

'Hello, Colin,' they hailed me, with an ingratiating smirk.

I returned their greeting without enthusiasm. Then I observed them suspiciously. Finally, to avoid their unnerving stare, both furtive and brazen, I found myself studying their jacket lapels. These were both of a worn, muddy nature, as if they'd been chewed by a dog, though I was pretty sure that Doran and Witherow were in fact the chewers. A private comfort, not something they'd risk under our master's eagle eye.

Mr Marston was particularly hot on what he termed 'dirty habits'. Not long since, he'd fiercely scolded a boy because he'd caught him nibbling at a ball of his own snot. From the strictures the terrified kid had received, you'd have thought there was no worse crime in the universe. And with the boys who stayed for school dinner, he always checked their hands twice, as though the dirt possessed its own devilment and had been hiding from him the first time.

'What have you been drawing, Colin?' Doran asked me.

I didn't want them using my first name. They had no right to do that, given the way they'd helped Olsen but, beyond a frown, I didn't react.

'Nothing much. As you can see.'

'I liked the picture you did of the wall,' said Witherow.

'Yes, so did I,' brought in his friend immediately.

'You did most of that, didn't you, Colin?'

'We both did it. About equal.'

They smiled slyly, as if they knew I was just defending Derek and had to say something like that.

'I bet you really drew the lion's share, though,' said Witherow.

I stayed silent. I wasn't going to fall for that one, take credit at Derek's expense!

'And painted it too.'

'But you need better pencils for those lines at the edge. You know, where they stretch into the distance. People should still be able to see them clearly.'

'HB.'

'What?' I said.

'Hard black.'

'We can get you some. We know a good place, don't we, Keith?'

'Yes, we do. What do you think, Colin?'

I just shrugged my shoulders, although it would have been far better to say a clear, resolute 'No' right then.

After I'd left the school building that afternoon, I saw Doran and Witherow near the playground entrance, kicking a ball about. This was in itself unusual, as they weren't known to be keen on sport of any kind. But the display was for my benefit, as I quickly realised.

'Hey, Colin, fancy a game?'

I shouldn't have been flattered to be invited but nevertheless, however reluctantly, I was. Even with Derek's friendship, it was still a new thing to be asked to join in.

As we started playing, Doran began to imitate Olsen who, for once, was nowhere around. It'd have been quite funny, if I could have forgotten their alliance. It also gave Doran the opportunity to break the rules we were more or less abiding by. He could barge, shove, handle the ball, because that's what Olsen himself would have done. Some other boys were with us now, tackling and dribbling, scoring imaginary goals.

'I thought you were friends of his,' I said.

'Friends?' spat Doran incredulously, as though he and

Witherow had never grasped my wrists tight at the lout's bidding at all.

'You told him about my "bad side", didn't you?'

For a moment he and his brother looked puzzled as if they didn't understand what I was on about, then Witherow gave a long drawn out 'Ah!' of delayed comprehension. He leant towards me, as if confiding a secret. 'But, you know, we're not free,' he said with a whispered air of drama.

'What do you mean?'

'Don't you think he bullies us too?' said Doran in the same kind of tone. The game flowed around us like a complete irrelevance. The two looked at me with an injured air, as if I should have shown more understanding, sympathy too, which was a bit rich coming from them.

Before I could attempt a response, Doran announced, in a louder voice: 'Svenny Olsen's a terror!'

It was hard to take issue with that at least.

The ball came our way. I managed to kick it strongly towards the sports field – a fluke – and we joined the others in chasing after it.

'That would have been a smashing goal, Colin!' shouted Doran over his shoulder.

'A dead cert!' added Witherow.

I wasn't a good football player but better than them, or so they let me appear. Their passes to each other were nearly always wide and slow, not hard to intercept.

'Well done, Colin!'

'Right, well done!'

Their praise sounded more than ever spurious to me and increasingly it got on my nerves, so it wasn't long before I made my excuses and left. I could feel Doran and Witherow's calculating eyes on me as I stepped through the school gateway onto the pavement but, when I turned round abruptly to test this out, they seemed intent on the game and were calling urgently for the ball to be kicked to them.

***

Mrs Fraser opened the back door and welcomed me into the kitchen. Becky had a play rehearsal on at school and the Skipper was still at work.

'Derek will be pleased to see you,' she said. 'He had a bad time at Mr Ginsley's. That old boy's getting too doddery to clean his own teeth let alone tamper with other people's. But we'll have to go one more time so he can check on the crater he's made in Derek's gum. It'll take some time to heal up.'

'Can Mr Ginsley do anything about that?'

'Well, he's given us some special tincture which he claims works wonders. I can't say I've got much faith in it. He's a farmer's son from around Marshchapel. His miracle cure is probably a version of his father's patent horse-rub.'

We joked about that for a while, then she told me to go up to see Derek, before he started getting impatient and banging on the floor.

I found him holding a hot water bottle tightly against his cheek which, when he took it away, looked flushed but not swollen. Derek was very sorry for himself and hardly even gave me the beginning of a smile, not exactly the welcome his mother had led me to expect. There was an odd shyness between Derek and me as I came and sat on the edge of his bed, an unusual constraint.

Tongue-tied, I studied the pack of playing cards jumbled on the tray across his lap; some books were piled up precariously beside his bed. Ostentatiously, he took a long drink of Lucozade and screwed up his face afterwards, as though it were the nastiest medicine you could imagine. Finally, he asked me what had been happening at school.

I gave him an edited account, passing on Mr Marston's

good wishes but missing out his sarcasm about Derek's absence – that wouldn't have gone down well in his present mood! I also omitted Doran and Witherow's attempt to curry favour. In a better frame of mind, he would have laughed at the story, if I turned it skilfully enough, however contemptuous of them he was. But now I feared he would have brooded on my tolerating their overtures at all.

He opened his mouth wide.

'Does it show?'

'I can't see a gap or anything.'

He stretched his mouth into a horrible rictus, like the mockery of a grin.

'Now?'

'I can just see the cavity.'

Which was indeed a bit messy and bloody, and I didn't want to look on it for long.

'But who's going to notice unless you're twisting your mouth like that?' I tried to reassure him.

'It hurts like hell.'

'It will do for a bit.'

He looked at me scathingly as if I'd never had tooth problems in my life.

'Thanks a lot,' he said dryly, sounding like our teacher but in a higher register.

The one book remaining on his eiderdown was *The Flight of the Heron* by D.K. Broster. I'd lent it to him a few days earlier.

He indicated the volume to me now.

'All that flowery stuff about lochs and heather and bog myrtle – whatever that is. Puts me off.'

'But that's mainly at the beginning,' I protested. 'You know, to set the scene. The story gets really exciting after that. '

'All right, I'll take another shot at all this Highland malarkey. I can't say I'm very interested in Bonnie Prince

Charlie and the Jacobites, but they may be so boring they'll help to numb the pain.'

Annoyed at his sneers, I insisted: '*The Flight of the Heron* is one of the best books I've ever read.'

'Yeah?'

That said everything he needed to say about my taste, or lack of it. I got up to leave. It was clear that Derek wasn't going to emerge from his ill-humour, so I should go before we started quarrelling.

I wished him a speedy recovery and said I'd see him at school tomorrow. He grunted, then put on such a woebegone, anguished expression that I could almost believe he was mocking his own pain, the familiar joking Derek returned. Then, thinking about it, I looked at him incredulously. Surely he wasn't going to try to swing two days absence from one troublesome extraction?

Glancing back at Derek from his bedroom door, I saw that he had indeed taken up *The Flight of the Heron* again and was flicking through the pages impatiently, sighing heavily, as if just to add to all his troubles, I'd chosen to inflict the world's most aggravating, unyielding novel on him.

***

Derek did come back to school the next day, much restored in spirits I was glad to see, describing to anybody who would listen his horrific experiences at the dithering old dentist's. Now he was the hero of the episode, a sparky, humorous one, rather than the abject victim, and we could all breathe a sigh of relief.

On my desk was the gift I'd been promised: a set of fine Faber HB pencils. Doran and Witherow were hovering nearby, wearing a look that befitted modest but expectant donors.

I couldn't help but thank them, though I should have

had the strength of will to refuse the present. Derek was over on the other side of the room at the time, chatting to some other boys, so he didn't see the transaction.

'Now you'll be able to get some really sharp lines on your drawings,' said Doran.

'But you need a little improvement elsewhere too,' commented Witherow.

Maybe I was being stupid, but it didn't click what this signified. However, that became all too obvious the next morning when I found a small packet of colouring pencils awaiting me in the same place.

On this occasion, Derek was right beside me. True, I was in two minds about these offerings, but Derek's immediate hostility put me on the defensive: it was my right to accept gifts from whatever quarter. I didn't have to ask his permission.

'And I suppose those creepers gave you the HB pencils you've been flashing around as well. Don't bother to tell me, anything silly like that!'

But why should I? My defiance was made worse by an onrush of guilt. I flourished the packet of colouring pencils in his face.

'What's wrong with that?'

'What's wrong! First of all, those two never do anything for nothing. They'll want something from you they're not letting on about yet. Secondly, they've probably shoplifted these pencils. It's very easy to do. You don't imagine the bloody smarmers would actually *buy* anything for you, do you?' he added in spite.

'They might,' I said sulkily. 'The pencils can't be all that expensive.'

'Too expensive for them. If they put a penny on their dead grandma's eye they'd charge interest on it.'

Wanting to avoid Derek's fierce, bullying expression I looked beyond him. Doran and Witherow were near the classroom door, watching us with more curiosity than anxiety, interested to see how our quarrel would develop.

'You always accuse me of getting mardy, Derek, but look at you.'

'I'm not mardy. I'm just pointing out the truth.'

'Well, something's got into you and it's not simply Mr Ginsley's dental pliers.'

'You don't need scum like those two,' said Derek in an odd, taut voice.

It was the tone that took me aback the most. It was hard and hurt and possessive, as if he were trying to clench his fist on something he valued which was threatening to slip out of his grasp.

There was no time for me to react anyway as Mr Marston had entered the room and was about to take the register.

'Fraser, *if* we could have your co-operation... time to plot your nefarious schemes with Palmer later on. Glad to see that the troublesome tooth allows you to be with us again. Pain receding?'

'Sir.'

I wrote down the word 'nefarious' with one of the new pencils, a red one, hoping that Derek would notice that little gesture of defiance. I got the spelling wrong at first, but managed to correct it. I looked it up later, to get the meaning exactly right: one more for my list of posh words. I'd try it out on Roy when next we met. If lucky, I might get an acknowledging nod.

For the rest of that school day, Derek and I avoided each other, as far as we could. Doran and Witherow were quick to move in, and I thought more than once of the contemptuous nickname he'd given them: the smarmers. How accurate that was! He'd put me on the alert about them, but I went along with their gestures of friendship all the same, wanting to rile Derek as much as I could. Getting my own back, or so I told myself unhappily.

He didn't walk part of the way home with me, as he usually did. Instead, he stalked out of the last afternoon class quickly, shoulders hunched and lips pressed down.

'What's got into Fraser?' asked Doran with mock-innocence.

'Have you two fallen out?' his chum inquired, as if the very thought was almost incredible.

'Of course they have! Don't be daft.'

'Derek's still feeling bad from yesterday,' I put in rather feebly.

'Fraser can be nasty, but I wouldn't worry about it.'

'I'm not worrying.'

'That's all right then.'

The smiles they put on now seemed to me their most repellent yet – servile, but also full of the pleasure of stirring things up.

I did my utmost to break free of them when I left for home; however, they insisted on escorting me down Willow Road. It was no fair exchange for Derek and I felt a sudden anguish that deadened my voice and made me move like a zombie. It didn't help that as the three of us left the playground, I saw Doran and Witherow glance quickly at Svenny Olsen who was skulking round that side of the area. This panicky feeling I had that they were leading me into his grasp! There'd be no Derek to rescue me this time.

But, as it turned out, I didn't even get Olsen's customary vengeful glare. He was surrounded by a court of petitioners, smaller boys eager to protest their grievances and implore him to be their champion. He was loftily ignoring them now – or pretending to, perhaps trying to decide which cases would be worthy of his concern – apart from the odd shove if they got too close to him. He hated anybody even putting a hand on his sleeve to get his attention and I'd seen more than one boy severely pummelled for such presumption.

But the brief look he exchanged now with Doran and Witherow was surely one of connivance – how could it be anything else? And yet I still walked between them as though, disturbingly, they had become my protectors.

***

The next thing at school, there was a fine new sketchpad spread out over my desk. Even at first glance, I could tell that the paper was of high quality. Doran and Witherow stood nearby, flaunting an air of modesty.

'That's for all the terrific pictures you're going to do, Colin,' said Witherow. Coyly he added: 'Who knows? You might make one specially for us.'

Before I could say anything, either mealy-mouthed or honest, there was a furious rush of movement and Derek was amongst us. His face was livid, but at least his anger wasn't focussed on me. For a moment I thought he was going to start clobbering Doran and Witherow there and then. I glanced at the clock on the wall; a few minutes to go before Mr Marston was due.

Derek pointed at the pad.

'Where did you get this?' he demanded of Doran and Witherow.

'Kirkby's in the Bullring, if it's anything to do with you.'

'How much did it cost?'

'Can't remember now.'

'I bet you can't! Have you got the receipt?'

'We did have but it must have got lost.'

'How much do you reckon, then?'

'It's none of your business, Fraser!'

'Yeah, stop sticking your ugly great snout in where it's not wanted!'

The other boys, attracted by the loud ill-feeling and the

drama it was engendering, were crowding round us. Mentally, I urged Mr Marston to appear, sweeping confidently in and calling us to order.

'Come on! How much?'

Very reluctantly, Doran said: 'Oh, about two bob.'

'Two bob!' Derek said with scornful disbelief. Then he paused for a moment, as though he wanted to be calmer when he made his accusation more plainly. 'Did you pay anything at all, in fact, or for the pencils? Or did you just pinch the whole lot?'

'Of course we paid!'

'You calling us thieves, Fraser?'

'If the cap fits.'

Now Doran and Witherow became highly indignant, puffing themselves up with their own fury which, if I hadn't been involved, would have been interesting to observe, so different was it from their usual slinking manner.

A shocking thing, they told their audience, to be accused of stealing when they simply wanted to give a present to a friend! That was a fine state of affairs to arrive at, wasn't it? Of course, Derek Fraser was fond of laying down the law, he was such a bighead!

And so on.

I winced when they used the word 'friend' again, singling me out as though any moment they'd call on my support. I edged away from them, hoping nobody would notice my movements, and soon placed myself close to Derek, observing Doran and Witherow protest their blamelessness with a spluttering, red-faced fervour that made the boys around us laugh and jeer.

'They'd never nick anything, not them!'

'Next stop Borstal!'

Finally, in angry exasperation, Derek threw the posh sketchpad at them. It skittered off the desk and Doran picked it up, examining it for damage.

'You'll pay if you've ruined that, Fraser,' said Witherow.

'Pay! More than you did, I bet.'

Now, getting nowhere with their display of innocence, Doran and Witherow became abusive. After calling Derek a few choice names, Doran said: 'There's nothing you like better than throwing your weight around, is there, Fraser? Everything's got to be done your way or not at all.'

In a different situation I might have acknowledged a modicum of truth in that, but I wasn't going to say anything now. I felt a renewed sense of shame – I should never even have been tempted by the things they offered me – which made it easier to reclaim my first loyalty.

'Well, we know someone who can do that sort of thing better than you, Fraser,' said Witherow. 'You were lucky that first time, but you won't be the next!'

'Get lost and take your miserable pal with you!'

At last there was a chance to show without any doubt whose side I was on. I spoke up, boldly for me: 'It's not long since you were giving out how horrible Svenny Olsen is with you too.'

'So much you know, you wet little bugger!'

Derek punched Doran in the chest, almost knocking him over, and shouted: 'You speak to Colin like that and I'll smash you out into the corridor!'

'Oh, poor dear little Colin, 'sneered Witherow.

'Fight! Fight!' some of the boys began chanting.

Perhaps it was this cheap incitement which made Derek pause, or perhaps just common sense prevailing, because all he did was swallow hard and glare at Doran and Witherow.

A good thing too because just at that instant Mr Marston entered, complaining about the row as he watched his pupils scatter back to their desks.

We'd forgotten in the heat of the altercation to return the pencils as well. They'd still been in my desk but, when I got back to the classroom after break, I found they'd gone.

Doran and Witherow must have sneaked them away, not wanting to waste any of their loot.

After school, Derek walked with me to the edge of the Shore Road, almost as though there'd been no interruption to this routine at all. But neither of us said much; there were long, awkward silences. He didn't crow over me, no I-told-you-so remarks and I didn't thank him for rescuing me a second time, nor for that matter did I complain about his fiery temper.

But it felt as if we were on the right way, even if it might take a while before we were completely easy with each other again.

The impetuous, boastful side of Derek emerged only once, at the end whilst we were waiting at the kerbside for the traffic to clear. When it did, and there was absolutely nothing coming either way, not even a bicycle, he pushed me into the clear space, shouting into my ear: 'See, I'm better than traffic lights!'

'That could have been dangerous, Derek,' I protested, but grinning as well.

'Yes, but it wasn't. And wouldn't ever be, not with me!'

He stuck his chest out and threw back his head to make his bragging a joke, or with the saving grace of one, and then ran off in the direction of the Park. He stopped to pull his balaclava out of his pocket and I waved to him from the other side of the road. He waved back like mad and jigged about on his feet as if he were dancing bare-footed on live coals. The helmet was over his head now, concealing virtually everything except his eyes, which I saw as being huge and searching, like a barmy hypnotist's. I could only guess at the expression he'd adopted.

X. In the Land of the Two Rivers at One A.M.

We visited the hide in the Land of the Two Rivers a couple of times. No one had been in there, so far as we could tell.

Derek claimed that, though Doran and Witherow were keeping their chastened distance, they were still on the lookout, doing their best to spy on us.

'Those shifty eyes! Perhaps you can't tell which direction they're really looking, but I can!'

I thought this was his imagination because the two had become hate-figures for him, whereas I just disliked Doran and Witherow, still ashamed of my brief association with them.

'And they're following us, I'm sure.'

'Oh, come on, Derek!'

Once or twice I noticed them behind us as we left school, but I never spotted them anywhere near the Land. Perhaps they were better trackers than I'd reckoned. I peered out of the hide but there was no one I could discern. Of course it was getting dusk earlier, but I was quite sharp in picking out thicker patches of dark, especially when they moved. I put my head out again, a few minutes later, but there was still nobody, not even the kids who played by the stream sometimes; neither old Mr Marston, trudging along on his lonely pilgrimage, slow chuntering steps the length of the upper path, his cloth bag hitting against his thin shanks, like a reminder he didn't need.

But I didn't think he'd given up his ritual. Just that he wasn't there the times we were.

'Wouldn't it be good if we came here early in the morning, during the sleeping hours, I mean. To have a feast.' Derek laughed with delight at his idea. 'True, it'd be even colder and darker then, but we could wrap up well.'

Normally, I wasn't the one who turned wild improbability into sober likelihood, but now it was me who said: 'Well, why shouldn't we do all that?'

And that's how that October adventure began.

Once we'd made the decision, we had the practical measures to work out, the ways and means.

The first thing to consider was leaving our houses without being noticed.

Derek's bedroom was at the front of their place, with a sheer drop out of the window. So he'd have to go down the stairs – (unless he knotted a sheet and hung it down outside which even the mettlesome Derek didn't contemplate!) – and for that care would be needed. Some of the stairs creaked, but he was familiar with those and claimed that, even in darkness, he'd be able to avoid them. His parents, once they settled down, were heavy sleepers, but the real problem was Becky. She was almost as sharp in slumber as she was when awake.

'The slightest noise and she's out of her bed wanting to know where the fire is, or screaming about burglars,' Derek claimed.

I smiled but could imagine he wasn't far wrong.

'Bring her with you then,' I said jokingly.

'Are you kidding! She'd be organising the whole thing for us, the great Becky Fraser expedition! Anyway, with her row going on – Becky's method of trying to keep quiet – we'd never get out of the house at all.'

Then he took me through his exit plan, step by step.

'I'll lie in my pit for a while, dressed of course and on the alert. Then, as the second wave of snores fills the house, I'll emerge, balaclava on and shoes tied to the back of my trousers. I'm not going to tiptoe clumsily along the landing, like a drunk in a strange house looking for the bog. No, I'll do a commando crawl...'

'Look out, Rommel!'

Derek ignored my facetious interruption, bound up in the drama of his escape.

'Testing the silence every second, almost floating over the carpet! The stairs are tricky, I grant you, because you can't really crawl down there. Likely as not, you'd break into a slither and end up crashing into the wardrobe at the bottom. So, I'll be on my two feet again – no touching of the banisters – and I'll go down the stairs very carefully indeed, like walking a descending tightrope!

'But once that's over, it'll be easy. Kitchen, back door, and then away. Not to forget my little bag of goodies, plus torch, which I'll have hidden from prying eyes outside already. Now, what about you?'

I didn't think that my departure would be so fraught with hazard, although you could never tell. You still had to be vigilant. All I should have to do, in fact, was get out of my back bedroom window and work my way down the sloping roof over the coalhouse, then lower myself onto the heaped wooden boxes I'd placed below, as inconspicuously as possible. I'd used this convenient route several times before, when the house was empty and I didn't have my key with me or just because I wanted to. It was always a very secret manoeuvre, though, and never yet the nocturnal truancy Derek and I were planning.

The Palmer residence had a long landing with a dip for the stairs in the middle. I was in the far 'wing', virtually separate, with Roy's empty room next to mine. My parents were right at the front, facing the street. They still more or less shared the same bed, although my father increasingly went to sleep in his office, slumbering noisily on the couch there.

***

It seemed plain sailing my end, then.

Yet, as I might have guessed, it didn't quite turn out to be. My parents had decided to have a late-night quarrel.

I had just eased my window up when the row erupted. At first I almost believed that the sounds were part of a bad dream projecting itself beyond my head, but they were external all right.

My bedroom door was closed, so I had to imagine my mother suddenly arriving on one side of the landing and my father on the other, as though on opposite sides of a firm divide – very ill met by moonlight. I'd seen the war movie with Dirk Bogarde when it came round again, and Mr Marston had told us where the tag came from, relating the story of Shakespeare's play, which seemed pretty soppy and stupid to me then.

I certainly wasn't going to do anything to find out what the quarrel was about. The usual stuff, I supposed: Dad's fecklessness, his lies and failures – the drinking, her father had warned her, been right about him all along; and, from the other corner: her nagging, mean-mindedness, the 'curdling' spirit Dad sometimes referred to, with considerable gusto in his venom, that could sour the freshest milk. Had she ever had a spark of joy in her? *Not since I married you!* I moved my lips silently over that one, as if in a rotten sort of prayer.

My mother began trying to shush my father's bellowing and finally succeeded. A little belatedly, they were both afraid that I'd be woken up. What worried me, though, was that their qualms of conscience might spur them into action and they'd rush along the landing to check whether my sleep had been disturbed by their wrangling, what my father sometimes dryly described as 'a little difference of opinion.'

But imagine them opening the door to find their son letting himself out of the window! It was all I could do to stop myself from giggling at the thought of their consternation, their guilty fear that I was running away from home because of them.

Then I decided that Mum and Dad's opening my door and checking on me, if they heard nothing from my room, was unlikely, and that with a bit of luck I could use the noise they were making, even if subdued to a fractious muttering now, to cover any I might make getting out and easing myself down the roof onto the boxes. Also – perhaps the trickiest part of the operation – once over the sill I needed to pull down the window from outside. Not close it completely, just to eliminate most of the draught which might otherwise penetrate through to the landing. Maybe I was being over-cautious. I'd already used rolled-up pullovers and vests to block the space between floorboard and the bottom of my bedroom door.

Slow but sure – I did manage to get myself to ground safely enough. Then I retrieved the things I'd left behind the garage: my windcheater, which I'd wrapped up in a plastic carrier, and my bag, not full of lamps like the old pilgrim's but various goodies for the feast, some sneakily purloined from the larder, others honestly bought. I'd also taken a couple of silver-plated knives and forks from the cutlery canteen in the front room. They were for best and had been my grandfather's. I was positive I could get them back in their place before they were missed. So Derek and I would dine in style!

I put my windcheater on, slung the bag over my shoulder and, with a quick look around and a pause to test the silence, I was on my way.

The silver birch that stood at the end of our short front garden, near the gate, was caught in the streetlight and looked more ghostly and yet more alive than I'd ever seen it before. Later, I put that down to the excitement and tension of our escapade, the unusual hour too. But, whatever it was, for a moment the birch, the gate and the streetlamp seemed to be caught in one image as if they really belonged to each other, or as though I were looking at myself from a short distance, making a composition for Miss Barber's class: a figure amidst objects, but none of these so reduced anymore.

When I was smaller, I'd liked stories where things talked, became like people, and, as I snecked the gate carefully and hurried away, I had the exhilarating feeling that this could happen any moment now, the whole world revealing its human voice.

***

Derek was waiting for me. He'd been at the hide for at least fifteen minutes, he claimed. He'd begun to think that I'd welshed on the deal and stayed snug and treacherous in my bed.

'Do you honestly think I'd do that?'

He pretended to consider the matter and only yielded when, as best I could in that narrow space, I brought my bag across his back.

'Of course not, Master, of course not! Oh, mercy, mercy!'

That was almost like a shout. Anybody could have heard us, particularly at night when everywhere was still and sound carried. I told him urgently to keep it down.

Derek had had no problems leaving: the crawl along the landing was masterful, the descent of the stairs perfect. Everything had gone as smoothly as he'd foreseen.

I couldn't help teasing him for his smugness.

'Are you sure Becky didn't follow you and isn't lingering around outside? Still, we've got enough food for three.'

'Nobody followed me!' he insisted haughtily. 'And, Cleverclogs, you *are* diabolically late.'

'Sorry. But I plead extenuating circumstances.'

'Good phrase. And what might they be?'

I told him about my parents quarrelling and the extra care I'd had to take, the delay involved. Derek appeared chiefly interested in the idea that anybody would bother having a slanging match so late at night. Why not store it up for breakfast-time when you were fresher and could really get going?

On my way, the streetlamps along Bradleigh Avenue had clutched in their gleam, concentrating each small radiance. It was the moon that got brighter, riding through a wide patch of cloudless sky. I didn't realise how strong it was until I'd stepped from the last edge of pavement onto the earth track, and I was in the Land. Then there was nothing to even remotely rival it, certainly not the intermittent flashes of Derek's torch within the hide. Moonlight illuminated the rise I was walking along and the ground that fell away from it down to my Lindsey Tigris and Euphrates, silvering everything over but still keeping it mysteriously dark at the core.

'I heard you approaching,' said Derek. 'You were pretty good but I've got ears like a Red Indian tracker when I'm on the alert.'

'What's left of them when Mr Marston's finished twisting your great lugs about.'

'Perhaps I could sue him for loss of hearing, fake total deafness.'

'You mean, like you do when he asks you a difficult question?'

'Oh no, that's just a switch-off. I'm away in my own world when he goes braying on.'

'He's got interesting things to say sometimes.'

Derek conceded that point, a bit reluctantly, but then burst out: 'We shouldn't be talking about school! It doesn't exist anymore. It's like it's been magicked away!'

'Some hope.'

I hardly heard myself making the commonplace response because there was a score – a small one – to be settled.

'All right,' I whispered, 'you might have heard me, but I saw you when I was coming up here. What did we say about things that'd give us away, Derek?'

'I couldn't find where I'd put my bag. I only switched the torch on a couple of times.'

'I've brought one too. We'll have to use some light to get the things out, but we'd better shade it with our hands.'

We remained completely in darkness for a short while, as if to prove that we could do it: huddled together in our windcheaters, wearing scarves too because it was so cold. Strangely, Derek hadn't brought his balaclava helmet.

'Wouldn't it be funny if old Marston came by now?' said Derek suddenly.

'He wouldn't be doing his ritual this late.'

'He might yet, though. Going cuckoo is a progressive thing.'

A box was our table and a dishcloth Derek had snaffled from home our makeshift tablecloth. He'd also found a couple of cardboard picnic plates. I showed him the heavy, old-fashioned cutlery I'd brought and he shone his torch on it admiringly.

'This'll be a banquet fit for kings!'

Derek fished out a tin of sardines, some biscuits and apples and a small bottle of fish paste. I'd bought a packet of pumpernickel from the one shop in Ketilsby then that was something like a delicatessen – and some slices of pink, tangy Danish salami at the same place, carefully wrapped in greaseproof paper by the assistant. If my father had found my little trophies he would have exclaimed with delight and scoffed the lot. He was the one who'd introduced both pumpernickel and Danish salami to me. For her part, my mother would have asked a lot of pointed questions, chiefly wondering why I felt I had to supplement my rations by buying food out of my pocket money. She'd have been worried that I didn't think her cooking sufficient – which it always was, whatever her mood. I'd also helped myself to one of her jars of home-made pickled onions. She had so many piled up at the back of the larder, I was sure she wouldn't miss just one.

Besides all this, we had some Tizer and plenty of chocolate with us, plus some very sticky dates which Derek had discovered in a drawer in their kitchen dresser when no one was around.

'But they've got a sort of fur on them, Derek! They must be from last Christmas!'

'No, I don't think so. Mam's birthday in August at the longest. They'll be perfectly all right if you just brush the gunge off.'

He didn't look too sure, though, as he peered closely at them. Recalling tales of horrible food poisoning convinced us to leave them aside; no point in taking any chances. Perhaps the night creatures who'd come in and work over the remains of our feast would be able to handle them, or we'd find their corpses to prove they couldn't when next we visited.

Tucking into our food, easing it down with mouthfuls of Tizer, helped to warm us up. Otherwise we talked – in low voices, stifling our laughter like kids out on a prank and expecting to be discovered, but pretending otherwise. I remembered the irate neighbour not far to the back of us, and wondered whether he was at his window, trying to track down the faint sounds he was hearing, even questioning himself if he'd heard them at all.

Children! What would children be doing out here at this cold night hour?

But the wind was rising and there was a good chance it would have blown away any sounds we were making now. We listened to it hurrying across the land like a fanatical searcher in pursuit of an elusive enemy. It seemed to claw at the scrubby vegetation near us, rattling the hide to show who was boss before moving on higher. The song it screeched was fierce but also mournful.

I suppose that this picture in my mind led to the idea of a chariot, and a memory of an illustration I'd seen in one of

Grandpa's books of an Assyrian warrior with a great curling beard, driving his chariot into battle.

After I'd mentioned that to Derek, it was only natural he would ask me about Mesopotamia. My 'Land of the Two Rivers' was strictly speaking, according to Roy, 'The Land *between* Two Rivers', but I kept the original name. The space separating our stream and its feeble tributary was tiny, but I wanted to suggest the whole area – and more, if my imagination were working at full steam.

My knowledge was sketchy, and I wasn't above confusing different periods and civilisations. Anyhow, I knew what a ziggurat was and I described that to Derek. I told him it was meant to be like a stairway to God. They worshipped right on the top and also had marriages there, which amused him.

'Imagine a bride being blown over the edge in her wedding-dress!'

I'd read a little about the law-giver Hammurabi too, whom I made into a kind of antique Cromwell, soldier and ruler, and, probably in the same book of Grandpa's, I'd come across the Sumerian Gilgamesh and his friend Enkidu. What I didn't remember properly or know for sure, I just jumbled up into a fresh mixture. It wasn't the time or place for separating fact from imagination anyway, and the stories didn't seem to suffer. Occasionally, the realist in Derek came to the fore and he expressed some incredulity, but I did my best to reassure him. I wasn't always wrong.

'This flood you're talking about, Colin, the one Gilga the Mess gets to hear about. That's pinched from the Bible. Noah and the Ark.'

'No, it was the other way about,' I insisted. 'The Hebrews took it from the old Mesopotamian story and just changed it a bit.'

Whilst listening, Derek lay prone, using his windcheater as a groundsheet. He had on a thick turtle-necked pullover in squares and lozenges of different colours. I hadn't seen anything like that before. At our place I wore pullovers of school grey or muted green. For variations of style there were my father's sloppy cardigans, my mother's neater ones and Roy's fishermen's jersey.

This startling pullover of Derek's was something his mother had seen on a market stall, which sold mainly Scandinavian goods. She'd bought it for him the previous Christmas, a size too big. That was one reason he hadn't worn it much, but he was growing into it now. Generally, it was too warm for inside but perfect for our den on a raw night.

'I hardly feel the cold at all!' he declared. 'Just on my face and fingers.'

This jumper (Derek was vague about its exact provenance, reluctant to plump for Denmark because of Olsen, which he admitted was unfair; finally choosing Norway and the image of a dashing skier) all but glowed like a chopped-up rainbow, as the torchlight fell over his upper body while he adjusted his position. Briefly, the gleam was on his face, making his cheekbones more prominent, his eyes hollow then glittering, the open mouth momentarily too full because, for just a trice, the lips and his protruding tongue seemed one. It was a changed image which made him seem older too, so that I could guess at what he might look like when he was grown up.

As my stories began to peter out, Derek stuck his head beyond the entrance of the hide. Now he was a sentry who'd kept a slack watch and needed to make up for it with special zeal.

He faced me again.

'Well, Derek?'

I was just about to spear one of the last pieces of salami. Grandpa's fork was greased over now; no longer so silver-looking.

'Enemy activity has been reported on all fronts,' he said in the solemn, rarefied tones of a BBC announcer. Then he switched to Ena Sharples, the old carper from *Coronation Street*. 'That Olsen – ooh, he's got something to answer for! He's gone and scoured the whole country to find a dozen other misshapen brutes like himself and, by heck, they're congregating against that stream down yonder, reckoning to come up here and sort us out!'

But this was a short diversion.

Clasping his hands over his knees and hugging his body to them, Derek abandoned *Coronation Street* for *Treasure Island*.

'Bags I be Squire Trelawney! I've got him off to a T.'

'Keep your voice down, Derek.'

'And you stop flashing that light about. You're worse than you claim I was.'

He was just about right, although I didn't tell him that. From the darkness came his voice: 'Shall I give you my impression of Squire Trelawney, then?'

'If you have to,' I replied, mocking his eagerness to perform with a disparaging sigh. 'At least it'll make a difference from Billy Fury or Mr Marston.'

'Mardy-cat! '

He gave a creditable version of the huffing and puffing patriotic squire, while I took the part of the quieter but shrewder Dr Livesey. Altogether, with an invisible Jim Hawkins, we repelled the grunting, slobbering mass of Olsens, sent them flying down the rise from our stockade as they called vainly on their barbaric gods for help.

'Shit-scared,' said Derek happily, chewing on a pickled onion. 'The lot of them! How about a worthy opponent for a change?'

I agreed, still surprised that he hadn't chosen the richest character in Stevenson's book to imitate, the immortal Long John Silver himself.

It was inevitable that our escapade should reach and pass its peak, start to pall. Feeling increasingly tired, we tried to prolong it, though, till the whole thing threatened to go wrong. Then we both agreed it was time to be on our way.

We left the remains of the feast where it was in the den. We could clear up the mess whenever we chose. But, carelessly, I forgot to take Grandpa's cutlery. Not a tragic lapse, I convinced myself later after the initial irritation, because I expected to be back in the hide very soon and I'd retrieve the knives and forks then.

Nobody had discovered our secret place up to now, and there didn't seem any reason why they should. I discounted the kids down by the stream. They hadn't shown any curiosity, dangerous or otherwise, so far, a mark of our skill at concealment perhaps as well as sheer luck. Besides, with the harsher weather coming, there weren't many of those kids left anyhow. About the only people who came up to the rise were us and old Mr Marston, and I couldn't imagine him sniffing round there and breaking in, unless he wanted a store for discarded lamps. Sometimes, in a mood that made me soft on magic, I imagined the place was somehow protected; no harm could come to it. Decreed, stamped and sealed.

We eased our way onto the path cautiously, as if malign creatures really were lying in wait for us, ready to pounce, but the truth was that neither Derek nor I felt in any danger whatsoever.

It was still a silver land outside, right down to the bushes and trees bordering the stream, a clarity in everything before the moon went behind a belt of cloud. The wind we'd revelled in had dropped, much less clamorous and intent on conquest now; even so, the cold had an extra gripiness to it. Derek zipped up his windcheater, though the thickness of his multi-coloured pullover prevented him from closing the neck completely.

'Will you be able to get back in all right?' he asked me. 'Your parents should have stopped quarrelling by now.'

'Sleeping like logs, I bet.'

'Nothing like a row to work up a good kip.'

We went along the track and crossed the border – earth to concrete – between the Land and the world of bow windows, discreet porches, tidy front gardens and hedges, the occasional small, unalarming tree. It was 'a very respectable area,' as my father was in the habit of contentedly saying.

Naturally, Red Roy scoffed at such smugness. It was enough to set him off on a rant about the tepid, narrow lives of the petty bourgeoisie (it took me some time to get my tongue around that one, but I did, a treasurable acquisition, and I taught the term to Derek in the end), their rank materialism and so on. It followed the same pattern as other outbursts, allowing for improvisation where the spirit took him. The important thing was the right belief and fervour, a pure one-sidedness, an absolute lack of doubt.

During these performances and the ensuing political wrangle with my father, Mum would either deliver herself of a few telling sighs or go off into the kitchen to brood, or both, but I don't think she fundamentally disagreed with her husband's view of things.

As for Roy, she couldn't be too hard on him. He'd get over all this grouching and sneering, this insistence on radical change. In Mum's view it was just a form of late adolescence: irritating and unpleasant, but something which would pass as Roy matured and, inevitably, 'settled down'.

Rounding the corner into Langtoft Avenue, Derek suddenly turned to me and asked, in a deceptively off-hand way: 'Do you think there'll be a war? I'm sure my Dad does, though he keeps on saying there won't be one. But I mean, if the Russians and Americans start going at each other, that's it! There won't be time to say it's all an accident, or "Sorry, let's make peace", will there?'

I had my fears like most people then, but mostly I tried to push the growing crisis over Cuba to the back of my mind. Sometimes, though, an uneasy feeling stayed with me, hard to subdue. To bolster my courage, raise my spirits, I'd look around me and think: Well, nothing has changed, nothing *will* change! It was better than whistling in a graveyard but it didn't always work. I'd seen pictures of nuclear mushroom clouds like everyone else, of Hiroshima and Nagasaki, and knew that the weapons both sides had now were much more powerful.

'It's all bluff, Derek. They wouldn't be so daft as to destroy the world.'

'They might find themselves in a situation where they can't do anything else,' he said, unwontedly gloomy. 'I heard a bloke going on like that yesterday.'

'An alarmist,' I said with more conviction than I felt.

'Yes, maybe,' Derek said eagerly, seizing at this straw. 'In fact, there was a programme on telly that...'

But I never found out what it was he'd seen because, just at that moment, lights swept round the far corner of the avenue, facing us at full strength. I thought it might be a car carrying people home from a late party, but Derek seemed to know instinctively who the vehicle contained. He pushed me into a driveway and pelted up the side of the house to the back garden, urging me to follow him. It was only a few doors from my place, but I didn't know the people there except to say hello to. An old couple, invariably polite but distant, as though they were deaf and didn't want to admit it.

'Cops coming!' whispered Derek to me.

'How do you know?'

'The way they drive, especially at night. I bet you anything it's them.'

They couldn't have avoided seeing Derek and me unless they'd had their eyes screwed backwards, and were driving blind! Now they'd zoom up, move in on us like hunters. Thoroughly alarmed, I foresaw the policemen delivering us to our parents; we'd be in double trouble then, one for sneaking off to our feast and, two, for being returned to them by the law. And there might well be a fuss at school too, Mr Marston ticking us off but abruptly stopping because this was something so serious we'd been summoned by the Headmaster. I'd never had to present myself to Mr Gordon as yet and I didn't imagine, from what other boys had told me, that the experience would be a pleasant one.

On that side we could see the beam of the lights getting closer. The car was slowing to a crawl, but not quite stopping. As it went by, the driver's window open, I wanted to bolt immediately, hoping that the car would turn the Bradleigh Avenue corner and leave altogether.

'Let's go now, Derek!'

'Wait. We're still in danger.'

He was right because back the police came and this time they stopped; the sound of a car door opening and closing. We daren't peep round anymore, just flattening ourselves against the wall as if trying to fuse with the bricks and mortar. We could hear the gate swinging. A torch now – straight up the path at first, then a bit to the side, focussing on the narrow gap between the garage and the fence. There might just have been enough room to squeeze in there, but it was a good thing we hadn't – we'd have been plucked out straight away, strong hands and questioning, admonitory voices. Even so, we were still very much unhidden. It could only be a matter of seconds and then the torch's glare would be on us.

The policeman inspected the back door, checking for attempted break-ins. Surely, however deaf they were, the occupants of the house would soon be alerted, if they hadn't been shocked into wakefulness already. Somewhere – it seemed far away – a dog barked, as though he were the sentinel of the whole avenue.

I could hear the sound of the police radio crackling. The constable advanced very slowly, suspiciously, almost as if marking time.

Derek's hand was on my sleeve. When he tightened his

grip further and immediately afterwards released his hold, I wanted to flee straight off, take what little chance we had left. I was faster than Derek but more liable to panic in a crisis. I could imagine him neatly shinning over the back fence while I'd mis-time my attempt hopelessly, giving way to useless rage.

But, against all expectations, we were in luck. A voice came from the gate, hailing the torch-carrying policeman, who was almost level with us now.

'Des, those kids who did a bunk from the remand home... they've got them.'

Our policeman snapped off his torch. He was so near to us we had to hold our breath like swimmers underwater.

'I could have sworn I saw two lads just about here.'

'Me too. You didn't see any signs?'

'No. But I didn't check the garden.'

'Ah well, leave it. We've got other things on our plate before we pack in, and I'm getting tired if you aren't. Come on!'

Grumbling a little, the policeman went down the path. I don't think I've ever heard receding footsteps with so much relief. For a while, Derek and I stayed exactly where we were, just in case this departure was a bluff. We heard the car drive away, this time towards the Shore Road, and it didn't come back. You could almost breathe the silence.

Derek felt my forehead, much as my mother did when she thought I had a fever.

'You're sweating buckets.'

'I bet you are too. '

He wiped my forehead with the back of his hand, laughing softly when I winced a bit, before drying himself with his handkerchief.

'My snotrag's too mucky for you.'

In the end we went down the driveway, but cautiously. The old occupants of the house still seemed to be asleep. I imagined them upstairs, so impeccably polite even in slumber that they wouldn't risk a snore.

On the pavement, we looked up and down Langtoft Avenue. No indication of the police car or its occupants. Derek gave the all-clear and, like triumphant but weary adventurers, we parted in front of my place.

***

Balancing carefully on the boxes, I hoisted myself onto the coalhouse roof and crawled up the short incline to the bedroom window. I raised it very slowly, half-inch by half-inch. There was a slight scraping sound even so. Anybody on the alert, really listening, would have heard something, but I didn't think it'd be enough to jolt my parents out of sleep. Unless one of them was awake already, and then… Whatever, I'd have to take the risk.

The house wasn't quite as peaceful as I'd hoped. When I wiggled over the sill and entered my bedroom, I heard a loud voice in rambling dispute from the other end of the landing. Mum and Dad couldn't still be quarrelling!

But it was Dad's voice only – from his office, I reckoned, where he must have taken refuge for the night. His door was probably ajar, whereas Mum's would be firmly closed, though I wasn't going to tiptoe down the corridor to check. Of course, she might have taken a sleeping pill, but Mum was a bit wary of them. She said they worked all too well and left her feeling groggy the next morning.

Dad still seemed to be arguing, yet with an invisible adversary this time. Softly, I opened my door a fraction. From what I could work out, Dad's sleep-ramblings weren't to do with my mother at all, not a one-sided continuation of their earlier wrangling. This was to do with business. I caught mention of typing paper and cream-coloured envelopes with crinkle-edged flaps. Very desirable, apparently. It appeared that Dad was offering a bargain price but was getting increasingly annoyed that his prospective customer remained unimpressed. Then there was a spell of incoherent mumbling before the final slide into whiffly unconsciousness.

All I can remember of the short period before I fell asleep myself was wondering about our exploits of that night and what I'd put down in my diary about it all.

XI. A PIRATICAL APPURTENANCE

The next school morning, stepping from the building to inspect the lines as usual, Mr Gordon displayed one striking alteration to his appearance. He was sporting a black eye-patch which made him look a bit like a pirate, a tidy sort of pirate admittedly, a besuited official with a touch of the desperado about him.

All the boys watched with fascinated attention, or tried to without being noticed by Mr Gordon or the teachers on duty. It was as though the whole playground were exploding with silent laughter. It even affected Mr Marston, if one could judge by the shades of difference in his behaviour: the extra, forced severity in his expression, the times he turned round to study the bricks of the school wall.

Once we were in the classroom, during that brief space of freedom before the register was called, the rumours began to run rife and, by break-time, they had become downright scurrilous, our imaginations in free flight because no authorised explanation whatsoever had been given to account for Mr Gordon's eye-patch. Naturally, we didn't expect the Headmaster himself to provide one, being the august presence he was. He wore the patch, in fact, as if it were the most normal item of attire in the world, as customary as the triangular tip of the handkerchief peeking from his front jacket pocket.

'His wife landed him one,' said Allington, the smallest boy in the class, in a piping voice of humorous certainty.

'Who'd blame her?'

'No, rubbish!' said a round-faced boy called Adrian

MacPherson, who went to the same Presbyterian church as Mr Gordon and his wife. Sometimes he gave us a report on how the Gordons disported themselves there but, as they remained staid and respectable, pious model citizens, these reports were never very interesting. Now, however, MacPherson was waxing as wild as Derek ever could.

'Old Gordon went out on the town and got into a fight in one of those horrible pubs near the docks. If he took the patch off, we'd be able to see the purple bruise. Of course, he was trying to poach some deckie's tart at the time.'

This version drew much hilarious approval. Our mirth had a kind of rebellious exhilaration about it – a victory in itself, though none of us really disliked Mr Gordon. We were in awe of him, but that was a different thing altogether.

How would he be watching us from his eyrie now? Using the heavy binoculars as a telescope? We imagined him putting up the glasses unthinkingly, amazed to find one eye completely dark. Derek gave a good imitation of Mr Gordon squinting irritably behind his eye-patch as if that action alone would restore sight, until he remembered. Would he – when the staffroom was empty apart from himself – take off the eye-patch, reveal his shame or wound, whatever it was, to the framed photographs of two of his predecessors staring at him from their honoured positions above the bookcase, and try to focus as he usually did? We decided that he'd shy away from such humiliating exposure, even in private.

Mr Marston worked hard to calm us down, as though he feared a serious revolt was imminent, but even he couldn't help joining in the fun, after his fashion.

Someone had got a brownish piece of cloth – it might have been a small handkerchief of sombre colour, but I'm not sure – and it was being passed surreptitiously round the group, some of my classmates trying it out as an improvised, if precarious patch over one eye.

Of course, it would have to be Derek whom Mr Marston caught in the act, but he was so flamboyant and deliberate too with this latest trick, the scrunt of cloth falling down his face repeatedly, that it was hardly surprising.

I think this was the first time it struck me that Derek *wanted* to be caught by Mr Marston. The idea must have crossed my mind before as a possibility, but now it seemed like collusion: the prank itself, Mr Marston's discovery of it and the consequent ear-tweaking and neck-pincering, even a lightish tattoo with a ruler on Derek's head. Both of them seemed oddly happy with this rhythm of things, playing their parts with gusto.

'Is there something the matter with your eye, Fraser?'

'No sir.'

'A sudden rheum perhaps? A gush of tears for all your many sins?'

'If it was that, sir, it'd be both eyes.'

'How true! Your knowledge of the human form and its qualities would no doubt astound the Royal College of Surgeons. By the bye, I wonder if you have maritime ambitions, Fraser?'

'What sir?'

'You know, the sea.'

'My dad used to be a skipper, sir.'

'And a very good one too, I'd think. But I wasn't thinking of the North Sea. A warmer climate for you, Fraser – the Caribbean, let's say. When you were trying to stuff that disgusting piece of material into your eyeball, I had a vision of you in that part of the world, in the old days of fable and splendid lore: rum and parrots and crutches, a lot of yo-ho-hoing. That kind of thing.'

Some of the other kids knew *Treasure Island* too, but most of them would only have seen the film version. I liked that as well, especially Robert Newton playing Long John Silver, but for me, in the rank of things, books came before films, even when secretly you might prefer the latter.

Mr Marston was actually smiling now, in a rare, unguarded way. It amazed and unnerved us. The class studied him, wondering how far we could believe in this suddenly relaxed form-master.

'Jolly buccaneering,' he said in a nostalgic tone.

'No sir. That's not my ambition, sir.'

'Curious. '

'He just wants to be Billy Fury, sir!' somebody yelled out, to a shout of laughter from those around him.

'Billy – who? Oh, you mean William Fergus of 4A. '

'No sir. The singer, sir.'

'Ah,' said Mr Marston slowly, caught between puzzlement and revelation. 'Fury – as in the state you lot often drive me into?'

'Yes sir! But pop music, top twenty hits, sir.'

'Interesting. So we have a young rock and roller in our midst, perhaps even a tearaway.'

Derek protested that he wasn't a tearaway with such hurt ostentatiousness that it only seemed like a variation of his usual showing-off, and tried to explain to Mr Marston about Billy Fury. For one dreadful moment, I thought he was going to get up from his desk and launch into his favourite impersonation there and then, leg-swivels and formalized hand gestures and all, giving the classroom 'Halfway to Paradise' or 'Jealousy' in a higher version of the singer's purring, plaintive voice.

In fact, some of the boys began to urge just that and it was there Mr Marston decided that the class really was beginning to get out of hand. The humorous digression was now over.

Quickly, he brought us back to what he was supposed to be teaching us that period: RK. He was giving an account of how Moses and the Israelites managed to cross the Red Sea, how it *might* be rationally accounted for.

'Yet don't forget, while you can explain certain

phenomena scientifically, that doesn't mean God isn't behind it all,' he warned his charges with raised, admonitory finger, a bit like a preacher at a tricky point in his sermon.

'God winds up the clock,' Derek whispered facetiously.

'What was that, Fraser?'

'I was just telling Palmer, sir, that God sort of works the machine, winds up the clock. But not every night.'

With one sweeping frown, Mr Marston stilled the titter that arose from the class.

'A little more than that, Fraser, I would think. But next time, why don't you give us all the benefit of your theological wisdom?'

'Sir.'

Mr Marston only returned to the matter of eye-patches once, towards the end of the lesson when he'd got Moses and his people safely into Sinai. With a sigh he closed the textbook, as though that were enough applied rationalism for the day.

Now he told us that being bereft of the use of one eye could have its uses, citing Horatio Nelson at the Battle of Copenhagen, how he ignored the orders of Admiral Parker to disengage, putting the telescope to his blind eye and declaring that he saw no signal. Thus, Nelson continued exactly as he wanted to and subdued the Danish fleet.

'The wretched Parker was recalled while the wise Horatio was appointed admiral and made a viscount.'

In admiring mime, Mr Marston closed one eye and held out a half-clamped fist before him as if he were holding an invisible telescope. At first, I thought he might be making some oblique reference to Mr Gordon, that the Headmaster might well be even more vigilant with one eye than with two, but then it struck me there was something strange in our teacher's story, perhaps revealing a subversive streak in him. He who was normally so hot on our obeying orders now seemed to be suggesting that the rewards would be all the greater for disobeying them.

I reckoned I was right because, as though suddenly realising the possible danger of what he'd just said, Mr Marston hastily strove to cover himself.

'However, Nelson was a military genius, only exceeded during that time by Wellington and Napoleon. Such men have to be allowed a certain licence. In this classroom I don't think we're amongst such rare spirits. Or would you disagree, Palmer?'

'Probably not, sir.'

'*Probably* not. Hmm, I wonder. Sensible, though, to qualify my statement. Even schoolmasters of some experience should leave a margin for error.'

He couldn't be twenty-seven or so, sounding like that, as if he were in his fifties like Mr Gordon! I knew our teacher acted a part in the classroom and enjoyed it, but all the same it was from him, like Derek's performances were, and it puzzled me as to why he should want to come on as a man twenty years older than he actually was.

We couldn't imagine him as a child, nervous and apprehensive as we sometimes were, being coaxed and cuddled by the beautiful German mother of the photograph, or being genially instructed in Meccano by a younger, less bizarre father. For us, Mr Marston BA arrived ready-made in this world, set to run on the same rails for ever. As Derek said, if he ever managed to get a wife he'd most likely be testing her on her spelling when they sat down to tea, or setting her history quizzes just as she was drifting off to sleep.

After school, Derek and I couldn't leave go of the pirate idea. He came round to our house for a while and, after we'd told my mother about Mr Gordon's eye-patch, bringing a smile even to her drawn, anxious face, we went up to my room.

My father was out; if he'd been at home he would have enjoyed Derek's elaborated account, booming with laughter, slapping his knees with delight.

'Such a bright spark,' he tended to say, when Derek had entertained him. 'He'll end up on the stage or television, don't you think, Colin?'

I'd agree with him enthusiastically. Of course, I was jealous that I wasn't the one who received such accolades, but pleased too, basking in Dad's praise of Derek as if it were my right, something more than just reflected glory. After all, I increasingly felt that I supplied Derek with lines and ideas, a bit like the straight man in a double act. And he was my friend, the special one, whom I'd introduced to the household.

Still thinking of Mr Marston's comments about buccaneering, we did bring Long John Silver to the fore at last. There was fun fitting out Mr Gordon as the wily sea-cook, with the piratical accoutrements Mr Marston had mentioned. D.K. Broster's story of the '45 might not have lit Derek's imagination, but *Treasure Island* certainly did.

'He doesn't only have to be Long John, though, does he?' I said. 'Just think – if tomorrow he comes on like Blind Pew, tapping his way along with a stick, clutching the black spot in his hand.'

'Great!' shouted Derek, immediately jumping up and acting it out.

'Who'd you have for Billy Bones, then?'

'Look, Blind Pew Gordon would shuffle to the end of 4B's line, probably giving a few of those gets a swipe with his stick into the bargain...'

'And guess who he'd find there, to receive the dreaded warning?'

'Svenny Olsen!' we both exclaimed together, assuming a scowling, baleful expression.

'If there was a strong north wind blowing in, our phizogs might stay like that,' warned Derek, only half-playfully.

'It bloody well hurts anyway,' I said, stressing the adjective as though I'd won my spurs by now and had a

perfect right to use it.
    'Don't swear, our kid,' said Derek. 'It lowers the tone.'

XII. KNIVES AND FORKS

My mother might not have counted the bottles of pickled onions in the larder but, as I soon discovered, she'd certainly checked on my grandfather's cutlery. It seemed to be an act of daughterly faith, as though the sight of the heavy gleaming things somehow sharpened his image for her. I'd thought that she just polished up this portion of her legacy about twice a year at most: Easter and Christmas.

So she'd discovered two knives and forks to be missing the next day but one after our feast. She re-counted the whole canteen and then again, to make triply sure.

No, she was not mistaken and they were not where we kept the ordinary cutlery either.

The storm broke.

'Where are they? Where the – are they?'

Both my father (truthfully) and myself (untruthfully) denied any knowledge of their whereabouts.

'They'll turn up,' said Dad, with an attempt at reassurance which only further infuriated my mother. 'Bound to.'

'Where do you think they've got to, then?' she said scornfully. 'Taken themselves off for a walk?'

'I don't know, woman! Why are you making such a fuss? It's not as if they're solid silver. You wouldn't get much for that lot if you tried to pawn them.'

'They're silver-plated,' said Mum firmly. 'And they've belonged to the family for two generations at least. They're antiques.'

'Well, I always found them to be a bit cumbersome, to be honest,' my father contributed, once again revealing a deadly talent for needling his wife.

'They're amongst the few things of any worth or style

we've got! Not that you would know much about that.'

'Ouch! '

Dad put his hand to his cheek as if he'd been slapped. Then he grinned across at me collusively, as you might to a partner in crime.

I wished he hadn't done that because it drew Mum's suspicious attention onto me.

'Have you seen these knives and forks at all, Colin?' she asked.

I thought of Derek in such a situation and, though I didn't have much of his flair or panache, that helped me to be defiant, brazen it out. I didn't stutter at all and barely even began to go red. Afterwards, it seemed a wonderful thing to me that I could curb my weaknesses by playing a part.

'Why would I, Mum? You can't accuse me...'

'I'm not accusing you.'

'As good as.'

'Colin!' warned my father. 'Don't be rude to your mother.'

That was rich coming from him!

'The last time we had the posh stuff out from the canteen...'

'The *posh* stuff?' interrupted Dad, stressing the word in a broad manner. 'Who's talking there, I'd like to know?'

'...was when Roy was over.'

'Are you suggesting he's taken them?'

'Of course not!'

'Now, that'd be something,' chuckled Dad. 'Silver – pardon me, silver-plated – knives and forks in his commie pigsty in Leeds!'

'Oh, shut up!' snapped my mother, and then turned to me again. 'Colin, for the last time, do you know anything about this?'

'No,' I lied unabashedly, even staring her straight in the eye until it was she who dropped hers first. That made me feel guilty and wretched for a moment because she looked hurt, but there was nothing I could say. I had to carry the act off. Contrition would come, if at all, when I could afford it.

'What about Mrs Rolt?' suggested my father, as if he'd had a fantastic brainwave. Mrs Rolt was our char, who came in twice a week. She was a highly respectable, hard-working Congregationalist, with some social pretensions. Making beds, sweeping and scrubbing floors were presented as good deeds she performed to help out my mother, much given to complaining about her bad back when Mrs Rolt was around. However, the virtuous lady charged well above the normal rates, Mum claiming she was worth every penny and more.

Dad got it in the neck now for making a joke in poor taste, Mum gave it as her opinion that he should go back to his stationery and cards and that, as for me – I should get ready for school and take the silly grin off my face forthwith because this wasn't a laughing matter!

It certainly wasn't, though I'd not been aware of the offending grin until she made me so.

***

I determined to head for the den the moment afternoon school was over and retrieve the knives and forks (that is, if they hadn't been whipped by some wandering plunderer), articles now raised to the dangerous status of heirlooms. I visualised the cutlery on the makeshift table staring up at me through the beam of the torch, and cursed myself again for being so careless.

I couldn't put the things back into the canteen immediately. That'd be too obvious, almost as bad as owning up. Better to wrap them in a cloth and hide them, behind the garage somewhere – *not* in my room – and then slip them back, cleaned to an identical shininess with the others, in a week, say, anyhow once the whole issue had begun to recede a bit.

I imagined Mum in due course, prompted by pious thoughts of Grandpa, checking the canteen again and finding every knife, fork and spoon present and gleamingly correct. Her suspicions might be awakened once more, but the relief would outweigh all that.

'And I counted them so many times! I must be going doolalley.'

And, if she were in an indulgent mood, I'd come in with: 'Well, you said it, Mum, not me.'

Perhaps a smile then – they were nice when they came – and a few words about how much the cutlery had meant to Grandpa.

But I was running ahead of myself.

Derek couldn't come with me to the hide; his mother wanted him for some errand or other after school. But, when I told him what had happened, he agreed I should go as soon as possible.

I was delayed for a while, however. Miss Barber had finally brought those prints by Douanier Rousseau she'd mentioned and wanted me to have a look at them, in particular one called "The Snake Charmer", which was interesting, even though I couldn't give it my full attention then. It showed a dark figure playing the flute and attracting the snakes, principally a huge one wrapped round a branch and bending towards the charmer, who was a woman with very fleshy legs, almost completely in darkness and difficult to figure out. There was also what I thought to be a flamingo amongst the serpents, which seemed to be attracted to the music too. All the same, I wondered what it was really doing there, but that was a question for another day. Miss Barber might answer at length and I wanted to be off as quickly and politely as possible.

When I finally got to the Land of the Two Rivers it was growing quite dark. I had no torch with me, but by now I felt that I could almost have trod that path blindfold.

I knew there was a box of matches, protected by a plastic bag, just to the right of the entrance. I just needed to strike a couple of matches and I'd be sure to find the missing things.

I'd scurried so hastily from school to the hide that I didn't think of anyone following me, didn't even stop for a second to listen and peer through the gloom, nothing like that. I was alone, or assumed I was, everything subordinated to my purpose of recovering the cutlery.

***

I pulled aside the branches and briars that were our 'door' and started fumbling round for the matches. Suddenly, a torch snapped on, straight in my eyes, blinding me. Then it dipped to the silver knives and forks on the box-table, exactly where I'd remembered them to be.

'Looking for these, kid?'

The torch changed direction for the third time when Olsen shone it on himself. He was girning, which made his broad, puddingy, acned face even more grotesque.

'Good place you've found – a bit draughty, but you can't have everything. A pity your Derek can't be with us to enjoy it today. I've got a score to settle with that little turd, but you'll do at a pinch. Oh yes, you'll do great! We still have to find out the answer to the big mystery, don't we?'

At first I couldn't speak. I started sweating. Fear gripped me; a ball and chain clamping my foot couldn't have been worse, it was like being paralysed. The torch focussed back on me but lower.

'Time for a chat. We can be friends if we cosy up a bit.'

At last I struggled out a sentence, pale and squeaky.

'How did you find this place?'

'A little bird. Two of them, in fact.'

'Doran and Witherow!'

'Now, now, kid. You know the old saying: No names, no pack-drill.'

He shone the torch on his face again, to leave me clear about his message.

'I had a scout round here early on. I didn't reckon that either of you would turn up that early, so I thought I'd leave the actual meeting until about now. And if it hadn't happened today, then I'd be here tomorrow, the next day, whatever. You can't put locks on briars and I don't think this den has a motor to drive away on, so there we are.'

I'd had this idea of sanctuary, although I probably wouldn't have called it that then. This was destroyed now, as Olsen was making plain.

He shone his torch around the hide. It created a flickering impression, like an old-style film. Then the light was back to himself again. He was sitting with his heavy legs spread out, the box small and precarious beneath him as if about to give way altogether. More and more his bulk seemed to fill what little space there was. I shrank back against the entrance, but I wasn't capable then of escaping to the outside. Olsen knew that perfectly well.

Cold air through the thinned foliage, coastal air, fresh and sharp, but it did nothing to lessen the reek that I caught off him now. It wasn't simply that he didn't wash much; there was something else, like the smell of hot sour bed linen that had covered somebody in a fever.

'You shouldn't treat those two so badly, you know,' said Olsen. 'They were only trying to give you something. Don't you like presents? I've had plenty of things from them. And I act as their storeman too. In fact, those pencils had been at my place for some time.'

It was on the tip of my tongue to say that it was Derek who'd quarrelled with Doran and Witherow, but I had enough pride – or perhaps shame would be better – not to try it on.

'Fraser fights your battles for you, but you egg him on

with those little girl manners.'

Olsen was beaming the torch on my face again, like the relentless wounding light of a torturer.

'Well, take your knives and forks, then.'

As though to encourage me, he lowered the torch once more and played it over the cutlery. I could see the food stains on the tines of the forks and thought how good the feast had been, how happy Derek and I were and how useless that seemed now.

Suddenly Olsen asked me, as if we were having a perfectly normal talk in a perfectly normal situation: 'How come you didn't go to grammar school?'

The answer was an obvious one so, suspecting a trap, I hesitated before giving it to him: 'I failed the exam. '

'Same with me, but you're a snooty sort of kid. You could have bought your way in somehow.'

'I don't think it works like that nowadays. Besides...'

'No?' He laughed cynically. 'Well, it does everywhere else.'

Then he became reflective.

'I didn't stand a chance anyway. Not because I'm a moron as people like Derek Fraser put around. I just couldn't be bothered. There'll always be jobs for the Olsens of this world, don't you reckon? *Real* jobs, not sitting in an office totting up figures all day long.'

The wind blasted through the hide in a sudden gust. A thin branch from the stunted tree moved in alarm, scraping my hair.

'Parky here.'

I gave no response. A mistake.

'I said it's fucking parky here!' Olsen bawled, enraged. 'Don't you react when spoken to? I call that rude.'

'Yes.'

'Yes, *what*?'

'I'm sorry. It is cold. Parky.'

He moved the torch upwards again, so that it shone

mainly on my hair.

'Do you ever go to a barber's?'

'I'm supposed to go soon, actually.'

'Oh, "actually",' Olsen mocked. 'There's nothing like being lah-di-dah, is there?'

The torch lingered on my hair, which was tousled, the front lock flopping over my forehead. I pushed it back.

'No, leave it,' Olsen said, in a softer tone. 'I shouldn't bother with the barber's for a while yet. Your hair looks good, almost blond in this light.'

Then it was back to the knives and forks.

'Your Mam missed these?'

'Yes.'

'Well, hadn't you better get them back to her?'

I leaned forward, but beyond that I still dithered.

'You know how to pick up kitchen tools, don't you? Or does Mummy also carry out that little task, as well as tying up your shoelaces and wiping your crack? Come on!'

As I retrieved the cutlery, Olsen clamped his free hand on my wrist. I was so shocked that I dropped one pair of the knives and forks. I still kept hold of the other, though.

It wasn't foresight– at least I don't think so – rather luck or chance, easy to turn into a benign fate afterwards if things went your way.

'But first we need an answer to my question – a burning question, no less!'

He took his hand off my wrist and began to fumble at my trousers, as he'd done before behind the temporary classroom.

'Because I really do think we'd better find out what you are. Get that established once and for all!'

His thick blunt fingers groped inside my waistband and with the energy of panic I began to struggle and pull away. Olsen became impatient, as if I were just being contrary. He hit me in the belly with his torch hand. That winded me and made me lurch half a step forward, my head falling on

Olsen's chest. I could smell him even stronger then and that and the effects of the blow nearly made me vomit. Olsen grunted, almost gratefully, as though I had altered my position to accommodate him. His fingers were delving lower, struggling with the flap in my underpants.

'That's better. I still reckon you're a girl sent over from their Seniors to spy on us. That's my view. Anyway, you squeal like a girl, if that's anything to go by.'

It felt like instinct when I stretched back my hand in that limited space and brought down the remaining knife and fork on his forearm. Olsen might have been complaining about the cold, but he only had a jerkin on over a plaid shirt, no windcheater or mac. With the force I brought to the act, both the prongs and the tip of the blade went through the material. Neither were particularly sharp, but enough to hurt and draw blood. Horrified, I could see the spots and small streaks of red appearing on his shirt.

It was funny too, as though I were having Olsen's forearm for dinner and it was proving to be a tough joint. Later, enjoying the story and its endless re-tellings, Derek would nickname me 'Colin the Cannibal' for a time. Between ourselves, that is – after all, there was a new secret to keep now. But that was when we could both laugh at what had happened, even if I rarely did so without feeling some disquiet.

Olsen's yell of pain was not easy to forget or relegate to the harmless areas of memory. His hand snatched up out of my trousers so that, moaning and cursing, he could save himself from further hurt. At last I had the gumption to spring back, dropping my weapons just inside the den, as if they were poisoned and would turn on me given half the chance.

I was still afraid of Olsen but mixed in with that was a kind of rough exhilaration because I knew this was my chance to escape him. Stumbling out of the hide, I ran back along the track. But what if Olsen, his fury at its height, chased and caught me? Replacing the missing cutlery in my grandfather's canteen seemed the least of my worries now.

Because of haste and fear, I was not as sure-footed as usual and I tripped, pitching to my knees in the mud and dirtying my trousers, the palms of my hands too. That would have been the exact moment for a pursuer to pounce, but there was no harsh breathing behind me, no galumphing but relentless paces.

I paused. I could hear Olsen bellowing. He was still in the hide, as if it were a tangled thicket he couldn't escape. Looking over my shoulder, I saw the torchlight moving wildly about inside and wondered with trepidation whether I'd hurt him more than I thought, conveniently deciding that it was probably the shock of the attack which was troubling Olsen now, more than the physical pain.

As I neared the border of the Land, he roared out my name.

I stopped, feeling safe enough now to cheek him.

'Did you want something, Olsen?' I shouted.

'Your fucking tripes! Come back here!'

'Sorry, I'm late. Beans on toast for tea and I don't like them cold.'

This was the kind of bravado that Derek could produce at any time, but it was new for me and felt good – less so at Olsen's next words.

'I'll get you, you murderous little bastard!'

But I did manage a spirited response all the same, that boastful phrase I'd heard on countless occasions but which I couldn't ever remember using myself before.

'You and whose army?'

Every playtime from now on, Derek and I would have to stick close to the master on duty and we'd contrive elaborate escapes for when school ended. We'd outwit the oafish Olsen all right! That was what I kept telling myself, but it was hard to ignore the fact that Olsen had the brawn and now, from his point of view, an absolutely legitimate motive for using it.

I didn't think Olsen would tell on me. For one thing, that wasn't his way. For another, my story would trump his – I mean, what he'd been trying to do. At that time, it didn't seem a moral question at all, but rather a practical matter.

There was no need to pelt along Bradleigh Avenue, as though I had a horde of devils behind me. I was pretty sure I was out of immediate danger, though not above giving the odd backward glance just to make certain. Besides, a number of people were about and they'd have thought it strange if they'd seen this figure running for dear life. Time to think about being more circumspect. All the same, I still kept up a quickish stride, like any boy late for his tea.

What if the wonderful den was a thing of the past now, spoilt for ever by Olsen's intrusion? Perhaps it'd be better if, in his maddened state, he simply wrecked it, uprooting the bushes and the spindly tree as well: a latterday Northern Samson, bringing down the whole thing on his head!

It was all a waste, then, the hide which I'd begun work on in my loneliness and exclusion, and which Derek had completed simply by the spirit he brought to it. But, as I approached our house, I began to resent this defeatism and fight against it. Why *should* I desert the hide overlooking the waste ground and my very own Tigris and Euphrates?

It was as if someone else, someone ever tougher like Derek, was urging courage on me. Who said you couldn't rebuild little patches you'd treasured, make them new again, or almost as good as new?- because, of course, they'd have to bear some scars; that was the logic of things. But you didn't have to flee all the time like a frightened mouse. With assertions like that thundering through my brain, it was easy to slap the gate to, make it sound like a falling axe, but I opened the back door into the warm kitchen much more cautiously.

I hadn't got back all that late for tea as it turned out, but I was spectacularly dirty, my school clothes messed up, so I got a thorough scolding from my mother: 'You really drive me to despair at times!' and so on. Naturally, I didn't tell her about what had happened, just making up some taradiddle about rough games with Derek.

Mum's displeasure with me was hardly enjoyable, but compared to what I'd been through with Svenny Olsen, and the revenge I guessed he intended to take (should he get the chance), this was plain sailing. So I accepted the harsh words with meekness. There was a time for safe havens, however unhappy.

XIII. The Absentees

Next morning, I kept an eye open for Olsen and his two sneaky minions as I crossed the park, keeping well to the centre of the green, and then cautiously started up the length of Willow Road. I didn't want to be careless and give Olsen the chance to step out and waylay me. I needed some running space between us.

As I reached the grim building with the long classroom windows on kip, I didn't turn in at the school entrance, instead continuing up the road to Derek's place. As I'd left our house early, he was still eating his breakfast when I called. He looked surprised to see me – we usually met in the playground these days. I could see that he'd passed a flannel across his face at least, judging by the wet lick of hair on his forehead, but he was still rubbing the sleep from his eyes.

'What's up?'

'Nothing. I just had a few minutes to spare.'

Naturally, he *knew* there was something wrong, but also realised that I couldn't speak freely in front of his mother and Becky, hovering around now with a sharp gleam of curiosity in her eyes.

'You look a bit peaky today, love,' Mrs Fraser said, examining my face anxiously.

'That's what my Mum said.'

'You're not going down with a cold, are you?'

'I don't think so. Hope not, anyway'

Understandably, I'd had a bad night: fitful sleep and horrible dreams. As far as I could remember, Olsen didn't appear in any of them, not directly. But he was there, all right, in each threatening shape that threw itself against me. When shocked awake, I hadn't cried out as I did when I was smaller and had nightmares, but it'd been a near thing.

Mrs Fraser offered me some breakfast. I thanked her but refused, saying I'd just had mine.

'Cup of tea, then, while Slowcoach here finishes his bacon?'

I accepted that, sipping at it as Mrs Fraser got Becky off to school, calming down some last minute worries the little girl had.

'Have you got your Grand-dad's stuff back yet?' Derek asked in a half-whisper, bending towards me.

'No, I haven't.'

'Why not?'

'I'll tell you outside.'

Chewing the rind of his rasher, Derek looked at me appraisingly, trying to guess what I had to tell him. Even with the nervy state I was in, holding back on Derek for a while (as the possessor of a secret growing more tantalising by the minute!) did give me some satisfaction, I must admit.

***

Once we were on the short way to school, he demanded: 'Come on, spit it out! What's happened?'

Stuttering a bit at the beginning, I told him everything, including the detail I thought I might fight shy of, what Olsen had been after.

'The dirty bastard!' exclaimed Derek furiously, yet he wasn't too surprised as he'd witnessed the first attack. 'He'll find himself locked up in clink, on bread and water, if he goes on like this!'

I made as much of my escape from Olsen's clutches, my means to freedom, as I could, really building it up, without actually telling any lies. I felt that if previously I'd sunk in Derek's esteem through my cowed, less than impressive performance before the bully, then I'd more than make up for it by this sensational revelation.

'You stabbed Svenny Olsen!' he shouted, both astonished and gleeful. 'With your Grand-dad's posh knife and fork?'

'Not so loud!'

I glanced round, but none of the kids, either seniors or juniors, flocking to school, seemed interested in picking out what we were saying.

'But that's nothing to be ashamed of. You ought to sing it to the skies!'

'And get into trouble for GBH?'

I'd learnt that from *Z Cars* on television and this was the first opportunity to flourish the acronym.

'GB – what?'

'Grievous bodily harm. It's a term the police use.'

'Well, what are you worried about, Inspector Palmer? For giving Olsen a taste of his own medicine? They should award you a medal for that! Not the Victoria Cross, perhaps – something close, though.'

We entered the school playground, laughing, all the same keeping on the alert.

'You didn't cut him very deep, did you?' Derek asked me in a low voice, suddenly anxious.

'No, I don't think so. It got through his shirt sleeve, but the prongs and the knife-blade were quite blunt.'

'You must have used a lot of force, then.'

'What would you have done?' I demanded of him, angrily.

'Me? I'd have slit his fucking throat!'

Most of the boys, including us, were drifting towards the space before the main entrance to the building, beginning to form up in a raggedy sort of way.

Derek was silent for a moment, gazing thoughtfully at the ground.

'Olsen'll be hopping mad now,' he said. 'I can't fend him off all by myself. I had the advantage of surprise before.'

'But together?'

Derek looked me up and down, a bit dubiously.

'You'd have to go for weapons rather than muscle. What'll it be this time? Axes and claymores?'

'I didn't *plan* that, Derek!' I said heatedly.

'All right, keep your hair on. Just a joke.'

'You'll go through life making that excuse. And just see where it gets you,' I brought out snidely.

'There are worse things. I might threaten to stick nuclear weapons up people's backsides, mightn't I? Like that horrible old Mr K in Moscow.'

He knew that would amuse me and gave a lummocky sort of smile – funny enough in itself sometimes, especially when he twisted his mouth about. Then it seemed as if it were almost separate from his face.

'Tell you what. You kneel behind *him*, close behind, and I'll push him over. I saw that in a Stan and Olly film once.'

'You'd need a strong shove.'

'And you'd need a strong back, with that weight tumbling down on you! No, I'm afraid we'll have to think of something else.'

Briefly, he put his arm across my shoulders.

'It's always darkest before the dawn,' he said solemnly.

That old chestnut! But when I glanced at him, I saw no signs that he was mocking the saying.

'I didn't know you were a philosopher, Derek,' I said, unable to resist a sarcastic tone.

It was as though he hadn't heard me. He was miles away and yet very present too, exactly where he needed to be.

'We'll just have to be on our guard,' Derek said. 'And if there's trouble, we'll find some way of dealing with it.'

I couldn't quite believe in his optimism, but I was grateful for it all the same.

We looked around for Olsen's hulking, ominous figure – usually all too discernible. The brutal righter of wrongs was still nowhere to be seen.

The line-whistle went.

Again Mr Marston took the 'parade', as I thought of it. Perhaps he begged the other masters for the honour of doing this duty for them. I wondered whether he had some connection with the army, or wished he had. He must have done National Service, I supposed; it had only been abolished a few years previously. Unless he'd failed the medical and was pining now for a pleasure denied him. There was always the Territorials, though.

Mr Marston wore shoes – brown, highly-polished, steel-tipped too, I reckoned – that tapped authoritatively on the concrete as he walked up and down, inspecting us. Like an officer's shoes. All he needed, apart from the military uniform, of course, was a swagger stick. He'd be able to wield that all right. Better than tweaking ears and twisting hair with his long, bony fingers.

'2A! Shoulders back, eyes ahead, hands behind the seams of your trousers! 3B! Don't gape like a procession of village idiots! Try breathing through your noses, not your mouths. Smarten up, the lot of you – straighter than straight!'

While trying to present an appearance that wouldn't offend Mr Marston's sense of decorum, I experienced a terrible pang of fear. Suppose Olsen hadn't come to school because he *couldn't*, that I'd injured him more seriously than I'd thought and he'd had to be taken to hospital? In those circumstances he wouldn't be slow to put the blame on me and concoct some rigmarole or other to exonerate himself.

'4A! You're not at a mothers' meeting – observe the line and seal your lips!'

Mr Marston took up his position at the front, the school now absolutely still.

Olsen's absence was the first strange thing that morning and soon came the second.

Mr Gordon didn't appear, eye-patch or no eye-patch. Instead, it seemed to me that Mr Marston took the exact length of time which the Headmaster would have needed for the scrutiny of his school, as though the upright Presbyterian had been made invisible to prowl the lines, to search out infringements all the better.

The boys, as far as they could under this strict control, were growing restive, wondering what was going on. We began to think that Mr Marston might be playing some sort of weird game with us, and then that he too was ignorant of what was really up.

But his stern, resolved face gave nothing away.

Finally, he barked out the order to lead off.

The third surprise of the morning was that when we reached the assembly hall, we found the Deputy Headmaster, Mr Bartlett, waiting for us on the makeshift dais, in the position his superior normally took. Mr Bartlett was a small, rather nondescript man, who seemed content to stay in Mr Gordon's shadow. The Deputy Head's area of expertise was the drawing-up of timetables and staff rosters, so I'd been told.

He addressed us in a thin, less than compelling voice. Mr Marston and the other members of staff, ranked along the assembly hall, were keeping us under flintier observation than usual, which we knew was a warning not to take advantage of the weaker man conducting the ceremony today.

'The Headmaster has been unavoidably detained on a matter of some importance and regrets that he cannot be with us this morning. I shall be taking over his normal duties. '

In lacklustre style, he led us into the hymn, prayer, Bible reading and delivered the briefest of homilies before finding a bit more energy for the school notices. After these, he dismissed us with evident relief.

The fourth surprise.

Doran and Witherow had desks on the other side of the classroom from Derek and me and, since the bust-up, we'd ostentatiously avoided looking in that direction, unless we had to. And that morning we'd been so preoccupied with searching for signs of Olsen, plus the changes in things, we hadn't thought about them at all.

Mr Marston began on the register, using his big fountain pen, fuelled with red ink, to tick off the names or put an 'A' against them for absence. There were only two of those. Doran came high on the class-list, but I noticed that Mr Marston was putting the letter against his name even as he called it out. The same applied to Witherow further down.

Usually, if Mr Marston got no response, he would pause, repeat the boy's name, then stare across at the empty desk, as though suspecting a deliberate affront. Once he'd proved to his own satisfaction that the boy in question really wasn't there, he'd make a sarcastic comment, as he had the day Derek had gone to the dentist, or ask wearily if anybody knew why so-and-so was absent: something else sent to try him, one more irritating irregularity.

But this time the teacher didn't bother with any of that. He knew perfectly well why the 'weasels', as Derek and I often called them, weren't amongst us, but he wasn't telling us, not yet.

Something odd was going on. I tried to read Mr Marston's expression with greater heed than usual, without success. He looked tired and grim, abnormally so – unless he was being 'seriously provoked', as he put it, by one of his charges or the stupidity of 2A as a whole, massed together in an 'unconquerable wall of ignorance'.

It was strange that I treasured some of his harsher censures almost like compliments. Perhaps I enjoyed the wording and the scathing manner because, secretly and smugly, I believed *I* must be excluded from general criticism, given the number of times I'd been singled out for praise. It didn't matter that, more often than not, it was jokily or ironically put – that was just a device to stop me getting swollen-headed, or prevent the other boys turning against me. Anyway, I wasn't teacher's pet, whatever the jealous might think. Derek occupied that position, in a curious, unsettling kind of way.

But the reason for Mr Marston's expression could have been anything: a bad night, a nervous stomach or, most likely, his aged and rather batty dad kicking up again.

***

At eleven o'clock, during that brief moment at the end of break when there was no teacher in the room, some of us examined Doran and Witherow's desks. They were completely empty: nothing in there whatsoever, not even a broken pencil. In fact, they even looked as if they had been dusted and wiped.

Now the rumours really began to fly. I recalled the ingratiating manner of the weasels, their chewed lapels and – shamefully again – my acceptance of their gifts.

These stories were of a wild, fantastic nature at first: from gory deaths under the wheels of recklessly speeding cars and savage bludgeonings by random maniacs, to crippling attacks by parents tried beyond their limits of endurance, or – a vision which pleased those with romantic Whittingtonian notions about escape to London – running away to seek their fortune in the capital, hitching the hundred and seventy miles down to the Big Smoke. It was a place which had the glamour of size, power and remoteness; it might have been a separate universe for most of us.

Finally, all this excitement settled down to a more mundane version of things, more plausible but still fascinating. This centred on Doran and Witherow's light-fingered tendencies and was assembled by boys who set themselves up as pundits because they knew someone who knew someone definitely in the know, if only given their status as cousins or neighbours.

***

It was essentially accurate, however, this account, so that when we eventually got the official line from Mr Marston, there was little to surprise us. I think he would have been reluctant to tell us anything at all, if he and Mr Gordon and the other teachers hadn't felt the need for 'the sharp corrective of truth' as a counter to 'virulent gossip', as our master rather loftily put it. 'He thinks he's Perry Mason,' Derek whispered to me.

'I should tell you all that your classmates, John Doran and Trevor Witherow, are unable to attend school because they are – to use the hackneyed phrase – helping the police with their enquiries. The affair is apparently to do with goods missing from several shops in the town. Mr Gordon would appreciate any information you might be able to give. As far as possible, this will be treated confidentially.'

'Are they going to be done for shoplifting, sir?'

'Nothing further need be said on the matter at the moment.'

He ordered us to take out our school atlases and do some quiet work for a while, picking out the main cities of France – leaving aside Paris, which he assumed we knew a little about. We should try to figure out how our chosen places 'survived and thrived'.

There was the sound of desk lids being opened and closed, a short bustle of talk.

'Take about half a dozen, let's say. And not all on the coast. And any connection with Britain you know of would be useful. All right, start now.'

But Derek was raising his hand to ask a question.

'Where's Svenny Olsen, sir? He's not helping the police as well, is he?'

I buried my head as deep as possible in my atlas, expecting an explosion. Derek had licence to be cheeky with Mr Marston but not to this extent, especially when you could see the teacher was worried.

But, remarkably, he answered calmly.

'Now, what prompts you to ask that, Fraser?'

'Olsen's not at school today either, sir.'

'Indeed. I'm touched by your concern. I wasn't aware that Sven Roderick Olsen attracted such loyalty.'

The class tittered, also amused by the way our form-master had stressed Olsen's full name.

'Why would you assume that I'd know Olsen's whereabouts, Fraser?'

'Just thought you would, sir. You once told us that you had your finger on the pulse of the school.'

'How vain boasts come back to haunt one! Only Mr Gordon has that privilege, I'd think. Of course Mr Bartlett too, in his methodical, painstaking way. Well, who knows? Perhaps Olsen's taken a trip to Odense to visit his grandparents, or check on the birthplace of one of the world's greatest storytellers. Who am I referring to, anybody?'

I knew that one, but hesitated to give the answer, fearing my worsening reputation as class know-all.

The silence grew. Mr Marston surveyed us, pacing before his rickety table at the front.

'Oh dear, dear. It seems we'll have to rely once more on the Sage of Willow Road Secondary. Care to oblige, Palmer?'

'Hans Christian Andersen, sir.'

There were exclamations around me then of mild self-blame, like when you don't get an easy clue in a crossword.

'We read stories by him in junior school, sir,' contributed MacPherson.

'I've read "The Little Mermaid", sir.'

'There's a statue of that. I've seen it on a foreign stamp.'

'And "The Emperor's Suit", sir!'

' "New Clothes", Allington. "The Emperor's New Clothes".'

'There's a film about Hans Christian Andersen, sir. With Danny Kaye.'

'An absolute travesty! An insult both to the writer and the Danish nation,' pronounced Mr Marston.

He proceeded happily and with spirit to explain why. It was a useful distraction for all of us. French cities didn't get much of a look-in that day.

***

Doran and Witherow had finally been caught on one of their thieving expeditions: two small, shabby, unlikely figures at the perfume counter of Ketilsby's only department store. A smart one too. They were adroitly – but not quite adroitly enough – secreting bottles of 4711 eau de Cologne about their persons, all of which they claimed were intended for their mothers' and grannies' birthdays which, strangely, fell closely together. Of course they'd meant to pay! They'd been saving up specially. It was just a careless oversight that they'd stuffed the small bottles away like that into their pockets.

The police found a considerable stock of stolen goods at the homes of the two boys. They must have tried to incriminate Olsen, or perhaps even attempted to shift the major part of the blame onto him, because the police also learned that he had indeed been the weasels' storeman, as he'd confided to me.

It would have been hard for Olsen to deny that he knew the goods he was hoarding for Doran and Witherow were stolen but, to his credit, he didn't even attempt to do so. It probably helped his case – and I could imagine Mr Gordon, who'd become his advocate if not his excuser, stressing this – that , in spite of what he'd told me, Olsen had taken no rake-off from these thefts at all, either in cash or kind. This puzzled Derek a lot. 'Olsen must have grabbed something! He demands enough bribes at school, doesn't he?' But I was beginning to get an idea of Olsen's strange contradictory pride, the boundaries he set himself and those he scorned.

In my mind's eye, I saw him bending forward in a chair, staring before him, his great fists clamped together as if he could squeeze out between them all the accumulated tension in the interrogation room. I imagined him nodding his morose agreement to the charges he could accept, growling away those he didn't, as though such offences were beneath him.

At one point, the senior investigating officer – I made him an inspector, straight out of *Z Cars* – would indicate Olsen's bandaged forearm and ask: 'What happened there, son?' 'Oh, just fooling about.' 'A stupid accident?' 'Yes, very stupid.' It didn't make me fear him any the less, but I was getting pretty sure now that he wouldn't give me away, whatever the pressure put on him. And, as this proved to be the case, I couldn't withhold a wary respect for Svenny Olsen.

Some of the playground experts claimed that once the police had finished with him, his dad – home between fishing trips – promptly lit into him and left bruises all over his face, and that when his mother came back from her shopping, she (no mean size herself) lit into both of them: Svenny for the shame he'd brought on the family, and her husband for being too free with his fists and, altogether, a useless father.

I never encountered Doran and Witherow again. The number of their offences was far greater than the police had been able to get out of them at the beginning. Bit by bit, they admitted to every act of pilfering they'd been involved in, from the grandest to the most humble, and for all I knew may have invented a few exploits on the way, just for the fun of it – though I couldn't imagine the fun showing on their faces, not when they were confronted by authority. It would be cringing-time then, but once they were together again, just the two of them? I wondered whether they were already planning fresh coups, distant raids post-punishment, in their collusively taciturn way.

'They had enough stuff hidden to start a market stall!' a playground chronicler declared. 'How did they keep their mams and dads from finding out?'

'Perhaps they didn't need to.'

And that led to the next heady rumour that Doran and Witherow's parents were in on the filching. It wasn't long before a story arose like a gospel which, as with all good gospels, you could never properly attribute to just one person: apparently, some boy who had a friend at the school had spied through the Dorans' window one evening and seen John's mother and father going through his share of the swag with him – all those pens, cheap watches, scarves, ties, whatever. At the end, they'd patted him on the back, congratulating him proudly on his skill. Who could say that the same kind of thing wasn't going on at the Witherows' household too? In my lively fantasy, these four adults were carbon copies of their sons, even down to the chewed lapels.

Of course, there was no evidence worth a bean that anything like this had taken place, but it was exciting to imagine Doran and Witherow's parents as local Fagins, all the same.

XIV. Fate and Mr Gordon

Doran and Witherow were to be sent to a remand home at Derby. I think we all expected Olsen to join them there, or to land up in a similar place, but it was largely Mr Gordon's efforts which prevented that.

In the Juvenile Court, Olsen was portrayed as the innocent dupe, a boy of limited intelligence with a fierce sense of loyalty to those he mistakenly considered his friends. I could just see Svenny Olsen before the magistrates, doing his best to look particularly gormless: a stranger to the baser machinations of the world. This kind of notion made Derek and me laugh, but at the same time put me into some moral confusion as I asked myself how far the pious and upright Mr Gordon had stretched the truth to breaking point and beyond to protect Svenny. It troubled me to think that compassion, especially 'official' compassion, could be wrongly placed.

In the event, Olsen didn't even get probation. Well, he did, in an extra-legal sense you might say, as our Headmaster, at a generous nod from the Court, virtually became his keeper.

And now that the Terror was shackled, maybe even on the way to being tamed, the boys in the playground, our classroom too, seemed released, eager to rehearse Olsen's past crimes; not in low whispers either but in tones loud and strident enough to be heard over the seagulls at low tide. Some of his past feats I was aware of, but others were new to me.

The investigation of the private parts of choice victims was all too familiar, unfortunately, but I'd been ignorant of his penchant the previous year for pinching bikes from the sheds in order to ride round the area in school hours, sometimes damaging the cycle he'd chosen, once knocking an old lady down and pedalling on regardless. He'd got off with a carefully rehearsed apology that time, and a couple of hours weeding in the old lady's garden.

In his first year at Willow Road, most of his school milk had gone in gobs of spit into other kids' faces. And so on and so on. More recently, he'd had a phase of throwing Junior pupils over the low railings in front of the building, imprisoning them there between bricks and pavement, as though in a cage, their panicky crying and howling bringing a lop-sided smile of derision to his lips.

This nasty game might have had serious consequences for Olsen but there'd been a tough teacher at Willow Road at the time, an ex-soldier who'd doubled as the crafts and PE master. He'd happened along and, catching Olsen in the act, had belted him across the head with such force that it rocked even the redoubtable Svenny on his feet.

So he was obliged to give up that particular bad habit but there were plenty left for him to savour, especially those where he thought he could justify his conduct.

The day after the dramatic absences I was looking out of the classroom window down at the street. It was the beginning of break, the rest of the class had left, even Derek, but I was lingering in the warmth as long as I could.

'Arthur' Askew was the master on corridor duty. I heard him coming along, then his footsteps stopping behind me, at the open doorway. I turned round to face him, my expression held in a mystery of triumph which evidently exasperated Arthur. One more boy up to something he shouldn't be! Slowly, the young man was learning his trade, or at least the policing side of it.

'Have you a sick note or teacher's permission to stay inside?'

'No sir. '

'Then your place is in the schoolyard. Come on, look lively!'

What I'd seen, briefly but tellingly, was this: Mr Gordon, on the far side of the road, waiting for the traffic to pass. He was flanked by two large people who all but dwarfed him and behind this trio was the familiar figure of Svenny himself. The Olsen gang.

At first sight, it looked as if the Headmaster was their prisoner rather than their leader. Then you could see he was laying down the law to them. His hands and lips were moving emphatically, the one working eye darting from father to mother and back again. They appeared glum and downcast, meek in that clumsy way big, aggressive people are driven to sometimes. Svenny's face was not much different, although he also gave off a stunned air, as if he simply couldn't grasp what was going on. How far this was genuine, how far calculated, was anybody's guess.

Another thing that struck me, thinking over these new impressions as I sped along the corridor and down the stairs, was the uncanny similarity in looks and build between Mr and Mrs Olsen. He was Danish, his wife Ketilbarian, but with their bulk and height, their fair hair and rough-hewn faces, they might have been brother and sister. I knew the early settlers of the town had crossed the sea from Jutland, but I couldn't believe that genetic roots could twine into each other after all this time so completely. I pictured them as survivors of an earlier, crudely heroic civilization. Perhaps they'd sought each other out, these two, after long and arduous searching, like creatures of a rare species whose mating choices were few.

I looked for Derek in the playground.

'Olsen's come back. And his parents are with him.'

'No!' Derek exclaimed with glee. 'Then you're for it, Colin my young cannibal, because they'll want to work you over for knife and forking their darling, delicate child – of course they know who the culprit is, don't kid yourself! And that's before they let Svenny get hold of you!'

How long the Olsens were closeted with the exhorting,

counselling Presbyterian elder, I don't know. I didn't catch sight of the parents again.

Now, however, their son was very much on display. Everywhere that Mr Gordon went, it seemed, Svenny was sure to be somewhere close by. He was the hundredth sheep and, relentlessly, he was going to be saved. All of Mr Gordon's concerns now appeared to centre on this shambling lump in his wake, but the feeling didn't show in any softening of his demeanour. In a way, his face was just as set as Svenny's, the latter's mainly displaying sullen acquiescence whereas Mr Gordon's expression was even more one of righteous authority, as though he received constant, sternly encouraging messages from on high, zeroing in by courtesy of the Supreme Headmaster Himself.

Apart from attending lessons judged absolutely essential, Olsen was plucked from 4B to be attendant on Mr Gordon. Svenny cut a chastened but still formidable figure.

'Captain Gordon's villainous first mate,' muttered Derek. 'The one who'll make you walk the plank, or feed you to the sharks.'

'Silence!' roared Mr Marston, hurrying back down the line towards his superior officer. Svenny Olsen had positioned himself in front of the bike-sheds, a few yards off. 'See me before registration, Fraser!'

'Sir.'

At least Olsen didn't pad along behind Mr Gordon as he inspected his troops. But he was there, a respectful four paces to his rear, as the Head nodded approval to Mr Marston, turned his back on the mass of boys and re-entered the school.

A cubbyhole had been found for the enyoked penitent. It was a small stockroom where he was set to work on various tasks, many of which seemed to involve some useful kind of destruction, like the ripping-up of old exercise books. Olsen undertook this job with considerable vigour as if he were finally bringing his numerous enemies to account.

Knowing that they were safe – unless Olsen went berserk and completely broke all bounds – some of the boys began to linger by the room whenever they could. The door was generally kept ajar, because it was smaller than a cell in there, crammed with textbooks; the small window wouldn't open either, so it got warm and pongy rather quickly, especially when you had powerful body smells like Svenny.

'Olsen won't try anything, because he knows it's the remand home if he does,' pronounced one second-form stalwart and this was taken up as a self-evident truth by his pals around him.

'Yes, he's not that stupid.'

'You could have fooled me! But maybe you're right.'

They knew too that, whatever the provocation, Olsen would never tell on them. He'd twist their necks one by one, sooner than do so.

The object of this game was to goad Olsen as sharply but quietly as possible – the staffroom was just around the corner. I'd read somewhere that in the eighteenth century, the aristocrats used to visit local loony bins for an afternoon treat, amusing themselves no end with the antics of the inmates and, although we hardly counted as such elevated folk, what we were doing was not so dissimilar – except, of course, that there was also something much more personal involved. We wanted to safely torment the boy who'd terrorised us. To begin with, I enjoyed this in a way, yet even then, fundamentally, I thought it wasn't right: just bullying in return, bullying in numbers.

Can you jeer silently? Well, we did or as near as possible. Once or twice, some of the other boys would even throw Olsen a biscuit or a piece of chocolate, as you might a wild beast in a cage. He'd survey such offerings with a knotted brow, as if he were willing them to disappear and, when they didn't, he'd get up heavily and, ignoring his persecutors shrinking back, pick up the bits and put them in the wastepaper basket.

Then he'd return solemnly to his place, as though lost in a dream of redemptive voices.

You had to give him credit for self-control, but even so I thought that vindictive goading like this might well lead to the snapping-point, especially when he recollected the pre-eminence he'd had – only days before – in the playground. If that really struck home, his endurance would just burst like a bubble, the humiliating contrast too much to bear!

But Svenny Olsen proved to be stronger than us, this new way too. He was steadfast in his resolution. Perhaps One-eyed Gordon was a kind of miracle worker after all.

I watched some boys leaving the group, looking thoughtful and a bit shame-faced. But nobody tried to curb Olsen's tormentors. Including Derek and me. He simply plucked me by the sleeve and we went, quickly getting into a game going on outside.

The Olsen-baiting didn't last much longer after that. His audience had increased daily as the word got around that the monster was cornered but not going to strike. In the confines of the corridor it began to seem like a crowd pressed up against the stockroom entrance. I could imagine the giggling and whispering, the pushing and shoving.

And this must have led to the keener attention of the master on duty. Previously, the boys had waited till he'd started off on his rounds before they dared to sneak up to Svenny's lair. Now, particularly when it was Mr Marston's turn (as it often seemed to be) the culprits knew they'd get short shrift and scattered as soon as they heard his footsteps far off. He did manage to capture some of the dafter first years, though, taking their names and referring them to their form-masters for further chastisement.

From then on the stockroom door was kept firmly closed. You could only hear Svenny at work, and nobody found that very interesting.

Derek and I joked about how long it'd take before Olsen suffocated in his own stink. He even suggested that we should have a whip-round to buy him some canisters of oxygen.

That gave us a good laugh as we went along Willow Road towards the park.

Far more sombre was something else he said to me about this time. It seemed so out of character that that alone gave it the ring of truth. His words both impressed and disturbed me so much I put a shortened version of them in my diary; sparked-off memory has given me the rest.

'Just think, if there is a nuclear war, then Olsen would be king afterwards. Or someone like him. Svenny the First!'

'Why?' I asked, mystified.

'Because after that destruction, if anybody survived at all, it'd be the strongest who'd rule. '

'The strongest and cleverest,' I insisted.

'No,' retorted Derek, with gloomy certainty. 'Thugs like Olsen would take over. There'd be no Robin Hood or noble knights, and King Arthur'd just go on sleeping. Besides, Olsen's not so stupid. Not beneath.'

This despondency of Derek's even rendered him ugly: mouth turned down at the corners, eyes narrowed in resentment and scorn.

'Well, what shall we do then? Maybe you can draw a picture that'll save the world, little...' he began to sneer.

'Don't say it!' I shouted in warning. It was a strained defiance but it stopped him. Now – a rare occurrence – it was my task to nudge him back into good spirits.

'Never forget I'm the knife and fork attacker, just itching to tuck into a fake Billy Fury!'

'Nothing fake about me, mate!'

Derek took up a familiar pose in the middle of the playground, one leg pivoted before him, outstretched hand cupping the air in anguish. ' "Last night was made for love,"

' he wailed plaintively, ' "and where were you?" '

The boys milling around were not short of suggestions.

'Round at my Gran's.'

'At the fish and chip shop.'

And from a more knowing spirit: 'Getting some night-time loving already.'

'You dirty bugger!' said Derek in mock-outrage, interrupting his song for a few seconds.

He had an appreciative audience and was happy again, his black vision banished or at least pushed away, like something he could well do without.

***

The most astounding thing in Mr Gordon's Save the Olsen campaign happened at the school assembly on the morning of Monday, the 21st of October.

Olsen followed the Headmaster into the hall and, instead of staying in the shadows, as inconspicuous as he could ever be, came to the front of the room with him, standing below the dais, hands clasped across his stomach, a solemn dutiful expression on his face. His fair thatch was combed neatly, with a clear parting, and he was wearing a smart tweed jacket, obviously new.

The hymn was good: 'Hills of the North, Rejoice!' – a real belter.

After Miss Barber and the school had more or less finished together, Mr Gordon announced: 'Sven Olsen will give us the reading this morning.'

A gasp of astonishment went up from the boys, and a murmur of excitement as Olsen ascended the platform. Miss Barber remained sitting at the piano, which was having increasing trouble with its wayward castors, how they never quite aimed in exactly the same direction.

Glancing up at the dais, she seemed anxious, as if she expected disaster – at the very least, Svenny foaming white at the mouth and rioting down from the rostrum. I looked at Mr Marston, standing at the side in the line of teachers, but I got no lead there. His face was as firm and closed as when he formed up the classes in the playground.

'Now, Olsen,' said Mr Gordon, moving aside from the lectern. 'Enunciate clearly and slowly.'

Svenny nodded slightly, as if he'd been familiar with the difficult word since his first bowl of Rice Krispies.

He read the Beatitudes from *St Matthew's Gospel*, stumbling occasionally but managing better than I would have expected. He'd been carefully rehearsed, though, that was obvious; perhaps hours spent under the Headmaster's tutelage, getting the short passage right. All the same, it was a bit much to have to hear the boy who'd terrorised the playground and beyond now urging the blessedness of the meek and the peacemakers. Beside me, Derek allowed himself a satirical grunt.

After Olsen had finished, Mr Gordon resumed his usual place, while his protégé humbly left the platform. Miss Barber's face relaxed and she looked as if she'd like to play the merriest tune she could think of, perhaps one of those from *Oklahoma* or *The King and I* that we heard her going through sometimes when classes finished at four o'clock.

Olsen was still standing in front of the school. That was the customary place for those singled out to be publicly disgraced and humiliated. But this was the complete opposite, a triumph of modesty and virtue! With a touch of delicacy which I'd never have imagined he possessed, Olsen even lowered his head slightly as Mr Gordon thanked him for the reading.

Then the Headmaster gazed over the room, surveying his charges, from the titches at the front to the big lads right at the back. He was not the kind of man to beam with pleasure, but his one-eyed face was suffused with exalted satisfaction. The hundredth sheep was safely in the fold.

We mumbled our way through the Lord's Prayer and

listened to Mr Gordon's little sermon. Today it was all about altering for the better if we really wanted to and accepted the help offered us. We could all overcome the worst in our nature and make the best shine out!

No prizes for guessing who he had in mind. But Mr Gordon kept his eyes scrupulously averted from Olsen which, of course, only gave the game away even more.

He finished the prayers at the end with a wider message.

'And let us pray that the leaders of the two great, troubled countries facing each other in such hostility also take to heart the words we've just heard from *St Matthew's Gospel* and advance cautiously and with humanity.'

Now Mr Gordon began dealing with more mundane, immediate matters: the school notices.

Standing before the dais, Olsen had his back to us, but at one point he turned to the side for some reason and, over the heads of the first formers in front of me, I glimpsed the look on his face. It was what my grandfather used to dismiss as 'holier-than-thou'; more than that, actually, like the phiz of a sanctimonious gargoyle.

I don't think many of those the Headmaster was addressing, either boys or staff, shared his confidence about the new, cleansed Olsen. Granted his awed respect for Mr Gordon, yet I was pretty sure that Svenny was play-acting for all he was worth. He knew on which side his bread was buttered. He just had to keep in with his mentor and last out his final school year respectably. No doubt he'd get a glowing reference and future support.

But if it was more than that? If the change was real and went much deeper than we supposed?

Derek dismissed even this inkling of doubt as sentimental 'sermonitis'.

Grudgingly, I admitted to myself that in Svenny's position, I might well have pocketed my pride and done the same as him. It puzzled me, however, that he had bamboozled Mr Gordon so completely. I'd assumed that stern righteousness endowed its possessor with insight of a moral nature, narrow maybe but powerful.

I hadn't realised that it could inflict a new form of blindness, but it looked like Svenny had. There was something to be said for the cunning of the hundredth sheep.

XV. MR MARSTON SOLVES THE CUBAN MISSILE CRISIS

The robot I'd imagined leaving behind to represent me in the line-up while my spirit soared free would at least have moved in a convincingly human way. But when we caught our first sight of Mr Marston (he'd not been on playground duty that morning, neither was he in assembly), it looked as if he'd swapped the man for a machine whose messages weren't getting through to its component parts.

He was paler than I'd ever seen him and there were dark bags under his eyes like bruises. His hair had been so hastily combed it made little peaks on his pate; there were ridges of scurf at the sides of his head. For once, the frown was not a sign of impatience with us but as though he were trying to control a thousand fierce little hammers working ruthlessly away inside his skull. The enemy within – there was also an enemy without, called light: bright and strong for an autumn day, driving down like golden gouges into his eyes. When he came into range a strong peppermint smell arose from his mouth.

'Looks like he's well into half-term already,' whispered Derek to me, grinning.

I didn't get the significance of Mr Marston's state to begin with, although I should have done. But Dad usually went very red when he'd had too much and sucked busily on eucalyptus sweets which he claimed did wonders for his laryngitis. My mother had run out of cutting remarks about how strange it was that his throat problem should always recur when he had a stinking hangover. These days she just sniffed contemptuously and dipped her handkerchief in rosewater.

But that was Dad. Most days he drank yet, through long practice, kept it more or less under control. The hangovers, during which he flopped about bewailing his lot, didn't happen very often. But I found it hard to imagine Mr Marston, a person we respected whatever our jokes about him, getting into such a state at all.

Some of the boys started sniggering and making drunken motions. Without seeming to understand what this disturbance signified, Mr Marston called them to order in an over-precise, tinny sort of voice.

And that's how he took the register too: no slurring or faltering, just this remote combiner of sounds, always about half a beat out of the normal rhythm with none of the scathing additions we were used to. I can't say that we exactly looked forward to these remarks but you missed them when they weren't there, like an odd sort of comfort.

After those first hints of mischief, we were mostly too shocked to play him up. Derek, although he tried to make comic capital out of it all later, became grave, even solicitous. He began staring at the teacher concentratedly, his mouth drooping a little.

When he'd managed the register, Mr Marston put back his head and gulped in breath, as if that task had cost him the last of his strength. I noticed the tiny cuts on his chin; evidently, shaving hadn't gone well that day either.

'I'm afraid I'm not feeling very chipper, boys. It must be the onset of a bad cold, perhaps even flu.'

'Shall I get you some aspirins from the first aid cupboard, sir?'

'No, Fraser, but thank you for the kind thought.'

'That's all right, sir.'

'Aspirins don't do much for me, I'm afraid. However, I did take the precaution of bringing a flask of coffee with me – strong black coffee. Normally, I wouldn't even drink water in the classroom, but today we might make an exception to the no liquid rule. Nothing like a gute Tasse

Kaffee, as my dear mother used to say.'

A catch in his voice, again a first. We watched in trepidation as he raised the flask and beaker in trembling hands and poured. He wiped away the spillage vigorously. It didn't amount to much, but we could see that our teacher was angry at his clumsiness.

'Was that German you were speaking, sir?'

'That little phrase? Oh yes. '

'Are you fluent, sir?'

'Not bad. Getting a bit rusty now.'

'Donner und Blitzen! Die, you filthy Engländer!' shouted Allington, who'd evidently been impressed by the war stories in his comics. He'd either lost control in his enthusiasm or was chancing his arm, taking advantage of Mr Marston's condition.

Derek clearly thought the latter. He jumped up from his desk, cheeks red with fury.

'Mr Marston's mother was German, a refugee from Hitler, and she died last year. So bloody well shut up, Allington! Otherwise, you'll get thumped!'

The teacher was gulping his first cup of coffee as if it were an elixir that'd grant him total sobriety. He raised his free hand, in acknowledgement of Derek's intervention but mainly to urge him to calm down.

Anyway, Allington was crushed and looked as though he were about to burst into tears.

There was an awkward silence then. Finally, MacPherson, pointing at the beaker, said with meek politeness: 'Does that really do something for your cold, sir?'

Mr Marston put the coffee down and wiped his lips.

'I suppose not, if you're being scientific about it. But faith can work wonders and, besides, it gees one up a bit. However, I've also brought something else.'

For one dreadful moment I thought it might be a bottle of whisky or something just as lethal but, after scrabbling around in his bag, he produced a jar of Vick ointment.

'I'd imagine that most of you are familiar with this stuff?'

'Yes sir!'

He seemed to be about to start a lesson on the common cold and its various treatments, and was just placing dabs of Vick beneath each of his nostrils when Mr Gordon's face suddenly appeared in the door-window. I gasped with shock. It wasn't only the piratical look, but that in the Headmaster's face there was absolutely no trace of the benignity he'd shown when Olsen read to us from the Bible. I was certain that he'd been listening at the door. Why hadn't Mr Marston just phoned in sick and avoided trouble that way? He wouldn't have had to get a doctor's certificate for one day off work.

Mr Gordon wouldn't be averse to rebuking a hitherto respected colleague, if he felt he had to. He might even send him home, like a naughty boy, accusing him of dereliction of duty! That was a sombre phrase which went again and again through my mind, leaving its disgrace there like slime.

Yet the Headmaster didn't come in. I 'made' him drop his fingers from the handle and imagined him warning himself that he should be careful: Marston numbered amongst his best subordinates, conscientious to a fault. Even a little pernickety at times. Better that way, the Headmaster surely mused, better that way. He could perhaps be allowed one fall from grace.

But Mr Gordon didn't leave either; still framed in the glass, a head without a body (a disturbing sight in itself!), staring searchingly at Mr Marston...

Who flinched as he turned and caught sight of the Awful Image. But it also served to jerk him back into some semblance of normality. The robotic figure who'd negotiated his difficult way into the classroom seemed to be fading before our eyes – familiar human lineaments were definitely reappearing!

With the skill of a tried comedian, Mr Marston waved the jar of Vick at the Headmaster's face and, in dumbshow, went through the symptoms of being heavily under the weather with a cold. He held his hands wide in apologetic helplessness, as if he shouldn't have been so silly as to place himself before the mouth of the germ-laden infector in the first place. For Mr Marston this was a very unusual display indeed. If the Headmaster hadn't been lurking about outside, I think 2A would have rewarded our teacher with a round of applause. As it was, Derek couldn't help giving a grin that threatened to crack his face in two, doing his best to hide it behind the raised exercise book.

Mr Gordon must still have been somewhat suspicious, but from the glances we sneaked at him we could see that his expression was mellowing a little. He watched as Mr Marston went to the board and started writing names and dates. The decisive chalk-strokes were the same as ever, and that must have helped to allay the Head's doubts too. It might, after all, be politic to postpone censure. A firm but diplomatic word at a later time could well be more effective; Mr Marston's embarrassment and contrition would be almost a bankable quality. More duties for him to undertake, more tasks to 'volunteer' for. Doing penance was a curious but potent thing.

Of course, this was all surmise on my part, but it did seem that, in the next few weeks, Mr Marston had even more administration to deal with than usual, plus the fact that he was given the task of organising the school Christmas show for the first time.

The eye patch gleamed with a steady black light, as if it contained a special force. Captain Gordon was performing a piratical piece of voodoo, a skill picked up on shoreleaves in the Caribbean, between his buccaneering sprees. Eventually, he appeared to be satisfied. Hidden by the door, away from our eyes, he scabbarded his cutlass and then restored a grateful, pure space to the windowpane.

The success of his bluff seemed to enliven Mr Marston quite a lot, that and the effects of the two beakers of caffeinated tar he'd just downed. We had him for the periods before break, the first one being history. We were still on the Middle Ages but not strip farming and the travails of the villeins, thank goodness. Today should have been better, because Mr Marston had promised to tell us about the Wars of the Roses. In fact, what he'd put on the board was a list of the dynastic rivals and chief battles of that time.

But today his heart just wasn't in it. He couldn't sustain either the energy or the concentration. I was disappointed, even a bit angry, because I'd been looking forward to this lesson. When Mr Marston hit his best form he could tell history like a living tale, all but transforming our drab classroom into the scenes he was describing.

I'd not heard President Kennedy's speech the previous night, although I'd caught excerpts from and comments about it on the wireless that morning, before I set off for school. And there were the headlines in my parents' *Daily Telegraph*, of course, but I'd got the message clearly enough, there was no way of avoiding it: the advance of the Russian ships, Kennedy's decision to impose a quarantine. What would happen when the vessels of the two superpowers confronted each other? The question everyone was asking. That'd be when the peace – and probably the survival – of the world hung in the balance. If Derek had said that, in his usual dramatic way, I'd have tried to scoff at him: the attention-seeking exaggeration you could only expect from Derek Fraser, alias 'Billy Fury' and no doubt a dozen others!

But I didn't think I'd have drawn much comfort from teasing him now.

'It doesn't look good, Colin, it doesn't look good at all,' my father had muttered at breakfast-time, as he read the front page of his paper. None of the noisy but resilient grievance that normally marked his anger, just a deep gloom as if the crisis had got to the very heart of him. This disturbed me more than anything.

However, by the time I got to Willow Road, my uneasiness was receding. Immediate things took over: the tasks I had to do, the shape of the school day ahead of me. There seemed to be some reassurance left in all of that.

Now I watched Mr Marston shaking the flask over his beaker, as if trying to urge out a final vital mouthful. He looked disappointedly at the few drops which emerged.

His condition was a shock, but a fascinating one in a horrible sort of way.

Kilbertson stuck up his hand.

'Sir, please sir!'

He was the serious kid who'd asked the question about Berlin. He seemed to see himself as something of a student of current affairs, or foreign crises at least.

'What do you think going's to happen, sir?'

'Oh, I'll be all right, by and by. Colds take their time. You know what they say – a fortnight or two weeks.'

'No, I meant Cuba, sir. What do you think going's to happen there?'

'Oh, right! Well, it's funny you should broach the topic, Kilbertson, because last night – in fact, the early hours of this morning too, if we're ruthlessly honest – I was at what you might call a Cuban missile party...'

He breathed in the Vick fumes stertorously, and rocked on his feet with much effort.

'Discussing the whole troubling business with a few trusted friends.'

'Can you have friends who aren't trusted, sir?' put in Derek pertly.

Mr Marston tried to check his irritation at being interrupted and adopted a philosophical, world-weary expression. Or perhaps it was just the thousand hammers again, hopefully down now to about 920 and sinking.

'Oh yes, Fraser, I'm afraid you can. All too easily. You'll discover that as you go through life. Some friends are to be enjoyed but never trusted.'

He was by the side of Derek's desk now, well enough to indulge one of his favourite classroom pastimes, namely ear-tweaking. But he was not quite back in kilter because the effort he put into the action was greater than usual, and the 'Ouch!' that Derek let out had nothing of pretence in it.

'Don't make such a song and dance, Fraser.'

'But that hurt, sir!'

'Nonsense! All you need is a bit of backbone.'

'All I need is a new ear!'

'That's enough.'

But he paused, not quite sure whether he hadn't overdone things, bending down, examining Derek's flushed lobe as if he saw the world there. Then he said, in a mock-imploring voice which made us laugh: 'Fraser, please don't ever grow up and leave us all behind. I beg of you!'

Derek was fond of boasting that he knew exactly how to play Mr Marston in his various moods and he showed that skill now. Clasping his ear in a dramatic way, he put his head down on the desk-lid in a good semblance of woe. Some of the boys giggled, instantly recognising Derek's talent for mimic hyperbole, but it fooled me for a few seconds, Mr Marston a bit longer. True that it was a fragile time for the teacher, yet Derek did manage to get him to do what I would have thought almost impossible: apologise. Straightforwardly as well, more or less.

'I'm sorry, Fraser. Perhaps my gesture was a bit too vigorous. Meant as fun, though.'

'Fun?' came a muffled, incredulous voice.

'Yes. Hmm – look, let's shake on it, shall we?'

Derek raised his head and watched Mr Marston's hand travel unsteadily over the desk. Then he shrugged his shoulders in a negative gesture and turned away, the mardy child to perfection. But I wasn't sure there was any play-acting in it now.

'Shake hands, Fraser. All right?'

Still no reaction.

'Fraser?' wheedled Mr Marston.

I began to feel embarrassed for both of them, but most of the class seemed to be enjoying it as a game.

'Come on, Derek!'

'Be a sport!'

At last Derek sat up like a wounded soldier, but one still capable of gallantry, and shook his master's hand. The class cheered, if temperately, not wanting to attract the attention of Mr Gordon who might still be hovering about somewhere in the corridor.

'No hard feelings, Fraser?' asked Mr Marston anxiously.

Derek answered that he'd try to make sure there weren't but suggested that, if Mr Marston really felt he had to, he should work on the other lug next time.

'The freedom of the earlobe, eh!' Our teacher gave a heartily false laugh, patted Derek on the back with relief, then took his place at the front again.

'About Cuba, sir?' asked Kilbertson, with strained patience.

'Ah yes, where were we? A few trusted friends – if Fraser will allow me to use the epithet without subjecting me to the rigours of a Socratic dialogue?'

'You what, sir?'

'Right. Imagine teachers from different schools across the town, meeting together in the spacious sitting-room of one of us, who has the good fortune (in more senses than one) to own a house overlooking the park. We're all set to thrash the whole matter out. Of course, it's going to take Kennedy and Mr K a bit longer, but don't worry. Our urgent telegrams are being sent to Washington and Moscow to guide them.'

Of course, he was joking – but was he? We stared at him, undecided whether to be amused, awestruck or finally convinced that all teachers were mad. Additionally, I wondered, not wholly facetiously, if at that moment there weren't a number of educators with pounding headaches and furry tongues holding forth, like wonky oracles, in classrooms all over Ketilsby.

Mr Marston turned to the blackboard and selected a piece of chalk. He was warming to his theme, the voice now carrying much of its old familiar strength.

'You've seen their pictures on television or in the papers, no doubt, but let's try to get a rough image of the two protagonists even so,' he said. 'There are massive power structures – political, economic, military – which exert great influence on them, yet such prominent men are not just ciphers. A lot does depend on these two individuals. '

He drew a rough sketch of an ovalish head with a strong jaw and generous but determined mouth. Not much like the American President, really, more easily recognisable from the haircut Mr Marston had given him, the thick, brushed-back bit at the front especially.

'Who's that meant to be, sir?'

'Well, I may not have the artistic ability of my good friend and colleague, Miss Barber, but it shouldn't be too hard...'

'President Kennedy, sir!' I called out, shooting up my hand and answering at the same time, eager for the real crux of the lesson.

'Thank you, Palmer. So if I've got the President up there, who's his opponent? Whose place is on the other side of the board?'

'The Russian, sir.'

'Getting close, Brody. He's Ukrainian, actually, but what's a country between friends? He's leader of the Soviet Union anyway. And he's called? Come on! His name begins with a K and I've already given you that.'

Several boys tried approximations of Khrushchev's

name. It sounded as if the class had been attacked by mass whooping cough. I thought, with some smugness, that I'd have to be the 'clever clogs' again, because I could pronounce the name better than the others, but Kilbertson got there before me.

'Nikita Khrushchev, sir. He's *planning* to destroy the world.'

'I wouldn't say he's planning to do it, Kilbertson, although he may very well succeed without really trying.'

'He's a communist, sir.'

'And President Kennedy is a capitalist, or at least descended from very prosperous entrepreneurs. Such terms don't tell us much. Both the US and the Soviet Union have empires, you could say, or at least huge areas of the globe under their sway. They're in fierce competition – for men's bellies, minds and hearts.'

'Who do you think will win, sir?'

'You can't judge history like a football match.'

'It'd be good if you could, wouldn't it, sir? Yanks 2, Reds 1.'

'If only life were that simple... Now, back to the matter in hand. However ruthless one has to be in getting to the top in politics, I still don't think it's the intention of either Kennedy or Khrushchev to smash the world to smithereens.'

'Do you like Russkies, sir?'

'I don't know any, beyond the characters in the books of the classic Russian authors, and it's hard to see them – even Raskolnikov – as devils in human form.'

'My Dad met some Russian soldiers at the end of the war in Germany, sir. He said they were all right. Very generous with the vodka.'

'There you are then,' said Mr Marston. '"Greater love hath no man" than that he share a precious drop with his ally. And I hope I'm not blaspheming.'

Even Allington was smiling now, although he looked a

bit puzzled at our teacher's last remarks. But he wasn't alone in that.

Back at the board, Mr Marston drew a fat round face like a bloated moon, giving it tiny eyes and a piggy nose. It was like the faces I used to shape in dough when Mum was making bread. He was trying for the mouth when his hand suddenly jerked up and down in a spasm, so that the cake hole Khrushchev used to splutter out all those threats with now resembled the edge of a badly-opened tin. Mr Marston looked at his hand in troubled surprise, then flexed it vigorously until reassured that it wasn't packing up on him. I was beginning to like the jagged lips – they seemed to show both a snarl and a wicked grin – but the teacher rubbed them out-and made Mr Khrushchev's mouth into a dull straight line.

'Not very good either, but let it stand. I hope I'm better with these arrows I'm drawing now, which represent Russian and American vessels. I don't have the right coloured chalks, unfortunately. Anyhow, take the arrows in yellow as standing for the Russians and those in blue the Americans.' Then he drew a rough, slightly rounded oblong in white, which he said symbolised Cuba, and placed a number of vertical yellow strokes there to suggest the missile sites that had been installed. 'Most of them are on the northern side of the island, that much closer to the United States. Not hard to understand why the Americans see such a build-up as a serious threat.'

Mr Marston turned round and stared out over the rows of boys before him. He looked melancholy, as if he'd done his best for us and failed. Desperately, I put my faith in the hammers.

'The Americans have at least a dozen destroyers facing the flotilla advancing towards them, plus a few aircraft carriers. To add to the fun, the ships with rockets for Castro are being shadowed by Russian submarines.'

Quickly he chalked in the requisite arrows.

His words – the diagram too – made confrontation between the two superpowers appear inevitable and all my self-protective feeling that somehow things would just go on as usual threatened to crumble to nothing in an instant. It was then that I felt really afraid for the first time. All of us must have experienced something similar.

Mr Marston was clearly alarmed by the scare he'd provoked: he'd gone too far, he should have known better, the good old mea culpa I'd learned from Roy. I watched our teacher make an odd calming gesture as if he were trying to pat down half a dozen footballs at once. We laughed at that, it looked so zany and frantic, but it did give us some relief even if it didn't dispel the basic worry.

'But let's suppose that Kennedy's blockade works and the Russians turn tail. Outright victory for our cousins on the far side of the big pond. Cheers in Washington and across what I believe is called the "free world". How would Mr Khrushchev deal with his humiliation? By stressing his deep concern for human survival, I'd imagine. Not necessarily insincere, but sounding a little strange coming from the man who caused all this trouble in the first place. He might well be able to garner some credit for moving away from the brink, yet the loss of prestige for Russia! And if Khrushchev agrees to dismantle the rockets already in Cuba without getting something substantial in return, then that would be altogether too much for Moscow to stomach. He'd be overturned as quickly as you can say "tovarich".'

'Say what, sir?'

But I remembered that word from Dad's dispute with the prodigal, Red Roy. So up went my hand again.

'It means "comrade", sir. In Russian.'

' "Comrade", you boys. Nothing more, nothing less. Incidentally, still reading *The Daily Worker*, Palmer?'

'No, sir. I mean, I never...'

'It's not a sin to peruse its thin pages, tovarich! Except that I'm not sure they believe in sin over there.'

My face was aflame. The class giggled at my embarrassment, but somehow I felt they were on my side too, as if I were an oddity worth protecting.

'Now, let's imagine the Americans giving way. The Soviets are allowed to steam into Havana as and when they please, landing their lethal goods. I don't think Kennedy would be forced from office exactly, though I wouldn't fancy his chances in the next election. And the military – a dominant force in the world's greatest democracy – would certainly put pressure on him to do something pretty drastic. What would that be, do you think?'

'Attack Russia, sir!'

'Nuke them, sir!'

'Hold your horses, you bloodthirsty little blackguards! Don't you see that'd bring massive retaliation and counter-retaliation? Both the Soviet Union and the US would be devastated. And I wouldn't fancy the chances of any of us caught in the middle, either.'

'Just attack Cuba then, sir?'

'Just, he says! But well-thought out, Kilbertson. I'd say an invasion of Cuba is definitely on the cards. Before sending in troops, they'd have to bomb the rocket- sites. The argument has been advanced that, whatever the Soviet protests, this would be the safer course of action.'

'Why, sir?'

'Because, Fraser, they'd be bombing what is Cuban territory, rather than sinking *Soviet* ships. It would be seen as unjustified aggression, but at least not a direct attack on Russia itself. So, what could the comrades do in response, apart from starting trouble over Berlin again?' He frowned. 'Yes, Palmer?'

'Wouldn't it be better if the two sides agreed to disarm, sir, at least partly?'

'Sealed with an honourable handshake, that's the stuff!'

Clearly, in his eyes, my suggestion wasn't the simple but profound idea I'd thought it was, but I couldn't understand why it made him so angry.

'Perhaps it would be better, my young visionary, if each side offered an armoured champion, as in chivalric days of yore, so they could slug it out to decide the future of the world. Much more preferable!'

Derek studied me anxiously.

'Don't look down at the desk like that!' he hissed. 'Stare him out. You've done nothing wrong.'

Gripped by scorn that had something of a despairing edge to it, Mr Marston banged his fist on the table and bellowed out to the room at large: 'So what's this we have here, in remote little Ketilsby, this fraught month of October, 1962? A voice like a choirboy at Christmas, agreeable that's true, but a voice proclaiming in the wilderness all the same. Palmer the disarmer!'

The class was too nervous of our teacher's wrath to laugh at the time, but for a while that had to become my nickname: Palmer-the-Disarmer. It followed me everywhere for a few days until it fell from favour and just petered out.

Now Derek was busily protesting on my behalf.

'That'd be the best, though, don't you think, sir? Palmer's only saying what everybody hopes for.'

Mr Marston's pale face looked even more irritated at first. He shook his head vigorously as if to clear it of fever and confusion. I imagined the scurf flying from his hair like white insects.

But what he said was a wearily gracious: 'Granted, Fraser. And granted, Palmer. Admirable sentiments, laudable – who'd deny such pure hearts? But here's where I'll have to introduce another term, new to you, I'd suppose: *realpolitik*. And please don't say "What?" in that baffled, gobsmacked way, Fraser!'

'Me? I wasn't going to say anything, sir,' retorted Derek in hurt tones.

'*Realpolitik* simply means something like "practical politics". We can't live in cloud-cuckoo-land, although it's probably a far nicer place than here. Nations have to negotiate from a position of strength, or believe they have to. Morally, that hardly stands up, I know, but then...'

Sitting at the desk, he seemed to collapse all of a sudden, slumping forwards, thin shoulders hunching towards each other, as if all the energy he'd somehow found in his delicate state had just upped and left him.

'Thank God, I don't hold high office, that's all I can say!' he groaned, head in hands. 'Schools are difficult enough. '

'But do you think we're going to survive, sir?' asked the doughty Kilbertson.

Mr Marston leant back in his chair and closed his eyes. He couldn't have been sightless to us for more than half a minute, yet it seemed like an age. We hung on his next words as if he were a prophet.

'Sir?'

'Oh,' said our teacher finally, in a strange, sleepy voice. It was as though he were being presented with a common-or-garden classroom problem which bored him stiff. Then he rallied a bit. 'Let's take Palmer's idealistic view. It's the crock of gold we'll never find, but he and Fraser are right. We've got to go on searching for it, even so.'

He sighed, shook the empty coffee flask just in case and then stuffed it in his bag.

'If only Kennedy and Khrushchev would simply sit down to a nice cup of tea! The ultimate remedy when trouble looms. For Mr K it could be poured from one of those beautiful old Russian samovars that'd spark off memories of his babushka – granny, to the uninitiated. For Kennedy it'd have to be something specifically American. Perhaps some instant muck or other, but if he enjoys it, why not? And, after they've drunk a cuppa and swapped anecdotes – a good way of establishing that both leaders are acceptably human – they'll down a few shots of vodka and bourbon until peaceful co-existence is finally established.'

Derek seemed delighted with this flight of fancy; Kilbertson, however, looked dissatisfied.

It was on this note of barbed if wistful flippancy that Mr Marston's Cuban pronunciamento abruptly ended.

He began scowling at his watch, as if judging it to be intolerably slow. We were well into the second period which was supposed to be English composition, although our teacher seemed unaware of it. He told us to do some handwriting practice in the time remaining; we should be prepared to show him the results when called upon to do so, (we never were). Then he fell into a semi-doze, only fully surfacing when the noise level rose too high. Derek stared at him with such concern I thought it was another of his jokes until, having fallen into a snigger, I was told in no uncertain terms to shut my gob and grow up!

***

When the bell for break went and the boys tumbled out of the classroom, Derek stayed behind, fussing over Mr Marston, promising him he'd feel better soon, be right as rain by evening, as though he were an expert on hangovers. I stalked off jealously, making up nasty lines to inflict on Derek later, how he sounded like a daft old granny, or as smarmy as Doran and Witherow at their worst. I'd tell Derek how *sickening* he'd sounded, yet of course, I didn't – that would have opened up too much.

But it did give me some sour consolation that our teacher was unresponsive, apart from telling his favourite not to worry and to slip along to the staffroom and ask Miss Barber to drop in, asap.

'Discreetly, Fraser, discreetly. No alarm bells, right? Good lad.'

Towards the end of break, as I was standing by myself near the bike sheds, eating a piece of chocolate, I saw Mr Marston leaving the school. I knew he wouldn't be back later because he had his bag – a battered old briefcase, really – in hand. He looked just as pale and ill as before, but at least he was moving normally now.

Miss Barber accompanied him, looking concerned but trying not to. They were speaking to each other in a soft, confidential way which would have told anybody that they were more than just friendly colleagues. It still surprised me, though. Teachers weren't meant to be anything other than teachers.

I followed them, keeping at a safe distance, shielded at first by the groups of boys at play. I lost that shelter when I went through the gateway onto the pavement. There Miss Barber lingered, seeing Mr Marston off.

He had an Italian motor scooter, in our view far too modern and fashionable a machine for him to ride. He looked funny perched up there now, but he managed it all right. On normal days, it seemed to give him a kind of freedom as he gunned the scooter – as far as such a thing could be gunned – down Willow Road. Derek used to joke about him graduating to a real motorbike in time and turning up at the school in the full kit, biker's leathers and a fearsome helmet like a space traveller.

Miss Barber observed him anxiously as he progressed away from us – none of the usual speedy panache, just a slow, almost sedate pace with the occasional slight wobble. Earlier on, it must have cost a superhuman effort and concentration of will for Mr Marston to get to school in one piece. You had to admire him for that.

Miss Barber, turning round, caught me spying.

'Yes, what is it?' she asked, unusually acerbic.

'Nothing, Miss.'

'What are you doing out here, then?'

'Just hanging about till break ends, Miss.'

'Well, go back into the playground. You know you're not allowed to leave school premises at break, unless authorised.'

'It's only the pavement, Miss.'

'You know the rule. Imagine if children started dashing out into the road and getting themselves run over.'

'Do you think Mr Marston will be all right, Miss Barber?'

Her face softened.

'Of course he will! You've no need to fret. These' – she hesitated slightly and then spoke the word as though it were in capital letters – 'colds, you know.' She regarded me with an appraising air. 'I don't suppose he felt well enough to teach you much this morning.'

'Not the usual lessons, but a boy asked a question about Cuba and Mr Marston told us a lot of interesting things about the Americans and the Russians, what's happening there.'

'Did he?' she said, smiling. 'Once a dedicated pedagogue, always one of that ilk. He'll be instructing his pallbearers, I'd like to bet. And I don't fancy St. Peter's chances of remaining unscathed either.'

But the way she spoke didn't sound scornful at all, as it might have done. In fact, her tone was affectionate, as though she were proud of him more than anything else, even his lapses. I wondered whether she'd encountered Mr Marston senior yet. That'd be a baptism of fire! If Miss Barber could survive the old lampman, she could put up with any of our teacher's shortcomings.

'Run off now, Colin, there's a good boy. The bell will go any moment.'

She pressed my upper arm, briefly, smiling again. I knew she was thanking me for my concern for Mr Marston. She wasn't beautiful, like his mother, but at that moment she was very close to it. I sped back into the school. The next picture I did in Art would be really good, I swore, the best, the grandest! It didn't matter in the least that I had no inkling what the subject would be.

***

Derek was in altogether a sparkier mood when I saw him next, which was a relief, even sparkier when I filled him in about Mr Marston's departure. His eyes glittered, as though I'd contributed a vital piece of information, the clue that would – mysteriously – make sense of the rest.

In the afternoon Mr Askew covered for the absent class-teacher. Derek took the lead in playing up the young assistant, but Arthur was getting tougher with practice and better able to keep us in check. The periods of near-anarchy, which Derek knew how to exploit to perfection, were interspersed with long tediums of order. Even so, he managed to get a double imposition slapped on him.

A group of us gathered round Derek afterwards and offered to help him do it. The plan we worked out was that he'd write the first paragraph (it was just a copying task) and then each of us would take a chunk following, using the same kind of pen, ink and school paper. Ten to one Arthur wouldn't read the stuff at all, was our bold assessment, but we were taking a risk all the same.

'Look carefully how I make the letters,' Derek instructed us, 'the loops and things, the way the writing slopes.'

We agreed that, whatever happened, such an exercise would test our forging skills at least.

XVI. Mrs Shufflewick and Other Heroes

After tea, I was allowed to go round to Derek's for a while. I joined the family in the kitchen where they were lingering over their meal. There was a nice smell of fried fish in the air and Mrs Fraser was just moving the chip pan off the stove when I walked in. Derek had evidently been telling them about Mr Marston because his mother turned to me and, in a tone of shocked amusement, asked: 'Is this true, Colin, about your teacher? Or is our lad letting his imagination run away with him again?'

Derek looked indignant and stared around with wide dramatic eyes as though appealing for fair play.

'Tell them, Colin!' he urged. 'Go on!'

Naturally, I backed him up but I was cautious in doing so, still reluctant to criticise teachers too overtly in front of adults. I reckoned my parents upheld them whatever they did – yet if I really believed that, why hadn't I told them about Mr Marston? I knew the answer to that one. I could see Mum all too easily, ringing up the councillor she was acquainted with who happened to sit on the Education Committee.

'Mr Marston didn't look well,' I said now. 'He was walking in a funny way at the beginning. He said that he'd been to a party with other teachers, and that he had a bad cold.'

'A bad cold my foot!' scoffed Derek. 'He had the hangover of the century!'

On the other side of the table, Mr Fraser roared with laughter. He rarely referred to Mr Marston but I'd got the impression that he thought him a bit of a stuffed shirt. Now his escapade seemed to humanise him in the Skipper's view, although no doubt he would have declared that such conduct shouldn't become a habit.

'Teachers have their faults like everyone else,' said Mrs Fraser, 'but they're not there to parade them in front of their pupils, behave like ninnies.'

'They should set an example, Mam,' said Becky piously.

'That's right, love.' Mrs Fraser sighed. 'And I thought Richard Marston was such an upright, conscientious person.'

'He is!' Derek and I tried to reassure her.

'But to appear before his class, drunk...'

'He wasn't what you'd call drunk,' temporised Derek. 'Just sort of ill after the event.'

'Well, I'm not going to quibble.'

'Let it go,' said Mr Fraser. 'Worse things happen at sea. And they certainly did in my time!'

'What, Dad?' asked Becky excitedly.

'Oh, they're tales for another day. Anyway, you've heard some of them already, the printable ones.'

'She wants the *unprintable* ones,' said Derek. 'A one-track mind.'

'Yes, dirt-track, we know. That joke's as old as the hills, Derek!' responded Becky pertly.

'Mr Marston didn't do... anything else silly, did he?' cut in Mrs Fraser, in a strangely embarrassed, hesitant way.

'What do you mean, Mam?'

'Well, you know. Acting about...' She left it lamely in the air and we kids were none the wiser. Perhaps only the Skipper knew exactly what she was hinting at, but if he did he wasn't telling us. Instead, he tried to lighten the mood.

'He pulled Derek's ear harder than usual. But whether that's what you'd call silly is another question.'

Derek needed no prompting.

'Can't you see it's still all red and swollen?'

He thrust his face out sideways-on, as if sporting some

hideous disfigurement.

'There's nothing wrong with your ear,' said Becky, 'except that you don't wash it properly.'

'Are you calling me a liar?' said her brother in a roughened voice, like a lout from the docks.

'No, I'm calling you a great fibber.'

Mr Fraser appreciated that one, chuckling.

'I bet philosophers have argued reams about the distinction between those two.'

Trying to prevent Mr Marston's lapse from becoming the stuff of legend that'd count against him for ever, I told them, as I had Miss Barber, how he'd talked to us about the Cuban missile crisis and how interesting it had been.

'Oh yes, he did,' corroborated Derek. 'He knows a lot about it,' adding mischievously, 'more, I bet, than those other teachers he was with all night long.'

'A drunken oracle,' said Mrs Fraser satirically. 'Who would have thought it?'

'Will Mr Marston be sacked?' asked Becky suddenly, looking up from the piece of cake she was eating with methodical concentration from corner to corner, so that eventually she'd arrive at the small chocolate piece in the middle. I liked her open, enquiring, crumb-bespattered mouth and couldn't help smiling at her. Luckily, as she was glancing from one parent to the other, she didn't catch that.

'Sacked? Unlikely, I'd think. Besides, I wouldn't want anything like that.' Mrs Fraser considered the matter. 'But Mr Gordon should have a word with him – and I'm sure he will! So long as your clever teacher behaves himself from now on, he'll be all right. I don't know anyone else in that school who can instruct you boys so well.'

'Arthur?' asked Derek, the gash-grin almost severing his face again.

His parents and Becky knew about the student-teacher.

'Give him a chance,' pleaded the Skipper. 'He's young, still an apprentice.'

'We never play our teachers up like that at our school,' said Becky primly.

'You don't have any like Arthur.'

'We don't have any Svenny Olsens either,' his sister retorted. 'Boys are so stupid!'

'Watch it,' said Mr Fraser. 'I'm a boy, of the ancient variety. Anyway, you wouldn't say Colin's stupid, would you?'

'Of course not! But Colin's an exception.'

'Be careful, Becky!' whooped Derek. 'You'll start him blushing again!'

'I knew Richard Marston long before he went to university,' said Mrs Fraser. 'His mother was alive then, of course. A lovely woman in every way, was Krista. Dad and her husband were bosom friends at that time. Inseparable.'

Derek got up from the table and did an imitation of old Mr Marston shuffling around.

'He moves like *he's* drunk.'

'That's not kind, Derek,' rebuked Mrs Fraser. 'He's old and ill, and sometimes not quite all there since Krista died.'

'I didn't mean anything,' grumbled Derek sulkily, taking his place again. But almost immediately he brightened up.

'Did you see Jimmy James on the telly last night?' he asked me. 'That's his act, imitating a drunk. He has a top hat on, posh clothes, but he's shaking and tottering around and when he tries to light a cigar it takes him ages because he can't focus right. '

He tried to go cross-eyed and raised a trembling hand, containing an invisible cigar, to his mouth. We all laughed, except Becky. Derek's mime didn't please her.

'I don't see what's funny about that,' she protested. 'I prefer Max Bygraves.'

'Max Bygraves!' scoffed her brother.

'He's nicer.'

'Comedians don't have to be nice! They just need to make you laugh.'

'They should make you feel happy too.'

'They do, the battier the better! Look, Becky, if you want a Max, then take Max Wall.'

'Ah yes,' said the Skipper nostalgically. 'Professor Wallofski. He's a good turn.'

From there the two of them went on to other comedians, some I was familiar with, some not. I didn't know much about Charlie Chester or Tommy Trinder, but I'd listened to the Goons and liked some of the funny voices they put on, and I'd seen Tony Hancock on television. He'd been a favourite of Dad's before he'd gone 'downhill', dropping his old scriptwriters and deserting the BBC for commercial TV.

Becky stuck up stoutly for *Ray's a Laugh*, which again drew Derek's scorn.

'It's tame,' he said. 'Like a weak cup of tea.'

Their father chuckled loudly.

'What's up?' Derek asked curiously.

'I've just remembered this joke – must have heard it on the wireless. I can't think where else... Mrs Shufflewick.'

That was a completely new name to me.

'Now, Frank,' said Mrs Fraser in a warning tone.

'How does it go?' Mr Fraser adopted, as near as he could, a falsetto voice: ' "I was standing at the bar, minding my own business, and all of a sudden the door opened -and this sailor walked in".'

'Frank!'

'It's perfectly all right, love. I'm pretty sure now I heard it on *Workers' Playtime* and the BBC wouldn't allow anything off-colour through, would it?'

I caught the wink he gave Derek and the air of excited collusion his son assumed when he thought he was being let in on something improper.

' "Anyway, this man walked in. I think he must have been in the navy because he kissed me on both cheeks. And I was doing my shoelaces up at the time".'

Derek burst out with laughter, banging on the table, making the crockery rattle. Mrs Fraser couldn't help smiling, although rather ineptly trying to indicate disapproval at the same time. Becky looked a bit puzzled, as though there must be something more to the joke than *that*, but loyally grinned along with her father. As for me, I desperately adopted an air of knowing amusement. It must have seemed very weak and contrived.

And then I made my first blunder, or gaffe as Roy was fond of calling such things.

'I don't know Mrs Shufflewick,' I admitted. 'I don't think I've ever heard her.'

'*Her*?' Derek stared at me incredulously. 'Her? She's a *man*! A man dressed up as a woman, like in a panto. Isn't that right, Dad?'

Mr Fraser nodded. Derek was vindicated.

Under the impact of his scorn, I felt myself reddening; the old betrayal. It became worse with the second gaffe.

'And I don't suppose you get the point of the joke either?' Derek jeered.

'Leave off him, Derek!' his father ordered.

I was floundering, but didn't weaken into a stuttering attack even so. Instead, I tried to put up some kind of defence.

'That's how people kiss on the continent, isn't it, on both cheeks?'

'From behind and bending down?'

'That's enough, Derek!' said Mrs Fraser sharply. 'Do you hear me?'

But, ignoring the admonitions of both his parents, Derek leapt from his chair again. He gave us his back and leaned forward, although not quite down to *his* shoelaces.

'Derek!' shouted his Mam, in the kind of voice that mothers and fathers have for final warnings.

Becky spanked him once on his protruding rump and said brightly: 'And that's for giving us your best side!'

It was that well-timed mockery, even more than his mother's anger, which made him sit down again so promptly.

'I was just showing Colin what the joke was all about, that's all,' he said, with a familiar air of injured innocence.

'Showing is the word,' said the Skipper dryly. Then: 'I'm beginning to wonder. Was it *Workers' Playtime*?'

'Not everyone has a filthy mind like you, Derek.'

'Well, Mrs Shufflewick has, Becky, and Dad who liked the joke and all the other people who laugh at him or her!' declared Derek. 'And so has Colin. He just won't allow himself to know it yet.'

'Calm down, son, and take a back seat for once,' the Skipper said. 'Otherwise, you'll have to go to your room. You're getting too rough.'

'And you've made Colin go red as a beetroot,' put in Becky, with a disturbing compassion, as though she'd been administering that quality for years. 'It's not fair. You don't deserve to have a friend like him.'

'And does he deserve to have a friend like me?'

'You bighead!'

The dangerous moment passed, Becky's fulsome attention turned away from me and normal bickering was resumed as soon as possible.

Anyway, that was how (they didn't teach you these things in the sedate schools I'd been to, not even in the playground) I came to understand that buttocks could be referred to, a little naughtily, as 'cheeks'. I'd never heard that in our house and, if I'd come across it elsewhere, the meaning had completely passed me by.

'Well, everyone knows what Mrs Shufflewick means,' concluded Derek gruffly.

'Perhaps it might be better if they didn't,' said his mother. 'And don't play the wise child either. I bet Colin's taught you a few things you didn't know, hasn't he? Cleverer ones too, like some of the big words you've been trying to pronounce.'

'Most of those are from Mr Marston,' said Derek. Then, under the pressure of his mother's firm gaze, he conceded: 'But some I did get from the Walking Dictionary here.'

We all laughed at that. I still felt put out of countenance, but I enjoyed the name he'd given me.

Good humour was restored in the Fraser household. The speed and completeness of that process never ceased to impress me. At home, quarrels were followed by hours of recrimination and brooding, sometimes days, but here it was as though rancour could be wiped away in a trice, easier than cleaning your face.

'That's better,' said Mrs Fraser with relief, 'although make sure you take your father's warning to heart, Derek.'

'And listen to your mother!' commanded the Skipper.

'Like you, Dad?'

'Always! I wouldn't dare do anything else.'

This brought teasing scepticism from both his children; it was all like a comfortable game now. Mrs Fraser rolled her eyes and gave me an exasperated look, as if saying: How on earth do you live with such people? Very well, I thought, very well indeed.

'Now,' she said, addressing us all. 'Settle down for once. Dad and I have a proposal to make. Your half-term starts on Thursday, mid-day, doesn't it?'

'If the world's still spinning,' said Derek, but he didn't sound gloomy.

'Before I go to bed, I'm going to say a special prayer,' announced Becky, suddenly solemn.

'That'll do the trick!' said her brother.

'Well, it's not a bad idea all the same,' said Mrs Fraser. 'But what I wanted to suggest is this – how about an excursion on Friday? And you're invited too, Colin. You'll be very welcome. Dad's got a day off work, so we can all go.'

'Where?' Becky and Derek asked eagerly.

'Just to Leeds – look around a bit and do some shopping. They're offering cheap-day returns, so we should take advantage of that. It does mean starting fairly early in the morning and coming back in the evening, but that won't matter for once. You can always have a nap on the train if you're tired.'

'My brother's a student in Leeds,' I said.

'We were thinking about that, love. If you wanted, you and Derek could go up to see him. '

I think Mrs Fraser was a bit surprised at my initial lack of enthusiasm, but then she didn't know much about the relationship between Roy and me. But the idea of visiting him began to take hold. After all, he might be in a good mood, away from the constrictions of Langtoft Avenue. If he wasn't, Derek and I could leave quickly and do some solid exploring.

'What about me?' complained Becky. 'Can't I go with them?'

'No you can't!' snapped Derek. 'You'd spoil everything.'

'I thought you were anxious to get some new clothes, young lady. Leeds would be far better for that than Ketilsby. You're spoilt for choice there.'

Becky looked thoughtful. Here was a serious temptation indeed.

'Well, I do, but…'

'What I suggest,' said Mrs Fraser, 'and I've talked it over with Dad, is that we have a bite to eat when we get to Leeds and afterwards see the boys off to.. . . where is it, Colin?'

'Headingley.'

'Right. Then we three'll wander around the shops and try to find a café which serves chocolate éclairs.'

This messy concoction was Becky's favourite, so that settled that.

'We'll meet the boys half an hour before the train goes.'

'What if the bus down to the station is late, Mam?'

'Then take an earlier one.'

'What are we going to do, hanging around all that time?' protested Derek. 'Let's say ten minutes or so.'

'Let's say thirty, Derek, and on the dot. Understood?'

'It's a fine thing if we can't be trusted.'

But his mother managed to extract a promise from him that we would be back at the time she stipulated.

'And when we next go on an excursion, Becky, you can choose one of your friends to bring with you.'

'Can I have a turn soon and bring one of mine?' asked the Skipper.

'Your uncouth, boozy pals!' replied his wife, entering into the spirit of the joke. 'They'd never get beyond the station bar.'

I had some immediate anxiety about Mum and Dad. I couldn't see them openly refusing me permission to go to Leeds with the Frasers, but might they try to stop me by making money an excuse? I had nothing saved up and Mum in particular constantly seemed to be counting the pennies these days. Besides which, while they were pleased I'd become friends with Derek and they liked him, I was beginning to feel my parents bridle a bit when I went on about the Frasers, as though such praise was an implied rebuke for the way I was treated at home.

There was some snobbery there too, although neither of them would have admitted it. Dad especially found it hard not to be condescending, which I thought unfair. I clenched my teeth every time he stressed what 'decent people' Mr and Mrs Fraser must be, never able to hide a tone of surprise. His slight Birmingham accent disappeared completely at such pronouncements. I didn't challenge him for fear of seeing the hurt, puzzled look that came over his face when he couldn't (or wouldn't) understand why I was angry with him.

Mrs Fraser noted the worry on my brow, although she'd have to guess at the causes of it. She jumped up and started off towards the hall.

'In fact, I'll just go and phone your home, Colin, to check that it's all right for you to come with us. I should have done that before, but we got chattering on.'

She left the door ajar, and so we could hear her voice quite clearly.

'Hello, Mrs Palmer? Shirley Fraser here. Yes, Colin's still with us. Oh, he's no trouble. Quite the opposite. Now, there's something I'd like to ask you about, if you can spare me a minute.'

The call was a success. Mrs Fraser came back into the kitchen, beaming.

'Well, that's settled. Permission granted. So long as you behave yourself, which I told your Mum you'd have no problem doing, unlike someone I could name, not a thousand miles away.'

'Mam! You're always picking on me!'

'And you look so badly done by, don't you?'

'I suffer within,' said Derek lugubriously, making me laugh.

'You ought to dose yourself with bicarbonate of soda then,' said Becky.

Mrs Fraser hurriedly covered her daughter's words, apparently not noticing: 'But we both think, your mother and me, that you should get in touch with Roy beforehand. Is there a phone at his digs, Colin?'

'I don't think so. At least he says there isn't.'

'There's not much time then, is there?' said Derek. 'It's Tuesday now. You'll have to send a telegram.'

'Rubbish!' retorted Mrs Fraser. 'There's three days yet. The post's not that bad. Anyway, telegrams are expensive and when you get one you always expect the worst.'

I knew exactly what she meant. The news of Grandpa's death had arrived that way.

'If Colin gets a letter off in time for the first collection tomorrow, it'll arrive in Leeds the following morning. You could ask Roy to go to a phone-box and ring you if he can't be there – or even if he can be, just to confirm.'

'Yes, that's a good idea,' I said doubtfully, unsure my brother would exert himself so far on my behalf.

'Anyway, it'll be a nice day out,' Mrs Fraser assured us. 'If I remember rightly, to get to Headingley you go past the University. It's got a big white building with a tower. Might be worth a visit.'

'Sounds fascinating,' said Derek sarcastically.

'It could be, you misery! Colin'll be a student there one day, like his brother.'

'Fat chance,' I managed to say before Becky burst in with: 'Oh no! Colin should go to Oxford or Cambridge.'

'Do you reckon?' said Derek. 'With all those toffee-nosed gits wearing gowns and mortarboards. '

Derek was getting his umpteenth rebuke for coarse language when, taking advantage of a brief lull in the struggle, I said goodbye to them all, thanking Mr and Mrs Fraser for the invitation, and rushed home to write my letter.

***

When I got back to Langtoft Avenue, I popped my head into the sitting-room where my mother was watching TV. I explained that I was going to write to Roy and climbed the stairs to my room.

The first version of my letter was too peremptory: we planned to arrive at Cross Chapel Street at such and such a time and we'd be staying for the afternoon. It sounded more like an inspection than a visit and additionally, when I read it over to myself, almost as if I were writing to someone I'd never met.

The second draft was still a bit distant but better overall, full of 'would you mind if...' and hopes that we wouldn't inconvenience Roy: the flowery stuff. I was quite proud of it myself, but I could imagine his lip curling with contempt at such petit-bourgeois prevarications. Yet I could also imagine that if Roy got the first version I'd get ticked off for boorishness and poor style, so on balance the second attempt seemed the lesser of two evils and that's the one I decided to send.

I stressed Mrs Fraser's suggestion that he should ring, making sure I firmly attributed it to her – (my friend's mother fussing a bit) – in case he should think I was trying to give him orders. Any bossiness between us had to come from the other direction; otherwise, it counted as an impertinence. Well, I was asking a favour of sorts.

Anyway, whatever happened, Derek and I would chance it. I would have been apprehensive about finding my way through a strange city by myself, but in his company it'd be exciting, two young adventurers on the loose and finding something to laugh about in everything.

But I can't deny I secretly hoped that we'd arrive on Roy's doorstep and be told by his landlady that he wasn't there, not due back until long after our return train to Ketilsby had gone. I'd have done the decent brotherly thing, not a blot on my record, and I'd be free – even the shadow of Roy's dominating soul banished to the horizon!

After sealing the letter, I went along the landing to my father's office for a stamp. He was working at his desk, surrounded by boxes of stationery and big packets of greeting cards. He picked out one or two and read the terrible verses on them. The get-well card he chose had the worst lines of all, making us both chuckle. At that moment, Dad seemed almost young again. I sniffed the air inconspicuously, wondering if the hospitality sherry had been recruited to heighten his mood.

'People go in for such drivel, though,' he said. 'And I'm not in the business of improving their taste. But let's suppose you were seriously ill and got *that* through the post! It'd be enough to make anybody turn up their toes and hope for a better world up yonder. Perhaps that's the idea, eh Colin? A lot of quick corpses and dodgy wills. Deep-seated cunning!'

We talked about the excursion to Leeds. He gave me some loose half-crowns and florins on his desk as spending money, telling me to go to Mum for the rest. Apparently, Mrs Fraser had told her how much the cheap day return would cost. Somehow I'd missed that bit.

'Do you know what happened today?' said Dad, as he separated a stamp from a sheet of them and passed it over to me. Judging by his expression, it was obviously something good. 'I met an old business friend of mine. Knew him years back. He's in the wines and spirits trade now, two off-licenses in the town already and one in Horncastle. He wants me to go in with him, locally, as junior partner and manager. Reckons I'd be a whiz with the customers – the human face of booze-purveying! Of course, your mother would say I'd drink all the profits, but even so it's a thought, isn't it? Very different from what I've done so far in my life, but then it's no bad thing to keep an eye open for what's new and challenging. Especially' – he motioned round at the boxes and packets – 'as this stuff is moving rather slowly at the moment.'

'Perhaps he was just saying that, Dad,' I responded, not wanting to either dampen his new hopes or encourage them too much.

'Maybe,' he admitted reluctantly. 'But he kept on coming back to the idea. And he was keen to arrange another meeting, a serious *business* meeting.'

He viewed me with a familiar arch sagacity, as though he'd all but got the deal in the bag.

Partly to avoid his eye, I looked down at the stamp, thinking how small it was and how dull: just the young Queen's head and shoulders and a surround of decoration. She was crowned, to be sure, but the meagre face value at the bottom of the scrap of paper seemed to take away from all that – an array of jewels for a couple of pennies!

'Have you got anything better than this, Dad?'

'What do you mean?'

'Well,' I hesitated, not knowing really what to say without making myself ridiculous. 'Something more interesting.'

'The Battle of Hastings in panoramic detail, along those lines? Look, you're sending a letter to your brother, not a royal charter. This stamp will do the trick. They're the ones I regularly use, but then I'm only a humble businessman. Besides, I don't know whether there are more attractive British stamps on the market. Not like those colourful French colonials in your album, anyhow. Stick some of those on if you like, but I don't think the Royal Mail will be pleased.'

He sounded peeved, but also as if he were pursuing a fresh humorous idea. He studied me as I licked the stamp, then pressed it down hard on the envelope.

'But you're right there, Colin. The glue's not very good.'

'I didn't mean anything, Dad. Thanks for the stamp anyway.'

'That's all right. No offence taken. But I don't think Roy will even glance at the Queen's head, which he's dishonour-bound to scorn.'

'I wasn't thinking of that.'

Dad mentioned that he had to leave early the next morning and that he'd post the letter for me, it'd be no problem. I told him I was just nipping out now to the box on the corner.

'I know it won't get there any faster, but...'

My father looked a bit hurt, yet he laughed all the same.

'That's what I like about family life. A son's trust.'

'No, Dad, I didn't...'

'Tell you what. I'll get on to Carrier Pigeon Express and they'll fly your missive to Leeds during the night. The bird will be leaving its signature on Roy's doorstop before the Workers' Friend has managed to struggle down to breakfast.'

I enjoyed the notion and my father seemed gratified.

'You're exactly like your Mum, Colin. A thing's only gone when she's seen it go.'

Downstairs, I checked and re-checked that the letter was addressed properly, solidly stamped and sealed. Then I put on my mac and went out.

At the post-box, I pushed the letter through the slit, letting my fingers stay a few seconds after release, as if the envelope might mischievously bounce up and escape. Then I stood for a while pretending to study the collection times under the streetlight, even though I knew at a glance what they were. No white corner of envelope peeked out from the aperture, biding its time. Derek had me down as an alarmist, yet he'd have thought me hopelessly barmy had he been there and cottoned on to my little manoeuvres.

But, finally, to show the unattending world how resolute and sane I could be, I turned round and walked the short distance back to our house, head held high, gaze directly forward. I didn't look back once, not even a quick glance over my shoulder.

Short of some evil-minded prankster setting fire to the contents of the pillar-box, my careful message to Roy would be taken to the central post office near Town Hall Square the next morning and sorted along with all the other mail; on Thursday it would be there in Cross Chapel Street for Roy to respond to or not, as he chose.

XVII. THE BATTLE OF THE TITANS

We were getting ready to break up for half-term. There was little attempt at teaching, the shortened session we were compelled to be at school. Nobody would have settled down to learning anyway. Instead, we had quizzes or played games like draughts or noughts and crosses, or read books we'd brought with us. Whatever storm clouds loomed internationally, the immediate world still looked good. Freedom, or a few valuable days of it, that was the promise.

Still the morning line-up, of course, if anything all the more vigorous today in an attempt at containing our jubilant spirits; every detail attended to, as if Mr Marston and Mr Gordon would be pining for their little ritual even during the short holiday.

Mr Marston was more or less back to normal now, still looking a bit peaky, though, and occasionally, when his mask slipped, somewhat sheepish.

I suspected that Mr Gordon, gleaming eye-patch still immaculately in place, needed the school assembly even more than our teacher did the line-up. The Headmaster hooked up to the occasion like a blood transfusion. He didn't get Svenny Beatitudes to do the reading again, but intoned a biblical passage himself and delivered a loosely connected homily on it afterwards, three and a half minutes longer than normal. It was something to do with the idea of using our liberty wisely and responsibly, for the common benefit. Just the words we were aching to hear.

Only the sombre Kilbertson, back in the classroom, reminded us that the Russians were still on course for Cuba and that the Americans were waiting for them, prepared to enforce the blockade whatever the cost. Kilbertson suggested that none of us might be around when the half-term ended, our bodies fried to a frazzle all over the ruined town, but then Brady riposted by saying that at least this would mean the school wouldn't be standing either. This raised a rebellious cheer, a very odd one logically.

Mr Marston happened to overhear the exchange.

'Just think of the hymn Miss Barber played with such verve this morning, Kilbertson – "Rejoice, the Lord is King!". A great piece, don't you think? Enough to defeat the demons in a graveyard at midnight.'

'Have you ever been in a graveyard at midnight, sir?'

'Now, strange to say, I have.'

'How many demons did you see there, sir?'

'Funny you should ask that, Allington.'

He smiled at our expectancy, then the crestfallen faces as we realised he wasn't going to tell us an exciting story.

'No, I think we'll save that for Christmas-time, if Kilbertson and the other two Ks allow us to get that far.'

'Rejoice?' queried Derek, crinkling up his brow in mock-puzzlement. 'Oh, you mean like at all-night Cuban parties, sir?'

'Not only, Fraser,' said Mr Marston, drawing in his breath and then letting it out slowly, as though testing his powers of forbearance. '*Generally*, if anything like that can really be done.'

And such was the holiday spirit that he even omitted to cuff Derek round the head or tweak the favourite, much-tried ear.

***

I'd looked forward to being with Derek for much of the rest of the day, but as it turned out the time we spent together was limited.

An ancient great-aunt was coming round for tea at five

o'clock and Mrs Fraser wanted both children to be there, smartened up and on their best behaviour. The old lady lived in a tall terrace house sandwiched between two bed and breakfast establishments, near the Promenade. She was a rich widow and apparently favoured voluminous fur coats; she wore so many gold rings, they looked like expensive knuckledusters!

'Because of her bad feet, this auntie lives on the ground floor, never goes upstairs. There's a huge commode in her bed sitting-room. The lid's covered with fur too.'

'Who empties it?'

'The faithful companion. A slavey, you could say. She sleeps on a filthy mattress in the attic.'

'Come off it, Derek!' I said, laughing.

'Well, all right. She's got a bed of sorts, but at least the windowpanes are cracked and there are spiders all over the place. And her feet are even worse than the old besom's. It takes her ages to get up and down the stairs. And with that commode to empty – what a job! '

With a lofty assumption of moral authority, Derek reckoned that his parents were simply trying to get money out of their well-heeled relative.

'I wouldn't be surprised if they make her drunk on sherry and persuade dear Auntie Ethel to change her will in their favour. They've already been promised something and now they're moving in to scoop the lot! I wouldn't fancy the downtrodden slavey's chances after this.'

He was talking with the pantomime beadiness of eye and grim dolefulness of tone he favoured when elaborating on some particularly 'dark' truth. We both enjoyed this wild fantasy of his parents as grasping villains and played out variations on the theme as we left the school. As so often, he walked with me to the Shore Road and then turned back.

Derek and I were both chock-full of energy as if we'd been penned up for months. In the early afternoon, after a hasty meal, I called for him on my bike and we cycled down to the resort end of Ketilsby, about two miles off. We didn't do much when we got there, just stared over the estuary for a while: beyond us the increasing stretch of wet sand, the thin line of retreating water, and in the background the low coast of Holderness.

Then we rode along the arcade before the bingo and one-armed bandit places. We weren't supposed to do this but most of them were closed up for the winter now anyway. Zigzagging between the slender iron pillars, we went on until we came to the end of the row. Derek and I were equal in that game, just having had to put a foot down once each to steady ourselves.

Here the Promenade came to an end, in a wider, half-rounded area. The view from this point was at a different angle to the rest. You could see the Dock Tower across the mud flats and scrubland, the masts of trawlers crowded in the docks beneath it. We tried to count them but it was too distant, the outlines blurred, misleading sometimes. Even that was exhilarating, although we pretended to be frustrated that we always arrived at different numbers; a happy uncertainty.

Just before we started back, Derek asked me if I'd heard from Roy.

'Give him a chance,' I said, more tolerantly than I felt, because there was a part of me which had hoped that Roy would rush out first thing on receiving my message and phone home. 'He would only have got my letter this morning.'

'Do you think he will ring?'

'I don't know, but we'll still go up to Cross Chapel Street, unless he says not to.'

Echoing my sentiments of Tuesday evening, Derek pronounced: 'Questing into foreign parts!' making the words sound like banner headlines.

I hadn't a clue what Leeds was like. From Roy's account it seemed to be all politics and protests and deadly serious books as thick as boulders. But it must be something more than that as well. Derek's way of putting it made the city sound mysteriously alluring, so I just nodded my head in eager agreement.

***

Dad was in his office upstairs, Mum in the back room sipping tea and reading and I was in the kitchen, ears half-attentive to the wireless, eating fresh crispy biscuits between swallows of orangeade.

Both my parents would be out for part of the evening at least. Mum had a meeting of the Townswomen's Guild and Dad was off to see some of his cronies at the Honest Lawyer on Baxtergate. Both Dad and I liked the sign the pub had. It showed a lawyer in early nineteenth century costume, holding his head under one arm, his body ending at the severed neck.

'One of the wisest lessons you could ever learn is in that picture,' Dad had told me more than once.

I didn't feel bad on my own, but even so I didn't fancy spending the next few hours mooching about the house, watching the telly irrespective of what was on, or scribbling away at a story just for the sake of it. I was definitely not in a writing mood.

And then I had an idea, one that both frightened and fascinated me.

I went into the back sitting-room and told my mother I was going round to Kilbertson's for a bit: 'He's a boy in my class. He's interested in history too.' Of course, I had no intention of going there. I knew where he lived, not far from Derek, but we hadn't much to do with each other. It was more that he was in my mind because of his gloomy outlook and his stand against the high spirits of the rest of us.

I'd already mentioned to Mum that Derek's great-aunt

was visiting them, so I felt I should have some excuse for being out. I couldn't tell her that I planned to go to the hide, about which she knew nothing anyway.

Mum put her book aside, glanced at the clock on the mantelpiece and gave me my instructions.

'Take a spare key, Colin, and please make sure you're back in good time. You need to get to bed early because tomorrow's going to be a long, busy day, don't forget. There's the rest of the shepherd's pie in the oven. That'll do for your supper, if you heat it up.'

'Right, Mum. I won't be late.'

Soon I was pulling our front door to, stealthily, as if I were on an important secret mission, and walking up to Bradleigh Avenue and along there to the Bumps.

So here I stood, then, dithering away outside the den, obsessively scanning branches and twigs as though I had to commit their pattern to memory, working myself up into a 'tizzy', to use one of Derek's choice words, when I imagined Olsen being there again, balefully maintaining his vigil.

It was no use telling myself that it was almost certain he wouldn't be; no use trying to take comfort from Svenny's change of heart (real or apparent) and Mr Gordon's control over him.

What I ought to do was just rush in like a whirlwind or a one-man marauding army, a challenge that even Svenny Olsen might be bowled over by – well, for a moment or so perhaps. The idea nearly made me laugh out loud, it was so ridiculous.

Still just about light. None of the boys around who sometimes played beyond the hollow by my Tigris and Euphrates. I scrutinised the dips and hummocks, all but seeing the sneaky forms of spies: Olsen's agents, ready successors to Doran and Witherow.

Not a soul.

Round the hide I went again, worrying myself to catch

Olsen's reek coming out from between the twigs and branches, my smell too that time: rank terror. Olsen sitting on the box, thick legs splayed, shining the beam of his torch on Grandpa's knives and forks: 'Looking for these, kid?' Then the light moving swiftly up to his own face, all the bulges and pits of his features, his tongue briefly lolling out like something made free and mad.

How ridiculous my behaviour was! I was here to settle a ghost, not raise a storm of them over my head, new scares multiplying out of the old. I meant to redeem the hide after all, or do my best to.

'Grasp the nettle, son! You've got to grasp the nettle. Go on!'

It sounded like a voice outside my head, although I knew it wasn't: a commanding sound, an amalgam of my teachers, chapel ministers, Grandpa and, perhaps a little surprisingly, of my Dad too. But altogether it formed something new I'd never heard before and wasn't sure I wanted to hear again.

So I flailed wildly at the entrance to show willing and then rammed my way in.

A darkness met me that seemed unreal, a slice taken out of night and moulded to the shape of the den. Panting now, afraid my breathing would either stop completely or get even faster, become uncontrollable. With a masterly effort, I managed to slow it down, taking in and expelling air with great deliberation.

There was no threatening reek. The sharp wind and the rain which got in everywhere had seen to that. If I bent close to the ground, I'd be able to smell the must of pressed-down grass and earth, but I chose not to, instead switching on my torch and tracking it around the small confines of our hide, like a searchlight.

It seemed ages since Derek and I had sat here telling stories, fancying excitedly what might be happening beyond our scanty yet somehow robust defences. I felt nostalgic for that now.

The only traces of Olsen's presence were the things he'd kicked around in his pain and fury, mainly the makeshift chair and table. Even my Grandfather's tobacco tin had been torn from its perch and lay on the ground now, lid open. I wondered whether I could detect some spots of blood nearby, from where I'd stabbed Olsen – but, if there had been anything, the wet had taken care of it.

Perhaps the best indication that the place was as cleansed of that horrible encounter as it could ever be were Grandpa's knives and forks, which I found lying around on the floor, glinting in the beam as if on show. There'd been no other human intrusion, then, no light fingers making off with their surprising trophies.

I picked them up and put them in my coat pocket. A sudden powerful gust swept through the den. I was starting to shiver; the effect of the cold but the tension of reclamation as well.

I'd got the cutlery safe, but as a last thought before departure I thought I'd take the tobacco tin too. Once I'd cleaned the gunge out as best I could, that went into my other deep pocket. The hide was as safe as it could be, I reckoned, and I'd shown that I could be there again, but even so I had a foreboding that we weren't going to be using it much anymore. Winter would be with us soon – a floor of ice and maybe a roof of snow! And then only a lunatic would brave it out here. Blame the weather, fine. That would be the easier thing to do.

***

Emerging from the hide, I saw old Mr Marston coming along the track. He wasn't chuntering away to himself this time, though he had his lamp-carrying bag with him. Our clever teacher's fumble-minded dad seemed more aware of his surroundings on this route than usual and, in due course, of the single human being standing uneasily before him. I was tempted to run off in the other direction but that would have been feeble; besides which, he was much too close to me for that now. I just had time to feel embarrassed, wondering what he thought I was doing hanging about here. His purpose was obvious.

I greeted him politely, rather foolishly addressing him by name. I thought I might just get away with a rather startled response before he hurried on, perplexed, to the ritual-ground. But it must have been one of his better days because he stopped and peered hard, clearly racking his memory in an attempt to place me.

Finally, he exclaimed jubilantly; 'I know you! Yes, I do! You're one of the boys who came round from my son's school.'

'We brought back some things he'd borrowed from you, Mr Marston. Derek Fraser and me. I'm Colin Palmer.'

'I remember perfectly well,' the old man said with almost ludicrous smugness, as if he should be congratulated on this feat of recall. 'You two lads. We had a right good chat, didn't we?'

I nodded, rather evasively.

Then, all of a sudden, his face clouded.

'Let me see, you're Alfred Reynolds' grandson, aren't you?'

'No, that's...'

'But your hair's different. Even with this poor light I can tell. Jet-black it was last time.'

He looked at me suspiciously.

'That's Derek, the black hair. And Mr Reynolds is *his* grand-dad.'

'Oh aye!' His face began to clear. 'Are you and young Reynolds...'

'No – Fraser. Derek *Fraser*.'

'Are you and young Fraser good friends?'

'Yes, we are!' Just in case I'd sounded too confident and

proud, which would be simply tempting bad luck, I added: 'At least, I hope we are.'

'Nothing better than that, my lad. Well, the love of a good wife comes first, naturally, but...'

Lost in thought, he gazed down the slope towards the stream. It was getting murky, almost like being back in the den, yet I could also see a mist forming in the hollow. More and more it seemed like the ashy-white back of a sleeping beast, a weird blanched and gigantic whale which knew how to float silently overland, as if that too were an ocean.

'But it's when the friend you trusted like your own pulse turns against you! Betrayal, no less. If Krista's dying was a journey to the edge of hell, then what Alfred did helped me on the way there!'

I was afraid of this angry grief. Before I could stop myself, I asked him: 'Do you believe in souls coming back?'

'Eh?' He contemplated my question at length, as though my abruptness had knocked him off balance, then responded in a manner both resolute and vague: 'Well, there's something there. But it's not often you can reach it, see what's in your head let alone before your eyes.'

'Many people,' I began stumblingly, fearful of sounding presumptuous. 'Many people would say it's against reason.'

Mr Marston laughed, drawing strength from what he saw as my naive remark.

'Reason! In spiritual matters, that's like a two-yard rope. It'll get you the six feet and no more.'

He invited me to walk along with him and I did so, knowing exactly where he was going but pretending not to.

'I've got my own little ceremony. Don't think me barmy.'

'No, I wouldn't.'

'Anyway,' he said, 'it's better than going to church to do it. Folk are too fond of locking up God and prayers and hymns. Sometimes they're not very happy when you take belief outside the building. Turn left here, Colin.'

I wondered whether the irate neighbour would make an appearance, shouting and threatening over the fence and, if so, how we'd deal with it.

'You and Derek – you're a sound couple of boys. Not like some I could mention.'

He knows, I thought, momentarily giving way to panic. He's just been leading me on and then, out of sight of everybody, he'll deal out punishment!

Yet I couldn't quite believe that and recovered quickly. Old Mr Marston wasn't skilled in camouflaging his feelings. Something would have given him away if he'd really thought I was one of the hooligan window-smashers.

He was making a curious sound now, not grief or anger or complaint or anything I generally associated with him. It was most like a kind of phlegmy chuckling.

'But you've got to say this for those little tearaways. The money keeps coming, coppers and sixpences. Not much in the latest instalment, though.'

That I knew already, of course. Derek and I had economised on Mr Marston's compensation, because we wanted to put aside most of what we'd got for the Leeds trip.

'On the back windowsill this time. I can't say I like that, Colin. Like prowlers, sending a message they can get in anywhere.'

'No, that's not right,' I said, quite sincerely, making a mental note to tell Derek he should restrain himself, just slip the donations through the front door flap when no one was looking. He was enjoying his flair for stealthiness too much.

We arrived at the old man's impromptu altar, as I'd come to think of it. Mr Marston put down his bag and took out the lamp.

'Help me with this, will you?'

I wasn't sure what I was supposed to do because the lamp was small and certainly not heavy. It turned out he wanted me to take it and push the thing as firmly as I could into the ground.

'Can't bend as easily as I used to. That's where you youngsters score over us every time.'

So I got down on my knees, tamping the earth around the lamp as if I were planting something. At his request, I checked the level of the oil and whether the wick was showing enough to burn readily. Given his creaking joints, I thought he'd ask me to light the lamp but he managed this himself, groaning loudly at the effort involved as he fumbled for his matches. He might enjoy having an assistant like me, but the main parts of the rite he reserved for himself.

After rising precariously to his feet, using my shoulder as a support, he stared before him as if he saw his dead wife there, or sensed her presence so strongly it was as good as sight. I still didn't like old Mr Marston much, and I didn't rule out the suspicion that he was play-acting a bit, but I felt far more good will for him than I had at our first meeting.

He started telling me about how he and his wife had frequently walked up here and how it had eventually become their favourite spot.

'Funny, isn't it? Krista and I went to countless more striking places than this little wilderness. Spectacular sights! Switzerland once, France – on the edge of the Pyrenees – several times with Richard, your teacher, when he was younger. Money was never plentiful, but we got through.'

He pondered for a moment, chewing his lip.

'Germany too. We went over there a few years ago, when Richard was still at university. Back to where Krista was brought up, in Frankfurt.' He sighed. 'But it was a mistake. Years and years had gone by, but all the same too many unhappy memories were sharpened up for her.'

He'd taken a jam jar from his bag and some rather crushed roses. My task was to lower the flowers he'd put in the jar to the ground and fix it there.

'There'll be rain again tonight. Enough for them to feast on' – he indicated the flowers. 'They cost quite a lot.'

'Did people treat you badly in Germany?' I asked, curious, my mind instantly conjuring up images of belligerent Nazis from stories and films.

'On the contrary. Smiling, helpful, polite, especially members of *that* generation. It made me cringe in the end, let alone Krista. There was never any talk between us about our going to Germany again.'

Mr Marston looked at his watch and tut-tutted in annoyance.

'Colin, nice as it is to talk to you, I'm afraid I have to be off. I must see my doctor and the evening surgery gets very crowded. Now, would you be so good as to do me one more favour? It won't burden you too much.'

'All right.'

'Well, when I go would you let the lamp burn on for a few minutes? It may sound daft, but I always feel that Krista likes to see that brightness. If I turned it off, suddenly and too soon, she'd think something was wrong.'

I must have looked at him as if he were completely off his chump because, rarely for him, he burst into a hearty laugh and clapped me on the back

'I could do with getting the lamp back, of course.'

'I can't remember exactly where you live, Mr Marston,' I lied. 'But I'll pass it over to Derek. He'll bring it round.'

It was amusing to think of landing Derek in it, just a little.

'Good lad. That'll be fine. There's no rush.'

He started going through his pockets. At first I thought he was searching for a handkerchief, but from his mutterings it became clear that he was looking for money: 'Now, where's that loose change I had?' Bus fare? But no, it wasn't. Horrified, I realised that he wanted to give me some money – perhaps the very coins that Derek had left on his windowsill! Although, it was more likely that Mr Marston, adding to the guilty pile, still kept those evidentially on show on his sideboard.

'You could make use of a little extra, couldn't you, Colin?'

'But, Mr Marston, I don't want... I was here anyway.'

'There we are! Just a small token of thanks for your assistance and appreciation of your company, my boy.'

'Please, Mr Marston!'

'No, no, go on with you! Don't be bashful. You deserve it.'

I should have insisted that I didn't but if he'd asked me why not and pressed me to explain and something of the truth had fallen out? You can imagine the trouble I would have been in then.

Things got worse.

'If only I could drag those two rotten tearaways before you, they'd bow their heads in shame!'

It was like being in the kind of bad dream where everything's topsy-turvy, at odds with truth, and you can do nothing about it.

'Mr Marston!' I wailed, the coins in my open hand.

He closed the fingers over my palm and pressed them as though trying to imprint the shape of the coins into the soft flesh.

'Right, Colin. I must go.'

And then, with a heartfelt plea to say a prayer for Krista before I left, how much she'd enjoy that, Mr Marston was walking away along the ridge, more swiftly than normal, worried that he'd be late for the doctor.

With the best will in the world, I couldn't dedicate a proper prayer to the soul of Krista Marston, just a few scrabbled words which sounded as dead as the grace said at school dinner by a boy picked out for the honour. I didn't often stay to school dinner but it was the sort of experience which lingered in your mind – or rather regions further down, from the mashed potato sticking to the palate like wallpaper paste to lukewarm custard slopping menacingly around in the belly.

I couldn't summon up enough belief now and yet disbelief seemed out of the question too. For me, Krista Marston was still the young woman of the photograph I'd seen in both the old men's houses: a face so beautiful it could have been that of the Virgin Mary, a Northern one rather than the dark-haired, olive-skinned women I'd seen in copies of Italian pictures. But they all meant the same, though. I didn't know how to express it then, but I knew this air of serene tenderness was the best sign of love there was, my parents' sniffiness about Catholic 'idolatry' notwithstanding.

And I felt troubled as well when I didn't give the burning lamp the time I was supposed to. But I couldn't keep from glancing back at the fence, expecting the tetchy, self-righteous neighbour to materialise any moment and bawl me out. There were certainly lights on in the house at the other end of the garden.

But it was dark in my Land, except for the thickened whale-mist in the dip. At times it seemed to shine as if it were lit from within. Perhaps I was dreaming of a rival lamp down there!

I made sure that the real tangible one was properly doused and put it in the bag Mr Marston had lent me. This time, too, the flame had behaved itself. I left the jam jar and the roses where they were.

What to do with the coins? They were still pressing into my palm. Several options crossed my mind but finally I threw them, one by one, into the darkness ahead of me.

It was more like a game of chance than an offering. Let some kid come across them tomorrow and spend them on chocolate or sweets, or an archaeologist in a thousand years, carefully cleaning the archaic coins before they were put on display in a museum somewhere.

***

Toting the bag, I started back along the rise, having made sure for the umpteenth time that I had Grandpa's cutlery with me. Once I'd restored these eating irons to their usual gleaming condition, I'd smuggle them back into the canteen. Mum would be surprised next time she counted; perhaps she'd even scold herself for having made a stupid mistake, half-convinced that she was going potty.

Anyway, the knives and forks would soon be back in use, Christmas probably. I wondered whether I should put some mark on the ones that had been my weapons, a faint scratch which nobody else would see or detect any significance in if they did. Naturally, with an extra sharp flick of the eye, I'd be able to recognise them, avoiding their use myself whilst enjoying the sight of someone else, preferably Roy, wielding them to cut their Christmas turkey with, forking the roast potatoes into an unsuspecting mouth, those tines and the silver blade that had drawn fresh human blood!

I fully intended to step the remaining distance to the pavement of Bradleigh Avenue and then go straight home, but in the end I didn't. What prevented me, caused me to linger? I just can't answer that, not even all these years later.

Suddenly, without any premeditation, I stopped near the den and hunkered down on my heels, as if I'd just completed a hike of miles and was tired.

I looked down at the mist, less static now, harder to see as a huge whale falling into slumber. There was still that curious light within it I was intrigued by. Now I saw shapes there, forming and dissolving, forming again, striving towards a definition I only gradually began to guess at.

A thing like a table was emerging, a crude table made perhaps of packing cases. And then I saw that, on either side of it, two men were sitting, on smaller boxes. Somehow, without any kind of embellishment at all, these had the air of being like thrones. I blinked, but no gilded armrests or lion's claw feet appeared.

There was an increasing familiarity about the figures down there: photographs in the papers, clips on TV, even the rudimentary cartoons Mr Marston had drawn on the blackboard. And now they seemed closer than they could possibly be, as if Mr Gordon had kindly lent me his field-glasses.

The short, podgy man and the tall, slimmer one with the slight crook to his back, were, of course, Mr Khrushchev and President Kennedy. They were arguing furiously; no sound but I could tell by the gesticulations alone that the quarrel was a strong one. Just occasionally, they'd stop waving their arms about and lean back as far as they were able, nodding at each other as though they should strive once more to find some common ground – it had to exist *somewhere*! These peaceful intervals never lasted long; soon they'd be back to their rancour.

And then something weirder than weird began to happen. The world's two most powerful leaders – born of mist, a wraithy Kennedy and a wraithy Khrushchev – commenced to arm-wrestle. I saw the two forearms, sleeves drawn back, the two elbows positioned on the table, the fists clenched into each other.

In relation to Kennedy, Mr Khrushchev was a very stubby sort of man, yet he was strong and determined and at first seemed to be getting the better of his opponent. Indeed, it almost looked as if Kennedy were intent on throwing the first bout, at least at the beginning, as if that might be seen as a mark of good sportsmanship. But he quickly fought back when he realised that this struggle had nothing to do with playing games.

Khrushchev had taken the superior position early, though, a psychological advantage as well as a physical one, and now he was slowly bending Kennedy's hand towards the wood. He was cheating because he'd risen from his seat to press more weight on his opponent. But you might have said that was almost forgivable, given Kennedy's advantage in height. The President, with his free hand, motioned him back and, after initially jeering, Khrushchev plumped himself down again but right at the edge of his rough stool.

Even so, the Soviet leader won that first one, suddenly smashing Kennedy's hand down on the wood and clamping it there, putting his whole strength into the effort. His face seemed to bloat to twice its size as though about to burst, but a wide grin of triumph was gashed across it.

Before the two hands clasped again, Khrushchev wiped his face with a handkerchief the size of a flag. Were they going to settle for the best of three or continue until one or the other was too exhausted to fight any more?

Once again, the faces tensed fiercely in an assertion of force and will. The soundtrack I had to provide myself: the grunts and curses, the way they urged themselves on as if they were shouting at beasts who weren't working hard enough for them. I watched the arms pushing painfully to and fro, so taut they could have been made of metal rather than flesh.

It took him some time, but Kennedy got that second tussle.

They were aiming for more than the best of three, I realised: total victory, the absolute submission of the enemy. I began to lose count of the number of bouts, they were so quick – besides that, the whale-mist had become more active, swirling around madly and nearly obscuring the combatants. Robbed even further of colour, at times they were no more distinct than faint pencil drawings on old paper. Then they'd come back into ashy clarity again for a while.

As far as I could judge, the score was about level, but now there came a bout locked in stalemate, the two forearms in unyielding parallel to each other. If they budged at all, it must have been in millimetres. Both Kennedy and

Khrushchev were blatantly cheating now, putting all the might they had left into the resolution of the struggle, their backsides up from their seats and their elbows lifting a little above the surface of the table before being jerked down again.

And then, with all this frantic effort, they lost their balance and fell over sideways, tumbling onto the ragged grass and the mud. At first their hands were still clasped, as though nothing could ever separate them. Locked together, it looked as if they'd roll down the slope that ended with my Tigris and Euphrates, two warring parts of the same being, right down to the bank and then, with a huge splatter, into the chilly stream!

Perhaps the same notion crossed their minds, I don't know, the fearful prospect of bruises and a wetting, because suddenly their hands broke apart and they staggered to their feet, the dumpy leader and the taller one, who was now welsh-combing his famous hair into place.

And they were both laughing, that was the truly amazing thing. It wasn't just wishful thinking on my part. I could *see* it, even through all the mist. Convulsed with mirth, they bowed to each other, mocking the formal courtesy as if that meant deepening it.

Immediately afterwards, Mr Khrushchev broke into one of those Russian dances where your bum virtually scrapes the ground and you fold your arms and kick out your legs. For such a stout, ungainly man, he performed with great vigour and skill.

Naturally, Kennedy had to respond. From the magazine picture I'd seen of him and his wife smartly attired for a White House ball, I thought he might try a partnerless waltz or something similarly polite and smooth but instead, to my surprise, he began what I thought must be a tap dance. But then, remembering that his ancestors came from Ireland, I realised that the smiling President was attempting a jig.

I knew this was the time to leave, when they were

dancing at each other.

I surprised myself too by giving a whoop and a cheer, like a brave sound cutting across oceans and deserts, something I still hear at odd moments, although not as often as I'd like to. Then I pelted, twisting and jumping – my own dance – along the rest of the track, Grandpa's cutlery clinking against the lamp in the bag.

At the border of the Land, just as I was about to step onto the pavement of Bradleigh Avenue, I looked back. It could just have been my mind's eye, but the whale-mist seemed to be growing huge, a great opaque mass with strands swirling around at the edges, like ash-coloured flames. The figures within were lost to me now: two strange Jonahs indeed, but happy at the end.

I hurried home, full of a secret joy, and that's how I remember it still, the whole uncanny but wonderful experience.

***

Mum was out, as I'd expected. However, Dad arrived not long after me, when I was still faffing around in the kitchen, twisting the wireless dial to no great purpose. He popped his head round the door to greet me, then went straight upstairs to his office. I heard him collide with a stack of stationery or cards and send the whole lot flying, the ripe cursing that followed. He was much earlier than I thought he'd be. Evidently, his session at The Honest Lawyer hadn't gone as well as it normally did. If I'd listened keenly, from the hallway, I might have heard the drawer where he kept his 'hospitality' bottle being wrenched open; a large restorative sherry would be needed and then at least another for luck. I hoped they'd work.

As for me, I felt ravenous, so I turned on the oven, positioning the shepherd's pie exactly mid-centre inside. I'd leave it to heat up longer than I needed to (liberated for now from the weight of my mother's gastronomic experience) until the mashed potato at the top was crusty, almost charred.

I was thinking about my dinner with pleasurable anticipation, chewing a clump of bread to stave off the hunger pangs, when Dad came into the kitchen. He was carrying a copy of *The Ketilsby Evening Telegraph*, for once not featuring local news in the headlines.

Dad tapped the paper ominously and threw it aside. For a moment he glared at me as if I were Fidel Castro himself, then his expression softened guiltily, his whole manner, and I stood in danger of a maudlin embrace, perhaps even a few well-oiled tears. I was happier when his phiz assumed a more generally lugubrious air.

Derek was fond of that word, 'phiz'. When I'd told him it was very old-fashioned slang he'd only used it all the more – over a week or two every opportunity he could.

Now Dad was going on about the disaster facing us all – 'humanity', as he put it -sparing me nothing of his dark prognostications. War wasn't even just likely now, it was a dead certainty. He laughed hollowly at his unfortunate punning. Armageddon was practically upon us, the last minutes of peace ticking away.

'Imagine the world we could have had, if politicians weren't so bloody moronic and savage.'

'But Dad...'

'Paradise, or as near as you can get!'

He regarded me sorrowfully, puzzled too by what must have been the calm expression on my face.

'It's you young people I feel sorry for most. All that life ahead which should be yours by right, and now this!'

If Mum had been present, she'd have told him to shut up at this point – that is, if she hadn't before – accusing him of scare-mongering, seeing disaster through the depths of a bottle.

But I wasn't upset at all. It would have been beyond my

powers to explain to either of them why not. In fact, I never told anyone about what had happened that early evening as I stared down into the whale-mist, not even Derek. He'd barely believed my story about the dancing lamp; he would have given even less credit to all this taradiddle concerning Kennedy and Khrushchev. Not that it was, I mean, but Derek would have thought I was romancing, devising a special imaginative extravaganza or, simply, that I'd gone completely off my trolley.

Yet because Dad was so distressed, I did try to use what I'd witnessed to help him; a kind of message post-haste from the oracles, difficult to handle at the best of times.

He seemed to be coming to the end of his doom-speech – out of breath, out of words, or simply because he'd frightened himself into silence? I had to get in quickly, while I could.

I'd been checking on the pie again. The potato was beginning to brown very nicely. Now I straightened up and said: 'Don't worry, Dad. Nothing horrible's going to happen over Cuba.'

He peered at me then, taken aback, as if I'd sprouted two heads and six ears. His expression was a map I could have treasured in other circumstances: sheer incredulity, bafflement, scorn, and yet with some wonderment too, as if I were the most naive boy in God's universe but just possibly – that rare freak — also a youthful seer.

Then a more prosaic but touching explanation must have occurred to Dad. I was trying to comfort him, that was it, taking over what more properly ought to have been his role, as father. A shadow of shame passed across his face.

However, he didn't try to apologise, which was a relief. More than anything, he seemed anxious to go back upstairs again, simply reminding me – an echo of Mum! – that I should get to bed early because of the travelling next day, (tactfully, not mentioning that there might not *be* a next day). He left the kitchen shaking his head, muttering stuff about, 'Out of the mouths of babes and sucklings.' He was in an unusually biblical mood tonight, the sombre side of the great book, that is.

Dad must have been half-way up the stairs when he called out. It was as though he felt he'd better thank me for my well-intentioned but utterly cack-brained words. 'Good lad! Good lad!' he declared and went off along the landing to his room, breaking out into the shrill, spiky whistling my mother detested and tried to banish from the house as best she could. It appeared that my father, however desperately, was making a brave effort to join in the mood of hopeful fantasy he thought I was trying to create.

Down the stairs, through the kitchen door, came the jaunty notes, like a dagger splintering wood. They should have belonged to one of the morale-boosting First World War songs Dad was fond of, but somewhat incongruously they were the bare musical bones of a Fred Astaire number, elegant and tuneful when Fred did it. All three of us had watched *Top Hat* on the box not long ago. Now Dad was putting on his top hat, white tie and tails – an oddly quixotic way of squaring up to Armageddon. But I rather liked the idea of him as a rotund Astaire tipping his hat in the face of what he was sure would be disaster, and thought it'd be great if he could turn about and playfully shoot down the gentlemen of the chorus with his cane, as happened in the film – all except the last one whom Fred got with an impromptu bow (that useful polished stick again) and an invisible arrow.

XVIII. THREE CROSS CHAPEL STREET

It was Mum who scolded me out of bed and into the bathroom early next morning, preparing me a quick breakfast and making sure I had my money and Roy's address; Mum who checked that I knew our telephone number off by heart, just in case I was 'in trouble'. I didn't really understand what she meant by that and probably neither did she, not in any detail, but the anxiety was real enough. Anyway, phoning the odd seventy miles back to Ketilsby wouldn't do much good if we did run into difficulties. Mum and Dad could hardly zoom over there like Superman!

'Derek's parents and Becky will be with us – except when we go up to Roy's.'

'It's that big "except" I'm worried about.'

'We'll get on a bus, get off it, find the place, knock on the door – that's all.'

'Let's hope so. Now, come on, hurry up! You've got a train to catch.'

She insisted on going with me to the station. Still drowsy, not yet in full command of myself, I couldn't do more than feebly grumble.

Mum had made some of Roy's favourites for me to take him: little cakes with cherries and icing on the top, scones and Scotch eggs, all carefully wrapped up and put in a big tin. She'd also cut some sandwiches for me – they went in a separate package, alongside a bottle of fizzy lemonade to help them down.

'What if I eat Roy's stuff too, all in one go?'

'Then you'd be sick. Besides, your conscience will tell

you not to do anything like that.'

'After special instructions from you, Mum.'

'With special instructions from elsewhere, as you well know, Colin. Now, get your coat and make haste.'

I struggled on the mac over my best jacket. Mum smoothed the material across my back. I didn't like her doing that, squirming away as soon as I could.

'You know what they used to do to children who were getting round-shouldered?'

'I'm not round-shouldered.'

'You will be, if you're not careful. They put a stick between their arms and made them walk around like that, chest out and shoulder blades almost touching. It was harsh but it worked.'

I pointed upstairs in the direction of their bedroom.

'Dad's round-shouldered.'

'Well, he would be, wouldn't he?'

My father didn't have much of a chest to stick out anyway. His belly would have to serve for that. Sometimes it put me off but at other times, when I imagined his latest dream of success and prosperity coming true, I found it a reassuring sight. That's how businessmen should be, especially with a waistcoat buttoned tightly over an imposing girth!

Outside, on the front porch, I hesitated for a few seconds, remembering his gloom of the evening before. My optimistic message seemed a bit glib now, but that was more the manner than the content. I didn't doubt the truth of what I'd seen and, if it made me laugh, all the better.

Anyhow, the world was still standing and didn't feel any different. Not the faintest smell of war.

We set off, myself carrying an unwieldy bag with our stuff in it, Roy's and mine.

As we went over the big green in the park – still with a thick cover of rime – the ducks set up a squalling from the pond. I didn't know whether we'd disturbed them or if they were just squabbling amongst themselves. It still seemed like the middle of the night to me, though when I finally unglued my eyes it was easier, like putting on a torch with a slightly dodgy battery.

Mum and me all but ran up Chantry Avenue. You could see the short square tower of the parish church over the roofs in front of us, and then we were close to the bus station and the railway line. The crossing was open. On the farther side we turned down a short alley to the right which led out to the old Lindsey Hotel and the taxi rank. I heard an announcement over the loudspeaker, but I couldn't pick out what it said. With a sinking feeling, I thought it must be about the Doncaster train, I was too late! But very soon, I saw the Frasers, bunched together, waiting outside the concourse.

'Hurry up, Colin!' Becky shouted and Derek waved his hands frantically.

There was just time for Mum and Mr and Mrs Fraser to exchange greetings. They assured her that they'd see me home in the evening.

'Don't worry. We'll take a taxi and drop Colin off.'

Mum said she'd probably be up; if not, I knew where the spare key was.

Then, with an appraising look at me and something like a smile for all of us, my mother was gone and I was being hurried through the ticket barrier. I felt a babyish pang at the separation, but thankfully it didn't show.

'Come on!' said the Skipper. 'We've got to get over the bridge to catch our train. Give me your bag of goods, Colin, there's a pal!'

He added it to the assortment of things he was carrying and started leaping up the steps ahead of us. Derek and I kept at his heels, Becky and her mum a few yards behind but hurrying too.

So we did get the train we wanted, although we cut it pretty fine. Luckily, we found a compartment to ourselves.

After claiming their seats, Derek and Becky went into the corridor, watching out the window as the train slowly pulled away. The compartment felt damp and stale from acrid fumes. Mr Fraser joined his children and started pointing out local landmarks to them.

On the side of the compartment where Mrs Fraser was sitting, there were two pictures which attracted my attention. They showed trains travelling with great speed and urgency, cotton-white smoke billowing from their funnels. Nice to look at but a bit strange, as the trains seemed to be whizzing past Caernarvon in one picture, Conway in the other, when you'd imagine they should be coming to a stop, prior to setting down visitors who wanted to see the castles. They looked like trains out of *Thomas the Tank Engine*; all they lacked were those cartoon expressions of happiness or acute worry. Screwing my eyes up, I could detect vague figures on the platform, but no sign of the Fat Controller in his top hat and cutaway morning coat.

'Good, Colin. You're smiling now. That's a positive sign for the day. You looked tired and harassed before.'

'I'm still a bit tired.'

'That'll soon wear off.'

I didn't tell Mrs Fraser why I'd started smiling.

'I overslept a bit this morning,' I told her instead.

'Well, we were getting a bit anxious, but I always thought you'd make it. Derek grumbled, of course, saying how typical it was of you, which I thought rich coming from him. The struggles I have to get that lad up in the morning!'

'I'm sorry.'

'No need to be. You got there and now we're all going to have a fine day out.'

Looking over at my side of the compartment, Mrs Fraser saw that somebody had left a newspaper. It might have been yesterday's, or one bought that morning by a short-term traveller, someone who had got on at the small seaside terminus and got off at Ketilsby main station. Either way, I was sure the paper wouldn't have any cheerful news about Cuba.

I saw her frowning at it. I wanted to tell her not to worry, that everything would all turn out all right, but I couldn't even express the message in that scrimped, mysterious way I had to Dad the previous evening.

Suddenly, Mrs Fraser leant across and picked up the newspaper, too quick for me to get a glimpse of what it said. She screwed it up into a tight ball, then put it in the bag she'd set aside for rubbish.

'Some people dump their litter everywhere they go!' she said. That was the only comment she made, but just for a while she looked away from me and gazed thoughtfully out of the window. This gave me the chance to study her a bit.

There were lines across her forehead, quite strong ones, but the auburn hair was as fresh as a girl's and she was still pretty, although some people might have judged her too plump. Better that, however, than the leanness I couldn't help associating with resentment and bad temper. I envied Derek his capable, sunny-natured Mam and felt, not for the first time, that I'd have willingly swapped places with him. And that, understandably, made me feel guilty, summoning up corrective instances of when my mother had been good to me, even tender when she nursed me through bad illnesses.

I didn't think that God listened in all the time, like a universal snooper with a perfect bugging system but, out on His sound-patrol as He always was – somewhere He might catch me at an unlucky moment.

'Has Roy been in touch?'

'No, he hasn't. There'll probably be something in the post today, though,' I added sounding rather doubtful.

'Ring back home when we get to Leeds. Just to check.'

'We'll go to his place anyhow,' I said.

'Oh yes, you should do that,' said Mrs Fraser

supportively. 'You'll be seeing something new and that's nearly always interesting. But I'm sure Roy'll be expecting you. It'll be fun to see your student brother, won't it?'

I wasn't sure that 'fun' was the kind of word I associated with Roy, or at least my relationship with him. I nodded a rather feeble assent.

The rest of the Fraser family came back into the compartment and took their places. Becky began a game of I-spy and that kept us amused for a while. Now I felt that I was really coming alive at last and began to enjoy myself. I even managed to put the worry about Roy into sensible perspective. Or started to.

***

We got the connection in Doncaster with five minutes to spare, and then there was the shorter, second stage of the journey to Leeds. We decided against the light lunch we'd planned, because we'd tucked into the sandwiches and lemonade, plus some currant buns Mrs Fraser had brought, and didn't feel hungry. Now the Skipper fished in his pocket for some extra money in case Derek and I wanted a snack somewhere. I looked around for a phone-box. I got through to Mum on the second try – the coins at first not going into the slot properly – and found out that there'd been nothing from Roy in the post. I told her that we'd go up to Cross Chapel Street and see what the situation was.

Mr Fraser had gone to enquire about buses to Headingley. I began to feel nervous again, as if once more I was at the edge of safety.

When the Skipper returned, he told us that Derek and I needed to catch a number one bus, which went from very near the station. We were to look out for the big white building of the University on the left, soon after which there'd be an open space, Woodhouse Moor he'd been told it was called, and then we'd be almost there. We should ask to be set down as close to St Michael's Church as possible. Nobody seemed to know where Cross Chapel Street was, but it couldn't be far off. Hadn't Colin said that his brother had told him he could see the spire of St Michael's from his bedroom window?

'Perhaps we ought to buy a town plan,' suggested Mrs Fraser.

'No need!' said the Skipper breezily. 'They'll find it soon enough. Good test of the boys' initiative.'

'They're only twelve, Frank.'

'Nothing to worry about if they keep their heads,' said her husband.

'If!' sniffed Becky, relenting in part as she caught my look. 'Well, I'm sure *you* will, Colin.'

Derek repeated his sister's words in a silly, unctuous voice, making big eyes and fluttering his lashes.

Mrs Fraser separated the two of them, scolding them into a temporary peace.

'Lads used to go to sea that age,' mused the Skipper, which didn't do much to reassure me or Mrs Fraser.

'Roy said there's a cinema only a few steps from his place, so we should watch for that too,' I contributed.

'Right!' enthused the Skipper, as if I were getting into the spirit of things, showing distinct signs of promise. 'Now, listen, we'll see you onto the bus. Then we'll meet here, by the bookstall, at five o'clock. Got that Derek? Synchronise watches!' He laughed, in ebullient good spirits. 'Five sharp, absolutely no dawdle-time. Understood? If we miss our train, we'll be arriving back in Ketilsby about three in the morning, if that. I don't fancy a cold night on Doncaster station.'

We found the bus-stop straight away and it wasn't long before a No. 1 pulled in. I almost dropped my bag, with Roy's precious goodies inside, as I climbed aboard waving goodbye, but grabbed it just in time. Derek was clambering up the stairs when he bent down to shout back in reply to his father's reminder.

'Yes, five o'clock – we'll be there!'

Just past the big white university block with the tower – called the Parkinson Building somebody sitting nearby told us – the bus slowed down to a crawl because of heavy traffic and, looking across, I saw a pub on the right called the Eldon. The name rang a bell, something else Roy had told me about. Apparently, he went there with his friends several times a week, swigging down pints of Tetley's bitter in small, fuggy, crowded rooms, discussing politics and literature and old Soviet films. I remembered him mentioning Eisenstein in admiring tones, and Mark Donskoi's Gorky trilogy. I was impressed with these exotic-sounding names and wrote them down immediately afterwards in my diary.

'Derek, quick! That's the pub Roy goes to.'

Derek craned his head to gaze round as the bus moved slowly past.

'Doesn't seem much of a place to me,' he judged.

'You can't tell just from that!'

'I bet I can. Anyway, Woodhouse Moor coming up so keep your eyes peeled for the church.'

We made St Michael's our marker. Once we'd alighted we had to go further in, away from the bus route. It was easy enough, all the same. Someone showed us the way to North Lane and told us we needed to go down there, nearly to the Lounge Cinema, and we'd see Cross Chapel Street on the right.

Terrace houses, three storeys high and narrow. Roy had told me that there were other students living in his house, plus the landlady and her family. But when we spotted number three it didn't seem big enough to contain so many people. Perhaps it went a long way back.

We climbed the steps up to the door. There were only a couple but to me it felt like a dozen.

'Well, go on, knock,' said Derek impatiently, when I

hesitated. 'He's only your brother, he won't bite you. At any rate, perhaps he won't be at home.'

'Yes,' I said, sounding too much as if I hoped he wouldn't be.

***

But he was there all right.

The door opened only a few seconds after my knock and Roy appeared, his tall thin shape looming over us, face screwed up in vexation at being disturbed. But in a trice his expression changed to astonishment when he saw me.

'Colin, what on earth are you doing here? You can't have run away from home! Not that I'd blame you but...'

Derek laughed and Roy switched his attention to him.

'Who's this? Another one fled away into the storm?'

I made the introductions and told Roy that we were in Leeds on a day trip.

'Didn't you get my letter?'

'Letter? What letter?'

He puzzled for a moment or so, then his face broke into an expression of illumination. It looked too deliberate to be genuine, but I couldn't be sure. All I knew was that Roy was somehow enjoying the situation, now that his shock at seeing me was passing.

'Wait a minute! You've jogged my memory. A letter with a Ketilsby postmark did arrive. I assumed it was from Dad, moaning on about my politics or bolshy attitudes generally. I knew it couldn't be a cheque, because I'm not due anything for a while yet.'

'Didn't you even open it?' I asked, almost despairingly. I was angry as well, especially after all the trouble I'd gone to.

'Or perhaps I feared it was a bill? There are one or two people back in Ketilsby I'm still being dunned by.'

'But the handwriting! It couldn't have been anybody else's but mine.'

'Fooled me there, kid brother. It looked far too neat for you.'

Yet his snideness went as he saw me going red, on the edge of stammering a protest.

'You're right, though, Colin. It was my carelessness,' he admitted with a rare magnanimity, immediately compromised by the Latin tag he brought in at times like this: 'Mea culpa!' I'd learned that from him too. It made Latin sound like a light-hearted, self-exonerating thing.

'Oh, carelessness! That's what it's called these days, is it? Well, wouldn't be the first time,' came a clear, melodious girl's voice from within the room.

'Shut up, Deborah! Don't you start!' Roy called back.

Deborah? There'd been no mention of her when he'd been over in Ketilsby. Was she someone new on the scene or had Roy been 'hiding' her?

'Me – what?' asked Derek, puzzled. 'What does that mean when it's at home?'

'Mea culpa, mea maxima culpa,' Roy sang out, like a radiant sinner.

The scholar of the family explained and got Derek to repeat the phrase a few times, laughing and teasing him when he fumbled it. The attention was off me now and I could feel the redness and the threat of stammering get less.

'Roy!' called Deborah exasperatedly. 'Are you going to keep the boys out there all day? Bring them in.'

'Yes, yes, of course. We mustn't stand here gabbing on the doorstep.'

Roy moved back and ushered us past him.

The front door led directly into a sitting-room, bigger than I would have imagined. There was a dining-table not far from the door and a settee in front of the fireplace. The fire itself was banked up and roaring flame when we stepped in, like a fierce but hearty welcome.

I looked round curiously. I didn't really know what I was expecting – something *radical*, I supposed, some sign of the

Revolution to come. But there was none that I could see. It might have been a respectable, if slightly shabby sitting-room anywhere, of the old-fashioned sort: two armchairs with antimacassars and framed pictures on the wall of the stag-at-bay variety.

We had similar reproductions at home, which Roy had sneered at and tried to make us ashamed of. That's how I knew such noble stags and sunsets over Loch Lomond and so on were supposed to be trashy, although to be honest I quite liked things like that myself. How did Roy put up with them here? He was far less tolerant than I was, or less 'sloppy-minded', as he liked to put it. Even so, I'd have bet any money that he didn't try the snobby stuff with his landlady, however nice she was.

At our entrance, the girl turned round from her place on the settee and smiled at us. She had a long oval face, made even more so by the falls of straight, jet-black hair on either side. Her complexion in contrast was pale and I think she'd put on a little black make-up around the eyes to emphasise that. Her hands were slender and white, the fingers delicate yet strong too, like a pianist's. They clutched the back of the settee as she observed us.

'A visit!' she exclaimed with delight. 'And an unexpected one by the sound of it. Oh, that's wonderful! I was getting *so* bored.'

Her voice was not deep, but as if she were trying to force it to be so. It sounded good, though, and a touch trembly at times too, like an actress dealing with difficult moments on stage. She was posh all right, her father a doctor at least, yet nicely and naturally superior, her way of talking a strong contrast to Roy's self-conscious Leeds tones, his nasal syllables the most believable. Deborah might have the same views as Roy – I noticed they both wore CND badges – but it didn't appear as if she cared about sounding defiantly proletarian; nothing like Roy's act of class devotion.

'Deborah, this is my brother, Colin. I must have mentioned him to you. As for the name his chum carries, Derek...'

'Derek Fraser,' I put in.

'You never told me they breed such polite children in Ketilsby, Roy.'

'Oh yeah, every one of the runty, ill-favoured little bastards a natural Lord Fauntleroy!'

This crudely bluff good humour didn't come over quite right, but my brother would have got good marks for effort at least.

Pensively, his attention instantly distracted as if he were now cast a thousand miles away, Roy picked up a thick book from a small table by the door. On the cover there was a picture of a tuft-bearded, bespectacled man with a visionary stare: Leon Trotsky and his *History of the Russian Revolution*. Roy's place in the tome was marked by an envelope – which, when he rather clumsily opened the book, fluttered to the floor. I tried to hex my letter's flight, just by eye-power, so that it'd fall slower and be more of an accusation. As I'd expected from what he'd said on the doorstep, it was unopened.

My painstaking letter, ignored, serving as a bookmark!

'Well, well, well, what have we here? The vital message after all!'

He tore it open and read the contents swiftly.

Luckily, Deborah spoke up for me.

'Oh, Roy! You are a clot! Why don't you check your mail?'

It was a rebuke but tempered by affectionate forbearance. In a way, it put me in awe of Roy, that he could inspire feelings like that in such a beautiful, if odd-looking girl. She gave me a full, welcoming smile as I stared at her.

'Keep me company, won't you, Colin?'

She patted the settee, as though that had been my

established place for ages. As bashful and awkward as I'd ever been, I moved over to join her.

'De-bor-ah,' said Derek, sounding the name in an elongated manner. 'What do people call you? Debbie?'

'Hardly,' the girl said disdainfully, as if the very idea were repulsive.

'Why not?' persisted Derek, but he got no answer from her beyond a dismissive shrug.

'In actual fact,' said Roy, 'in Hebrew the name means "bee". So that always reminds me, Derek, to buzz around for a bit and then go for the nectar.'

He set up a loud drone before zooming frantically in Deborah's direction – much to Derek's amusement, although I found this newly playful Roy rather unnerving. Deborah leant firewards with a cry of mock-horror, clutching my hand. That bit was nice.

Once the game was over, I gave Roy the tin.

'Look at all this, Deborah!' he said, when he'd taken off the lid. 'A veritable cornucopia of culinary delights!'

He passed round the tin in an unwonted gesture of open-handedness. We were allowed to plunder the cherry-topped cakes to our hearts', and stomachs', delight. Everything was up for grabs – bar the Scotch eggs, which Roy reserved for himself.

'My favourite! No one makes Scotch eggs like my mother. A family recipe finessed down the generations' – this would have surprised Mum – 'plus that touch of kitchen magic that only she can provide.'

I couldn't help looking at Roy with incredulity. Back in Ketilsby he was never given to lavish personal praise like this, however humorous. Stern eulogies of Lenin and Trotsky were more his line.

Deborah released my hand and rose from the settee. She was tall and slim, with hips scarcely wider than those of Derek and me. She wore a green jumper over fawn-coloured slacks. Roy had started explaining the meaning of 'cornucopia' to Derek, who was busy nodding his head in comprehension while stuffing his face.

'Nescafé?' asked Deborah. She moved over to an electric kettle on a trolley at the back of the room.

From the dining-table, at either end of which Derek and he had seated themselves, Roy directed a few questions to me about the situation at home. Still rather tongue-tied in front of Deborah, I wasn't very forthcoming.

'I suppose one could conclude from your taciturn remarks, Brüderlein, that things are no better and possibly only a little worse?'

'Yes. More or less.'

'More or less. That really clarifies things.'

Once more Deborah came to my defence.

'Colin's made the effort to come and see you, Roy.'

'So he has. And carrying the precious Scotch eggs in this workaday chalice!' He tapped the bottom of the tin rapidly as if it were a drum. 'For that alone, all his sins – past, present and future – are forgiven him. Remind me to write out a plenary indulgence before the lads depart.'

Inevitably, the talk came round to Cuba. Yet, although it struck me that Roy and Deborah could doom-monger with the best of them, they seemed strangely calm in the face of the crisis – after all, they hadn't had the assurance I'd been given, those shapes in the whale-mist. Roy was full of the telegram appealing for peace which Bertrand Russell had sent to Khrushchev and Khrushchev's reply. He was sure that the old sage's contribution and the Soviet leader's measured response would have a beneficial effect. Even then that seemed naive to me, but I was impressed all the same with the daring notion that philosophers, and ninety years old at that, could help to change history for the better.

'Khrushchev has made a bad gamble,' Roy told us. 'But who knows what pressure he's under in the Presidium? Besides, looking at it all in the cold light of reason, why shouldn't the Soviets have rockets in Cuba if the Americans have them in Turkey?'

'You'll never get the Yanks to agree with that!' said Deborah. 'Cuba's their backyard.'

'But that's Fidel's point!' argued Roy. 'That the US *shouldn't* just regard Cuba as its fief. They have no right to meddle there. Things have moved on from Batista's time.'

'Fidel – that's Castro, isn't it?' interjected Derek. 'The bearded bloke, like a beatnik except he wears army uniform.'

Roy and Deborah laughed at that, me too. Derek was obviously taken with Castro's dramatic, swaggering style; his policies would have to come a poor second.

Deborah had returned to the settee with her coffee and mine, so we were twisted round and sipping at the hot liquid while we listened to Roy pontificating.

'Who needs Bertrand Russell?' she smiled at me satirically, but I noted that she hung on Roy's every word all the same. He concluded his oration by positing some kind of accord between Kennedy and Khrushchev, though nothing like the one I'd witnessed on the waste ground.

Deborah stroked me lightly on the cheek, which I found exciting but somehow shameful, as though the gesture revealed a weakness in me. 'Skin smoother than silk.' She turned back to the fire and called over her shoulder: 'Colin's features are much finer than yours, Roy. Nose, cheekbones, chin – everything.'

'That'll change if he ever has need of a razor and becomes a full-blooded male!'

'Goodness, it's Tarzan now, is it?'

A little later, when Derek asked Deborah where she came from, she replied vaguely: 'Oh, just south of London. Stockbroker belt. Nowhere important.'

'We're off to London tomorrow,' Roy told us. 'But not to see Deborah's parents. We'll be crashing down at a friend's.'

'Darkest Soho,' put in Deborah, with an air of

naughtiness.

'Have you something on in London?' inquired Derek.

'Demonstration against the Cuban thing,' said Roy, 'the sheer madness of nuclear brinkmanship. '

'At least we can help to show what people think,' contributed Deborah.

'Some people,' corrected Roy. He fingered his CND badge and then, taking his hand away, pointed at it, as though identifying himself by means of this stark black and white symbol.

'Because it's interesting how the Great British Public reacts when they see this.'

'What do you mean?'

It was me urging him on this time.

'Well, you get the *Daily Express*-type Tories shrieking into your face: "If you don't like it here, you bloody student layabout, then go and live in your beloved Russia!" That kind of crap. But a surprising number of people are sympathetic, if timid about it. They almost *whisper* their support in your ear! Of course, they'd baulk at actually demonstrating alongside the rest of us. Not quite respectable, don't you know!'

'Respectable!' laughed Deborah gaily, as though long since free of that stifling concept.

'But they should take a closer look at the Aldermaston marchers,' Roy said. 'Plenty of well-mannered decency there, Quakers amongst the Communists, troubled bank managers marching with solid union officials: one right cause, one uplifting resolve!'

He was half-clenching his fist and moving it heavenwards, but unfortunately there was no soap-box to complete the picture. He had an attentive audience though, however small.

But Derek had an urgent practical question.

'Are you going down by train? That'll cost you.'

'No, Derek,' said Roy, a little impatiently, brought down

to banal everyday matters. 'We're going to hitch-hike.'

'Have you got a picture of that Cuban bloke? He's not first cousin to that one over there, is he?'

My embarrassing friend pointed at the image of Trotsky on the cover of the book.

'Not by blood he isn't.' retorted Roy. 'Ideologically, Trotsky and Fidel? Well, that's arguable. Yes, I do have a poster of Castro, big cigar, army fatigues and all, but it's upstairs. That's the house-rule, Mrs Apley allows us to put up whatever stuff we like – short of the obscene! – in our bedrooms but not here. It's our sitting-cum-dining room to use, but it's her decor and remains so.'

He grimaced round at the deer-in-the-glen pictures, the sunsets, the rippling becks with their peculiarly metallic flashes to denote movement of water. They were all very neatly framed.

'Come on, Derek. I'll show you that poster.'

They made for the back door of the room which led to the stairs and, on our floor, the Apleys' kitchen and parlour. Roy called back that they wouldn't be long.

'You stay with me, Colin, unless you've got a thing about weirdy beardies,' said Deborah. 'Roy's never going to have face fungus, if I have any say in the matter – whoever his heroes are.'

'Don't you admire them?'

'Naturally I do! But bearded politics is one thing and scratchy skin's quite another.'

After Roy and Derek had finished clomping up the steep staircase, Deborah and I got talking properly, and I felt more and more at ease with her. There was nearly always an amused air when she studied me, but any open teasing was reserved for Roy and, once or twice, for Derek. She told me how glad she was I had such a good friend although, in her experience, 'Livewires, even if loveable, can also be exhausting.'

That made me smile.

'What?' She feigned surprise and incredulity. 'Are you saying that's true of Derek?'

'Yes!'

'Still, you wouldn't be without him, would you?'

She didn't need me to answer that.

Deborah told me about the lecturers she had, the wide range of university societies you could join, the celebrated speakers who were invited and the rare films that were shown in the Students' Union.

'I mean, they'd not be all that uncommon if people treated film intelligently, but you're hardly likely to find *The Battleship Potemkin* playing at the local fleapit, are you?'

And then she was off describing a folk club that she and Roy enjoyed going to, the performances held in a big room above a 'boozer', as she put it, not far from City Station.

'We had Dominic Behan last week,' she said. 'He was terrific.'

Some time ago, I'd seen this bloke's picture in the paper: cheeks and jowls swollen, eyes like buttons, lips made thin as though being swallowed by the bloated flesh around them. There was a caption beneath the picture about his being a famous writer and how he'd been involved in a spectacular drunken episode. It sounded like this was the latest in a long line of them.

'I didn't know he was a singer too,' I said.

'Well, he does sing, and he's very talented. But...'

'I thought he wrote plays for the theatre.'

'No, no,' said Deborah, 'you mean *Brendan* Behan, his brother. Dominic's as lean as Brendan's gross. They both have a wonderful way with words, though.'

She said she'd lend me an EP she'd bought by Dominic Behan, when she'd finished learning the songs on it.

'Are you interested in singing, Colin?'

I said that I wasn't really, not so much, and from there it wasn't far to confiding that I preferred writing stories. I was hesitant at first, but when she accepted what I said quite seriously, as if we were equals, I grew bolder. Hitherto, I'd only told Derek about them. Now Deborah was paying me a flattering attentiveness, making me feel very special.

'You must send me some,' she said. 'Don't be shy about it because I honestly would like to read them. Here's my address.' She scribbled it on a scrap of paper – '14 Clarendon Park Road, top flat' – which she then pushed down in my jacket top pocket. 'You needn't worry about Big Brother.'

We heard the two of them coming down the stairs. They both seemed invigorated when they entered the room, Derek going on excitedly about the pictures and books Roy had shown him. If he'd gone upstairs as a 'normal' boy, whatever that means, now he strutted about the room like a proto-revolutionary, particularly when my brother stuck a beret on him with a small red star fixed to it.

I couldn't help feeling angry at the way Derek took centre-stage, his Look-at-me! display. It was his nature but I felt it badly after my close talk with Deborah; jealous fear of being pushed back into the shadows. So, before I could bite my lip, I said to him, in a nasty, snide voice: 'A bit different from Billy Fury, Derek.'

'Billy who?' asked Deborah, puzzled.

'Fury.'

'Billy Fury. Is he a friend of yours?'

'I wish he was!' said Derek wistfully, stopping in his tracks. 'No, he's a pop-singer, the greatest since Elvis.'

'Oh yes, I think I've seen him on telly,' said Roy, but not sounding too sure about it.

'I do an impersonation of Billy Fury,' announced Derek, smirkily.

I groaned, hating him at that moment. But then I thought that the Royal Command performance had to come sometime, so long as it was just the once and didn't lead to a bagful of encores that would ruin the afternoon. Anyway, I deserved most of the blame. It was me who'd foolishly cued him in.

At least Derek had the small grace to take off his red star beret when he performed. Deborah and Roy attended closely, fascinated but more than a little appalled, I think, at the sheer brassiness of Derek's act: the exaggeratedly stylized mime, the caressing of the invisible microphone, the strained light voice trying to imitate the compelling, plaintive purr of the deeper and much more famous one.

'Phew!' exclaimed Roy when Derek at last came to a stop. Roy wiped his brow with the back of his hand. There wasn't any sweat there, but I knew what he meant.

Both he and Deborah applauded. I didn't even go through the motions.

'This boy's got talent – sign him up!' she said, through the corner of her mouth like some tough American impresario.

'It's clear what you're going to become, young man,' Roy said. Then he grew thoughtful and stroked his chin. 'But, you know, you need better music. People shouldn't have to settle for this kind of crud. '

'I don't settle for it,' proclaimed Derek indignantly. 'I love it!'

'It's what they go for, Roy,' put in Deborah, taking Derek's side which prompted me to say that I didn't go for it all that much.

'You wouldn't!' shouted Derek, turning on me as if I were the worst traitor in the world. 'I suppose you prefer that horrible fiddle and piano-playing in Hinkley's.'

'Maybe I've just seen you do your Billy Fury bit too often, that's all,' I replied, taken aback by his harshness.

'And maybe you've got cloth ears and eyes as blind as pebbles!'

Roy intervened and told Derek and me to calm down.

'What I meant was, why can't boys like you have songs that are just as tuneful but less moronic? Apart from anything else, music can be an extremely useful social tool.

Even with Elvis,' he mused, 'at least at the beginning. That raw sexual energy! He taught people that fucking was good.'

After this resounding use of the taboo word, Derek and I fell uneasily silent. Even he didn't come out with that term much, and then only somewhere like the school playground or on our way to the Shore Road when he wanted to garland Svenny Olsen, or some other absent hate-figure, with all the abuse possible – and shock me as well, two pleasures in one. He never came out with 'fuck' in his home or mine, not even in the privacy of our bedrooms, as if there too walls had the proverbial ears.

I thought Deborah might chide Roy for being so coarse, but she took him up in quite a different way.

' "Raw sexual energy"!' she said derisively. 'Roy, have you been at the D.H. Lawrence again?'

'Not recently. I wonder if Elvis read him, down in Mississippi. Don't think so, somehow. A great writer, Lawrence, if you put aside his Führer complex and the religious balderdash he was so fond of.'

'Is that the bloke who wrote the dirty books?' asked Derek.

'No, it isn't,' said Roy. 'That's what some people claim, of course – the pathetic Victorian leftovers!'

Both Derek and I had heard of D.H. Lawrence because of the *Lady Chatterley* trial two years previously. Derek had told me that at the newsagent's he worked for sometimes, the proprietor had sold piles of the book, each copy wrapped in plain brown paper.

'Who to?'

'Men. All men. Most of them middle-aged, sidling into the shop with furtive, dopey grins on their faces.'

'Right, boys,' said my brother now. He could have been young Mr Marston at that moment, calling his class firmly to order. 'I'll introduce you to something that's intelligent, melodious and easy to learn.'

'Oh goody, a singsong!' enthused Deborah, clapping her

hands like a small girl in anticipation of a treat.

So we started on 'The Hammer Song', Roy belting out the words and repeating them in order for Derek and me to pick them up. Soon we four were announcing to the world our intention of hammering out justice and freedom and brotherly love, making a fine old racket, which Deborah at last tried to modify – without success. In fact, Derek really got into the spirit of the thing, banging rhythmically on the dining-room table, to indicate the redemptive strength of the hammer.

Deborah finally stuck her hands over her ears as the row got even worse, our high voices even riding above Roy's powerful baritone at times. As though to give her support, the door at the back opened and a woman's face appeared round it, plump, bespectacled and smiling. She made quietening motions with one hand while waving round the other as if conducting a choir. Pausing, she nodded in a friendly fashion to Derek and me and then was gone as quickly as she'd shown herself.

Our singing petered out on a self-conscious, raggedy note.

Now Deborah took charge.

'Getting a bit wild there, although our hearts, if not our lungs, were in the right place. Mrs Apley's a lovely person and the last thing we want to do is antagonise her. Don't forget,' she said, pointing to Roy but looking at Derek and me, 'she's got four of these young men to look after. It's a good thing the other three are the kind of students who work long hours in libraries and laboratories and come back exhausted.'

'Well, I have been known to put in a few hours at the Brotherton library myself,' said Roy, pretending to be miffed.

'So it's my turn to choose,' continued Deborah. 'Let's have something in a softer mode.'

It was one of the songs she and Roy had learned on the

Aldermaston marches and it sounded almost as soothing as a lullaby until you listened carefully to the words. The only verse I can remember, all these years later, is the following:-

' "Don't you hear the H-bombs' thunder

Echo like the crack of doom?

While they rend the skies asunder,

Fall-out makes the earth a tomb".'

They were very solemn, these lines, but the beauty of Deborah's singing seemed to offset that. At the very moment she was prophesying universal destruction, she was somehow promising a full, rich life as well. I thought immediately of what I'd seen in the whale-mist the previous evening and wondered whether, if the confidence between us grew from its good beginnings that day, I'd ever tell her about that.

Derek and I were getting hungry again now. Deborah made us a thick chunky sandwich round each and Roy passed round his box of goodies again, (still reserving the rest of the Scotch eggs as his special treat).

The remaining time in the house went happily by. Roy and Deborah had intended to show us round the Students' Union, but that'd be cutting it fine. Soon we'd have to set off back to the station. Roy and Deborah said they'd come with us.

At the front door, as we stood ready to go down to the bus-stop, my brother suddenly checked himself and went back inside.

'Half a mo. Be with you in a jiffy,'

We heard him going upstairs. When he re-appeared he was carrying two small CND badges, exactly like the ones that he and Deborah wore. These he pinned to the lapels of our coats – Derek's and mine – like medals, as if he were bestowing symbols of valour on us. His manner was jokey (he pretended to be a rather unlikely French general, giving us both a mock-Gallic kiss) but I knew that was like a balance to the seriousness of the gesture.

Twisting the lapel up, I examined the badge: a white sign on a black background which looked at first like a bird's claw or an arrow. Roy told us that these were the semaphore signs, joined together, of N and D: nuclear disarmament.

It was strange wearing this badge at first. I felt singled out, proud even, but also embarrassed. Obviously, Derek didn't have that problem. With envy, I watched him swaggering along towards the bus-stop, sticking his chest out so that no-one except the sightless could miss his new acquisition. I think he only wished that the badge was ten times as big and illuminated as well!

When we got to City Station, we were already some minutes late and I could imagine the Skipper pacing up and down, consulting his watch every few seconds, muttering away in growing annoyance. But, less interestingly if less threateningly too, Mr Fraser was not even beginning to fume. Perhaps he'd made allowance for a few minutes tardiness from the beginning.

This time there was no need for a hectic dash to our platform. Introductions were carried out, pleasantries swapped, and then Roy and Deborah accompanied the Frasers and me to the barrier where the ticket inspector was waiting.

Saying goodbye, Roy patted me on the shoulder in a rare brotherly move and told me to thank Mum for all the nice things she'd sent. He planned to come over to Ketilsby fairly soon, he said, and quite probably – he gave an unwontedly shy glance at Deborah – 'not alone.' He asked me to be discreet but, if I wanted, I could 'casually' mention that he now had a regular girlfriend.

'Yes, you prepare the way, Colin,' Deborah chimed in, bending down to me. 'You'll be good at that, if you put your mind to it.' She kissed me on the forehead and clasped my face in her hands. I'd been hoping for some sign from her and would have been disappointed had there been nothing. Well, this was it! –and more than I'd expected. I think I travelled on air for much of the journey home.

After Deborah had finished, Becky looked across at me peevishly, her parents smiled as at something surprising but touching and Derek, predictably, grinned and guffawed like the worst kind of playground oaf. When we got on to the Doncaster train, he said in a stage-whisper behind me, breathing smells of coffee and cake into my neck: 'Looks like Little Boy has got a new Mummikins!' With the train gathering speed, he tried to make the final word fit the rhythm of it, until Mrs Fraser rebuked him and the Skipper cuffed his son into silence. Even in that semi-playful mood, a touch of the Skipper's paw was not to be taken lightly.

XIX. Badges and Wrestlers

There were two things of note on the way back to Ketilsby.

First, the CND badges Roy had given us.

After we'd described our day to the others and they'd told us what they'd been doing, Becky set up a clamour about them. She wanted a badge too, and got me to promise that I'd ask Roy to send another. It was against my better judgement because I felt Mr and Mrs Fraser's disapproval. This soon became open.

'No, Becky, you're far too young,' her mother intervened.

'Then the boys must be too young as well!' she protested.

'Yes, I think they are,' the Skipper said forthrightly. 'No offence to Roy, Colin. I'm sure he's sincere in his beliefs. Who isn't something of a communist when they're that age?'

'But he isn't,' I said. 'Not a paid-up member. He does agree with some of their ideas, though.'

'So do I,' the Skipper replied, 'in theory at least. It's the practice I worry about.'

'He didn't mean anything bad, Mr Fraser.'

'Of course not!' he reassured me. 'All this peace-marching and so on – there's something honourable about it, even if many folk reckon it's naive. But you lads need to grow up a bit before...' He broke off, struggling for an appropriate word: 'Before you become partisan like that. Just give it time – and much consideration.'

'Do you want us to take these off then, Dad?' asked Derek, strangely meek for him.

But before the Skipper could say anything, Mrs Fraser broke in.

'I've got an idea. A compromise. We English are supposed to be good at that, although you wouldn't know it sometimes.'

She came over to where Derek and I were sitting, deftly unpinned the badges and as deftly fixed them to the inside of our lapels.

'Now they're concealed from all suspicious or doubting eyes, but if you want to be reminded of this CND business, all you've got to do if flip the lapels to the reverse. It'll be like a silent password.'

Mr Fraser seemed quite tickled at the idea.

'This way you'll soon recognise your kind. Like Masons,' he added, a bit confusingly for me.

At first, Derek and I flicked the badges to and fro as though our lives depended on it. Becky enjoyed the game hugely and, not to be excluded from the action, bounced over to our side of the compartment, seizing hold of my lapel and twisting it round again and again, to answer her brother's display of his badge. The way she was tugging at my best jacket, I feared that she'd wrench it out of shape, wondering what Mum would say if she did. She and Derek were going on now as if they were playing Snap. It was even more monotonous than the usual game, and I was glad when her interest in this diversion started to flag. Besides, she was too close to me, almost in my lap, and I felt nervous about that.

Letting go of my lapel for the last time, Becky asked me what the design on the badge actually meant. Somehow, we hadn't explained that and, even more surprisingly, she hadn't asked.

'Isn't it obvious, you nitwit?' said Derek cockily.

I told her about the semaphore. Becky sat back again, between her parents, a thoughtful expression on her face. She claimed she'd been taught some semaphore and wasn't sure my explanation was correct. I told her that that was Roy's story.

'I can't swear it is correct, but Roy's usually pretty good on information.'

'And he's a university student,' said Mrs Fraser. 'He should know a lot.'

Roy's educational status seemed to carry weight with Becky and, after due frowning reflection, she conceded that Roy was probably right.

'Probably!' jeered Derek. 'Don't take any notice of her, Colin. She's only trying to put the wind up you. I know her tricks.'

Before another dispute could break out between them and develop into a full-blown squabble, Mr Fraser mentioned that there was a wrestling tournament at the Pier the following evening. This was the second important thing on the return journey and, as it turned out, more significant than we could ever have imagined at the time.

Just then we were coming into Doncaster, and the Skipper and Derek didn't properly get into discussing the attractions on the bill until we were settled on the Ketilsby train.

None of the wrestlers' names, often outlandish, even preposterous, meant anything to me. However, I found it interesting that it was the villainous fighters who attracted Derek and his father the most, even as they busily condemned their dirty tricks. Each criticism came to seem like a strange sort of compliment.

Mrs Fraser was scornful of all this wrestling talk.

'You two, you're never happy unless you're watching somebody being bashed about. Well, you won't find me going to gawp at all that rubbish! Becky and I will nip round to Aunt Rose's – she's always glad to see us. Or if not that, then we'll just stay in and find something to watch on telly.'

Neither prospect pleased Becky, who had never been to the wrestling yet and clearly felt that it was high time she became initiated.

'Give over yowling, Becky!' Mrs Fraser said impatiently. 'All those disgusting fat men throwing themselves around and pretending to be hurt!'

'They're not all fat and they *do* get hurt sometimes,' objected Derek.

'Why can't I go, Mam? I want to!'

Becky was tired and fractious and seemed to be working herself up into a tantrum.

Mrs Fraser looked across at me. I was learning to recognise that special gleam in her eye when she was nursing a fresh, and perhaps daring, idea.

'What about you, love? What do you think of all this wrestling tomfoolery?'

Shrugging my shoulders, I said that I didn't know anything about it, apart from what Derek had told me and the holds he'd tried on me. Inadvertently, these last words struck a humorous chord with everybody, even the mithering Becky.

'It's a wonder he's not broken every piece of your body!' exclaimed the Skipper. 'Never let him put an Irish whip on you, or the scissors. Could be fatal!'

'Derek tried pressure points on either side of my neck once,' I told them, 'but it was useless. He said it'd paralyse me, but I hardly felt anything.'

Becky squealed with pleasure at this blunt exposure of her brother's failure.

'I just hadn't practised enough, that's all!' retorted Derek defiantly. 'You wait till next time, Colin Palmer! You'll be a quivering heap on the floor, I can promise you that now!'

'Derek, why are you so bloodthirsty?' asked his mother. 'I thought Colin was supposed to be your best friend.'

'Who says he's not? He's hardly my worst enemy, is he?'

'You lay a finger on Colin and you'll have me to deal with!' warned Becky, putting on a fierce yet stony look and wagging a stern finger before her brother. She was imitating

Ena Sharples from *Coronation Street* and it made us all laugh, Derek included.

And then, after we'd calmed down, the Skipper suggested that I go with him and Derek to the Pier. After a little hesitation, I said I'd like to, providing my parents agreed.

'If Colin's going as well...' Becky left her sentence unfinished. Its message was clear enough, however, and it was one I was pretty sure her mother had anticipated. Perhaps Mrs Fraser thought it'd be a means of giving in without loss of face; also that Becky and I, unschooled in the skills and tricks of professional wrestling, might help to bolster each other's resolve.

'All right then, Becky. I'm not willing to argue any further. You can go, but be it on your own head. Don't blame me if you get bad dreams afterwards. Is that understood, my girl?'

'Yes, Mam. There won't be any problems, honestly.'

Becky looked very smug, now that she'd got her own way. She grinned across at me as if we'd planned it together.

Mrs Fraser said: 'Just ask your parents, then, Colin. I'm sure it'll be all right.'

'Get yourself round to our place a good half hour before the bouts begin,' the Skipper instructed me, 'and we'll see you home afterwards. We can take the car. Plenty of parking near the Pier.'

'We're monopolising you,' said Becky, proud of the polysyllabic word.

Derek seemed mischievously intrigued at the idea.

'We may as well kidnap old Cleverclogs here and now and have done with it,' he said.

'This kind of wrestling is a show, Becky,' advised the Skipper. 'Not unlike variety at times. And if it does get a bit rough, then I'll put my sombrero over your face to shield you.'

'You don't have a sombrero,' said Becky with surprise,

falling into the trap.

'Strewth, so I don't! I could have sworn I bought a huge one last time I was in Mexico City.'

'You were never in Mexico City!' said Becky, happily playing along and snuggling up to her father.

'Are you sure? Well, we'll find something, to be on the safe side.'

I thought to myself that if he just stretched his great red hand across Becky's face, the palm alone would be enough to screen her from virtually any shock.

'Why don't we ask Grand-Dad to come with us?' asked Derek eagerly. 'He likes the wrestling. '

Everyone thought this was a good idea.

'Of course, he might be there anyway,' said Mr Fraser.

'No, I don't think he'd bother going by himself,' commented Mrs Fraser, sadly. 'Apart from his preaching, he's too much alone these days. Since the great quarrel with Mr Marston, he's had no one to pal around with.' She sighed, adding: 'Yes, yes, you take him! Even that ropey old knockabout at the Pier will do him good.'

'Grand-Dad knows a lot about boxing too.'

'Oh, we've all heard about that,' said the Skipper archly, hinting at the times when Mr Reynolds, angry red quiff to the fore, did battle with the unrulier members of his al fresco congregation. I wondered idly whether he had official permission to preach so close to the dock gates, or whether the police didn't bother him because he'd become something of a fixture. Maybe, with hazy memories of Sunday school, they even thought that it might have some improving effect, the odd brawl to the contrary.

After a period in which Derek, Becky and I were getting drowsy and dozing off for odd minutes before we jerked into wakefulness again, Mrs Fraser announced that she could see the lights of the factories along the river. It wouldn't be long before we were home now.

I followed her gaze as she peered out of the window but

between me and the lights I chiefly caught a shadowy version of my own face. For a moment or so, it was as if I were a ghost: just a vague outline, with pits for eyes and hollows beneath my cheekbones and the dark landscape flowing through it, at its far verge the blobs and smears of white and orange.

Then, as if he needed to make sure he'd settled all Becky's apprehensions, perhaps mine too, the Skipper told us an anecdote that took us past the outskirts of Ketilsby, right up to when the train finally pulled into the station, grinding and wheezing to a halt.

His story concerned another wrestling tournament he'd been to at the Pier – some years ago now when Derek was too small to accompany him. The Skipper was friendly with one of the promoters, 'the moneybags who doled out the wages,' and, apparently, it had been an evening of great entertainment. 'Bodies all over the place,' he enthused. 'At least two monsters on the bill, and a tag-match where all four fighters threw caution to the winds, punching and kicking and jabbing...'

'Frank!' warned Mrs Fraser.

'Don't worry, Irene,' the Skipper reassured her. 'I'm coming to the point now and it's a very nice one.'

After the show was over, the promoter took Mr Fraser backstage with him to pay off the wrestlers. The Skipper claimed that, with their ferocious antics fresh in his mind, he expected to find the grapplers still at loggerheads, being restrained by their handlers from inflicting further damage on each other, but -

'Not on your life!'

Looking over the promoter's shoulder, Mr Fraser saw that all the fighters, from stars to unknowns, were sitting peacefully around a long trestle table, eating massive plates of fish and chips and drinking mugs of tea. They looked tired but somehow reflective, like baffled, bruised philosophers, as they focussed now on their food and drink.

The next amazing thing for the Skipper was that they didn't appear so much like a collection of men who'd *made* peace, but rather as though they'd never been out of humour with each other in the first place; not even the slightest hint of a grudge.

'And the ugliest, most vicious-looking wrestler, the leader of one of the tag teams – well, at that very second, he was leaning over the table towards an opponent whose ribs he'd been trying to crack only minutes before, politely asking him if he'd pass the pepper and salt!'

The story pleased us all in various ways. It made me and Mrs Fraser laugh as at some happy absurdity, Derek enjoyed scoffing, believing and yet not believing his father's account at the same time, the Skipper was simply content that his tale had gone down satisfactorily and appeared to be having the desired effect, and as for Becky – she sat quietly, a broad smile on her face as if she were visualising the scene, detail for detail, most particularly the courteous passing of the salt and pepper after such turmoil in the ring.

XX. TOOTHACHE AND BIBLICAL MATTERS

There was something wrong with Grand-Dad Reynolds from the beginning. He stumbled out of his house almost as if pushed. At his side Derek, who'd been sent to ring the doorbell, was chattering away but the old man, clutching a scarf over his jaw, took no notice of him whatsoever. He groaned mightily as he eased himself into the car beside Mr Fraser. We three children were sitting together at the back.

'What's the matter?' asked the Skipper, alarmed as we all were now.

'Toothache!' growled Mr Reynolds. 'Free of it for over a year and I even had a check-up recently. They didn't find much, but they couldn't have been looking very hard, could they? And now it flares up right after my dinner, with the dratted filling dropping out!'

'Lucky you didn't swallow it, Grand-Dad,' said Becky.

'Well, if I had, at least I'd know where it was. It rolled off the table onto the floor and I just can't find the thing anywhere. A great clump of metal like that.'

'They'll make you another filling,' the Skipper said soothingly.

'The trouble is, I can't get to a dentist until Monday.'

'There must be an emergency service.'

'Probably is, I don't know. Anyway, I'll hang on till next week. I'm not going to be thrown down by pain.'

'You can do it, Grand-Dad!' Derek encouraged him. 'You're an old soldier.'

'Well, strictly speaking, an old sailor. And they're even tougher! But you're right too, Derek, I am a sort of soldier. Enlisted in God's army, the best the world could ever have!'

For some reason, this declaration made Mr Reynolds laugh. Perhaps it was the idea of one of God's warriors being tormented by something so mundane as a rotting tooth that set him off, I couldn't tell and didn't even have time to ponder the question then, because we were faced with a more immediate peril.

Mr Reynolds' bellow of a laugh had been directed at the window screen which, given the foul reek that suddenly assailed it, I'm surprised didn't shatter instantly into terrified fragments. The rest of us got the ricochet and that was bad enough.

'Good God!' cried the Skipper. 'The charnel house beckons. Are you sure you're all right for the wrestling, Dad?'

'Of course I am, Frank! The tooth's giving me gyp, but it's nothing I can't handle. A bit of grappling should take my mind off my infirmities. Children!' he called to the back as the Skipper gunned the car into action. 'Now, think of your Bible – tell me, who did Jacob wrestle with?'

'The angel,' replied Becky promptly, quicker off the mark than me. 'Like the sign of God.'

'Spot on!' said her grandfather. 'There'll be a shilling for that.'

'Well, I'd have got there in the end,' grumbled Derek. 'I use deduction, Sherlock Holmes-style. Takes a bit of time, that's all.'

'Here's a chance to equal the score then,' said Mr Reynolds conciliatingly. 'What part of Jacob's body did the angel touch?'

'Most of it, if they were wrestling,' replied Derek very reasonably, although we knew it wasn't the answer the old man wanted.

'Point taken,' Mr Reynolds conceded. 'So let me re-phrase that. Ouch!' He pressed his hand tightly over his scarf, as if trying to draw out the pain by force of touch. 'I mean, the mark that stayed with Jacob for ever. The hollow of his...? Come on, it's in *Genesis*, I'm giving it away!'

I knew the answer to this one too, being also a Sunday school cleverclogs. But to my sneaky satisfaction, Becky was hesitating, gnawing at her lips. My instinct was to bring out the right answer and take the credit, yet I must have discovered an intellectual generosity within myself somewhere because, instead, I hastily whispered to Derek: 'The thigh! The hollow of the *thigh*!'

'You're helping him, Colin!' protested Becky.

'No teaming-up back there!' commanded Mr Reynolds, twisting round, his red quiff gleaming in the streetlights like the crest of a helmet. His stern eyes caught my guilty ones.

'Who's this, then? Oh, I know him all right. That nice lad you brought round, Derek.'

'He's not so nice when you get to know him.'

'Yes, he is!' Becky insisted, rising to the bait. 'Don't you believe Derek, Grand-Dad.'

Mr Reynolds was about to say something but the tooth took over again.

'Have you got anything for that?' asked the Skipper.

'I had a glass of rum just before you came. And I dosed myself with tooth tincture which seems to be burning away half my mouth.'

'Strewth! Well, that little cocktail, plus the decay, must account for the fragrant aroma. Look, Dad, you can always nip out to the bar if it gets too bad. A good strong Scotch – undiluted – that'll help more than all the rum and tincture jollop.'

'I might do that, Frank.' Mr Reynolds paused for a moment and then said: 'Anyhow, I don't think we'll see many angels wrestling tonight. Our old Pier Pavilion's hardly Peniel, is it?'

'Peniel?' queried Derek.

'Where Jacob and the angel fought.'

'I guessed that, Grand-Dad,' said Becky smugly.

'Like heck she did!' her brother scoffed.

We'd turned onto the Promenade, at the far end from the Pier, after travelling the Skipper's special 'short cut'. Mapping it out stretch for stretch, it was actually a touch longer than if we'd come straight down the Shore Road, but it was one of Mr Fraser's little vanities that he was skilled in knocking the edge off journey times, as if that proved something.

In a longer intermission than usual between one stabbing pain and the next, old Mr Reynolds chose to tell us a salutary story.

'I was trying to reach out to a few endangered souls by the Docks yesterday,' he said, 'when this lad was brought to me by his headmaster. He'd been in trouble but the teacher saw signs of good in him, reckoning that the Gospel message might not fall on stony ground. In return, perhaps I could find something useful and worthy for the lad to do. But my first sight of him – he made the biggest deckies look like saplings! And the glare! As if he were looking for someone who'd done him the worst wrong in the world.'

A strong suspicion – in fact, a near-certainty — began to form in my mind, Derek's too, I'd bet.

'When those two arrived, I was preaching about the camel and the eye of the needle.'

He paused, as if he expected Derek to ask him to explain, but my friend had had enough of showing ignorance and kept silent.

'The lesson being never to put your trust in wealth – never to believe that you can buy yourself into grace,' pronounced Mr Reynolds.

I didn't think that, on our pocket money, we were in any danger of falling prey to that temptation, but who knew what fortune might bestow on us?

'Camels and needles and grace, eh?' said the Skipper dryly. 'Couldn't fail with your average deckie.'

I smiled to myself when I considered how my mother might have been less reluctant to let me go to the wrestling tournament had she known I was going to get free biblical instruction on the way.

'That hulking great lad!' continued Mr Reynolds. 'I wouldn't have believed it to begin with, but he turned up trumps in our prayers like a zealot of old! Even so, my choice of "Onward, Christian Soldiers" as the next hymn wasn't quite right.'

'Why not?' asked Becky, starting to hum the tune.

'Because he took the soldiering a mite too seriously. There were a couple of young fools close by, d'you see, who'd taken too much beer on board and were horsing around. I'd have dealt with them soon. A few strong words and, if that weren't sufficient, a claret-tap, moderately powered.'

'A claret-tap?' said Becky, quite as mystified as Derek and me.

'A short, sharp blow to the nose,' the Skipper informed us, 'resulting in blood.'

'But delivered in righteousness!' said Mr Reynolds firmly.

'If you say so,' said Mr Fraser, 'but isn't there something in the Good Book about turning the other cheek?'

It seemed that Grand-Dad Reynolds was just about to settle that problem when the Skipper swerved out into the middle of the road to avoid a car that, in his view, was 'criminally' parked. Now we were well over the white line and he had to jerk the vehicle back to avoid a van coming the other way.

"Look out, Dad!' shouted Derek. 'Or you'll have us all dead!'

Becky and I were too terrified to speak; Mr Reynolds was working on his jaw again and seemed oblivious to anything else. When we were safe once more, Derek added a sarcastic wonderment that his father had ever been able to pass his driving test in the first place: 'You must have bribed the examiner!' He got told off for his cheek, but no punishment was threatened as if, privately, the Skipper had doubts about his driving abilities as well.

'But this new helper of mine,' said Mr Reynolds, going back to his story. 'The rowdies started calling him names, mocking him – but not for long.'

'What happened?' asked Becky anxiously.

'I hope this isn't going to be a tale of mass slaughter, Dad,' said the Skipper.

'No, no! He just banged their heads together like a couple of cymbals and I'm not saying the sound was all that dissimilar either. True, the young crusader was all for dragging them halfway round Irby Square before I dissuaded him. No problems there. He became as meek as a lamb with me, but I'm not surprised he's been getting into scrapes at his school.'

Derek and I looked at each other, secretly complicit.

'So now I've got an apprentice, a trifle frisky perhaps, but serious to the depths of his soul about redemption. At the end of the meeting I gave him a small Bible – I always carry a few to give out and — can you believe it? – he told me there wasn't a single copy in his home. Totally Godless! He's promised me he'll be back for the next gathering.'

Who was this large ungainly helper, inspired by Muscle and Light? Well, Derek and I knew the answer to that one and Grand-Dad Reynolds' next comment only confirmed it.

'Another funny thing. His headmaster was wearing an eye-patch, like a pirate. Wouldn't tell me what the matter was. Perhaps his wife gave him a shiner!'

He laughed out loud, enjoying the idea greatly.

'Now, what was the lad's name? Something Scandinavian…'

'Svenny Olsen!' Derek and I bawled out together, collapsing back in our seats, dropping our jaws almost free of their sockets and bolting our eyes as if they were on wires – like cartoon characters expressing shocked astonishment.

'That's it! That's the one! Is he a friend of yours or something?'

'Friend? Not likely!'

Before Mr Reynolds could ask for an explanation, the Skipper announced: 'Believe it or not, we're here,' and very slowly engineered his way into a free parking space between two other cars.

XXI. Saturday Night at the Pier

A continuous stream of people was going through the outer entrance and along the pier itself to the building at the end. This was the famous Pavilion, which had a curved roof and a white brick and plaster gable at the front. I looked up at the gleams of light from the side-windows – they were small and round like portholes and this helped me to imagine the place as a kind of ship, wide and top-heavy, and the walk up to the entrance as a ridiculously elongated gangway, stretched so far out of true it was as if we were in a dream where everything was distorted. Soon we'd be on board, the passengers watching the receding lights on the shore as we set off. There'd be a turn right after the estuary but, instead of the forbidding North Sea, mysteriously we'd find ourselves scudding over the warm Pacific Ocean!

Derek was telling his grandfather about the terrible reputation Svenny Olsen had at Willow Road – and still did have because most of the boys (and, I'd guess, the masters too) were unconvinced by the contrite version of himself he was presenting now and thought he was simply taking advantage of Mr Gordon's pious, austere nature.

But Mr Reynolds was clearly not of the doubting party, insisting that 'worse sinners, much worse' had been reclaimed and exhorting us to show compassion. I wondered how much he'd show if I told him about Svenny's penchant for diving his hand down other boys' trousers and also what he'd think about me, the 'nice lad', if I described my knife and fork-wielding antics.

At the entrance to the Pavilion, after collecting and paying for the tickets he'd ordered, the Skipper bought three programmes. He and Becky would share one, likewise me and Derek, and Mr Reynolds would have the last for himself.

There was a tall man standing near the ticket-woman, who was perched on a stool at her table. He was dressed in a smart suit like a bank manager. His cuff-links shone golden from bony wrists and his shirt gleamed with an expensive whiteness. We kids smiled when this man and the skipper shook hands, pleased that we were on the edge of a circle of prominence. For a moment I thought he might be the 'moneybags' of Mr Fraser's story, but Derek whispered to me that he was just the compère, the one who announced the bouts and introduced the fighters.

'Enjoy the show, Frank! You too, lads, and the little girl. Daughter, Frank? As pretty as the proverbial picture. First time here? Won't be the last, I can guarantee you that. It doesn't take long for the glorious wrestling game to get into your blood!'

Mr Reynolds had got caught up in the crush of people behind us. But now he hurried up and re-attached himself to our group.

'You have a good evening as well, sir.'

The compère patted the old man on the shoulder in friendly deference and ushered us through.

'Three generations of wrestling fans,' he announced to the people near him. 'That can't be bad for the health of the nation!'

***

The Skipper had got us good seats, not right at the ringside where we'd get a crick in the neck from staring up, but a few rows back where the angle of vision was less severe.

'Safer too,' said Derek. After I asked him why he gave me a sort of explanation, grinning all the while: 'It's when the bodies start flying out of the ring... they're hefty blokes, these scrappers. If you got one of them zooming your way, it'd be like Svenny or one of his colossal parents landing in your lap!'

Our seating order was as follows: me on the left, then Derek, then Becky and the Skipper and, on the last seat before the middle aisle, Grand-Dad Reynolds.

I surveyed the ring, the ropes and the padded corner posts, then the seats ahead of us. They were rapidly filling up, the latest additions being half a dozen middle-aged women right at the front. There were no husbands with them, in fact no males at all. I found this phalanx of formidable women, in their bulky hats and thick overcoats, somewhat disturbing. They looked like the kind of worshippers who sat beneath the pulpit in my mother's chapel; they didn't belong at the Pier at all. I pointed them out to Derek.

'Oh, those old bags!' he said dismissively. 'They're always here – the same seats – every tournament. They're the most bloodthirsty fans of the lot!'

Finally, the lights in the hall dimmed while those over the ring brightened like imitation suns. The compère slipped between the ropes to take up a position at the centre of the ring. Somebody handed him a microphone. The intermittent crackling noise ruined parts of what he was saying, so I got mixed up about the rules, but I understood that the bouts were decided by two falls or two submissions; there were also knock-outs and disqualifications. The static coughed painfully over the information about number and length of rounds: six of them, I thought, lasting four? five? minutes each.

It didn't really matter. I could always check with Derek, the self-proclaimed expert. Now the compère was enthusing about 'the galaxy of grappling talent' provided for our entertainment that evening.

After he'd laboured mightily to whet our appetites, he

introduced the referee – a small, compact man in shirtsleeves, bow tie and black trousers – and the first wrestlers. They'd entered the ring towards the end of the compère's speech and gone quietly to their corners: Geoff Porter and Brian Field.

'A big hand for these splendid young athletes, ladies and gentlemen, just starting out on their wrestling careers!'

The clang of the bell for the first round. By my side, Derek kept up a running commentary, informed remarks like: 'He's got him in an arm lock now. Doesn't do much good, but gives them both a breather' or:- 'That was a cross-buttock. A sure weakener if carried out properly.'

The bout was much tamer than I'd expected, with an almost pernickety adherence to the rules. I began to think that Derek and the Skipper had talked up the wrestling too much. Sensing my disappointment, Derek sought to reassure me.

'Don't worry. They often start the show like this, breaking in the new boys. You just wait till later on, kid! Things'll really wake up then.'

The Skipper was Becky's mentor. She nestled into his side as he explained the moves. He seemed determined to praise the fighters as good sportsmen, but I'm sure he craved the excitement we did and, to judge from the dissatisfied stirrings in the hall, the crowd generally.

As for Mr Reynolds, half-way through the third round he groaned loudly and I'm positive it wasn't just the troublesome tooth. After all, he knew something about combat and had had the faith to take Svenny on as his revivalist bouncer. Now the old man rose to his feet and told the Skipper that he was just going 'up yonder' for a while.

'Take it easy, Dad,' the Skipper advised him. 'Slowly but firmly does it.'

Mr Reynolds nodded at this sage suggestion and promptly disappeared from view.

During the next round there came a raucous shout from behind us: 'For God's sake, liven it up, lads! We've had tripe for supper!'

This drew supportive hoots of derision and from then on restraint was at an end, Geoff Porter and Brian Field being subjected to a rising tide of mocking criticism which at least relieved the tedium. I expected the Skipper, whatever he inwardly felt, to show disapproval at this, for Becky's sake. But, glancing along the row, I saw that he was grinning, trying to hide it at times but not succeeding very well.

That first fight ended in a draw. Just before it finished, I became vaguely aware of some figures moving into seats just across the aisle from where our old preacher had been placed. It was too dim to identify them by the ring-lights, but anyway there was no reason for me even to attempt doing so. Just latecomers, that was all.

But when the Pavilion lights went up after the opening bout, Derek nudged me and whispered excitedly in my ear: 'Do you see what I see?'

I followed his gaze. The three seats directly across the aisle were now occupied by the two Marstons – the elder looking expectant but confused, the younger just plain embarrassed – and, next to him, Miss Barber, interested, alert, sketch pad on her lap. Derek seemed to be strangely piqued at her presence.

'I thought you liked her,' I said.

'She's all right in small doses,' he conceded. 'But she's doing all the running with the ear-merchant. Bossing him around from morning till night.'

'Mr Marston?' I asked him incredulously. It was our teacher he was referring to, the one who normally spent his working day ordering other people around. And how did Derek *know* this about Miss Barber?

Grand-Dad Reynolds arrived back with a slight stumble. He'd taken the Skipper's advice all right. When he realised who was now sitting adjacent to him across the aisle he was gobsmacked, as Derek was fond of saying, then aboil with fury. But, as yet, he gave no further vent to that.

Derek was trying to explain tag-match rules to me. A lot seemed to depend on the beleaguered fighter in the ring trying to touch fingers with his partner beyond the ropes, stretching out his hand for the slightest connection so that the other one could take over. Naturally, his opponent would try to prevent that by the most vigorous means possible. Derek painted a graphic picture of a tortured body dragging itself over the canvas, inch by inch closer to the ropes, struggling towards salvation and terrified of failing.

One team was called the Viking Giants. They had blond hair, extraordinarily long for that time. I thought at first that these masses of flaxen locks might be wigs, but Derek scoffed at the idea.

'Wigs!' he exclaimed. 'And how do you think they'd keep them on during a fight? You wouldn't find glue strong enough for that! No, it's their own hair and, as they're big tough blokes who'd eat you as soon as look at you, who's going to make jokes about it? Not to their faces anyhow.'

The Vikings' blond hair appeared too bright to me, almost phosphorescent.

'Do you think they've dyed it then?' I asked Derek, apprehensive that he'd dismiss this idea too.

But the master of grappling lore chewed the notion over carefully, scrutinising the Vikings as they showed themselves off to the crowd. In the end, he admitted that they might have done, but added fiercely: 'That doesn't mean they're jessies, though! They wouldn't have muscles like that if they were!'

There was something dubious about his reasoning, but I'd no proper arguments against it and didn't really want to have, so it was easy to let the matter go.

Their opponents were introduced as the Leprechauns, two brothers from Dublin called O'Donnell. Obviously, their colour had to be green, with a shamrock outlined on the back of their robes. Perhaps I was being a bit literal-minded, but I'd always thought leprechauns were small like goblins, whereas the O'Donnell brothers were barely shorter than the Vikings. However, they were true to their image in the way they capered around on being introduced to the audience, making large mimes of slyness and mischief.

This bout was much more interesting than the first one, full of drama and tension.

The Viking Giants quickly got a fall and, a round later, the Leprechauns equalised. They were still level at the beginning of the last round.

And then, after about a minute, the Vikings, their bright manes flicking to and fro, broke one of the cardinal rules and joined each other in the ring. To roars of opprobrium and excitement, they picked up the small, dapper referee and started using him as a battering-ram against the leprechaun standing there. His brother volubly protested and vaulted over the ropes to join his sibling. The referee was dropped unceremoniously on the canvas and the four scrappers laid into each other with everything they had. I could feel the crowd going berserk.

'They'll get the book thrown at them for this!' Derek shouted as if I were sitting at the back of the hall.

Becky was clutching the Skipper's hand tightly, aghast but fascinated. As for Grand- Dad Reynolds he was sunk in gloom, his hand pressed against the throbbing side of his face. Yet his lips were moving as though he were making a silent prayer or, more probably, judging from his expression, a silent curse that should have withered his enemy on the spot. His face was turned resolutely to the ring, but I had my doubts as to whether he was taking in much.

The overhead lights suddenly went on. I glanced across the aisle. Our teacher showed boredom and distaste, Miss

Barber a professional, artist's interest and Mr Marston senior looked as if he were gripped by fever and shock.

The referee lay for some time on the canvas, apparently out for the count that he should have been telling over other bodies. Then he scrambled to his feet like a man pushed into wakefulness by the ringing of an alarm-clock. His bow tie was badly askew and there was a thin trail of blood on his shirt sleeve. He staggered around the four corners of the ring, keeping as best he could out of the way of the furious fists and legs of the wrestlers. The referee was crossing his hands and forearms horizontally in a kind of scissors motion.

'That's it,' Derek said. 'The fight's over. Disqualification.'

Clearly, both teams were honour-bound to protest but, this duty done, they left the ring quickly to a cacophonous farewell of boos, catcalls and applause. Through the microphone, sounding clear for once, the compère confirmed the official verdict. The audience showed its approval, a mass of lively people, now beginning to be well entertained.

So, in that sense, the interval came in very satisfactorily, but it was outside the ring, you might say, where the real fighting commenced.

Becky had been overwhelmed by the last chaotic part of the tag-team contest. The Skipper asked her worriedly if she wanted to go outside for some fresh air. She shook her head and for further answer pressed her face more tightly into the Skipper's comforting chest. He stroked her hair and forehead, coming out with his standard remark about professional wrestling being simply a form of rough play. Then he looked across at me.

'Are you all right, Colin?'

Derek answered for me.

'He loves it, Dad! He's a real convert.'

The Skipper seemed a bit doubtful as he examined my

expression, but smiled all the same.

'That's all right, then.'

But, with these shifts in his concentration, it wasn't surprising that Mr Fraser had relaxed his vigilance over Grand-Dad Reynolds.

We'd been lulled into a sense of false security, because up he shot now and was across the aisle in a trice to confront his enemy. He leant so closely into Mr Marston's face that I thought he was going to spit into it.

'You killed her, you *killed* her, that's what you did!'

It was a terrible sound, like a burning soul in hell. Frightening to me, Becky also, but not for her brother.

'Here we go!' he said, rolling his eyes in the direction of the two old men. His face was full of a disturbing sort of glee. 'The management have thrown in an extra scuffle for nowt.'

'Come back, Dad!' shouted the Skipper. 'Don't make an even bigger spectacle of yourself!'

I watched Mr Marston senior jerk back in his chair as if struck. Our teacher looked at his father with concern but, as far as I could tell, his chief feeling at that moment was embarrassment. Miss Barber just stared hard, as if trying to commit every detail of Mr Reynolds' distorted expression to memory.

Now old Mr Marston, wanting to make up for his initial signs of fear, levered himself into a firmer sitting position and shouted defiantly: 'That's a terrible thing to accuse me of. The worst lie you ever told in your whole life!'

'I'm not talking about knives, poison or guns. Hardness of heart can be just as lethal.'

'You can't accuse me of that either.'

'Can I not?'

'No!'

'Think of the way you went on at Krista when she was ill, all that bullying. Nastier than you'd treat the meanest skivvy...'

'She was drawing away, giving up. I wanted to bring her back, that's all.'

'That sweet woman who'd looked after you hand and foot. A blind bit of gratitude you ever showed!'

'I knew how to appreciate my wife,' said Mr Marston stiffly.

'Whited sepulchre!'

'I'm not proud of the mistakes I made. There were times when I was too rough, I admit. But I thought that might shock Krista out of her apathy.' He paused. 'And you've never been at fault, I suppose?'

'You're a sadist! You enjoyed humiliating her.'

'You what!'

Mr Marston half-rose from his chair, but was straight away plumped down again by his son and Miss Barber.

Both sides were now physically restraining their particular obstreperous old man.

The Skipper, in fact, had his two large hands full: one attempting to drag the enraged Grand-Dad Reynolds away, the other protectively around Becky's shoulder. The rumbustious bout between the Viking Giants and the Leprechauns had been difficult enough, but this quarrel was much worse: venomous and all too *real*. There was no way you could see it as any kind of game.

At last, Mr Reynolds was returned to his seat, his son-in-law's hand around his wrist like a padlock.

I looked beyond him. Mr Marston was clutching his father's jacket sleeve and muttering urgently to him. From the other side, Miss Barber bent over the aged face solicitously, drying the sweat on his forehead with her handkerchief and otherwise fanning him with her sketch-pad.

Derek's sympathy was differently focussed.

'I feel really sorry for our teacher. Think what he's going through, shown up like that. Do you think he wanted to bring his barmy old dad in the first place, or even come himself for that matter? It'd be her who'd insist on both, right? Miss Bossypants Barber! Simply because she wants to draw some silly pictures!'

'Come on, Derek. You've got Miss Barber on the brain. She's not like that.'

'You reckon? She's doing her best to turn him against us. She'll make him hate 2A in the end.'

'Why?'

'Women. They can't help it.'

'Can't help what?' I asked, perplexed.

'Ask Grand-Dad when he's sane again. He knows chapter and verse.'

And that was all the explanation I got because now the auditorium lights began to weaken, those over the ring to gain strength, and the third fight was about to start.

This should have been exciting because it was between a masked wrestler – the Dark Demon of Marseilles – and a 'blue eyes', as I'd learned from Derek the heroes were called: a clean-limbed young warrior called Johnny Birstall.

But I didn't feel easy after the disturbance in the interval, not yet anyway, and the moves and strutting in the ring seemed like tired acting to me – although there was one flying drop-kick by Johnny Birstall which I'd still consider a gem, as beautiful as anything you'd see in circus acrobatics.

The Demon, (paunchy, loath to move from his position in the middle of the ring), finally got a knock-out that even to a novice like me seemed patently bogus. So the Dark Demon of Marseilles remained with mask intact, his face still a secret, raising his arms in barely acknowledged triumph, while Johnny Birstall shook his head ruefully on leaving the ring as if somehow he'd fallen into a trap and messed up the chance of a lifetime.

'Where's Marseilles when it's at home?' asked Derek.

'South of France,' said the Skipper. 'A big port.'

I saw that he hadn't unclamped his hand from around Grand-Dad Reynolds' arm, even though the old man was just staring morosely into space again, as if waiting for messages from afar. Regarding him then, he seemed even incapable of wiping his nose to me, let alone returning to the battlefield.

'This next bout will be good,' Derek informed me. 'They always save the best for the last.'

I studied the programme. (Derek allowed me to take it after the tournament. I have it before me as I write, little the worse for the years.) Here's a picture of Magnus Smythe: 'The powerful farmer's boy from Wiltshire — but he's no Yawning Yokel!' He must have been in his middle twenties then, broad-featured, smiling widely, with a thatch of fairish hair. And here's his opponent on that far-off night at the Pier Pavilion: Jason Pulverstein. It's a slightly out of focus picture as though Pulverstein, doubtful about having his likeness taken, had started to move away at the last moment. Beneath the blurred photo, however, there's a big build-up. Pulverstein is described as the 'Scholarly Scrapper', the wrestler with a library of three thousand volumes, somebody who knew 'his Shakespeare backwards', but also as someone who had his eyes keenly focussed on the practical here and now, a man with acknowledged financial acumen: 'the North's very own Wizard of Wealth'.

'But if he's so rich and successful, with his finger in so many pies,' said Derek, 'what's he's doing slugging it out at places like the Pier?'

I asked him whether he'd ever seen Jason Pulverstein before. He shook his head and consulted his father. The Skipper had never come across him either, adding that it was Pulverstein's first appearance in Ketilsby. He didn't think that he'd been on the wrestling scene for long.

'He's reckoned to be very strange but definitely on the up and up. That's what I heard anyway.'

Mr Reynolds had started muttering again and was now staring balefully across at the Marston party. A little desperately, the Skipper tried to jolly the old man along.

'Buck up, Dad! The wrestlers are coming out now. This'll be the crown of the evening, the last fight!'

'The last fight,' repeated Mr Reynolds grimly. 'You never said a truer word, Frank.'

None of us found this very reassuring, but our attention was distracted by the sight of Magnus Smythe striding towards the ring in all his tanned, stalwart glory, smirking at the crowd in a silly way, as if quite sure he had its approval from the outset. He almost leapt into the ring and quickly took up position in his corner, muscular arms stretched along the ropes beside him.

Jason Pulverstein hadn't yet displayed himself in full view, still hovering somewhere in the shadows.

The compère's voice came over the crackling, snorting microphone.

'And now, ladies and gentlemen, your attention please – the Fight of the Night!'

He introduced Magnus Smythe, and then looked over with feigned surprise at the opposite, still empty corner. Then he peered beyond the ring, hand shading his eyes like a lost explorer. He seemed anxious, as if Jason Pulverstein had done a bunk. Finally, after more waiting and peering, the compère sent a great 'Ah!' of relief down the mike.

'And here he comes at last! Jason Pulverstein, ladies and gentlemen! Never say that books and brawn, mind and muscle, can't belong together' – had this tall, smartly-dressed man written the text of the wrestling bill? – 'because here's a living contradiction to that wrongful assumption! Assist the Professor into the ring, somebody!' A second obligingly parted the ropes and helped Pulverstein up. 'Here's a young man who, appearances perhaps to the contrary, is destined to go a long way and might even make wrestling history.' He followed Pulverstein's rather pussy-footed steps across the canvas with smiling indulgence. 'Ladies and gentlemen, making his début at the Pier but rapidly acquiring a big reputation throughout the North and more marginal parts of England – London, beware! – please give a warm welcome to the unusual, the truly surprising, Jason Pulverstein!'

I suppose I must have expected someone as spectacularly ghastly as the Dark Demon of Marseilles, but taking a closer look at the fighter the compère had praised as he emerged more clearly into the lights, I was totally flummoxed. Here was a figure that in a thousand years I'd never have guessed was in the grappling game: a dumpy, pasty-faced man, looking at least ten years older than he could really be, clad in a grubby robe that my mother would have promptly washed and dispatched to the nearest jumble sale. Add to that the thinning hair, the heavy horn-rimmed spectacles, which he handed to his second, a general air of sheepish, blink-eyed unease, and you had a person who would have caused consternation in the most credulous of wrestling crowds.

After the applause they'd been urged to give died down, a hush fell over the spectators. Then the jeering and derisive whistling broke out. The fans were angry; a cheap trick had been played on them.

'Who's this puffball?'

'Was it him I saw shuffling out of the Sally Am this morning?'

'What does this whiz kid deal in, then? Scrap and old rags?'

The bell went and Magnus Smythe swaggered into the centre of the ring. But Jason Pulverstein stayed where he was, squinting myopically across the canvas; he almost shrank from the roaring darkness around him. Then he abruptly turned his white blotchy back to the ring, the meek face bent forward over the ropes as if he were praying.

Magnus Smythe, eager to do battle, was disgusted at this craven gesture. In a slow strut he moved closer to Pulverstein's corner, taunting him. Getting no response, he appealed indignantly to the audience whose support, of course, he received in good measure.

Yet still Pulverstein didn't shift.

Strong legs firmly astride, Magnus Smythe put his hands on his hips, adopting an exaggerated air of contempt that made his blandly handsome face ugly and off-putting. The clamour around him grew even louder, various courses of action being suggested by the audience, all of them stark and violent. But even a beginner like me could see that he was standing too close to Jason Pulverstein now, well within range of the Scholarly Scrapper and Amazing Modern Midas. Bold or foolhardy?

The latter, it seemed to prove, because suddenly Pulverstein grasped the ropes on either side of him and kicked back with his legs. These were podgy, unsightly limbs, blanched and blotched like the upper part of his body, hardly appearing capable of supporting him when he'd made his uncertain way into the ring. Now, though, in this instant, they were as lethal as a maddened horse's; better, because they flew up as if defeating gravity. Jason Pulverstein's wrestling boots struck Magnus Smythe right in the centre of his chest with a sharp smacking sound you could hear over the noise of the crowd.

The farmer's boy was toppled. With an alacrity that few would previously have expected of him, Pulverstein was on top of his opponent, pressing his shoulders to the canvas.

That was a dramatic fall all right, hardly into the first round. I couldn't make up my mind whether it was rehearsed or genuine. Anyway, thereafter the Wiltshire man treated his opponent with cautious respect. Pulverstein tried now to resume his former meek demeanour but his cover had been blown by that astounding backwards kick.

The Skipper was thrilled – we kids too – but he made the mistake of taking his restraining hand off Grand-Dad Reynolds' arm. Fury lending him wings, the old man was over the aisle quicker than you could blink.

Just at that moment, Pulverstein stepped outside the

ropes, holding up a warning hand to Magnus Smythe. It was his turn to be outraged by a breach of fairness. Standing at the very edge of the ring, Pulverstein mimed a jab that he claimed had been directed at his kidneys, on the off-side of the referee. Boos and mockery for him and renewed cheers for the hero as Magnus Smythe protested his innocence.

The Skipper went in irritated pursuit of Mr Reynolds. Derek kept Becky back from following him. She accepted his command to stay put without demur. For Becky that was very unusual.

So we three watched the Skipper on the other side of the aisle, trying to drag Mr Reynolds away from trouble again.

Then our attention was distracted by one of the large middle-aged women in the front row, infuriated by Jason Pulverstein's refusal to get back into the ring. Rising to her feet, she shouted: 'You coward, you rotten coward! Get back in there and *fight!*'

I didn't actually see her take the pin out of her hat, but you couldn't miss her lumbering up to the wrestler with what looked like a miniature stiletto in her hand; neither could you miss her sticking the point of it into the porridgey skin of Pulverstein's thigh. Not deeply, but enough to draw a genuine scream of pain from the new grappling sensation.

Becky gave a gasp of horror, but the Skipper wasn't there to comfort her, and Derek and I were too agog with rather queasy excitement to do anything to help.

Jason Pulverstein glared down at the woman and was starting to snarl out curses when the referee hastened over and ordered her back to her seat. Two of her companions escorted her there and then flanked her in narrow attendance, like warders. As for Pulverstein, he got back into the ring and was promptly met by a hefty fore-arm smash from his opponent.

Meanwhile Grand-Dad Reynolds and old Mr Marston

were bellowing insults at each other and the attention of the nearer part of the crowd was veering between the fighters in the ring and the two antique warriors squaring up to each other outside it.

With all the row I could only pick out sentences here and there, for example Mr Reynolds' raw bellow: 'You barred me from your house! You wouldn't even let me see her!' and Mr Marston's counter, which seemed to come after the next paragraph of mutual insult: 'That was the last thing Krista needed in her state, you wailing and moping about our home like a great booby!'

I remembered that beautiful, serene face in the framed photograph both old codgers displayed on their walls, how this contained the soul too and would bring men to fight over it and make excuses for what they did. It didn't matter, in one sense, that Krista Marston ended as an exhausted woman, ravaged by sickness. It'd be that face I'd admired so much, and been in awe of too, which would remain.

Now Derek dragged me after him, Becky at our heels, to where the Skipper, our teacher and Miss Barber were once more trying to restore some kind of order. Derek evidently felt that it was time for us children to add our groatsworth.

For a while, Magnus Smythe and Jason Pulverstein wrestled on, even pepping up the fight in an attempt to bring back the crowd's attention to where it should be. But the fans were becoming increasingly attracted to the unscheduled event erupting below the ring. Droves of them were leaving their places now and making their way up to the front.

In the end, the two wrestlers felt unable to continue. This crowd-pleaser was too much for them. They appealed angrily to the referee to do something and followed him to the ropes nearest us, overlooking the area of dispute. The referee told Grand-Dad Reynolds and Mr Marston to ease off and get back to their seats immediately, or they'd be thrown out.

'People have paid good money to come and see us,' added Jason Pulverstein. 'Why should you be allowed to spoil their enjoyment?'

Somehow I expected him to have a thin, broken scholar's voice to match the act he'd given us at the beginning, but I should have known from that he wouldn't sound as you might think. His voice was, in fact, deep and resonant, an amalgam of Roy at his most Leeds-inspired and Grand-Dad Reynolds when he belted out the Truth at the Dock Gates.

But his intervention, plus that of the referee, had little effect. Fury and outrage had taken possession of the two old men.

People were calling for the compère to step in and put things to rights. He was the senior authority in the place after all. But he was nowhere to be found.

'He's not at the bar. He's generally propping it up.'

'Scour the pubs across the road!'

'He's done a runner with the takings!'

'Where *is* he?'

The question was taken up as a chant, still largely good-humoured but insistent.

Our teacher had sunk back into his seat as far as he could, trying perhaps to shrink himself into a clutch of mere atoms, the bliss of invisibility. But, of course, that journey was blocked and he stayed prominently where he was, his face nervous, stricken even.

Without warning, he gave Derek and me a strange look – one of appeal, I think, but there seemed to be accusation there too. We also had to take some of the blame; we'd helped to set our wild mangy dog onto his wild mangy dog, even if more through negligence than intent.

I could imagine him mutely begging us not to tell the boys at school about what was happening, although he must have known that was a dead letter to begin with. The news would spread quickly enough. Anyway, there were probably other Willow Roaders in the audience, let alone their dads, and no doubt Mrs Hatpin was somebody's auntie.

I felt sorry for Mr Marston, though. Derek did too, but went further than me because he actually showed his concern. Turning away from the mêlée, he bent close to him, murmuring words I couldn't catch, presumably encouraging ones, and then even had the temerity to pat History-is-Fun BA (our teacher!) on the shoulder in a sympathetic gesture, as an adult might a child.

I drew in my breath sharply. Derek would never have dared anything like that if Mr Marston had been in his normal state. Whatever the motive, that pat looked cheeky and presumptuous to me – Derek bringing his hand away swiftly as though he'd encountered one of the fabled giant scurf-flakes didn't make it any better.

'Come on then!' roared Grand-Dad Reynolds, red coxcomb stiffened for war, barging his way through a clatter of chairs and adopting a belligerent posture like an old-style pugilist. 'Let's settle this once and for all! May the Lord empower the blow of righteousness!'

Rising to the challenge, Mr Marston senior managed to shake off the restraining hand of Miss Barber and lunged towards his opponent.

'I'll see you, Alfred Reynolds! And if my Krista is looking on, she'll bless me for bashing your eyes shut, your evil mouth, your whole treacherous face!'

'That she won't!'

'Yes, she will!'

In reality, they landed very few effective blows, righteous or unrighteous. It was a messy sort of scrap, like mardy kids going home from a bad day at school and thoroughly out of temper with each other. But then the Skipper was there and clamping his father-in-law from behind with a fierce, relentless chest-grip. Judging by the wheezes and gasps of his prisoner, I thought he was crushing the last breath out of him. Perhaps he'd been secretly tempted to for years. And, as if inspired by the Skipper's example, Miss Barber and the Cuban Missile Crisis pundit closed in on their own warring party.

But, despite restraint, the fists were still flailing and the whole struggle became like a tug-of-war, lurching this way and that beneath our side of the ring. The crowd loved it, cheering and egging us on, eager to give their view about which side would win, generally favouring the Skipper and his team. Even though I knew we were involved in something completely stupid, I couldn't help taking some pride in this.

Above us, through the microphone, the referee was calling to the far ends of the auditorium, appealing for help that never came: a man deserted in urgent need, panic fraying the edges of his voice.

Oddly enough, the two wrestlers who might have descended from the ring and through their strength and skill broken up the tug-of-war seemed totally nonplussed, as if this radical departure from the scheme of things had caused them to lose their bearings. They retreated to their corners, waiting on events. The much-needed compère was still nowhere to be seen.

It was Derek and Becky who brought the crisis to a resolution. For once, they acted in perfect harmony, becoming as close to fusing into one person as they could, an impression reinforced by their close resemblance. They didn't even exchange a complicit look; they just *knew* what they should do.

Abruptly, Derek and Becky abandoned the tug-of-war and pushed their way between the old men, still doing their shackled best to punch and slap each other.

'Stop it! Stop it now!'

Derek pitched his voice stronger, to make himself heard above the din – higher too, so that he and his sister even sounded the same now. And it worked, this urgent chorus of theirs, the startling authority of it. The noise began to subside throughout the auditorium, as if the crowd believed that the children's command applied no less to them than it did to Grand-Dad Reynolds and Mr Marston senior.

My two young allies looked impressive standing there, pure and strong, almost angelic – if angels are allowed dark hair and rosy-brown faces. It was too much for me, though. I began to edge away from them.

'You're behaving worse than drunks in the street,' scolded Derek, turning from his Grand-Dad to his teacher's father and back again.

'You should be setting an example,' contributed Becky primly. 'You've both lived long lives. We want to ask you about things, look up to you!'

She drew praise from the audience then for her forthright but tender common sense. But that sweet, sentimental tone only made me feel a little queasy.

'Fighting won't help,' pronounced Derek. His father's mouth twitched in amazement, as if he would never have suspected his son of such a lofty sentiment in a month of Sundays.

'Not that serious kind of fighting,' Becky elaborated. 'It never does.'

Derek nodded his head in emphatic agreement, but straight away I remembered the figure in the playground whose decision to tackle Svenny Olsen had helped me out of a dangerous situation. Derek to the rescue and that hadn't been through high-flown feelings, an appeal to turn swords into ploughshares.

'It won't bring back the woman you both loved,' said Becky in a voice of treacle that you could barely have stirred with the strongest spoon. Yet it thrilled Auntie Hatpin and many others around us, as I plainly saw.

'Just listen to that little lass!' someone behind me said admiringly.

One glance at Derek and Becky showed me that there

was no mischief in their eyes. At that moment they believed every word they uttered. There should have been some sceptical voice amongst the adorers, some dryly humorous attempt at sanity, but if there was I didn't hear it – except within me, and that was powerless.

Anyway, their intervention was successful. Give it a little time and it would be cried up as a miracle.

When I next dared to look, I saw that the two old men had let their fists fall and moved apart. You could see the rage in their bodies dying by the way their faces went pale. They looked abject now, even horror-struck as if they really had been on the edge of tearing each other to pieces.

'That's better,' said one of the children. For the life of me I couldn't have picked out which of them it was. Then, even though I had such torn longing for Derek and Becky, I was smuggling myself back through the near reaches of the crowd, hastened on by the fear – backed by no evidence whatsoever – that Mr Marston senior was on the point of searching me out. After all, I was his acolyte in a way. I'd helped him, up there on the ridge in the Land of the Two Rivers, and he'd told me things that were close to his heart, how Krista and he used to come to that spot, the ceremony he'd taken to carrying out after her death. *And* I'd seen the lamp dancing up and down, which I wasn't sure he ever had.

'You've got to make peace, become friends again!'

They're going to tell them to shake hands, I thought, and they'll put their saintly mitts over those gnarled, liver-spotted ones to seal the bargain!

That didn't quite happen, thank God, although it would have brought the house down if it had: a perfect finish.

'You'll try, won't you?'

Becky's voice, sounding a note of uncertainty, which Derek immediately corrected.

'You *must* try!'

All the lights, both in the hall and over the ring, had

been switched on by now, and to me they seemed to be growing ever more glaring by the minute. It was at this point that the compère made a long-awaited reappearance – a flustered, red-faced spider of a man, clambering hastily up into the ring. However, it was clear from his first words that he'd been told what was going on.

'Bless these wonderful children!' he exhorted through the wheezing microphone but, with his free hand, indicated Derek and Becky as if they were the top prize at a fair. Even so, there was a roar of approval from the assembled fans. I imagined that sound, that collective exultant voice, bursting through the walls of the Pavilion and hurtling over the estuary to Holderness.

After apologising for his absence, the compère was keen to stress that it hadn't been through 'dereliction of duty' but instead 'a rather ticklish administrative matter' that had come up.

'Oh, that's what they call it nowadays, is it?' came the eternal waggish comment from the crowd.

The compère smirked along with the laughter as if they could consider him a bit of a lad if they liked but he wasn't going to say anything either way. Then, holding up his hand, he appealed for the people's attention.

'We'll go on with the tournament soon,' he began, 'but first I'd like to ask those responsible for the two excitable pensioners... well, if their minders or whoever would kindly escort them from the building without further ado and make sure they're kept in a secure place (preferably somewhere the other side of the Pennines!), I think we'd all breathe a deep sigh of relief!'

The crowd enjoyed the sally, but I noticed that Derek and Becky were looking at the compère disapprovingly, not caring, I suppose, for the light, dismissive fashion in which he'd referred to Grand-Dad Reynolds and Mr Marston.

'We've decided to leave the main lights on for another ten minutes or so and, during the extra, unscheduled interval and for this golden, glittering period only, all drinks at the bar will be half-price!'

By this gesture of largesse, the compère brought (and bought) his clients completely over to his side. From above, he watched with satisfaction as people rushed away up the central aisle to order their drinks. Before Derek could persuade the Skipper to join them and get something for all of us, the compère leaned over the ropes and beckoned Mr Fraser towards him.

'No offence, Frank, but please get those old tearaways out of here.'

'I didn't exactly plan it this way, Doug.'

'No, of course you didn't, of course not,' the compère said placatingly. 'But all the same... Now, where are those little paragons? Ah!'

He motioned to Derek and Becky so that they came up and stood beside their father. The compère beamed down at them.

'You've got a couple of real gems here, Frank. Listen – ring the office before the next show and there'll be free tickets for you and the kids. The one after that too, let's not be niggardly! Just mention my name. But I'm afraid that's all I can manage, children.' He spread his hands in a mock-despairing gesture, the gold cuff-links glinting in the light. 'I'd like to do more but haloes come expensive these days.'

Laughing, the Skipper and Derek looked considerably more gratified than poor Becky. This wasn't her idea of a reward!

'That's very generous of you, Doug.'

'Not at all. Don't give it a thought.' Then he stared down at Derek, puzzled. 'But there was another boy with you, wasn't there?'

Yes, there was, but he was set to fade from immediate view, looking as if he intended to join the bargain-hunters pressing up to all the gleaming bottles and glasses at the far end of the Pavilion.

Derek turned sharply on his heel at Doug the compère's question, apparently realising for the first time that I was no longer with them. Becky too – she even cried out in alarm as if I were lost; worse than lost, mysteriously subtracted from our group forever. It was her eyes that searched the most keenly over the place and they were the ones which found me.

'There he is!' she cried: relief and triumph.

No escape. But I wasn't sure that I wanted to retreat any further anyway.

Derek summoned me peremptorily, but it was Becky who dashed forward and, clutching my hand, extracted me from the crowd. This created a minor diversion in its own right: the spectacle of the radiant little peacemaker reclaiming a bashful friend.

Grinning, the Skipper said: 'You don't have to give more than name, rank and number, Colin. The Geneva Convention or something.'

It was too late for me to get the compère's blessing as, after a mellow farewell to the Skipper and his offspring, he'd stepped back from the ropes to confer with the wrestlers, both looking rather glum. I couldn't catch any of the words as the three of them were huddled together, only some of the facial expressions and gestures, but he seemed to be setting out a proposition and cajoling them to quickly accept it.

An important decision was being taken. Nodding at his fighters, the compère called for the mike and tapped it vigorously before raising it to his mouth again. The thing did crackle and wheeze a bit less, to begin with at least.

'Ladies and gentlemen, I have an announcement to make.'

He paused, harvesting the drama of the moment.

'Friends, there's grappling magic yet to come! Magnus Smythe and Jason Pulverstein have agreed to start the bout afresh. We're all of the same mind that it would be wrong simply to pick up where we left off, as if that unfortunate disruption never happened. The rhythm, the atmosphere, of the contest were broken, we can't deny that.'

He stilled the spatter of applause that followed this statement.

'So I'm proud to tell you that Jason Pulverstein, out of the generosity of his sportsman's heart, has agreed to waive his one fall advantage. Now, isn't that something?'

Jason Pulverstein didn't look particularly chuffed at the compliment bestowed on him but, his thick-rimmed glasses resumed for the while, he did acknowledge the crowd's appreciation by giving a weary sort of Roman's emperor's salute.

Magnus Smythe gazed admiringly at his opponent as if he'd never in his life poured scorn on him. And the battling scholar gradually began to look less disgruntled. Perhaps he'd reminded himself that he was scheduled to get the bout anyway, only that now it'd take a bit longer. Moreover, perhaps Doug the persuasive compère had hinted that there'd be a bonus in it too.

The lights in the Pavilion were just beginning to dip as we went up the central aisle, the Skipper guiding our aged delinquent before him. Head bowed, quiff wilting, Grand-Dad Reynolds was into the muttering again, but it was so low and rapid his words were like a foreign language to me.

We children followed, Becky and Derek in front. Behind me came Miss Barber who tapped me on the shoulder once as we made our progress. I twitched the shoulder nervously, but she didn't seem to notice that as she said merrily: 'We'll be laughing at all this, Colin, when we look back.' I didn't tell her a hidden part of me was doing that already, though hardly in the easy, carefree way she meant.

At her heels was old Mr Marston, propped up by his son's hand. Our teacher was still not saying anything, not a word, not even the commonplaces you might expect at such a trying time. Familiar with Mr Marston BA's daily performances as Derek and I were, it was unnerving to find this eloquent man struck dumb, as if language had betrayed him altogether.

Our passing was accompanied by smiles and encouraging remarks from members of the audience. I was aware of the blur of faces above the aisle seats but mostly kept my eyes fixed firmly ahead, unlike Derek and Becky who cast frequent glances to one side or the other, acknowledging public approval with a graciousness that should have made anybody in their right mind suspicious.

All I wanted at that moment was to be free of the place: the fighters, the fans, the kerfuffle our two old men had kicked up, the ludicrous tug-of-war, those two judging angels descending amongst us and, yes, throw in sharp-suited, smooth-talking Doug the compère for good measure, even the empty, totally blameless ticket-table we were skirting by now as we approached the exit. Just to be out and away!

***

So it was a relief to feel the fresh air, gusty and invigorating, as we walked over the boards of the Pier and listened to the water striking against the struts beneath us. From the Pavilion we heard the crowd roaring with excitement as the fight got going again and either Magnus Smythe or Jason Pulverstein made a spectacular move.

On the Promenade once more, we gathered close together, shivering against the chill. Mr Marston senior shivered more than anybody else but, as he was still in shock, it wasn't simply the cold that was fingering his bones. Our teacher stood by him, sentenced to an eternity of guard duty. It was the Skipper and Miss Barber who did most of the talking, with Derek and Becky butting in now and again. At last, they were showing signs of tiredness.

'Don't worry,' Miss Barber told the Skipper. 'I'll make

sure our venerable gentleman gets home safely.' Then, after a hesitation, she indicated the Marstons in turn, twitching father and silent, withdrawn son: 'Well, that they're both all right.'

'Put a bromide in their Horlicks,' suggested Mr Fraser facetiously.

'Something like that.'

She laughed and turned to us.

'Bye, Colin and Derek. See you back at school on Tuesday. I bet all this will give you inspiration for new pictures, won't it? A different kind of circus, I suppose. I've certainly picked up a few ideas.'

She patted the sketch pad, now safely lodged in the wide deep pocket of her coat. Suddenly, she realised she'd left one child out and that, embarrassingly, she was short of a name. The Skipper came to her aid.

'Becky! Of course. Bye to you too, Becky. You did very well back there. You and this irrepressible young scamp!'

I think she was tempted to ruffle the 'scamp's' hair but something in his look made her stay her hand.

' "The child is father of the man", as the poet said,' she continued, 'and just occasionally you can see he's right.'

' "The child is father"...?' puzzled the Skipper.

'Wordsworth,' said our Mr Marston, giving voice at last. 'From "My heart leaps up when I behold". Seventh line of a brief but telling poem. Nine lines in all. Very famous. In every book of quotations, I should imagine.'

He speaks! And even with that superior, reassuring air of pedantry Derek and I were familiar with. I was so grateful that I could have stood an impromptu lecture on Wordsworth there and then, even given the sharp wind from the estuary, whipping up the edges of our coats and trying to burrow right through to the skin.

I waited eagerly for his next words, but after that brief pronouncement there wasn't even a cough. Our teacher had returned to his Trappist state. Yet at least he'd given us a sign; surely he'd be all right again in the classroom on Tuesday morning. Invisible but most certainly present, the schoolmaster's strengthening mantle would fall naturally around his shoulders again.

Wouldn't it?

The Skipper drove me straight home, up the Shore Road this time, at considerable speed. Mr Reynolds sat in front as before, clutching his mouth tightly as if not only trying to subdue the painful tooth but also his manic chuntering. I *thought* I'd heard him going on about the lion lying down with the lamb, but that was largely guesswork – or wishful thinking.

'Sorry about all that, Colin,' the Skipper said when we pulled up in Langtoft Avenue. My house was in darkness, apart from the dim light left on in the hall. 'The evening didn't turn out quite as expected, but I trust we got you interested in the wrestling game even so.'

'Oh yes!' I said, hoping I sounded sincere. 'Jason Pulverstein's going to be a big star!'

It was my first public judgement as a grappling fan.

'You're not wrong there,' said the Skipper, pleased at such enthusiasm. 'Next time we go it'll be free, thanks to Doug, although we'll have to leave that old vigilante behind. 'He indicated Mr Reynolds with a jerk of the head. 'Anyway, we'll see you soon, no doubt. Goodbye for now.'

I made my goodbyes too and got out of the car. Derek said he'd be round to see me on Monday morning while Becky gave me the most cloying smile imaginable. Mr Fraser revved up the engine of his vehicle until it sounded like a rocket ready for take-off. I wondered whether it'd wake up Mum, who'd be only half-asleep at best until she knew I was safely home.

Before I closed the door, I heard Becky say: 'Time to drop Grand-Dad off now.'

'No, it isn't,' replied her father firmly. 'He's coming back with us. I dread to think what he might get up to, if left alone in his state. And tomorrow – who knows?' Grimly, he added: 'We could be taking him over to Lincoln.'

At last, the car bucked forward and then, more smoothly, charged away along the street.

I guessed what the reference to Lincoln meant and it had nothing to do with visiting the Castle or the Cathedral. In the city there was a big mental hospital: Bracebridge. It was the biggest of its kind in the county – a 'loony bin' as we termed it in our callously juvenile way, enjoying visions of the mad being locked up in their howling, screaming thousands. In our dismissive view, it was a place where you were sent to be punished rather than treated, let alone cured.

I told myself that the Skipper was just venting his anger with Mr Reynolds through a rough, sardonic sort of humour, but I couldn't be sure. As for Derek and Becky, they hadn't seemed disturbed at the implied reference to Bracebridge, but then they were still floating around on their clouds of glory, not quite back with us as yet.

It was a shocking notion for me, though, because I wanted Mr Reynolds to be restored too, like our teacher would be. This stocky, righteous old man with the blazing red quiff, enjoining the boozy layabouts at the Dock Gates to come to God – I might even find myself relishing all that, so long as I was standing well on the sidelines, comfortably distant from the baleful glare and twitching fists of his bulky young assistant.

XXII. THE BEST OCTOBER

When I woke up next morning, after a long sleep full of wrestling dreams, the world was still standing, and in fact the day was crisp and bright. And even if that proved to be deceptive, I still had the inspiration of the whale-mist to cling to. It was like the hob in a game of tag, something you couldn't violate.

That Sunday news began to come through about Mr Khrushchev's climb-down, his acceptance of President Kennedy's terms – this was the black and white view of it anyway. No more rockets would be sent to Cuba and the sites already constructed there would be dismantled. Peace wasn't sure yet, but at least it was a beginning, a step back from the brink. And if the Russians had made the initial move, then...

My father started to claim that he'd known all along that something like this would happen: even the most bloodthirsty of politicians would see sense in the end – that is, until I reminded him of the doom-laden pronouncements he'd actually been making. He tried to laugh these away.

'Just sounding off,' he claimed. 'To untempt the devil, as it were.'

But he grinned when he saw that I was less than convinced by this attempt at self-exoneration. However, he wasn't the only one trying to be wise after the event.

Naturally, we had no idea of what was going on behind the scenes, the secret deal being hammered out, the essential quid pro quo: the rockets would go but the Americans would assure the Russians in return that there'd be no invasion of Cuba, their 'backyard' as Deborah had termed it in Cross Chapel Street.

Everybody was full of praise for President Kennedy, his cool self-possession and resolute nerve in face of the worst crisis since the Second World War. Nobody that I knew praised Mr Khrushchev, (though young Mr Marston might have done so in private). The Soviet leader had brought humanity to the edge of disaster, so people believed, and in the end had been forced, humiliatingly, to see sense. How could you find nice words for someone who'd given us all such a scare? You could make jokes about him and that was about it.

But not for me. Somehow, I had a soft spot for the dancing Ukrainian. I'd seen a better side to him in the whale-mist and if that's a sentimentality, I was prepared to let it stand. I mean, it wasn't as if I were fighting Khrushchev's case publically, before a hostile 'free world'.

***

At breakfast that Sunday with my mother, I gave her a carefully edited version of the wrestling at the Pier Pavilion, omitting the escapades of the two old men altogether. (I'd have to warn Derek to hold his tongue about all that if he encountered Mum when he came round on Monday. A whisper at the door when I let him in should be enough.)

As for the audience, I reduced them to a mass of cheerful, mannerly bystanders, not a coarse comedian or hatpin-wielder amongst them. The two angels had no billing either.

Bustling around, glancing at the kitchen clock and checking that she had some small change for the collection plate, Mum was still a bit sniffy about the vulgarity of the entertainment and wondered pointedly how Becky had managed to put up with it all. At least Mrs Fraser had had the good sense not to go with us.

'Oh, Becky just lapped it up!' I said, presenting an innocent face.

My mother looked at me sceptically, but didn't say anything further. She was in a hurry, dreading as she did getting to chapel even a minute late: bad manners and something of an affront to God Himself.

After she'd gone, it struck me with a pang of alarm that the mayhem-at-the-Pier Pavilion story might well get into the local paper. It was the sort of thing they'd revel in – and if Mum saw that!

But I was to be in luck, although it was tempting to put it down to a benign providence. There'd been a spate of robberies in Ketilsby over the weekend, most of them in big houses around the Park, one of the victims being an ex-mayor and another a wealthy trawler owner-cum-philanthropist. So there was much space given to that story, plus that concerning renewed trouble on the docks, the threat of a strike by the lumpers. Also, last but certainly not least, there was a pageful of pictures of a local girl who'd become a TV soap opera star and had returned home for a school reunion at the Girls' Grammar. She was pretty in a carefully cultivated way, but I was chiefly grateful to her for the amount of space she took up in Monday's paper.

Thus, to my relief and satisfaction, I found that the report on the wrestling tournament had been whittled down to a few lines: no wild old men, no pure children redeeming the evening. Just bare facts as to the bouts and a few lines on the 'amazing phenomenon' of Jason Pulverstein and how there were plans to bring him back to the Pier as soon as possible. Rightly or wrongly, I saw Doug the compère's influence in this piece. A few free drinks for the journalist, perhaps.

There was a brief mention of a stoppage in the final bout, but thankfully no accompanying explanation. That show was over.

By the way, Jason Pulverstein won his fight by two falls to nothing. What a surprise! But the bout was allowed to run its full course, so the fans couldn't complain they weren't getting their money's worth. All in all, quite the contrary.

On Sunday morning Mum was usually out of the house for about two hours – she liked chatting to friends after the service. I went up to see my father in his office. He'd not long since got washed and dressed and was munching at a plate of biscuits when I went in. He asked me how I had got on at the Pier Pavilion. I told him, warning him about the much milder account I'd given my mother: please would he be careful, therefore, in what he passed on to her? I declared that I wasn't really being underhand or anything, but that I wanted to make sure the omissions and white lies held up.

'Peacemaker or Machiavelli?'

'What, Dad?'

'We do have an encyclopaedia downstairs, Colin.'

Then he pronounced the Italian name very slowly but with a rich fullness as if he were evoking the most delicious gastronomic treat possible.

But I had more immediate things to worry about. I went on at him to promise me.

'Ducking the possible brickbats, eh? Keeping mum to Mum!' he cackled, putting a stagey finger to his lips, then – finally – giving me his word of honour that I could rely on him to make any ticklish aspect of the tale simply vanish.

While I was describing what had happened at the Pier Pavilion, Dad kept breaking in with expressions of joyful incredulity – along with sprays of biscuit crumbs: 'Better than Laurel and Hardy!' and 'Who needs a Brian Rix farce? Go on, lad!' I think he believed I was embellishing and I suppose I did here and there, but not much. Not that Dad cared, so long as it fitted.

I shone in that brief time with him. It was like the best moments when I was writing my stories: immersed in other worlds – those of my making, whatever I took from life around me or the books I'd read.

It was better in a way, because Dad went on laughing like a man who'd found a pile of gold sovereigns in his back garden. Music to my ears. Now I knew how Derek felt when he had an audience under his spell, even if it was only in the school playground.

My father seemed particularly to relish the pathetic scrapping of the two old men. I began to feel a bit guilty then because there was a sad side to it as well which, playing up to Dad's enjoyment, I wasn't doing justice to.

Maybe he'd been thinking along the same lines because, when I'd finished, he did comment that, although Grand-Dad Reynolds and Mr Marston senior were obviously 'two of nature's anarchists', it would have been nicer if they'd just said their respective angry pieces, exchanged a few jabs and hooks into thin air and then had some drinks together and made up.

'It would have robbed us of a lot of laughter, but saved them... what word shall we use, Colin?'

'Shame, Dad?' I suggested, rather tentatively.

But he nodded approvingly, straightening his tie, brushing his shoulders and front.

He looked rotund but smart, togged up in a freshly cleaned and pressed suit. He was getting ready to go for his Sunday mid-day session at The Honest Lawyer, and was now sipping his pre-expedition sherry.

He gave me a little taste, tipped me half a crown for amusing him so much, (my first fee for a story, even if it was an oral one), a yarn which Dad judged to be good enough for *Punch*. Then, indicating the sherry bottle, he advised me to clean my teeth again, double-thoroughly, 'just in case'.

'You've got to learn the methods of self-protection that have served the male of the species from time immemorial, my boy. Mothers – and wives – often mean well but they can be tricky.'

After a final check on his appearance, Dad turned to me

for inspection.

'Do I look presentable, Colin?'

'On your way to being decorated at Buckingham Palace, Dad.'

He regarded me with a pleased but arch expression.

'Now that would be a thing!'

He said goodbye, moving rapidly out of the room and along the landing to the stairs.

Just at the head of them he called out that I should ask Mum to put some lunch in the oven for him, to keep warm if he wasn't back in time, and that he'd like to hear my Pier Pavilion story again – the office door closed, just between ourselves – and that I should tell him more about Jason Pulverstein, who sounded weird enough for a dozen tournament extravaganzas.

I said that I'd do my best. I didn't think there'd be another half-crown in it, but I had my prize anyway. The second performance would take place after tea, when Dad went up to do his 'accounts', my mother glued to the television downstairs.

The front door was snecked to and I heard Dad's footsteps receding down the path, the click of the gate – that was when I felt his appreciative laughter at my story fade into nothing, when the loneliness came.

Normally, it took me a while to push this black mood aside and that had to be through activity, boring or not it hardly mattered. It could be a deed as simple as re-arranging the books on my shelves, (Rosemary Sutcliff and Geoffrey Trease well to the fore, William still holding his own but Biggles slowly slipping down the ranks), or the production of wild sketches, often just flurries of lines like a hurricane advancing.

But today I was buoyed up by something really strong: the feeling that I'd never liked my father more than in the short period we'd just spent together.

The month soon to end had been the best October ever

for me, however far the world outside shook on its axis. I hoped it was the same for Derek. Commemoration was too solemn a word, but we should try to celebrate it somehow in the future. For instance, we could start the *real* year there, as though each following October would be just as alive, although rationally we'd know how unlikely that'd be. Still, it'd be something to measure ourselves against. A private joy, something secret and all the better for that – not even a badge half-hidden behind our lapels! The accepted calendar began to seem arbitrary to me. After all, people of different religions started their true year at other times and I'd read somewhere that in the Northern hemisphere there were those who used to begin it in March, to catch the springtime. So surely a place could be found for Derek and me and our special October? We wouldn't be disturbing anybody. Well, no more than usual.

I'd discuss this unique-to-the-heavens idea with Derek when he came round on Monday. He might be scornful at first because it hadn't originated with him but he'd agree in the end, particularly if he were able to elaborate on my suggestions so that he could all but co-opt the grand notion as his own.

That Saturday evening at the Pier had made our friendship a bit strange, but Derek would descend from the angelic heights and be back to normal soon. I wasn't so sure about Becky. It might take her up to the 11+ before she was right again. She'd *have* to get to grips with mundane matters then.

That Sunday morning I couldn't conceive, nor for a long time afterwards, that Derek and I would ever be less close than we were; and drawing apart, slowly like a torture, becoming worse than strangers to each other – that would have been the stuff of nightmare. Our world of two was still extant and ready to take on all comers. Let it thrive for an age!

A little later, I went up to my room at the back of the

house and tried to write an account of the evening at the Pier Pavilion, but got tired and discouraged. The story had seemed so spirited when I'd told it to Dad. Now it was becoming flat and laborious, like a school composition I didn't want to do.

I wasn't particularly put out. Just my mood, I told myself, the sense of anti-climax following a special excitement. There'd come a time when I could shape it properly for the page, shape *everything* of significance that had happened to us.

What I didn't know then was that the occasion for tackling these boasts lay vistas ahead, much further than I ever could have dreamed of as I stared out the window, trying to find fascination in the odd sparrow hopping across the lawn or the fact that the neighbour had left his dustbin lid at a slight angle, like a huge and roguish cap.

Author's Note

If you enjoyed *The Best October*, please consider reviewing it on Amazon. Reviews – even a quick note that you liked it – are a great way of spreading the word and very much appreciated.

If you'd like to stay in touch, my e-mail address is:
dwdebney@gmail.com

Best wishes,
Jack Debney

ABOUT THE AUTHOR

Jack Debney was born in Cheshire in 1941. He was brought up in Grimsby, where his mother's family was long established. He was educated locally and then at Leeds (BA) and Warwick (MA) Universities. Jack worked as a lecturer of English literature in Alexandria, Egypt, in Athens, Greece, and in Marburg, Germany. Jack Debney is married and has two children and three grandchildren.

BY THE SAME AUTHOR

Clowns and Puritans, 1999
The Crocodile's Head and Other Stories, 2002
The Alexandrian Charlie Chaplin and Other Stories, 2005
Jannicott, 2010
Postcard from Salò, 2012
Kharshouf and Other Stories, 2015
My Pal Jeremiah, 2017
The Best October, 2017

Available on Amazon
http://www.amazon.com/author/jackdebney

Printed in Great Britain
by Amazon